Only With You

Books by Julia James

Harlequin Modern

Securing the Greek's Legacy
The Forbidden Touch of Sanguardo
Captivated by the Greek
A Tycoon to Be Reckoned With
A Cinderella for the Greek
Tycoon's Ring of Convenience

Secret Heirs of Billionaires

The Greek's Secret Son

Mistress to Wife?

Claiming His Scandalous Love-Child
Carrying His Scandalous Heir

One Night With Consequences

Heiress's Pregnancy Scandal

Visit the Author Profile page
at millsandboon.com.au for more titles.

Only With You

USA TODAY BESTSELLING AUTHOR

JULIA JAMES

MILLS & BOON

First Published 2019
Second Australian Paperback Edition 2024
ISBN 978 1 038 91976 2

First Published 2019
Second Australian Paperback Edition 2024
ISBN 978 1 038 91976 2

First Published 2018
Second Australian Paperback Edition 2024
ISBN 978 1 038 91976 2

Published by
Harlequin Mills & Boon
An imprint of Harlequin Enterprises (Australia) Pty Limited
(ABN 47 001 180 918), a subsidiary of HarperCollins
Publishers Australia Pty Limited
(ABN 36 009 913 517)
Level 19, 201 Elizabeth Street
SYDNEY NSW 2000 AUSTRALIA

Printed and bound in Australia by McPherson's Printing Group

CONTENTS

Billionaire's Mediterranean Proposal

MILLS & BOON

Julia James lives in England and adores the peaceful verdant countryside and the wild shores of Cornwall. She also loves the Mediterranean—so rich in myth and history, with its sunbaked landscapes and olive groves, ancient ruins and azure seas. “The perfect setting for romance!” she says. “Rivaled only by the lush tropical heat of the Caribbean—palms swaying by a silver-sand beach lapped by turquoise waters...what more could lovers want?”

DEDICATION

For Joyce

CHAPTER ONE

TARA SASHAYED INTO the opulent function room at the prestigious West End hotel along with the rest of the models fresh off the catwalk. They were still gowned in their couture evening dresses, and their purpose now was to show them off up close to the private fashion show's wealthy guests.

As she passed the sumptuous buffet she felt her stomach rumble, but ignored it. Like it or not—and she didn't—modelling required gruelling calorie restriction to keep her body racehorse-slender. Eating normally again would be one of the first joys of chucking in her career and finally moving to the countryside, as she was longing to do. And that dream of escape was getting closer and closer—escape to the chocolate-box, roses-round-the-door thatched cottage in deepest Dorset that had belonged to her grandparents and now, since their deaths, belonged to her.

In her grandparents' day it had been the only home she'd ever really had. With her parents in the armed forces, serving abroad, and herself packed off to boarding school at the age of eight, it had been her grandparents who had provided the home comforts and stability that her parents had not been in a position to provide. Now, determined to make it her own 'for ever' home, she was spending every penny she earned in undertaking the essential repairs and restoration that were required for such an old house—from a new thatched roof, to new drains…it all had to be done.

And now it nearly was. It only lacked a new kitchen and bathroom to replace the very ancient and decrepit units and sanitary ware and she could move in! All she needed was another ten thousand pounds to cover the cost.

That was why she was taking on all the modelling assignments she could—including this evening one now—squirrelling away every penny she could to get the cottage ready for moving in to.

She could hardly wait for that day. The glamour of being a fashion model had worn off long ago, and now it was only tiring and tedious. Besides, she had increasingly come to resent being constantly on show, all too often attracting the attention of men she had learned were only interested in her because she was a model.

She sheered her mind away from her thoughts. Jules had been a long time ago, and she was long over him. She'd been young and stupid and had believed that it was herself he'd cared for—when all along she'd simply been a trophy female to be wheeled out to impress his mates…

It had taught her a lesson though and had made her wary. She didn't want to be any man's trophy.

Her wariness gave her a degree of edginess towards men which she knew could put men off, however striking her looks. Sometimes she welcomed it. She wasn't one to put up with any hassle. Maybe something of her parents' emotional distance had rubbed off on her, she sometimes thought. They'd always taught her to stand up for herself, not to be cowed, overawed or over-impressed by anyone.

She certainly wasn't going to be overawed by the kind of people here tonight, knocking back champagne and snapping up couture clothes as if they were as cheap as chips! Just because they were stinking rich it didn't make them better than her in any way whatsoever—no way was anyone going to look down on her as some kind of walking clotheshorse!

Head held high, poker-faced, she kept on parading around, as she was being paid to do. The evening would end soon, and then she could clear off and get home.

Marc Derenz took a mouthful of champagne and shifted his weight restlessly, making some polite reply to whatever Hans Neuberger had just said to him. His mood was grim, and getting worse with every passing minute, but that was something he would never show to Hans.

A close friend of Marc's late father, Hans had been at his side during that bleak period after Marc's parents had been killed in a helicopter crash, when their only offspring had still been in his early twenties. It had been Hans who'd guided him through the complexities of mastering his formidable inheritance at so young an age.

Hans's business experience, as the owner of a major German engineering company, as well as his wisdom and kindness, were not things Marc would ever forget. He felt a bond of loyalty to the older man that was rare in his life, untrammelled by emotional ties as he had been since losing his parents.

It was a loyalty that was causing him problems right now, though. Only eighteen months ago Hans, then recently widowed following his wife's death from cancer, had been inveigled into a rash second marriage by a woman whom Marc had no hesitation in castigating as a gold-digger. And worse.

Celine Neuberger, here tonight to add to her already plentiful collection of couture gowns, had made no secret to Marc of the fact that she was finding her wealthy but middle-aged husband dull and uninteresting, now that she had him in her noose. And she had made no secret of the fact that she thought the opposite about Marc…

Marc's mouth tightened. Celine's eyes were hungry on him now, even though Marc was blanking her, but that did not seem to deter her. Had she been anyone other than Hans's wife Marc would have had no hesitation in ruthlessly sending her packing. It was a ruthlessness he'd had to learn early—first as heir to the Derenz billions, and then even more so after his parents' deaths.

Women were very, *very* keen on getting as close to those billions of his as possible. Ideally, by becoming Madame Marc Derenz.

Oh, at some point in his life, he acknowledged, there *would* be a Madame Derenz—when the time was right for him to marry and start a family. But she would be someone from the same wealthy background as himself.

It was advice his father had given him: to do what he himself had done. Marc's mother had been an heiress in her own right. And even for mere *affaires*, his father had warned him, it was best never to risk any liaison with anyone not from their own world of wealth and privilege. It was safer that way.

Mark knew the truth of it—only once had he made the mistake of ignoring his father's advice.

Celine Neuberger was addressing him now, her voice eager, and he was glad of the interruption to his thoughts. He had been recalling a time he did not care to remember, for he had been young and trusting then, and he had paid for that misplaced trust with a heartache he never wanted to experience again.

But what Celine had to say only worsened his mood sharply.

'Marc, have I told you that Hans has promised to buy a villa on the Côte d'Azur! And I've had the most *wonderful* idea!'

Celine's gushing voice grated on him.

'We could house-hunt from *your* gorgeous, gorgeous villa on Cap Pierre! *Do* say yes!'

Every instinct in Marc rebelled at the prospect,

but he was being put on the spot. In his parents' time Hans and his first wife had often been guests at the Villa Derenz—convivial occasions when the young Marc had had the company of Hans's son, Bernhardt, and had made enthusiastic use of the pool and gone sea bathing off the rocky shoreline of Cap Pierre. Good memories…

Marc felt a pang of nostalgic loss for those carefree days. Now, all he could say, resignedly, and with a forced smile, was, '*Bien sûr!* That would be delightful.' He tried to make the lie convincing. 'Delightful' was the last word to describe spending more time with Celine making eyes at him. Having to hold her at bay.

A triumphant Celine now pushed even further in a direction Marc had no intention of letting her advance. She turned to her husband. 'Darling, don't feel you have to stay any longer—Marc can see me back to our hotel.'

Hans turned to Marc, a grateful expression on his face. 'That would be so kind of you, Marc. I have to phone Bernhardt—matters to do with the forthcoming board meeting.'

Again, how could Marc object without giving Hans the reason?

The moment Hans had left Celine was, predictably, off the leash. 'Now, tell me,' she gushed, smiling warmly up at him, 'which would suit me best?' She gestured at the perambulating models.

Marc, knowing his mood was worsening with every passing moment in this impossible situation he'd been dumped in, lanced his gaze around to find the nearest model, whatever she was wearing, determined to give Celine the least opportunity for lingering.

But, as he did so, suddenly all thoughts of Celine went right out of his head.

During the fashion show itself he'd paid no attention to the endless parade of females striding up and down the catwalk, focussing instead on his phone. So now, as his eyes caught the figure of the model closest to where they stood, he felt his gaze riveted.

Tall, ultra-slender—yes. But then all the models were like that. None like this one, though, with rich chestnut hair glinting auburn, loosely pinned into an uplift that exposed a face he simply could not take his eyes from.

The perfect profile—and then, as she turned to change direction, he saw a strikingly beautiful face with sculpted cheekbones, magnificent eyes shot with sea-green, and a wide, lush mouth that was, at this moment, tight-set. The expression on her amazing face was professionally blank, but as his eyes focussed on her he felt his male antennae react instinctively—and on every frequency. She was quite incredible.

Without conscious volition he raised his free hand, summoning her over. For a second he thought she had not seen his gesture, for she was moving as if to keep stalking around as the rest of the models were doing. Then, tensing, she strode towards him. He could not take his eyes from her…

The thoughts in his head were flashing wildly. OK, so she was a model—and that put her out of reach from the off, because models were nearly always *not* from the kind of privileged background he insisted that any woman he showed interest in be from. But this one…

Whatever she had—and he was still analysing it, with his male antennae registering her on every frequency—it was making it dangerously hard for him to remember the rules of engagement he lived by.

As she approached, the impact she was making on him strengthened like a magnet drawing tempered steel. *Dieu*, but she was stunning! And now she was standing in front of him, a bare metre or so away.

He scrutinised her shamelessly, taking in her breathtaking beauty. And then he caught a flash in her eyes—as if she resented his scrutiny.

His own eyes narrowed reactively—what was her problem? She was a model; she was being paid to be looked at in the clothes she was wearing. OK, so in fact she might have been wearing a sack, for all he cared—it was her amazing beauty that was drawing his attention, not her gown.

But, abruptly, he veiled his appreciative scrutiny. It didn't matter how stunningly beautiful she was. He had not summoned her for any reason other than the one he gave voice to now. The *only* reason he would show any interest in her.

'So, what about this one?'

He turned to Celine. The sooner he could get the wretched woman to spend Hans's money on a gown—

any gown!—the sooner he would be able to get her back to her hotel and finally be done with her for the evening.

His eyes went back to the model. The number she was wearing was purple—a kind of dark grape—in raw silk, draped over her slight breasts, slithering down her slender body. Again Marc felt that unstoppable reaction to her spectacular beauty. Again he did his best to stop it—and again he failed.

'Hmm…' said Celine doubtfully. 'The colour is too sombre for me, Marc. No.' She waved the model away, dismissing her.

But Marc stayed her. 'Please turn around,' he instructed. The gown was a masterpiece—as was she—and he wanted to see what she looked like from the back.

The flash in those blue-green eyes came again, and again Marc wondered at it as she executed a single revolution, revealing how the gown was almost backless, exposing the sculpted contours of her spine, the superb sheen of her pale skin. And as she came back to face them he saw an expression of what could only be hostility.

What is it with her? he found himself thinking. Annoyance flickered through him. Why that reaction? It wasn't one he was used to when he paid attention to a woman—in his long experience women *wanted* to draw his attention to them! His problem was keeping women away from him, and without vanity he knew that it was not only his wealth that lured them. Nature had bestowed upon him gifts that money could not buy—a six-foot-plus frame, and looks that usually had a powerful impact on women.

But not on this one, it seemed, and he felt that flicker of annoyance again as his gaze rested on her professionally blank face once more.

For a second—a fraction of a second—he thought he saw something behind that professional blankness. Something that was not that hostile flash either…

But then it was gone, and Celine was saying pettishly, 'Marc, *cherie*, I really don't like it.'

She waved the model away again, and she strode off with quickened stride, her body stiff. Marc's eyes followed her, unwilling to lose her in the throng which swallowed her up.

A pity she was a model…

For all her amazing looks, which were capable of piercing the black mood possessing him at having been landed with Hans's wretched adultery-minded wife, the stunning, flashing-eyed beauty was not someone, he knew perfectly well, he should allow himself to pursue…

She isn't from my world—let her go.

But a single word echoed in his head, all the same. *Domage...*

A pity…

Tara wheeled away, gaining the far side of the room as fast as she could. Her heart-rate was up and she knew why. Oh, she *knew* why!

She shut her eyes, wanting to blank the room. To blank the oh-so-conflicting reactions battling inside her head right now. She could feel them still, behind her closed eyes, slashing away at each other, fighting for supremacy.

Two overpowering emotions.

Impossible to tell which was uppermost!

The first—that instinctive, breath-catching one—had come the moment she'd seen that man looking at her…seen him for the first time. She certainly hadn't seen him at the fashion show, but then she never looked at the audience when she was on the catwalk. If she had—oh, she'd have remembered him all right…

No man had ever impacted on her as powerfully—as instantly. Talk about tall, dark and devastating! Sable-hair, cut short, a hard, tough-looking face with a blade of a nose, a strong jaw, a mouth set in a tight line. And eyes that could strip paint.

Or that could rest on her with a look in them that told her that he liked what he was seeing…

She felt a kind of electricity flicker through her and her expression darkened abruptly. The complete opposite emotion was scything through her head, cutting off the electricity.

Liked it so much he just saw fit to click his fingers and summon me over so he could inspect me!

She fought for reason. OK, so he hadn't actually clicked his fingers—but that imperious beckoning of his had been just as bad! Just as bad as the way he'd so blatantly looked her over…

And it wasn't the damn gown he was interested in.

That opposite emotion, with a jacking up of its voltage, shot through her again. As if she was once again feeling the impact of that dark, assessing inspection…

She threw the switch once more. *No—stop this, right now!* she told herself. So what if he'd put her back up? Why should she care? That over-made-up blonde he'd been with had treated her just as offhandedly, waving her away. So why get uptight about the man doing so?

And so what, she added for good measure, that she'd had that ridiculously OTT reaction to the man's physical impact on her? He and Blondie came from a world she wasn't part of and only ever saw from the outside—like at this private fashion show. Speaking of which…

She gave herself a mental shake, opened her eyes and continued with her blank-faced perambulations, showing off a gown she could never in all her life afford herself. She was here to work, to earn money, and she'd better get on with it.

Oh, and if she could to stay on this far side of the room… Well away from the source of those emotions in her head.

'Marc, *cherie*, now, *this* one is ideal! Don't you think?'

Celine's voice was a purr, but it grated on Marc like nails on a blackboard. However, at last, it seemed, Hans's wife had found a gown she liked and was stroking the gold satin material lovingly, not even looking at the model wearing it. This model was smiling hopefully at Marc, but he ignored her. He was not the slightest bit interested.

Not like that other one.

He cut his inappropriate thoughts off. Focussed on the problem at hand. How to divest himself of Hans's wife at last.

'Perfect!' he agreed, with relief in his voice. *Could they finally get out of here?*

His relief proved short-lived. Celine's scarlet-tipped fingers curled possessively around his arm.

'I've seen all I want here. I'll arrange a fitting for that gold dress while Hans and I are in London. But right now…' she smiled winningly at Marc '…do be an angel and take me to dinner! We could go to a club afterwards!'

Marc cut short her attempts to commandeer him for the rest of the evening. Never one to suffer irritation gladly, he knew his temper had been on a shortening fuse all evening. It was galling to see his father's old friend in the clutches of this appalling woman. How on earth could Hans not have seen through her?

But then dark memory came, though he wished it would not. Hadn't *he* been similarly blinded once himself?

Oh, he could tell himself he'd been young, and naïve, and far too trusting, but he'd been made a fool of all the same! Marianne had strung him along, playing on his youthful adoration of her, carefully cultivating his devotion to her—a devotion that had exploded in an instant.

Walking into that restaurant in Lyons, Marianne thinking I was still in Paris, seeing her there—

With another man. Older than Marc's barely two and twenty. Older and far wealthier.

Marc's father had still been alive then, and Marc only the prospective heir to the Derenz fortune. The man Marianne had been all over, cooing at, had been in his forties, and richer even than Marc's father. Marc had stared, the blood draining from his face, and had felt something dying inside him.

Then Marianne had seen him, and instead of trying to make any apology to him she had simply lifted her glass of champagne, tilted it mockingly at Marc, so the light would catch the huge diamond on her finger.

Shortly afterwards she had become the third wife of the man she'd been dining with. And Marc had learnt a lesson he had never, never forgotten.

Now, his tone terse, he spoke bluntly. 'Celine, I already have a dinner engagement tonight.'

Hans's wife was undeterred. 'Oh, if it's business I'll be good as gold,' she assured him airily, not relinquishing her hold on his arm. 'I sit through enough of Hans's deadly dull dinner meetings to know how!' she added waspishly. 'And we could still go clubbing afterwards...'

Marc shook his head. Time to stop Celine in her tracks. 'No, it's *not* business,' he told her, making the implication clear.

Celine's eyes narrowed. 'You're not seeing anyone at the moment. I know that,' she began, 'because I'd have heard about it otherwise.'

'And I'm sure you will,' Marc replied, jaw set.

He did *not* want a debate over this. He just wanted to get Celine off his hands before his temper reached snapping point.

'Well, who is it?' Celine demanded.

Marc felt his already short fuse shortening even more. He wanted to get out of here—now—and get shot of Celine. Any way he could. The fastest way he could.

He said the first thing that came into his head in this infuriating and wretched situation. 'One of the models here,' he answered tersely.

'Models?'

She said the word as if he'd said *waitresses* or *cleaners*. In Celine's eyes women who weren't rich—or weren't married to rich men—simply didn't exist. Let alone women who might possibly interest the likes of Marc Derenz.

Her eyes flashed petulantly. 'Well, which one, then?' she demanded. She was thwarted, and she was challenging him.

It was a challenge he could not help but meet—and he called her bluff with the first words that came into his head. 'The one in the dress you didn't like—'

'*Her?* But she looked right through you!' Celine exclaimed.

'She's not supposed to fraternise while she's working.'

Even as he spoke he was cursing himself. Why the hell had he said it was *that* model? The one who had stiffened up like a poker?

But he knew why. Because he was still trying to

put her out of his head, that was why—trying and failing. He'd been conscious of his eyes sifting through the crowded room even as Celine was cooing over the gown she was selecting, idly searching for the model again. Irritated both that he was doing so and that he could not see her.

She was keeping to the far side of the room. Not coming anywhere near his eyeline again.

Because she is avoiding me?

The thought was in his head, bringing with it emotions that were at war with each other. He shouldn't damn well be interested in her in the first place! For all the reasons he always stuck to in his life. But he could remind himself of those reasons all he liked—he still wanted to catch another glimpse of her.

More than a glimpse.

Another thought flickered. Was it because she hadn't immediately—eagerly!—returned his clear look of interest in her that she was occupying his thoughts like this? Had that intrigued him as well as surprised him?

He didn't have time to think further, for Celine was counter-calling *his* bluff.

'Well, *do* introduce me, *cherie*!' she challenged.

It was clear she didn't believe him, and Marc's mouth tightened. He was not about to be outmanoeuvred by Hans's scheming wife. Nor was he going to spend a minute longer in her company.

With a smile that strained his jaw, he murmured, 'Of course! One moment.' And he strode away across the room with one purpose only, his mood grimmer than ever. Whatever it took to shed the clinging Celine, he'd do it!

His eyes sliced through the throng, incisively seeking his target. And there she was. He felt the same kick go through him as had when he'd first summoned her across to him. That racehorse grace, that perfect profile—and those blue-green eyes which now, as he accosted her, were suddenly on him. And immediately, instantly blank.

And not in the least friendly.

Marc didn't give a damn—not now. His temper was at snapping point after what he'd put up with all evening.

He stood in front of her, blocking Celine's view of her from the other side of the room. Without preamble, he cut to the chase. Whether this was a moment of insanely stupid impulse, or the way out of a hole, he just did not care.

'How would you like,' he said to the model who was now staring at him with a closed, stony look on her stunningly beautiful face, 'to make five hundred pounds tonight?'

CHAPTER TWO

TARA HEARD THE WORDS, but they took a moment to register. She knew only that they'd been spoken with the slightest trace of an accent that she hadn't noticed in his curt instruction to her before.

She had still been trying to quench her reaction to the man who had just appeared out of nowhere in front of her. Blocking her. Demanding her attention. Just as he'd demanded she walk across to him and Blondie and twirl at his command.

OK, so that was her job here tonight, but it was the *way* he'd done it that had put her back up!

As now he was doing all over again—and worse. Because she did not *want* to feel that kick of high voltage again, that unwelcome quickening of her pulse as her eyes focussed, however determinedly she tried to resist, on that planed hard face and the dark eyes that were like cut obsidian.

The sense of what he'd just said belatedly reached her brain, as insulting as it was offensive.

She started to open her mouth, to skewer him with her reply—no *way* was she going to tolerate such an approach, whoever the hell this man was!—but he was speaking again. An irritated expression flashed across his face.

'Do *not*,' she heard him say, and there was a distinct tinge of boredom in his voice, as well as curt irritation, 'jump to the tediously predictable assumption you are clearly about to make. All I require is this. That you accompany myself and my guest back to her hotel, where—' he held up a silencing hand as Tara's mind raced ahead to envisage unspeakable debaucheries '—she will get out and you will stay in the car with me and then return here.'

The words were clipped from him, and then his eyes were going past her towards one of the fashion designer's hovering aides. He summoned him over with the same imperious gesture he'd used to draw her over to show off the gown she was wearing.

The man came scuttling forward. 'Monsieur Derenz, is there anything you require?' he asked eagerly.

Tara heard the obsequiousness in the man's voice and deplored it. The last thing rich guys like this one needed—let alone those with the kind of tough-looking face that he had, who expected everyone to jump at their bidding—was anyone kow-towing to them. It only encouraged them.

'Yes,' came the curt reply. 'I'd like to borrow your model for a very temporary engagement. I require a chaperone for my guest, Mrs Neuberger, as I escort her to her hotel. Your model will be away for no more than half an hour. Obviously I'll pay you for her time and take full financial liability for her gown. I take it there'll be no problem?'

The last was not a question—it was a statement. The aide nodded immediately. 'Of course, Monsieur Derenz.' His eyes snapped to Tara. 'Well? Don't just stand there! Monsieur Derenz is waiting!'

And that was that.

Fulminating, Tara knew she didn't have a choice. She needed the money. If she kicked off and refused then her agency would be told, and as this particular fashion designer was highly influential, there would be no hope that her objection to being shanghaied in this manner would be upheld.

All the same, she glared at the man shanghaiing her as the aide scuttled off again. 'What *is* this?' she demanded.

The man—this Monsieur Derenz, whoever he was, she thought tautly—looked at her impatiently. She'd never heard of him, and all the name did was confirm that he was not British—a deduction that went not just with his name and slight accent, but also with the air of Continental style that added something to his stance, and to the way he wore the clearly hand-made tuxedo that moulded his powerful frame in ways she knew she must not pay any attention to…

'You heard me—my guest needs a chaperone. And so do I!'

Tara could see his irritation deepen as he spoke.

'I want you to behave as if you know me. As if—' his mouth set '—we are having an affair.'

This time Tara did explode. *'What?'*

That dark flash of impatient irritation seared across his face again. 'Cool it,' he said tersely. 'I merely need my guest to be…disabused…of any expectations she may have of me.'

'She'd be welcome to you!' Tara muttered, hardly bothering to be inaudible.

How had she managed to get inveigled into this? Then something pinged back into her mind.

'Did you say five hundred pounds?' she demanded. No way was she going to come out of this empty-handed—not for putting up with this man commandeering her like this.

'Yes,' came the indifferent reply. 'Providing you don't waste any more of my time than this is already taking.'

Without waiting, he helped himself to her arm and started to walk back with her across the room, to where Tara could see the blonde woman who, apparently, had the idiotic idea that this man being tall, dark, handsome—and presumably, judging by how obsequious the aide had been, very rich—in any way compensated for his high-handed behaviour and peremptory manner.

As he walked her towards the unwanted blonde he bent his head to her. 'We have been together only a short while…you are reluctant to leave your work early, being highly conscientious—and if you pull away from me like that one more time your money is halved. Do you understand me?'

There was a grim note in his voice that put Tara's back up even more. But he was still talking.

'Now, tell me your name.'

It was another of those orders he clearly liked giving.

'Tara,' she said tightly. 'Tara Mackenzie. And I need to get my bag and coat first—'

'Unnecessary.' He cut her off. 'You'll be back here soon enough.'

They had reached the blonde, who was looking, Tara could see, like curdled milk at their approach.

'Ah, Celine—this is Tara. Tara—Frau Neuberger.'

His voice was more fulsome, and there might well be relief in it, Tara thought.

'Tara's been given the all-clear to leave early, so we can drop you off at your hotel. *Alors, allons-y.*'

He cupped a hand around Celine's elbow and drew them both forward simultaneously, his guiding grip allowing no delay. Moments later they were on the pavement outside the hotel, and Tara found herself stepping into a swish chauffeured limo. She settled herself carefully, mindful of her horrendously expensive gown, arranging the skirts so they did not crush.

The man she was supposed to be giving the impression that she was having an affair with—however absurd!—sat himself down heavily between her and the blonde—who, Tara was acidly amused to see, was faffing about with her seatbelt in order to get the man she wanted to make some form of body contact and fasten it for her. Sadly for her, it seemed he did not return the desire.

'Marc, *cherie*, thank you!' Tara heard the woman gush.

OK, Tara connected, Marc Derenz. She still had no

idea who he might be, but then so many of the richest of the rich were completely unknown to the wider world. To the plebs in it like herself. Well, what did it matter *who* he was? Nor did it matter that he seemed to possess the kind of physical appeal that was so annoyingly able to compete with her resistance to his peremptory and quite frankly dislikeable personality.

She glanced at him now, as the car moved off into the London evening traffic. His profile was just as tough-looking as his face—and the clear set of his jaw indicated that his mood had not improved in the slightest. She heard him make some terse reply in German to the blonde at his side, and then suddenly he was turning to Tara.

Something flickered in his eyes. Something that made Tara's insides go gulp even though she didn't want them to. Suddenly, out of nowhere, she felt the close physical proximity of this man—felt, of all things, that it wasn't Blondie who needed a chaperone, it was *her…*

That flicker in those dark, dark eyes came again. And this time it was more than just a flicker. It was a glint. A glint that went with the set of that tough jawline.

'Tara, *mon ange*—your seatbelt…'

His voice was a low murmur, nothing like as brusque as it had been when he'd spoken to Blondie, and there was only one word for its tone.

Intimate...

Out of nowhere, Tara felt herself catch her breath. She heard her thoughts scramble in her brain. *Oh, dear God, don't look at me like that! Don't speak to me like that! Because if you do...*

But there was something that was even more of an ordeal for her than the husky, intimate tone of his accented voice that was doing things to her that she did not want them to do—because the only reason she was here in this plush limo was to provide fleeting cover in a situation that was none of her making and that would be over and done with inside half an hour, tops…

Only it seemed that Marc Derenz was utterly oblivious to what she didn't want him to do to her—to the effect he was having on her that she *must* not let him see! Because her reaction to him was totally irrelevant! Totally and absolutely nothing to do with her real life. And totally at odds with the way she *should* think of him—as nothing but a rich man moving other people around for his own convenience and not even bothering to be polite about it!

But it was impossible to remember that as he leant across her, reaching for her seatbelt, invading her body space just as he invaded her senses. She could feel the hardness of his chest wall against her arm, see the cords of his strong neck, the sable feathering of his hair, the hard-edged jawline and the incised lines around his mouth. She could catch the expensive masculine scent of his aftershave. His own masculine scent…

Then, in a swift, assured movement, he was reaching for the seatbelt and pulling it across her. And in those few brief seconds the breath stopped in her lungs.

Oh, God, what has he got—what has he got?

But it was a futile question. She knew exactly what he had.

Raw, overpowering sexuality. Effortless, unconscious, and knocking her for six.

It was all over in a moment and he was back in his position in the middle of the wide, capacious seat, turning his attention to Blondie, who was relentlessly talking away to him in rapid French. Tara could see her long red nails pressed over Marc Derenz's sleeve, her face upturned to his—claiming his attention. Ignoring Tara.

The woman's rudeness started to annoy her—adding to her resentment of the way she'd been commandeered for this uninvited role. Well, if she was supposed to be riding shotgun, she had better behave as if she were!

Cutting right across Blondie's voluble chatter, she deliberately brushed her hand down Marc Derenz's sleeve. It was an effort to do so, but she forced herself. She had to recover from her ludicrous reaction to his fastening her seatbelt for her. She had to recover from her ludicrous reaction to his overpowering masculinity full-stop.

After all, she told herself robustly, she'd lived with her looks all her life and had been a model for years—she was a hardened operator, able to give short shrift to men importuning her. No way was this guy going to cow her just because he had the looks to melt her bones. No, it was time to prove to herself—and, damn it, to him too!—that she wasn't just going to meekly and mildly put up and shut up. Whatever it was about him that riled her so, she wasn't going to let him call all the shots.

In which case…

'Marc, baby, I'm sorry I gave you a hard time over leaving early. Forgive me?' She leant into him just a fraction, quite deliberately, and put a husky, cajoling note into her voice.

His head swivelled. For a moment she saw an expression in his eyes that should have been a warning to her. But it was too late to regret drawing his attention to her.

'You'll have to accept, *mon ange*, that I have severe time constraints in my life. *Hélas*, I have to be in Geneva tomorrow, so I wanted to make the most of tonight.'

He sounded regretful. And intimate. It was an intimacy that curled right down her body. He didn't have a strong French accent, but, boy, what he had worked…

And then Blondie was jabbering in German, and he turned to her to reply.

Relief drenched through Tara. If that was him simply *acting* the role of attentive lover…

She dragged her mind away, steadied her breathing. Oh, sweet Lord, whatever he had, he definitely had what it took to get past her defences.

Her expression changed. It was just as well that his personality didn't match his looks—he had all the winning charm of a ten-ton boulder, crushing everyone around him! And it was even more just as well, she was honest enough to admit, that her acquaintance with this man was going to be extremely short-lived.

She'd see this exercise through, get back to work, and be a useful five hundred pounds the richer for it. All feeding into the Escape to My Cottage in the Country fund. She made herself focus on that subject for the remainder of the thankfully short journey, doing her best to ignore the very difficult to ignore presence of the man sitting next to her, and grateful that he was being monopolised by Blondie, who was clearly making the most of him.

As the car pulled up under the portico of the woman's hotel Tara sat meekly while the other two got out. Marc Derenz escorted Blondie indoors, to emerge some minutes later and throw himself back into the car, this time on the far side vacated by Blondie.

'Thank God!' Tara heard him say—and he sounded as if he meant it.

Tara couldn't resist. He was such a charmless specimen, however ludicrously good-looking. 'Such a bore, aren't they?' she said sweetly. 'Women who don't get the message.'

Dark eyes immediately swivelled to her, and Tara reeled inwardly with the impact. It was like being seared by a laser set to stun. Despite the effort it cost her, she gritted her teeth, refusing to blink or back down.

He didn't deign to answer, merely flicked out his phone and jabbed at it. A moment later he was in full flood to someone he clearly wanted to talk to—unlike herself—and Tara assumed from his businesslike tone, that business was what it was.

She leant back, not sure if she was feeling irritated by his manner or just glad the whole escapade was almost over. Even so, she unconsciously felt her head twist slightly as the car moved back out into the traffic, so she could behold his profile. Again, she felt that annoyingly vulnerable reaction to him, that skip in her pulse. She jerked her head away.

Oh, damn the man! He might radiate raw sexuality on every wavelength, but his granite personality was a total turn-off. The minute she was out of here and had the money he'd promised her she would never think about him again.

Five minutes later they were back at the hotel where the fashion show was being held and she was climbing out of the limo. Pointedly, she held her door open—no way was he driving off without paying her.

'You said five hundred,' she said, holding out her hand expectantly. The only reason, she reminded herself grimly, that she had anything to do with this man was for money! No other reason.

For a moment he just looked at her, his face closed. Then he got out of the car, standing in front of her. He was taller than her, even with her high heels, and it wasn't something she was accustomed to in men.

She felt her jaw set. There was something about the way he was looking at her. As if he were considering something. She lifted her chin that much higher, eyeballing him, hand still outstretched for her pay-off.

His dark eyes were veiled, unreadable.

'My money, please,' she said crisply. What was going on? Was he going to try and welch on the deal? For a sum that would be utterly trivial to a man like him?

Then, abruptly, she realised why he was not reaching for his wallet. Because he was reaching for her hand.

Before she could stop him, or step away, he'd taken hold of it and was raising it to his mouth. His expression as he did so had changed. Changed devastatingly.

Tara felt her lungs seize—felt everything seize.

Oh, God, she heard her inner voice say, silently and faintly and with absolute dismay, *don't do this to me...*

But it was too late. With a glint in his obsidian eyes, as if he knew perfectly well that what he was doing would sideswipe her totally, he turned her hand over in his, exposing the tender skin of her wrist.

Eyelashes far too long for a man with a face that tough swept down, veiling those dark, mordant eyes of his. And then his mouth, like silken velvet, was brushing that oh-so-delicate skin, gliding across it with deliberate slowness. Soft, sensuous, devastating.

She felt her eyelids flutter shut, felt a ludicrous weakness flood her body. Desperately she tried to negate it. It was just skin touching skin! But her attempt to reduce it to such banality was futile. Totally futile. The warm, grazing caress of his mouth on the sensitive surface of her skin focussed every nerve-ending in her entire body just on her wrist. She was melting, dissolving...

He dropped her hand, straightened. 'Thank you,' he murmured, his voice low, his eyes holding hers.

The darkling glint in them was still there, but there was something more to it—something that kept her lungs immobile. 'Thank you for your co-operation this evening.'

There was the merest hint of amusement in his voice. She snatched her hand away, as if it had been touched by a red-hot bar of iron, not by the sensuous, seductive glide of his mouth.

She had to recover—any way she could. 'I only did it for the money!' she gritted, going back to eyeballing him, defying him to think otherwise.

She saw his expression harden. Close. Whatever had been there, even if only to taunt her, had vanished. Now there was only the personality of that crushing boulder back in evidence.

With a clearly deliberate gesture he reached for his wallet in the inner pocket of his tailored dinner jacket, and an equally deliberately flicked it open. Stone-faced—determinedly so—Tara watched him peel off the requisite number of fifty-pound notes and hold them out to her.

She took them from him, her colour heightened. There was something about standing here and having a man handing her money—any man, let alone this damn one!

He was looking at her with that deliberately impassive expression on his face, but there was something in the depths of those dark veiled eyes of his that made her react on total impulse. The man was so totally charmless, so totally forbidding, and yet he had so *totally* shot to pieces her usual cool-as-ice reaction to any kind of physical contact with a man. She'd *let* him do all that wrist-kissing, *let* him taunt her as he had and hadn't even *tried* to pull away from him.

Now, in an overpowering impulse to get some kind of retaliation, she lifted the topmost fifty-pound note from the wad in her hand. Stepping forward, she gave her saccharine smile again and with deliberate insolence tucked the fifty-pound note into his front jacket pocket and patted it.

'Buy yourself a drink, Mr Derenz,' she told him sweetly. 'You look like you could use one!'

She turned on her high heel, stalking away back into the hotel, not caring about his reaction. If she never saw Marc Derenz again it would be too soon! A man like him could only be bad, bad news.

A man who, like no other man she'd ever met, could turn her into melting ice-cream with a taunting wrist-kiss and a veiled glance from those dark eyes—and who could equally swiftly make her mad as fire with his imperious manner and rock-like personality.

Yes, she thought darkly, *definitely* bad news.

On *so* many counts.

Behind her, stock-still on the pavement, knowing the doorman had been covertly observing the exchange and not giving a damn, Marc watched her disappear from sight, the skirts of her gown billowing around her long, long legs, that glorious chestnut hair catching the light. In his memory he could still taste the silken scent of the pale skin at her wrist, the warmth of the pulse beneath the surface.

Then, his expression still mask-like, he turned away to climb back into his car, and be driven to his own hotel.

As if mentally rousing himself, he reached for the crumpled note in his breast pocket. He slipped it back into his wallet, depleted now of the four hundred and fifty pounds that were in her possession. As his wallet held his gaze, he felt as if the contents were reminding him of something important to him. That he would be wise not to forget.

How much he had wanted to silence that acidly saccharine mouth of hers, taunting him in a way that right now, in the mood he'd been in all evening, had *not* been wise at all… Silence it in the only way he wanted…

No. Tara Mackenzie was not for him—not on any terms. All his life he'd played the game of romance by the rules he'd set out for himself, to keep himself safe, and it was out of the question to consider breaking them. Not even for a woman like that.

After all, he mused, had it not been for the wretched Celine he would never even have encountered her. Now all he wanted was to put both of them behind him. For good.

It would be less than a fortnight later, however, that he would be forced to do neither. And it would blacken his mood to new depths of exasperatedly irate displeasure…

Tara was looking at kitchens and bathrooms online, trying to budget for the best bargains. However she calculated it, she still definitely needed at least another ten thousand pounds to get it all done. And even living in London as cheaply as she could—including staying in this run-down flat-share—it would take, she reckoned, a good six months to save that much.

What I need is some nice source of quick, easy dosh!

She gave a wry twist of a smile tinged with acerbity. Well, she'd made that five hundred pounds quickly enough—just for keeping the oh-so-charmless Marc Derenz safe from Blondie.

Memory swooped on her—that velvet touch of his mouth on the tender inside of her wrist…

A rasp of annoyance broke from her—with herself, for remembering it, for feeling that tremor that it had aroused go through her again now.

He only did it to taunt you! No other reason.

With an impatient resolve to put the wretched man out of her thoughts, she went back to her online perusal. Moving to Dorset—*that* was important to her. Not some obnoxious zillionaire who'd put her back up from the very first. Nor some man who could set her pulse racing…a man who was so, so wrong for her…

A thought sifted across her mind. Would there ever be a man who *was* right for her, though?

Yes, she thought determinedly—one day there *would* be. But she wasn't going to find him here in London, in her life as a model. No, it would be someone she'd meet when she'd started her new life in the country. Someone who didn't know her as a model at all, and who didn't see her as a trophy to show off with. Her thoughts ran on. Someone who was, oh, maybe a vet—or a farmer, even—at home in the countryside…

She pressed her lips together, giving a smothered snort. Well, one thing was for sure, it would not be Marc Derenz. And, anyway, she was never going to set eyes on him again.

A sharp rapping on the front door of the flat made her jump. She gave a sigh of irritation. Probably one of her flatmates had forgotten her keys.

She put her laptop aside, padded to the door, and opened it.

And stepped back in total shock.

It was the last person on earth she'd ever expected to see again.

Marc Derenz.

CHAPTER THREE

MARC'S MOOD WAS BLACK. Blacker even than it had been that torturous evening at the fashion show, with Celine trying to corner him. He'd hoped the brush-off he'd given her would mean she'd give up. He'd been wrong.

She was still plaguing him—still set on inviting herself to the Villa Derenz on the blatant pretext of house-hunting. It had been impossible to refuse Hans's apologetic request—and now he'd been landed with them arriving this week.

Marc's reaction had been instant—and implacable. He'd blocked her before—he would just have to do it again. However damn irritating it was to have to do so.

His eyes rested now on the means he was going to have to use. Tara Mackenzie.

He knew her name, and it had been easy enough to find out where she lived. He cast a disparaging eye around the dingy apartment. The front door opened on to the lounge, which was cheaply furnished and messy—belongings were scattered on battered settees, and a rack of washing was drying in front of the window.

His gaze swept round to the woman he'd tracked down.

And he veiled it immediately.

Even casually dressed, in jeans and a loose shirt, Tara Mackenzie was a complete knockout. Every bit as stunning as he remembered her. The same insistent, visceral response to her that he'd felt at that fashion show, that he'd been doing his damnedest to expel from his memory, flared in him again. Deplorable, but powerful. Far too powerful.

He crushed it down.

She was staring at him now, with those amazing blue-green eyes of hers, and had opened her mouth to speak. He pre-empted her. He wanted this sorted as swiftly as possible.

'I need to talk to you. I have a business proposition to put to you.'

His voice was clipped to the point of curtness. Just as it had been before at the fashion show. Tara's hackles rose automatically. She was still reeling from seeing him again—still reeling from the overpowering impact he was having on her, that seemed to be jacking up the voltage of her body's electricity as if she'd suddenly been plugged into the mains.

This time he was not in a hand-made tux, but in a dark grey killer business suit that screamed *Mr Rich and Powerful! Don't mess me about!*

Just as the look on his face did. That closed expression on his hard-planed, utterly unfairly devastating features and the obvious aura of impatience about him. His automatic expectation that she would meekly listen to whatever it was he was about to say.

He went on in the same curt, clipped voice, his faint accent almost totally supressed. 'Extend the role you adopted at the fashion show and you can make five thousand pounds out of it,' he said, not bothering with any preamble.

Tara frowned, and then she smiled, enlightenment dawning. It wasn't a genuine smile, but it helped her control that voltage hammering through her.

'Blondie still pestering you, is she?' she put to him.

She saw his expression tighten at her sardonic observation. Obviously he was annoyed, but he was acknowledging, tacitly, what she had said.

'Well?' It was his only response.

'Tell me more.' Tara smiled sweetly.

The electricity kindled by his utterly unexpected arrival had sparked a kind of exhilaration in her. It dawned on her that he was resenting having to approach her. And that, she knew, feeling another spark inside her, was really quite gratifying...

Just why that should be so she did not pause to examine.

He took a short breath, his eyes still like lasers on her. 'A week of your time—ten days at the most. It would be...residential,' he said, 'but entirely...' His eyes suddenly closed over their previous expression. 'Entirely synthetically so. In other words, on the same basis as before.' A tight, non-humorous smile tightened his mouth. 'For appearances only.'

Was there a warning in the way he'd said 'only'?

Tara didn't know and didn't care. It was entirely irrelevant. Of course it was 'appearances only'. No other possibility. Any woman thinking anything more of him would need her head examined!

'You would,' he continued, in that businesslike voice, 'be my house guest.'

Tara's eyebrows rose. 'Along with Blondie, I take it?'

He gave a brief nod. 'Precisely so.'

'And I get to run interference?'

He nodded again, impatience visible in his manner but saying nothing, only letting those laser eyes of his rest on her, as if trying to bend her to his implacable will.

And then suddenly, out of nowhere, there was something in them that was a like a kick in her system—something that flashed like a warning light in her head…as if she stood upon the brink of a precipice she hadn't even realised was there.

Just as suddenly it was gone. Had she imagined it? That sudden change somewhere at the back of those unreadable slate-dark eyes? Something he'd swiftly blanked? She must have, she decided. There was nothing in his expression now but impatience. He wanted an answer. And fast.

But she did not like being hustled. She took a breath and met his eyes, though she was conscious of the way she'd crossed her arms firmly over her chest, as if keeping him and his imposing, utterly out of place presence at bay.

'OK, do I have this right? You will pay me five thousand pounds to spend up to ten days, max, as your house guest, and behave—strictly in public only—' she made sure she emphasised that part '—as if I am your current squeeze, just as I did on that limo ride the other night, while your *other* house guest—Blondie—gets the message that, sadly for her, you are not available for whatever adulterous purpose she would like you to be. Is that it?' She raised her eyebrows again questioningly.

His expression did not change. He merely inclined his sable-haired head minutely.

Tara thought about it. 'Half up front,' she said.

He didn't blink. 'No. You might not show up,' he said flatly.

His eyes flicked around their shabby surroundings and Tara got the message. Someone who had to live in a place like this might indeed walk off with two and a half thousand pounds.

She made herself look at him. The man was loaded. He had to be, the way he behaved, the lifestyle he had—chauffeur-driven limo, hanging around at couture fashion shows in swanky hotels. No way was she going to be short-changed by him. After all, pro rata, the five hundred pounds for the bare half-hour previously was *way* more generous than this offer.

'Ten thousand,' she said bluntly.

It would be chicken-feed to a man like him, but a huge sum for herself. And exactly what she needed for her cottage. For a moment she wondered if she'd overplayed her hand. But then, maybe she should be glad if she had. Could she *really* face spending any more time in the company of this man? The reasons not to were not just her resistance to his rock-like personality…

Caution started to backfill the ridiculously heady sense of sparking exhilaration she had felt. Caution that came too late.

The voltage in those eyes seared. Then abruptly cut out. 'OK. Ten thousand,' he gritted out. As if she'd just pulled a tooth from his steeled jaw.

That spark of exhilaration surged again inside her, overriding the vanished and defeated caution. Boy, was he mad she'd pushed the price up!

She felt herself smile—a genuine one this time. And then, abruptly, her triumph crashed. With a gesture that was vivid in her memory, he was coolly extracting his gold-monogrammed leather wallet from his jacket, peeling off a fifty-pound note. Then a second one.

Reaching forward, with a glint in his eye that gave her utterly insufficient warning, even though it should have, he tucked the two notes into the front pocket of the shirt she was wearing.

'A little something on account,' he said, and there was a purr in his voice that told her that this was exactly what she knew it was.

His comeback for her daring to tip him with his own money.

She opened her mouth to spit something at him but he was turning on his heel. Striding from the room. Informing her, as he rapidly took his leave, that arrangements would be made via her agency.

Then he was gone.

Taking a long, deliberate breath, she removed the

two fifty-pound notes from her breast pocket and stared at them. That, she reminded herself bluntly, was the nature of her relationship with Marc Derenz. And she had better not lose sight of it. The only reason he'd sought her out was to buy her time, because she could be useful to him. No other reason.

And I wouldn't want it to be for any other reason!

Her adjuration to herself was stern. Just why it was that Marc Derenz, of all the men she'd ever encountered in her life, could have this devastating effect on her, she didn't know. She knew only that no good could come of it. Her world was not his, and never would be.

It was hard to remember her warning to herself as, a week later, she turned to look out through the porthole of the plane heading for the Côte d'Azur. Their destination had been a little detail Marc Derenz had omitted to inform her of, but she had no complaint. Just the opposite. Her mood was soaring. To spend a whole week at least on the fabled French Riviera—and be paid for doing so! Life didn't get any better.

She didn't even care that she was being flown out Economy, in spite of how rich the man was. And, boy, was he *rich*! She'd looked him up—and her eyebrows had gone up as well.

Marc Derenz, Chairman of Banc Derenz. She'd never heard of it, but then, why would she have? It was headquartered in Paris, for a start, and it was not a bank for the likes of her, thank you very much! Oh, no, if you banked at Banc Derenz you were rich—

very, *very* rich. You had investment managers and fund managers and portfolio managers and high net worth individual account managers—all entirely at your disposal to ensure you got the very highest returns on your millions and zillions.

As for her destination—the Villa Derenz was featured in architectural journals and was apparently famous as being a perfect example of Art Deco style.

It was something she could agree with a few hours later, as she was conducted across a marble-floored hall and up a sweeping marble staircase like something out of a nineteen-thirties Hollywood movie.

She was shown into a bedroom, its décor pale grey and with silvered furniture. She looked about her appreciatively. This was *fabulous*. It was a sentiment she echoed when she walked out onto the balcony that ran the length of the frontage of the villa. Her breath caught, her eyes lighting up. Verdant green lawns surrounded the brilliant white building, pierced only by a turquoise circular pool and edged by greenery up to the rocky shoreline of the Cap. Beyond, the brilliant azure of the Mediterranean confirmed the name of this coastline.

She gazed with pleasure. No wonder the rich liked being rich if it got them a place like this.

And I get to stay here!

She went back inside to help the pair of maids unpacking her clothes. They weren't her own clothes—a stylist had selected them, on Marc Derenz's orders, Tara assumed, as being suitable for the role she was going to play. For all that, she would definitely enjoy wearing them. Actually wearing them for herself, not for other women to buy—it would be a novelty she would make the most of.

She would make the most of everything about her time here. Starting with relishing the delicious lunch about to be served to her out on the balcony, under a shady parasol, followed by a relaxing siesta on a conveniently placed sun lounger in the warm early summer sunshine.

Where Marc Derenz was she didn't know—presumably he'd turn up at some point and she would go on duty. Till then…

'Don't burn.'

The voice that woke Tara was deep and familiar, and its abrupt tone told her instantly that concern for her well-being was not behind the statement.

Her eyes flared open, and for a moment the tall figure of the man who was going to pay her ten thousand pounds for staying in his luxury villa in the South of France loomed darkly over her.

She levered herself up on her elbows. 'I've got sun cream on,' she replied.

'Yes, well, I don't want you looking like a boiled lobster,' Marc Derenz said disparagingly. 'And it's time for you to start work.'

She sat up straight, feeling her arms for the thin straps of her swimsuit, which she'd pushed down to avoid tan marks on her shoulders. As she did so she felt the suit dip dangerously low over her breasts. And she felt suddenly, out of nowhere, a burning consciousness of the fact that those hard, dark eyes were targeted on her, and that all that concealed her nakedness was a single piece of thin stretchy material.

Deliberately, she busied herself picking up her wrap, studiedly winding it around herself without looking at him. Whether he was looking at her still she did not care.

I'm going to have to get used to this—to the impact he has on me. And fast. I can't go on feeling so ridiculously self-conscious. I've got to learn to blank him.

With that instruction firmly in mind, she finished knotting her wrap securely and looked across at him. Against the sun he seemed even taller and darker. He was wearing another of his killer business suits, pale grey this time, with a sharp silk tie and what would obviously be twenty-four-carat gold cufflinks and tiepin.

Tara made herself look and sound equally businesslike. 'OK,' she said. 'What's the next thing on the agenda, then?'

'Your briefing,' Marc Derenz replied succinctly.

His pose altered slightly and he nodded his head at a chair by the table, seating himself on a second chair, crossing one perfectly creased trouser leg over the other.

'Right,' he started in a brisk voice as she sat where he'd bade her. 'There are some ground rules. This, Ms Mackenzie, is a *job*. Not a holiday.'

Marc rested his eyes on her impassively. But he was masking a distinctly less impassive emotion. Arriving here from Paris to find her sunning herself on the balcony had not impressed him. Or, to be precise, she had not impressed him with her lack of recognition that she was here to fulfil a contractual obligation. In every other respect he'd been very, *very* impressed…

Dieu, but she possessed a body! He'd known she did, but to see it displayed for him like that, before she'd become aware of his presence, had been a pleasure he had indulged in for longer than was prudent.

Because it didn't matter how spectacular her figure was, let alone her face, this was—as he was now reminding her so brusquely—a job, not a holiday.

Certainly not anything else.

His thoughts cut out like a guillotine slicing down. In the days since he had hired her to keep Celine Neuberger at bay he'd had plenty of second thoughts. And third thoughts. Had he been incredibly rash to bring her here? Was he playing with matches near gunpowder?

Seeing her again now, viewing that fantastic body of hers, seeing her stunning beauty right in front of him again, and not only in the memories he'd done his best to crush, was…*unsettling.*

Abruptly he reminded himself that she was not a woman from his world, but a woman he'd admitted into his life briefly, under duress only, and not by free choice. That that did not mean he could now break the rules of a lifetime—rules that had served him well ever since the youthful fiasco over Marianne that had cost him so dearly. Oh, not in money—in heartache that he never wanted to feel again.

But I was young then! A stripling! It was calf

love, nothing more than that, and that's why it hit me so hard.

Now he was a stripling no longer, but a seasoned man, in his thirties, sure of himself, and sure of what he wanted and how to get it. Sure of his relationships with the women he selected for his *amours.* Women who were nothing like the one now sitting opposite him, taking money for her time here.

That was what he must remember. *She* would—that was for certain. It was the reason she was here… the reason she'd accompanied him from the fashion show. She'd made it perfectly clear then—and again when she'd so brazenly upped what he'd been prepared to offer her to come out here now. That was warning enough, surely?

However stunning her face and figure—however powerful her appeal—his relationship with Tara Mackenzie must be strictly professional only. She was here, as he reminded himself yet again, only to do a job.

It was, therefore, in a brisk, businesslike tone that he continued now. 'The Neubergers are arriving this evening. From then on, until they leave, you will assume the role you are here to play. What is essential, however,' he went on, 'is that you understand you are here to *act* the part only. You are *not* to imagine we actually have a relationship of any kind whatsoever or that one is possible at all. Do you understand me?'

Tara felt herself bridling as his dark eyes bored into hers. He was doing it again! Putting her back *right* up. And not just in the way he'd said things—in *what* he had said.

Warning me off him. Telling me not to get ideas about him. Oh, thank you—yes, thank you so much, Monsieur Derenz. It was so *necessary to warn me off you! Not.*

Would she really ever consider a man with the personality of a lump of granite, who clearly thought every woman in the world was after him?

Indignation sparked furiously in her. 'Of course, Monsieur Derenz. I understand perfectly, Monsieur Derenz. Whatever you say, Monsieur Derenz,' Tara intoned fulsomely, venting her objection to his high-handed warning.

His eyes flashed darkly and his arched eyebrows snapped together in displeasure. 'Don't irritate me more than you already have, Ms Mackenzie,' he said witheringly.

'And don't *you*, Monsieur Derenz,' she shot back, bridling even more at his impatient put-down, 'entertain the totally unwarranted assumption that I have *any* desire to do anything more than *act* the part I am here to play! And,' she continued, refusing to be cowed by the increasingly black look on his face, 'I expect *you* to do likewise. There is to be *no* repeat of that little wrist-kissing stunt you pulled just before I went back into the fashion show!' She saw his expression stiffen and ploughed on. 'No unwarranted body contact at all. I appreciate that my role must be convincing—but it is for *public* view only.'

Even just *pretending* to be on intimate terms with

him was going to be a challenge. A challenge that, now she was seeing him again, was making a hollow form inside her. Oh, *what* did the wretched man have that got to her like this?

Deliberately, she made herself think not about how drop-dead devastating he was, sitting there in his killer suit, drawing her hapless gaze to his hard-featured face with the night-dark eyes, but of how obnoxious his manner was. Yes, that was a much safer way to think of him!

The best way of all, though, would be to do what he was doing, annoying though it was to admit it—treat this entire matter as simply a professional engagement.

So, with a deep breath, and a resumption of her cool tone, she asked in a no-nonsense, businesslike way, 'OK—so, the Neubergers… You'd better tell me what I'll be expected to know.'

He didn't seem to like it that she'd taken control of the conversation—but then, she thought acidly, Marc Derenz was clearly used to calling all the shots, all the time. Maybe his employees—and she was one herself, after all, however temporary—were not expected to speak before the august chairman of Banc Derenz.

However, he answered her readily enough, in a no-nonsense tone matching her own.

'Hans Neuberger is head of Neuberger Fabrik—a major German engineering company based in Frankfurt. He is a long-standing family friend and he knows this villa well from many previous visits. Celine is his second wife—Hans was a widower—and their marriage is a relatively recent one…less than two years. He has adult children from his first marriage—'

'Who hate Celine's guts,' put in Tara knowingly.

He made no reply, only continued as if she had not spoken. 'Celine has persuaded her husband to house-hunt for a villa here, and on that pretext she has invited herself to stay, with predictably obvious intent.'

His tone was icy and Tara found herself chilled by it. Even more so as he continued in the same cold voice.

'I will not conceal from you the fact that I consider Hans's marriage to Celine…ill-advised. The woman targeted him for his wealth, and she presumes to target myself—' his tone dropped from cold to Arctic '—as a source of…*entertainment*.' His voice plunged to absolute zero. 'This demonstrates just how ill-advised their marriage is. Were Hans Neuberger anything other than, as I have said, a long-standing family friend, there would be absolutely no question. I would have no hesitation in sending her packing.'

Tara took a slicing breath. 'No, no question at all…' she muttered.

It was unnerving to see just how cold Marc Derenz could be—and how ruthless. Imperious in manner, intemperate in mood—yes, she'd seen that already—but this display of icy ruthlessness was something else…

He got to his feet. 'As it is, however, I am required, for Hans's sake, to proceed by taking a more…*subtle* approach.'

Tara gave a tight smile. 'To demonstrate to her that the…*vacancy* in your life is fully occupied?'

His eyes rested on her, dark and unreadable. 'Precisely,' he said.

He got to his feet. He seemed taller than ever, looming over her. He glanced at his watch—doubtless one of those custom-made jobs, she assumed, that cost more than a house. Then his eyes flicked back to her. She got the feeling that he'd suddenly veiled them, and found herself doing likewise with her own. Instinctively she reached for her discarded sunglasses, as if for protection.

'Cocktails at eight, Ms Mackenzie. Do not be late. I don't appreciate tardiness,' he instructed brusquely.

With that, he left her. And as she watched him stride across the balcony Tara suddenly felt as if she'd gone six rounds with a heavyweight.

She picked up her book, conscious that her heart-rate was elevated. One thing was for sure—she was going to earn her money here.

As she settled back in her lounger a stray thought flickered. *I should have asked for danger money—I think I'm going to need it.*

But whether that would protect her from Marc Derenz's unyieldingly flinty manner, or from his much more devastating impact on her, she did not care to examine...

CHAPTER FOUR

MARC WAS IN his office, staring moodily at his computer screen, paying the display no attention. He kept a fully kitted-out office in all his properties, so that he could keep constant tabs on his business affairs.

It had been his habit to do so ever since his vast inheritance had landed on his too-young shoulders. If he hadn't kept a tight grip on everything, shown everyone he was capable of running the bank, he'd have been sidelined by his own board. Doing so had made him appear hard-nosed, even arrogant sometimes, he was aware, but imposing his will on men a generation older than him had been essential. Even now, over a decade on, the habit of command was ingrained in him, whoever he was dealing with.

Including women who were being paid handsomely to do a very simple job, and yet who seemed to find it impossible not to simply take on board his very clear instructions without constantly answering him back!

His mouth tightened. This nonsense with Hans's wife was causing him quite enough grief as it was.

To have Tara Mackenzie constantly interrupting him, gainsaying him, answering him back, was just intolerable!

He gave a sigh of exasperation. She had better adopt a more gracious and compliant attitude once the Neubergers arrived, or she would never convince the wretched Celine that they were an item.

Why can't she just be like other women are with me? he demanded of himself in exasperation. All his life women had been eager to please him. So why was this one so damn *un*-eager? With her stunning looks, she could have made him far better disposed towards her.

Maybe I should win her over...

Whatever her self-righteous protestations, she had, he knew with his every well-honed male instinct, reacted just the way he'd intended when he'd kissed that tender spot inside her wrist that evening of the fashion show… It had had exactly the effect on her he'd wanted. Started to melt her…

So maybe I should do more of that, not less...

The thought played in his mind. It was tempting… oh, so tempting…to turn that obstreperous antagonism towards him to something much more…*co-operative…*

It would be a challenge, certainly—he had no doubt of that. But maybe he would welcome such a challenge. It would be an intriguing novelty, after all. So different from being besieged by over-eager females…

He thrust the thought from him, steeling his jaw. No, that would *not* be a good idea! Did he *really* have to run through all the reasons why Tara Mackenzie, whatever her allure, was out of bounds to him?

No, he did not. He pulled his keyboard decisively towards him. All he had to do was get through this coming week, using the woman he was paying an exorbitant amount of money, to keep the wretched Celine off his case.

Tara Mackenzie was here to do a job, and then leave. That was all.

All.

Decision reaffirmed, he went back to his work.

Tara cast a professionally critical eye over her reflection. And *professional* was the word she had to keep uppermost in her mind. This, she reminded herself sternly, was just as much a job as striding down a catwalk. And Marc Derenz was simply her employer. She frowned momentarily. Thankfully only for a week or so.

For a week I can put up with his overbearing manner!

And, of course, for the ten thousand pounds he was paying her.

She nodded at her reflection, that showed her in a knee-length royal blue cocktail dress, from a very exclusive luxury label, her make-up immaculate, hair in a French pleat, and one of the pieces of top-brand costume jewellery she'd found in the suitcases around her neck. Yes, she looked the part—the latest woman in Marc Derenz's life. Couture-dressed and expensive.

So—time to go onstage. One of the maids had told

her she was being waited for downstairs, so she made her way to the head of the Hollywood-style staircase. From the top she could see a white-jacketed staff member opening the huge front doors and stepping aside to let Marc Derenz's guests enter, just as Marc himself issued forth from another ground-floor room.

And stopped dead.

Immediately Tara could see why. This was not the Neubergers arriving—this was Frau Neuberger *toute seule.*

Celine—*sans mari*—was dressed to kill in a tailored silk suit in crème-de-menthe, five-inch heels, and a handbag that Tara knew, from her modelling expertise, had a waiting list of over a year and wouldn't give you change from twenty thousand pounds…

'Marc, *cherie*!' Celine cooed as she came up to her host, who was still standing frozen, and lavished air kisses upon him. 'How *wonderful* to be here!'

'Where is Hans?' Tara heard him ask bluntly, at which Celine gave an airy wave.

'Oh, I told him we had no need of him! We'll do *perfectly* well on our own!' She patted Marc's cheek insouciantly with her bare hand, lingering over the contact with her varnished fingernails.

Tara wanted to laugh. Celine was in high fettle, despite the thunderous expression on her quarry's face. Well, time to disabuse her of her hopes.

She started forward, heels tapping on the marble stairs. A wide, welcoming smile parted her lips. 'Celine, how lovely to meet you again!' she exclaimed. 'We're so glad you were able to come!'

She reached the hallway, marshalling herself alongside Marc Derenz. Her pulse was not entirely steady—and that was nothing to do with Celine Neuberger and everything to do with the way Marc Derenz had looked at her as she'd walked down towards them. The way his hard dark eyes had focussed totally on her, as if pinning her with his gaze. A gaze that this time was not like a laser, but more… Appreciative. Liking what it saw. More than liking…

She felt a flush of heat go through her limbs, and then, collecting herself, reminded herself that of *course* Marc Derenz had looked at her like that—*he* was in role-play just as much as she was! She bestowed an air kiss upon Celine, whose face had contorted in fury at Tara's appearance.

'I just *adore* house-hunting! We'll have *such* fun together! I can't wait!' she gushed, ignoring the other woman's obvious anger at her presence there. 'Why not describe what you're after by way of a villa over drinks?' she invited Celine cordially, hoping that Marc Derenz would lead them to wherever it was that cocktails were going to be served. She hadn't a clue—and if Celine realised that it might give the game away.

Thankfully, he did just that, ushering them both into a sumptuous Art Deco salon, where wide French windows opened onto a terrace bathed in late sunshine. Celine, all but snatching her glass, immediately started to talk animatedly in German to Marc, clearly intent on cutting out Tara as much as she could.

Marc's expression was still radiating the same

thunderous displeasure it had been since he had seen Celine arrive without her husband. For her part, Tara cast a jaundiced eye at the woman.

Honey, you'd be welcome to him! He's arrogant and bad-tempered and totally charmless! Help yourself, do!

But of course that was out of the question. So, knowing she had to act—quite literally—she stepped forward, a determined smile on her face, placing a quite clearly possessive, hand on Marc Derenz's arm.

'I'm hopeless at German!' she announced insouciantly. 'And my French is only schoolgirl, alas. Are you telling Marc what you're looking for in a house here?'

As she spoke she was aware that the arm beneath her fingertips had steeled, and his whole body had tensed at her moving so closely into his body space. She pressed her hand on his sleeve warningly. Celine was never going to be fooled if she stayed a mile distant from him.

And he needn't think she *wanted* to be in his body space! His utterly unnecessary warning from the afternoon echoed in her head, informing her that she was to remember she was only here to *act* a part. Not to believe it was real.

I wouldn't want it to be real anyway, sunshine, she said tartly but silently to him.

In her head—treacherously—a single word hovered. *Liar.*

You might not like him, the voice went on, *but for some damn reason he has the ability to turn your knees to jelly, so you just be careful, my girl!*

She pushed it out. It had no place in her thoughts. None at all. She was *not* looking for Marc Derenz to pay her what he so clearly imagined would be the immense compliment of desiring her for real. So there was no need at all for him to have warned her off.

And all this—all she was going to have to act out for the duration—was just that. An act. Nothing more.

An act it might be, but it was hard going for all that.

All through dinner she made a relentless effort to be Marc Derenz's charming hostess—attentive to his guest, endlessly gushing and smiling about the delights of searching for zillion-dollar homes on the French Riviera to this woman who clearly wished her at the bottom of the ocean.

Tara was doggedly undeterred by Celine's barely civil treatment. Far more exasperating to her was Marc Derenz's stony attitude.

OK, so maybe he was still blazingly furious that Celine had turned up on her own, but that didn't mean he could get away with monosyllabic responses and a total lack of interest in the conversation Tara was so determinedly keeping going.

As they finally returned to the salon for coffee and liqueurs, she hissed at him, 'I can't do this all on my own! For heaven's sake, play *your* part as well!'

She slipped her hand into his arm and sat herself down with him on an elegant sofa, deliberately placing a hand on his muscled thigh. She felt him flinch, as if she'd burnt him, and a spurt of renewed irritation went through her. If *she* could do this, damn it, so could he!

She turned to him, liqueur glass in her hand. 'Marc, darling, you're being such a grouch! *Do* lighten up!' she cooed cajolingly.

Her reward was a dark, forbidding flash of his eyes, and an obvious increase in the reading on his displeasure meter as his expression hardened. Her mood changed abruptly. Actually, she realised, there was something very satisfying in winding up Marc Derenz! He was so *easy* to annoy.

A little frisson went through her. She might be playing with fire, but it was enticing all the same…

She turned back to Celine, who was fussing over her coffee. 'Marc's just sulking because he doesn't want to go house-hunting,' she said lightly. 'Men hate that sort of thing—let's leave him behind and do it ourselves!'

But Celine was having none of this. 'You know nothing about the area,' she said dismissively. 'I need Marc's expertise. Of course ideally,' she went on, 'we'd love to buy here, on Cap Pierre—it's *so* exclusive.'

'So much so that there is nothing changing hands,' was Marc's dampening reply.

Dieu, the last thing he wanted was Celine Neuberger anywhere on the Cap. And the next last thing he wanted, he thought, his mood darkening even more, was Tara's hand on his thigh.

It was taking all his resolve to ignore it. To ignore her, as he had been trying to do ever since his eyes had gone to her, descending the staircase with show-stopping impact, and he'd caught his breath at her beauty, completely unable to drag his eyes away from her.

All his adjurations to himself that Tara Mackenzie was out of bounds to him had vanished in an instant, and he'd spent the rest of the evening striving to remember them. But with every invasion by her of his personal space it had proved impossible to do so. As for her hissing at him like that just now—did she not realise how hard it was for him to have to remember this was only a part he was playing? And then, dear God, she had placed a hand on his thigh…

How the hell am I going to get through this week? Was I insane to bring her here?

But it didn't matter whether he had been insane or not—he was stuck with this now. And, tormenting or not, she was right. He had to behave as if he were, indeed, in the throes of a torrid affair with her—or else what was the point of her being here at all?

So, now, trying to make the gesture casual, he placed his free hand over hers. Was it her turn to tense suddenly? Well, *tough*.

To take his mind off the feel of her slender fingers beneath the square palm of his hand, he said, making his voice a tad more amenable, 'I'm sure you and Hans will find what you're looking for, though, Celine. How about higher on the coastline, with a view?'

Pleased at being addressed directly, even if did cast a sour look at him all but holding hands with Tara, Celine smiled engagingly.

'A view would be essential!' she stipulated, and then she was away, waxing lyrical about various houses she had details for, animatedly wanting to discuss them.

Marc let her run on, saying what was necessary when he had to, aware that the focus of his consciousness was actually the fact that his fingers had—of their own accord, it seemed—wound their way into Tara's… His thumb was idly stroking the back of her hand, which felt very pleasant to him, and her palm seemed be hot on his leg, which felt more than merely pleasant…

He could feel himself starting to wish Celine to perdition—and not for the reason that he had no interest whatsoever in a spot of adultery with his friend's wife…

Because he wanted Tara to himself…

He could feel his pulse quicken, arousal beckon…

Maybe the cocktail he'd imbibed, the wine he'd drunk over dinner, the brandy now swirling slowly in his glass, had loosened his inhibitions, faded the reminder he'd been imposing on himself all evening that he had not brought Tara here for any purpose other than to shield him from Hans's wife.

But what if I had?

The thought played in his mind, tantalising… tempting.

Then, with a douche of cold water, he hauled his thoughts away. He lifted his hand away too, restoring Tara's hand to her own lap with a casual-seeming move. He got to his feet. He needed to get out of here.

'Celine, forgive me. I have a call booked to a client in the Far East.' He hadn't, but he had to call time on this.

Celine looked put out, but he couldn't care less. Tara was looking up at him questioningly. Then she took the cue he was signalling. He saw her give a little yawn.

'We'd probably both better call it day,' she announced to Celine. 'I'm sure you're tired after your journey.'

She was making it impossible for Celine to linger, and Marc ushered them both from the room, bidding his unwanted guest goodnight.

Then he turned to the woman who was not his guest, but his temporary employee, however hard she was making it to remember that.

'I'll be about half an hour, *mon ange*,' he murmured, knowing he had to give just the right impression to Celine. Knowing, with a part of his mind to which he was not going to pay any attention, that, however much of a siren call it was, he did not want it to be a mere 'impression' at all…

He silenced his mind ruthlessly, by force of will, turning on his heel and heading for his office, where he was *not* about to make phone call to the Far East, but another, far more urgently needed communication.

The whole evening had been nothing but a gruelling ordeal—and not just for the reasons he'd thought it would be. Not just because of Celine.

Because of Tara.

And what she was tempting him to.

Which he must resist or risk breaking the most essential rule he lived by.

As Tara gained her bedroom relief filled her. Dear Lord, but that had backfired on her—big-time! Hissing like that at Marc to be more convincing in his role-play! Had she been nuts to demand that? To take the initiative he would not?

Memory was hot in her head, as if it were still happening—sitting up close and personal beside him, so that the heat from his body was palpable through the fine jersey of her dress. And then, after so stupidly getting a kick out of winding him up with her taunt about being a grouch, putting her hand on his thigh.

Hard muscle and sinew…and a strength beneath the material of his trousers that had made her want to snatch her hand away as if she'd touched white-hot metal. But she hadn't been able to, because his own hand had closed over hers, imprisoning it between the hard heat of his thigh and the soft heat of his palm.

And then she'd felt her throat catch as that casual meshing of his fingers with hers, that slow, sensual stroking of his thumb, had lit up a thousand trembling nerve-ends in her…

No! Don't think about it! Focus, instead, on getting to bed.

Tomorrow was going to be another long day. Just putting up with Celine was ordeal enough—let alone Marc as well.

Putting him out of her mind as best she could,

she got on with getting into her night attire, carefully hanging up the beautiful dress she'd been wearing, then removing her make-up and brushing out her hair. The familiar rituals were soothing to her jagged nerves—as much as they *could* be soothed.

Aware that she was still on edge, and knowing why and deploring it, but unable to calm herself any more, she headed for the palatial en suite bathroom to brush her teeth. As she did so she glanced askance at the door inset beside it. It was no surprise that she'd been put into a bedroom with what must be a communicating door to wherever it was that Marc Derenz slept, because otherwise it would look too obvious that she wasn't really there in the role she claimed. But all the same it was unnerving to think that only a flimsy door separated her from him.

Without thinking too much about what she was doing, let alone why, she went to test it. Locked—and from the other side. A caustic smile pulled at her mouth. Oh, it was definitely time to remind herself that whatever Marc Derenz did in public in order to put out the impression that they were having an affair, in private he was obviously keeping to the arrogant warning he'd given her—not to take his attentions for real…

Well, that was a two-way message, and it was time to remind him of it! She reached for the bolt on her own side, meaning to shoot it closed. And jumped back.

The door had been pulled open from the other

side, and Marc Derenz was stepping through into her bedroom.

Her eyes flashed in alarm. 'What are you doing?' she demanded.

She saw his brows snap together in his customary displeased fashion, as if she had no business challenging his walking in unannounced to her bedroom. Quite illogically, she welcomed it.

It's better to dislike him than to—

Her disturbing thought was cut short.

'I need to speak to you,' he announced peremptorily.

He was still in his dinner trousers, but he'd taken off his jacket and his tie was loosened. It gave him a raffish look. As did the line of shadow clearly discernible along his jawline.

Tara felt her stomach hollow. It just did not matter how disagreeable he was. Marc Derenz really should not be so bone-meltingly attractive…

And he shouldn't be in your bedroom either.

The realisation hit her and she took a step back, suddenly aware that she was in her pyjamas. Oh, they might be modesty itself, with their wide silk trousers and high-collared *cheong-sang* top, but they were still nightwear.

'Well?' she prompted, lifting her chin. She didn't like the way his dark eyes had swept over her, then veiled instantly. Didn't like the way she was burningly aware that they had… Didn't like, most of all, the way her nerves had started to jangle all over again…

'I've been emailing Bernhardt—Hans's son.' Marc's voice was brusque, as if he wanted to get this over and done with. 'I've told him in no uncertain terms that he must make sure Hans joins us. I won't have Celine here on her own. Even with you here to—'

'To protect you,' completed Tara helpfully.

Another of his dark looks was his reply, before he continued as if she had not interrupted him. 'Thankfully Bernhardt agrees with me. He's going to tell his father he'll stand in for him at a board meeting so Hans can arrive tomorrow evening. It's all arranged.'

She could hear relief in his voice, and saw a snap of satisfaction in his eyes.

'So we just have to get through tomorrow, do we? Trailing along while Celine looks at houses?' Tara said.

She was trying to silence the jangling of her nerves at his unexpected presence—in her bedroom, with her only in her night attire. She fought to make her voice normal, as composed as she could make it.

'Or are you going to find a way of getting out of it? I don't mind coping with her on my own if you want to bottle it,' she added helpfully.

His expression darkened again. 'No, I'll have to come along as well. If I don't she'll end up landing Hans with some overpriced monstrosity!' He gave an exasperated sigh.

Tara couldn't help but give a laugh, though it earned her yet another darkling look. 'I'll take a bet she'll go for the most garish, opulent pile she can find,' she said, preferring to have a dig at Celine than let herself be distracted by Marc Derenz's overpowering, and utterly unfairly impactful presence in her bedroom. 'Gold bathrooms and crystal chandeliers in the kitchen.'

'Very likely,' he replied grimly. 'Oh, hell, why on earth did he marry the damn woman?' he muttered to himself.

'Well, she's certainly a looker,' Tara conceded, still trying to make normal conversation. 'Over-done-up, to my mind, but presumably it appeals to your friend.'

He shook his head. 'Not Hans,' he said. 'The last thing he wants is any kind of trophy wife.'

Tara couldn't keep the caustic note from her voice. 'Are you sure? Most men like to show off the fact that they can acquire a woman that other men will envy them for.'

Marc's eyes narrowed. 'Is that your experience?'

She shrugged her shoulders. 'It's pretty common in the world I come from—models are, after all, the ultimate trophy females to make a man look successful.'

Was there bitterness in her voice? She hoped not, but being with Jules had made her wary. What would a man like Marc know, or care, about men like Jules, who needed to feel big by draping a model on their arm? *He* certainly wouldn't need to.

A man as rich and as drop-dead gorgeous as he is doesn't need to prove a thing to anyone!

The thought was in her head before she realised it was there.

Then it was wiped right from her mind. Marc Derenz had taken a step towards her.

'Can you blame them?'

There was something different in his voice, in his stance, in the way he was looking at her.

Suddenly, out of nowhere, every nerve in her body was jangling again—louder than ever. What the hell was she doing, talking to him like this? Standing here in her bedroom, wearing only her silk pyjamas, while Marc Derenz stood there far too close to her, looking so unutterably damn *sexy* with his loosened tie, his jacketless shirt, the hint of a shadowed jawline…

She caught the scent of his aftershave—something expensive, custom-designed, a signature creation made for him alone…

And his eyes—those deep, dark eyes—like slate, but suddenly not hard like slate, but as if a vein of gold had suddenly been exposed in their unyielding surface…

She couldn't drag her own eyes from them…

Couldn't drag breath into her lungs…

Could not focus on a single other thing in the universe than those dark, gold-lit eyes resting on her…

The room seemed to be shrinking—or was it the space between them?

He started towards her again, lifted a hand. She caught the glint of gold at his cuffs, echoing that same glint in those dark eyes of his that were now holding hers…holding her immobile, breathless, so she couldn't breathe, couldn't move…

She could only hear the blood surging in her veins,

feel electricity crackle over her skin, as if all he had to do was touch her—make contact…

'Can you blame them?' he said again.

And now there was a husk in his voice, a timbre to it that did things to her insides even as his outstretched hand reached towards her, a single finger drawing down her cheek, lingering at her mouth.

His eyes were playing over her face and she felt a kind of drowning weakness slacken her limbs. Making it quite impossible for her to move a muscle, to do anything other than simply stand there…stand there and feel the slow drift of his fingertip move across the soft swell of her lips. Only his touch on her mouth existed…only the soft, sensuous caress…

'*Pourquoi es-tu si, si belle?*' His murmur was a low husk as he lifted his other hand to slide it slowly, sensuously, around the nape of her neck, through the tumbled masses of her loosened hair. 'Why is it that I cannot resist your beauty?'

She felt her eyelids flutter, felt her pulse beating in her throat, felt her lips parting even as his fingers splayed across her cheek, cupped her jaw to tilt her face to his lowering mouth which she could not, for all the world, resist…

Her eyelids dropped across her eyes, veiling him from sight. She was reduced only to the kiss he was easing across the mouth she lifted to his… Reduced only to the feathered silk of his touch, the hand at her nape cradling her skull, the fingers woven into her hair.

It was like that lingering wrist-kiss all over again,

but a thousand times more so. A million sensations swirled within her at the sheer velvet sensuality of his kiss…his mouth moving on hers, tasting her, exploring her. She was helpless—helpless to resist. The heady scent of his aftershave, his body, was in her senses, in the closeness of him as he shaped her mouth to his.

She felt herself leaning into him, letting her own hands glide around the strong column of his back, feeling the play of muscle and sinew, with only the sheer cotton of his shirt to separate her palms from the warmth of his flesh.

She could not stop—would not. Blood was surging in her…her pulse was soaring. She was drowning in his kiss, unable to stop herself, unable to draw away, to find the sanity she needed to find…

And then, abruptly, he was pulling away from her. Stepping away so sharply that her hands fell from him, limp at her sides, just as her whole body felt limp.

Dazedly, Tara gazed blankly at him. She had no strength—none. All her limbs were slack and stricken. Inside her chest her heart was pounding, beating her down.

She heard him speak, but now there was no husk in his voice, no low, sensual timbre. Only a starkness that cut like a knife.

'That should not have happened.'

She felt it like a slap—but it was a sudden awakening from her deathly faint and her eyes flared back into vision, her mind into full consciousness of what she had permitted…given herself up to…

She saw him standing there, stepped back from him. There was a darkness in his face, in his eyes, and his features were pulled taut—as forbidding and shuttered as she had ever seen them.

Then, with the same sharp movement with which he'd pulled away from her, he was turning away, body rigid, his expression still tight as steel wire, walking with heavy, rapid strides to the door. Walking through. Snapping it shut behind him. Without another word.

Leaving her alone, heart pounding, lungs airless, his words echoing in her head—resonating as if it had been she who'd uttered them.

Dismay hollowed her.

Marc plunged down the staircase. *Dieu*, had he been insane to let that happen? Hadn't he warned himself repeatedly that he must keep his response to her hammered down, where it could not escape?

Anger with himself consumed him. Anger he welcomed—for it blotted out more than any other emotion could, blotted out the memory of that irresistible kiss.

Well, you should have resisted it! You should—and must—resist her! She is not here for such a purpose! It would be madness to indulge yourself. Indulge her...

Every reason for his warnings to himself about the dangerous folly of letting the desire that had seized him from the first moment her show-stopping beauty had hit upon his senses marched through his head at his command.

He kept them marching. He must allow nothing else to occupy his mind. Nothing except work. That would keep him on the straight and narrow.

Gaining the hallway, he yanked open the door to his office. The Far Eastern markets would soon be starting up. They would absorb him until he was sufficiently tired to risk heading for bed. *Tout seul.*

His mouth tightened. Most definitely alone.

And it must stay that way. Anything else was a folly he would not commit.

Would not.

CHAPTER FIVE

TARA STOOD IN the over-hot garden of the over-ornate villa they'd just toured, feigning an enthusiasm she did not feel in the slightest. But that was preferable to letting her thoughts go where she did not want them to go. To the memory of that disastrous kiss last night.

She gave a silent groan. Had she been crazy to let Marc Derenz kiss her? *Why* had she let him? Why hadn't she stopped him? Why hadn't she told him to go to hell? Why…?

Why did I kiss him back?

That was what was so disastrous—that she'd *let* him kiss her. And returned it!

Angrily, she catalogued all the reasons why she had been so insanely stupid as to have let that kiss happen. Capping it with the one she'd always had to remember, ever since she'd made the mistake of trusting Jules.

Men who see me only as a model are bad news! And I won't be any man's trophy to show off! I won't!

But even as she yanked that warning into her head she felt it wavering. Hadn't she already accepted that

Marc Derenz had no need of a trophy female—not with his wealth, his looks.

Yes, and doesn't that just make him even worse? she shot back to herself. *Thinking every woman in the world is after him?*

She pressed her lips together. Well, not her! She had *not* needed that final warning from him in the slightest.

'That should not have happened.'

And it wasn't going to happen again—that was for certain! Somehow, whatever it took, she was going to get through the rest of this week, collect her money and get away—away from the wretched man.

Until then she had to keep going.

She put her mind back to the role she was supposed to be playing.

'Four of the bedrooms don't have balconies,' she pointed out to Celine helpfully. 'Do you think that rules this one out?'

Celine ignored her. It had been obvious to Tara that she'd been doing her best to do so all morning. Instead she turned to Marc.

'What do *you* think, Marc, *cherie*?' she posed with a little pout. 'Does it matter if not all the bedrooms have balconies?'

'No,' said Marc succinctly, his indifference to the issue blatant. He glanced at his watch impatiently. 'Look, would you not agree that it's time for lunch?' he demanded. He was clearly at the limit of his patience.

Tara found herself almost smiling, and welcomed

the release from the self-punishing thoughts going round and round in her head. He was so visibly bored and irritated—and, whilst she could not blame him, she knew with a waspish satisfaction that this time it was not she who was drawing his ire. Besides, at least when he was being bad-tempered he wasn't being amorous…

His ill humour, she noted with another caustic smile, seemed completely lost on the armour-plated Celine however. All through lunch—at a very expensive restaurant in Nice—Tara watched the woman determinedly making up to him, constantly touching his sleeve with her long scarlet nails, making cooing noises at him, laughing in an intimate fashion and throwing fluttering little glances at him…

All to utterly no avail.

He sat there like a block of stone, his expression getting darker and darker, until Tara wanted to laugh out loud. She herself was doing her level best to drag Celine's attention towards her instead, chattering away brightly, waxing lyrical about the houses they'd viewed, the ones they might still view, obdurately not letting Celine blank her as the woman kept trying to do.

That her brightly banal chatter was only adding to the visible irritation on Marc's face did not bother her. What else did he expect her to do, after all? She was here to run interference, and that was what she was doing. And, after all, the way wretched Celine was behaving, the whole situation was just ridiculous! He really needed to lighten up about it.

As the woman turned away now, to complain about something or other to a hapless passing waiter, Tara could not suppress a roll of her eyes at Celine's endless plays for Marc's attention. Then, abruptly, his eyes snapped to hers, catching her in mid-eye-roll.

She saw his mouth tighten and one of his laser looks come her way. She gave a minute shake of her head in resignation, a sardonic twitch of her lips, and for a moment—just the slightest moment—she thought she saw something flicker in the slate-grey depths of his eyes. Something that went beyond a warning to her not to come out of role. Something that she had never seen before. A flicker so faint she could not believe she'd seen it.

Humour.

Good grief, did the wretched man actually have a sense of humour? Somewhere buried in the recesses of his rock-like personality?

If he did she didn't catch any more sight of it. After lunch was finally over Celine gushingly begged Marc to head for Monte Carlo. With ill grace he complied, and Tara found herself glad of the excursion. Not only was it a lot better than looking at over-priced, over-decorated villas for sale, but she'd never seen Monte Carlo, and she looked around her with touristic scrutiny at the grandeur of the Place de Casino, her gaze lingering on the fabled casino itself.

'It's where fools go to lose their money,' a sardonic voice said at her side.

She glanced at Marc, whose expression mirrored his disparaging tone of voice. 'Now, *there* speaks the sober banker!' she exclaimed lightly. 'All the same,' she added, 'sometimes those fools come out millionaires.'

'The winners win from the other gamblers who lose.' His tone was even more crushing. 'There is no free money in this world.'

'Unless,' Tara could not resist saying, 'one marries it… That's always been a favourite way of getting free money.'

Her barb was wasted. Celine's attention was focussed only on the luxury shopping mall opposite the casino. Like a heat-seeking missile, she headed towards it. As Tara made to follow she caught a frown on Marc's face. She presumed it was because he was now facing a prospect every man loathed—shopping with women.

Impulsively, she tucked her hand into his elbow. *'Courage, mon brave!'* she murmured humorously, leaning into him.

She only meant to lighten him up, maybe even to catch a glimpse of that crack in his steel armour that she'd evoked so unexpectedly over lunch. But clearly his mood had worsened too much for that.

Her hand was abruptly removed and he strode forward, leaving her to hasten after him into the mall.

She gave a sigh. And a twist of her mouth. It had been stupid of her to do that. And not because it had annoyed him instead of lightening him up. Because *any* physical contact at all with the man was not a good idea in the least…

Not after last night. Not after that kiss—that disastrous, dangerous, completely *deranged* kiss that she should never have let happen!

No, any physical contact with him that wasn't forced on her by the necessity of playing the role he was paying her to play, was totally *défendu*. Totally forbidden. And she mustn't forget it. Not even to wind the man up. Or try and lighten him up. It was just too risky…

Because, however overbearing and obnoxious he could be, she was just too damned vulnerable to what he could make her feel.

Sobered, she followed him into the mall.

'*Fraulein*, how very good to meet you!'

Hans Neuberger was shaking Tara's hand genially, his face smiling. He had a nice face, Tara decided. Not in the least good-looking, and late middle-aged—a good twenty years older than his wife—but with kindly eyes.

She smiled warmly back. 'Herr Neuberger,' she returned.

'Hans, please!' he said immediately, and she liked him the more.

They were in the magnificent Art Deco salon once more, and Hans Neuberger had just arrived. He'd kissed Celine dutifully on the cheek, but she'd turned away impatiently. Tara thought her a fool to treat her kindly husband with such open indifference.

'Hans! I'm glad to see you!'

Tara turned. Marc was striding in, holding out his

hand to his guest in greeting. She stared, disbelief etching her features.

Good God, the man could smile! As in *really* smile! Not the cynical, humourless indentation of his mouth she'd seen so far, or that infinitesimal chink she'd seen at lunchtime, but an actual smile! A smile that parted his mouth, reached his eyes to crinkle them at the edge. That lightened his entire face…

She felt her breath catch.

Gone, totally, was the hard-faced, bored, impatient, ill-tempered expression she was so used to. Just… gone. It made him a *completely* different person—

She reeled with it, still hardly believing what she was seeing. And she felt something shift inside her, rearrange itself. Marc Derenz…*smiling!* It was like the sun coming out after thunderclouds…

She stared on, bemused, aware that her pulse had suddenly quickened and that it had something to do with the way Marc's smile had softened his face, warmed his eyes… It warmed something in her as well, even though it was not directed at her in the least.

But what if it were—?

No. She shut her mind off. It was bad enough coping with the utterly unfair impact the man had on her when he was being his usual ill-humoured self. She could not possibly think how she would cope if he were capable of being *nice*, for heaven's sake!

It was a resolve she had to stick to throughout dinner. She was helped in that by focussing her attention on Celine's husband. Hans Neuberger really was far too nice to be landed with a shrew like Celine. He was clearly hurt and bewildered by her dismissiveness, and Tara did her best to divert him.

'I think Marc said you're based in Frankfurt? All I know about it is the huge annual book fair. Oh, and that it was the birthplace of Goethe.'

Hans's kindly face lit up. 'Indeed—our most famous son! And Germany's most famous poet—'

Celine's voice was sharp as she cut across him. 'Oh, for heaven's sake, Hans, don't start boring on about poetry! Who cares?'

The rudeness was so abrupt that Tara stared. Hans was silenced, looking stricken. Tara felt immensely sorry for him and rallied to his defence.

'I'm afraid I know very little about German poetry—it didn't really come into my English Literature course at university, alas,' she said politely.

'Speaking of university…' Marc's voice interjected now, as he picked up the baton. 'Has your youngest—Trudie—graduated yet?'

As Hans answered Tara saw Marc throw a glance at her. There was something in his eyes she'd never seen before. Appreciation. Appreciation, evidently, for coming to Hans's rescue as she had.

She blinked for a moment. Then gave a minute nod.

For the rest of the meal she did her best to shield Hans from his unpleasant wife, drawing him out about Goethe and the German Romantics, comparing them with the English Romantics of the same period. Marc joined in, widening the discussion to include French poetry too, keeping the conversation going.

Celine seemed to be in a foul mood—though whether that was because she was clearly being cut out of a conversation she was incapable of contributing to, or whether it was just because her husband had arrived, Tara wasn't sure and didn't care.

What *was* clear, though, was that Celine was not about to let her husband's presence get in the way of her determined pursuit of Marc Derenz, and she was still focusing her attention solely on him.

She continued to do so, quite blatantly, the following day. She dragged them all out for yet more house-viewings, then insisted on heading to Cannes, so she could trawl through the luxury brand-name boutiques strung out along the Croisette.

'She really is,' Tara heard herself say *sotto voce* to Marc, as Celine preened in front of a mirror, 'the most tiresome woman ever! Poor Hans can't possibly want to stay married to her!'

'She's like a leech,' he snapped shortly. 'And Hans is too damn soft-hearted for his own good!'

'Can he really not see her true character?' Tara mused disbelievingly.

Marc's face hardened. 'Men can be fools over women,' he said.

She glanced at him curiously. He couldn't possibly be referring to himself—she knew that. A man like Marc Derenz was made of granite. No woman could make an impact on him.

'Marc, *cherie*!' Celine's piercing call sought to summon his attention. 'Your taste is impeccable! Should I buy this?'

'That is for Hans to say, not me,' came his tight reply.

'Oh, Hans knows nothing about fashion at all!' was Celine's rudely dismissive retort.

Tara stepped forward, seizing a handbag from a stand. 'This would go perfectly with that outfit,' she said. And it was not for Celine's sake, but for the sake of her hapless spouse, hovering by her side.

Celine was hesitating between outright rejection of anything that Tara suggested and lust for the shiny gold bag. The latter triumphed, and she snatched it from her.

'Magpie, as well as leech,' Tara murmured, her head dipped towards Marc.

Did she hear a crack that might just be laughter break from him, before it was abruptly cut off? She stole a look at him, but the moment was gone.

At least, though, the handbag had clinched it and Celine was ready to depart.

It still took for ever, it seemed to Tara—and probably to Marc and Hans as well, she thought cynically—before they could finally return to the villa. Another grim evening loomed ahead of them, with Celine openly discontented because Marc had flatly vetoed her repeated suggestion that they head for the casino at Monte Carlo.

But her petulant mood improved markedly when, after dinner, she took a phone call that made her announce, 'That was the Astaris. They're on their yacht in Cannes. They're giving a party tomorrow.' A frown crossed her brow. 'I haven't got a *thing* to wear for it!' She turned towards Marc. '*Do* run me into Monte, tomorrow, *cherie*! I'm sure Tara can stay here and discuss poetry with Hans,' she added pettishly.

Not surprisingly, Celine's blatant ploy to get Marc to herself for yet another shopping expedition failed, and the following morning all four of them set out for Monaco.

This time, thankfully, Celine availed herself of a personal shopper, who read her client perfectly so that she could emerge triumphantly with a gown that would cost her husband an outrageous sum of money. Full of herself, Celine then demanded that they lunch at the principality's premier hotel, overlooking the marina packed with luxury yachts, and proceeded to plague her husband to buy something similar.

It was obvious to Tara that this was the last thing Hans wanted to do, and she took pity on him by deliberately interrupting the flow of his wife's importuning.

'Tell me,' she asked, 'what else is in Monte Carlo besides the casino, luxury shops and yachts?'

Hans's face brightened. 'The Botanic Gardens are world-famous,' he said.

'Have we time to visit?' Tara asked. It would be nice, after all, she thought, sighing inwardly, while she was here, actually to see something of the Côte d'Azur other than expensive villas, expensive shops and expensive restaurants.

'What a good idea!' Celine put in immediately. 'Hans, you take Tara to the gardens and Marc and I can—'

'I thought you wanted to talk to a yacht broker?'

Marc cut across her brutally, pre-empting whatever scheme Celine was about to dream up to get him on his own.

Celine sulked visibly, then ordered Hans off to find out who the best yacht broker in the principality was. Dutifully the poor man went off to ask the hotel's concierge. Perking up at her husband's absence—however temporary—Celine leant across to Marc, resting her hand on his sleeve in her possessive fashion, stroking it seductively.

'A yacht is *so* essential these days—you must agree!' she oozed. '*Do* help me persuade Hans, *cherie*!'

There was a cajoling, caressing note in her voice, and her scarlet nails curved over his arm. Her over-made-up face was far too close to his, her eyes greedy for him, openly lascivious—and suddenly, out of nowhere, Tara had had enough. Just *enough.*

There was something in her that absolutely revolted at seeing Celine paw at Marc the way she did. Something that was the last thing she should feel about him—but feel it she did, and with a power that shook her.

Parting her lips in an acid grimace she leant forward. 'Celine,' she said, sweetly, but with a bite to her voice that could have cut through steel wire, 'call me old-fashioned, but I would prefer you, please, to take your hand *off* Marc!'

Immediately Celine's eyes snapped to Tara. There was venom in them. And in the words she snapped out too.

'Oh, my, how *very* possessive! Anyone might think you have *ideas* about him!'

It was a taunt—an obvious one—and Tara opened her mouth to retaliate. Except no words came. Only a spearing dart of emotion that should not be there… should not exist at all.

And then, suddenly, Marc's voice cut across her consciousness. She felt her hand being taken, turned over, exposing her wrist. Before she knew what he intended he had dipped his head, grazed his mouth across that tender skin, sending a million nerve-endings firing in her so that she could only stare at him, eyes widening…

'I very much hope Tara *does* have ideas about me… very possessive ideas!' she heard him say. 'For I most certainly do about her!'

His voice had dropped to a low purr, and now his gaze was holding Tara's with an expression of absolute intentness.

Was he trying to convey a message? She didn't know—could only feel all those nerve-endings still firing inside her like a hail of fireworks as the dark gaze on her suddenly lifted, shifting to Celine. Tara felt his hand, large and strong, enfold hers, meshing his fingers into hers…*possessively.*

She saw him smile—a smile, she suddenly thought, that had a twist of ruthlessness to it. A ruthlessness that was entirely explained when she heard him speak.

'You can be the first to know, Celine.' That same deep, steely purr was in his voice. 'Tara is my fiancée,'

Fiancée? Tara heard the word, but could not credit it. Where had *that* come from?

Urgently, she looked at Marc, burningly conscious not just of what he had dropped like a concrete block on them all, but even more of the tightly meshed fingers enclosing hers. Possessively…very possessively.

With a corner of her consciousness she heard a hissing intake of breath from Celine.

'*Fiancée?* Don't be absurd!'

Her derision stung. Stung with an echo of Marc's voice telling her not to get ideas about him, telling her this was playacting only and for no other purpose.

And it stung with much more. With the way his mouth had felt like velvet on the tender skin of her wrist just now, taunting her…tempting her…

Of its own volition and entirely instinctively, with an instinct as old as time and as powerful as the desire she felt for the man who had brought her here, Tara felt her mouth curve into a derisive smile, a mocking laugh.

Because he did not desire her for himself, but only to block another woman's access to him.

She felt her hand lift to Marc's cheek, felt herself lean towards him. Felt her mouth reach for his, open to his, to feast on it, possessive with passion and naked desire…

How long she kissed him she did not know, for time had stopped, had ceased to exist. There was only the sensation of Marc's mouth, exploding within her, the taste of him, the scent of him, the weakening of every part of her body as desire flamed inside her…

Dazed, she drew back, gathering what senses she could, knowing her heart was pounding in her breast but that she had to say something. Anything.

Deliberately she gave that mocking little laugh again. Clearly Celine had wanted proof of the engagement Marc had suddenly and out of nowhere imposed upon the scene.

'We were going to keep it secret—weren't we, darling?'

Her glance at Marc was brief. She did not meet his eyes…did not dare to. Then she looked back to Celine across the table. She had to stay in role, in character—that was essential, however hectic her pulse was after that insanely reckless kiss that she had been unable to prevent herself from taking from him.

'Don't say anything to Hans, will you?' she said to Celine. 'Marc wants to tell him himself—before we announce it formally.'

The expression on Celine's face was as if she had swallowed a scorpion—or a whole bucketful of them. Then Hans was coming back to the table. He started to say something about yacht brokers but Celine cut across him. She was furious—absolutely seething.

Tara's glance went treacherously to the man she had just kissed with such openly passionate abandon…

But then so was Marc…

CHAPTER SIX

MARC YANKED ON his DJ and strode to the connecting door, pulling it open and striding into Tara's bedroom. He still could not believe he'd done what he'd done. Telling Celine that Tara was his fiancée! And then letting her kiss him—*again*. Had he gone mad? He must have. But had there been *any* other way of getting Hans's damn wife to lay off him?

Even as he'd made that momentous announcement he'd been appalled at himself. Danger had shimmered all around. Every precept he'd lived his life by had been appalled.

And now he had to do what he was intent on doing—make it absolutely crystal-clear to Tara Mackenzie that he had spoken entirely on impulse, exasperated beyond the last of his patience by Celine. It was a final means to an end—nothing more than that. Being his fiancée was every bit as fictional as his original proposition.

His mouth set in a grim expression. That devastating kiss she'd given him had not been fictional in the least! It had been searingly, devastatingly *real*…

But he absolutely could *not* risk that. Risk anything like that at all! Not with Tara—the woman he should have nothing to do with whatsoever outside the playacting he was paying her for…

She can't be anything in my life—I can't risk it. And I can't risk her thinking she can be anything in my life. Wanting any of this to be real...

His eyes went to her now. She was sitting at the dressing table, putting on her lipstick. She was quite at home in his villa, in this bedroom with its luxurious atmosphere, with its priceless pieces of Art Deco furniture, the silver dressing table set, the walls adorned with paintings from the thirties by artists whose prices in auction rooms were stratospheric.

Tara looked perfect in the setting—as if she belonged there…

But she doesn't belong. I hired her to play a part, and the fact that the part has suddenly become that of my fiancée changes nothing!

That was what he had to remember.

That the searing desire he felt for her was not something he could permit.

Part of him registered that, yet again, she was looking totally stunning. The russet silk halter-necked evening gown left her sculpted shoulders bare and skimmed the slender contours of her spectacular body, and her glorious hair waved lustrously over her shoulders in rich abandon.

Her head swivelled sharply as he strode in, and she dropped her lipstick on a silver tray.

'We need to talk!' Marc's voice was brusquer than he'd intended, but he did not care.

Tara's chin lifted, her eyes defiant. She got to her feet and got in first. 'Don't look at me like that!' she said. 'I know I was impulsive, kissing you like that, but—'

He strode up to her, took her shoulders. He'd had to wait *hours* for this moment! He'd had to endure babysitting Hans at the yacht broker's so he didn't end up buying a damn yacht for his appalling wife, then endure the car ride back to the villa, and then endure Tara disappearing up to her room to shower and dress for the evening. He was not going to wait a single interminable moment longer!

'It was *totally* unnecessary!' he barked.

'It was totally *necessary*!' Tara shot back. She wrenched herself free. 'Look, you'd just dropped that on me out of the blue! Saying I was your fiancée! I didn't know what to do—only that I had to follow your lead and make it look real!'

'*Dieu*, it looked real, all right! It damn near earned a round of applause from everyone there! And, worse, it nearly got seen by Hans.' He took a rasping breath. 'Hans must *not* know anything about this—do you understand? Because it isn't real! You *do* understand that, don't you?'

His eyes were skewering hers and his hand slashed the air for emphasis.

'There is *no* relationship between us! *No* engagement! Do *not* think otherwise!'

He saw her expression tighten, her eyes flash.

'Of course I do!' she snapped.

'Then *behave* like you understand it!' he shot back. He drew a deep, if ragged, breath to calm himself, get himself back under iron control. Because if he didn't…

She was standing there, breasts heaving, eyes fired with retaliation, looking so incredibly beautiful that with a single impulse he could have swept her up into his arms and buried his mouth in hers, feasting on those lush, silken lips…

And he dared not—dared not do anything of the sort. It would be madness. All he could do was what he did now. School his features, take another breath…

He held up a hand, silencing any utterance she might be going to say. He needed to say his piece first. 'OK, so I dropped a bombshell…went off-script. And OK…' his expression changed '…if I must I can accept that you acted on impulse to give credibility to what I'd just thrown at you.'

His breathing was still heavy, but he forced it back. Went on with what he had to say.

'But from now on, although we've told Celine we're engaged, we absolutely *must not* let Hans think so!' He took another ragged breath, ran his hand through his hair. 'Or he will believe it.'

His mind slewed away from the prospect of Hans believing that he and Tara were engaged to be married… the hassle and misunderstanding it would lead to…the absolute impossibility of it ever being real, Hans would not understand.

That was what he must cling to now—the fact that

his outburst of sheer exasperated temper, when he had been goaded beyond endurance by Celine, was for *her* consumption only, serving only to convince her to give up any hopes of an adulterous affair with him.

'So,' he said now, 'are we clear on that? We've let Celine think we are engaged—that I've proposed to you and you've accepted—but, as you so adeptly persuaded her, that I am waiting to tell my old friend Hans myself, and we'll be announcing it formally later on. And on that basis…' he took a final heavy breath, his eyes skewering Tara '…we'll get on with the rest of this damn evening. Which I am *not* looking forward to—Celine's appalling friends and their even more appalling party to endure!'

He held out a hand to Tara, not wanting her to say a word…not wanting her to do anything but meekly go along with what he was paying her to do—acting the part of his fiancée.

For a moment it looked as if she was going to argue with him—something no employee of his had ever dared to do. And Tara was no different from *any* other employee—that was what he had to remember. What *she* had to remember.

Then stiffly, ignoring his outstretched hand, she marched to the door, pulled it open.

He caught up with her, and they walked down the stairs. *'Smile,'* Marc urged grimly, *sotto voce*, 'you're my secret fiancée, remember!'

He saw her mouth set in a smile—tight, but there, even if it *was* totally at odds with the glacial expression in her eyes.

As they walked into the salon he saw Celine was already there, looking gaudy in a new gold lamé gown, Hans, totally ignored by her, stood dutifully at her side.

A basilisk glare shot from Celine to Tara beside him, far stronger than any animosity she'd displayed so far towards the woman she perceived as getting in her way. Marc's mouth compressed tightly. Well, maybe his announcement and Tara's outrageous kiss had hit home—even if he was still furious that she'd had the temerity to do such a thing off her own bat.

His simmering anger—and the prospect of a party with a bunch of Celine's friends—made him stiffer than ever in his manner, and his 'Shall we set off?' was made through gritted teeth. His jaw tightened even more when he felt Tara slip her hand into his arm. And nor did his black mood improve when they boarded a yacht lit up like a Christmas tree, music blaring and the deck heaving with just the kind of people he disliked most—those who showed off their money as conspicuously and tastelessly as possible.

Celine, however, was clearly in her element, and she swanned around, discarding Hans as soon as she could, knocking back champagne as if it was water. Marc watched her flirting openly with other men and did his best to keep talking to Hans and to avoid as much as possible any contact with anyone else.

Including Tara.

He was burningly conscious of her standing at his side, not saying a great deal—partly because of the noise of the party and partly because he was quite deliberately talking business with Hans, attempting to block his friend's view of his wife, currently cavorting on the small dance floor with unconcerned abandon with some man. He had no idea who and doubted Hans did either.

But, for all his efforts to ignore Tara, he could still catch her elusive fragrance, hear the rustle of her gown as she shifted position, and he knew that he wanted only to turn his head so his eyes could feast on her…

Was it the hypnotic rhythm of the music, or the champagne he'd imbibed to get him through this ordeal, or the oh-so-occasional brush of her bare arm against his that was building up inside him a pressure he was finding it harder and harder to resist?

He didn't know—only knew that Tara standing beside him was a torment.

I want her. I should not want her, but I do. It's madness to want her, and I know it—and it makes no difference. Whatever it is about her, she makes me forget all the rules I've lived my life by...

'Marc, *cherie*, dance with me!'

Celine had abandoned her partner, was sashaying up to him. Her eyes were glittering and the overpowering scent of her perfume was cloying. She leaned towards him, as if to lead him out onto the dance floor.

'Dance with Hans,' he answered shortly. 'I'm about to dance with Tara.'

The moment he said it he regretted it. The last thing he needed to endure was taking Tara out on the dance floor. But it was too late. Celine's eyes flashed angrily at his blunt refusal as he turned to Tara.

'*Mon ange?* Shall we?' His voice was tight, and the expression in his eyes warned her not to refuse him.

He saw her stiffen, saw her obvious reluctance to be taken into his arms and danced with. It fuelled his anger. He reached out, helping himself to her bare arm, and guided her forward. Stiffly, she looped her arms around his neck, barely touching him, and his hands moved to rest on her slender hips.

He could feel the heat of her body through the thin fabric of her gown. Feel, too, how stiffly she was moving as they started to dance. He made himself look down at her face, which was set in stark lines, as if dancing with him were the most repugnant thing in the world.

'Celine is watching us,' he gritted. 'Let's make this a bit more believable, shall we? After all,' he added, 'we're an engaged couple now, aren't we? So give it all you've got, *mon ange*.'

His taunt was deliberate, and she knew it—he could see by the sudden flash in her eyes. It gave him a perverse satisfaction to see it, to know with every male instinct in him that there was only one reason why she was reluctant to make this look real.

And it was not because he repelled her…

It was time to make that clear to her—and if it helped convince Celine too…well, right now he didn't give a damn about Hans's benighted wife or keeping her away from him. Right now only one intention fuelled him. Consumed him…

His hands at her hips drew her towards him, closing the distance between them, and one palm slid to the small of her back to splay across her spine. The supple heat of her body was warm beneath his palm.

For a split second, he felt her resist—as if she would not give in to what he knew from the tremor that ran through her and the sudden flaring of her eyes her body was urging her to do. Then, with a little helpless sigh in her throat, her resistance was gone and she was folding against him, her hands tightening around his neck, her eyes gazing up at him.

He felt her breasts crest against his chest—felt his own body reacting as any male body would react to such a woman in his arms! A woman who was driving him crazy with wanting her, being denied her…

His splayed hand at her spine pinioned her to him and his thighs guided her in the slow, sensual rhythm of the dance. He heard her breath catch again. Her lips were close to his, so tantalisingly close. He felt his head dip…wanting so badly to feel that silken velvet he had tasted only once before. He hungered for it with a desire that was now surging in him, to taste her again…to sate himself on her…

He pulled her more closely against him, knowing that she knew—for how could she not know just how very much he desired her…?

His lashes dipped over his eyes. He said her name—low and husky with desire… Relief was flooding through him—relief that finally she was in his arms, in his embrace, that she was pressed as closely to him as her body would be were he making love to her…

The rest of the world had disappeared. Hans, Celine, the whole damn yacht had disappeared. Only Tara was here—the woman who had stopped the breath in his lungs the first time he'd set eyes on her. The woman he wanted now more than any other woman.

His eyes were holding hers, not relinquishing them, watching her pupils expanding, seeing the dilation of desire in those incredible blue-green eyes of hers…

His mouth lowered to hers, seeking the sweet, silk velvet of her lips…so hungry to feel them part for him…for her to yield the sweetness of her mouth to his once more… Desire was like molten lava in him…

And then, abruptly, she was yanking herself away from him, and there was something flaring in her eyes now that was not desire—that was the very opposite of that. She strained against him, dropping her arms from him, removing his hands from her body. She seemed to be swaying as he looked down at her, face dark with her rejection.

'The music has stopped.'

She got the words out as if each one were a stone. He stared at her blankly, then heard her go on, her eyes like knives now.

'And if you *ever* try that on again with me I'll… I'll…'

But she did not finish. Instead, with a sudden contortion of her face, she walked off the dance floor, seizing up a glass of champagne from a passing waiter and knocking it back.

'A lovers' tiff? Oh, dear!' Celine's voice was beside him, her false sympathy not concealing her spite.

He ignored her, his eyes only for Tara, clutching her flute, refusing to look at him. His senses were still aflame, afire, and yet as the noise of the party filled the air, as the thud of music started up again, faster this time, he turned to Hans.

'Let's get out of here,' he said bluntly.

Ruthlessly, he shepherded them ashore, summoning his driver as he did so, and then piling them all into the limo the moment it drew up.

Tara had got in first, and was making herself extremely busy with a seatbelt. Her colour was high, her mouth set tight, long legs slanted away from his direction. As he threw himself into his own seat—diagonally opposite Tara—he saw Celine's gaze whip between the two of them. Speculation was in them as she took in Tara's withdrawal, her hostile body language.

Marc shut his eyes. He was beyond caring now. Let Celine think whatever the hell she wanted! His thoughts were elsewhere.

He wouldn't get any sleep that night—it would be impossible—but he didn't care about that either…

The moment they arrived back at the villa Tara all but bolted up the stairs, and he heard her bedroom door slam shut. Hans also took himself off. Marc made for the sanctuary of his office—anything to get away from Celine, who had gone to help herself from the drinks trolley in the salon.

He was just pushing open his office door when he heard her call out behind him.

'Marc, *cherie*—my poor, poor sweet!'

He hauled himself around. Celine was issuing towards him, a liqueur glass in her hand. Her eyes were glittering as she made for him. Every muscle in his body tensed. His black mood instantly tripled in intensity. Dear God, this was the last thing he needed now.

'Celine, I have work to do,' he ground out.

She ignored him. Came to him. Draped one bare arm around his shoulder. Her over-sweet scent was nauseating to him, her powdered half-exposed breasts in the skin-tight gold dress even more so.

He yanked her arm away, propelled her backwards. She was undeterred. He could smell alcohol mingling with her perfume.

The glitter in her eyes intensified. 'Don't marry that woman, Marc. You can't! She's not right for you. You know she isn't. She thinks she can treat you the way she did tonight. Push you away. You don't want a woman like that, Marc!'

She swayed towards him, trying to reach for him again. He seized her wrist, holding her at a distance. His face was thunderous, but she was still trying to touch him, to clutch at him with her scarlet nails.

'You want *me*, Marc! I know you do!' she cried, her voice slurring, 'I would be so, *so* good for you! Let me show you.' She swayed again, as if to throw herself into his arms.

'Celine, you are married to Hans,' he growled.

Dear God in heaven, was he to endure this now? On top of everything else? Fighting off Celine, with her rampant libido loosened by the alcohol she'd consumed all evening?

Her face twisted. 'Hans?' She all but spat out the name. 'He means nothing to me! *Nothing!* I should never have married him! I can't bear him. I can't bear him to touch me! He's old and pathetic and boring!' Her voice was vicious, cruel. 'I want to divorce him! Get him out of my life! I want a man like *you*, Marc—only you!'

Marc thrust her from him, stepping aside, filled with disgust at her. 'Get to bed, Celine. Sleep it off. You are the last woman on this earth I'd be interested in, and I wouldn't be even if you weren't married to Hans!'

He heard her gasp in stunned disbelief and outrage, but he was turning away from her, plunging inside his office. Slamming the door shut behind him. He leant back against it, slipping the lock. Not trusting Hans's unspeakable wife not to try and follow him in.

He swore fluently. Cursing her. Cursing the whole world. Cursing, most of all, the fact that upstairs, in a bedroom he must not let himself go anywhere near, was the one woman on earth that he wanted.

Who was tormenting him beyond endurance.

Tara woke. Instantly awake after dreams she dared not remember.

I can't bear this! I can't bear this any longer!

To have to act this role with Marc—only act it! Act it and keep him at bay at the same time. To tell herself over and over again that it was just role-play, nothing more than that!

Except it wasn't, was it? She could no more fool herself that she was acting than she could tell herself that *he* was!

Memory burned in her of that slow dance to end all slow dances… Their own bodies had betrayed them, shown them that neither of them were *acting…*

No! She mustn't think of it! Must not remember it!

She was here for one reason only: to protect Marc Derenz from another man's wife. And she was doing it for money, as a paid employee. *Anything* else was not real.

Whatever their bodies told them.

She hauled her mind away. So what? So what if she could not stop her body's reaction to him? If she could not stop that electricity surging within her whenever he looked at her, touched her? It didn't matter—not a jot—because none of this was real.

And even if it were real, she told herself, her thoughts bleak now, she could not let it be real. She was an outsider to this world. Her life was in England and she was moving to the country, starting afresh, getting out of the fashion world. Out of the orbit of men like Marc Derenz.

However powerful and devastating his impact on her…

With a heavy sigh she got up, went through into

the en suite bathroom. There was another gruelling day ahead of her. She had better brace herself for it.

Yet as she headed downstairs a little while later she noticed there seemed to be a different atmosphere in the villa. It was quieter, for a start, and as she crossed the salon to reach the terrace where breakfast was always served she realised she could not hear Celine's dominating voice yapping away.

She walked out. There was only Marc, sitting in his usual place at the head of the table, drinking his coffee, perusing the morning newspapers.

Tara frowned. 'Where are Hans and Celine?' she asked as she took her seat. Her expected sense of awkwardness after the night before had vanished in her surprise at not seeing his guests there.

Marc looked up. He hadn't heard her step out on the terrace. His eyes went to her, riveting her like a magnet, then instantly veiling.

'They've gone,' he said.

Tara's frown deepened as she reached for the jug of orange juice. 'What do you mean? More house-viewing?'

Marc sat back, folded his newspaper and set it aside with a deliberate movement. His mood could not be more different from his mood when he had ploughed up the stairs last night, thrusting the vision of the drunken, vicious-mouthed harpy that was Celine from him, wanting only to seek oblivion from what Tara had so tormentingly aroused in him.

The news that had greeted him this morning had wiped all that from his mind, leaving only one emotion. And that had brought with it only one decision that now burned in him, just as the memory of Tara kissing him had, of how their bodies had clung to each other in that devastating slow dance…

With Celine and Hans gone, and Tara tormenting him with his desire for her, there was only *one* decision he now wanted to make—and to hell with all his endless damn warnings to himself! To hell with the lot of them!

She was gazing at him now… Tara with her sea-blue eyes set in that breathtakingly beautiful face of hers, her lush lips parted, a frown still on her brow as he answered her question.

'No,' he said.

The emotion he felt was in his voice, and he could see that it had registered with Tara as well, for her expression had changed.

'Gone,' he elaborated now. 'As in Hans has flown back to Frankfurt, where he will be consulting a divorce lawyer. As for Celine—I don't know and don't care. Presumably to find herself a divorce lawyer as well.'

Tara stared. *'Divorce?'*

'Yes.' Marc smiled.

And Tara, to her disbelief, realised that it was a genuine, hundred-carat smile.

It wasn't just the shock of what he'd said but the dazzling impact of his smile that froze the jug in her hand. 'I don't understand,' she said weakly.

He lifted his coffee cup again, tilted it towards her. 'Congratulations,' he said. 'To both of us! It did the trick—*my* announcement to Celine yesterday that you were my fiancée and *your* oh-so-convincing behaviour that went with it!'

He took a mouthful of coffee and continued in that voice that was so different from any she had heard from him before.

'It rattled Celine into making one last desperate attempt on me. When we got back last night she threw caution to the winds—and herself at me. Full-on. She told me she didn't want Hans any more, that she only wanted me. What I didn't realise at the time,' he went on, 'when I was disabusing her of her hopes, was that Hans overheard her saying she wanted to divorce him.' He took a breath. 'So he is going to oblige her and file for divorce himself.'

Tara's face lit. 'That's *wonderful*! I couldn't be happier for him!'

'Nor me,' said Marc. His expression changed again. 'Celine will try and take him to the cleaners, but Bernhardt will make sure she gets as little as possible. He's been on the phone to me already, thanking me profusely.'

His eyes rested on Tara. They were warm in a way she'd never seen before. So was his voice when he spoke again.

'And I have to thank you too, Tara.'

His expression was veiled suddenly and his voice suddenly changed again. Now there was something in it that sent flickers of electricity through her, that quickened her pulse, made her eyes fix on his.

'You don't need me to tell you how damnably tormenting this whole thing has been! But…' he gave a heartfelt sigh, rich with the profound relief that was the only emotion in him right now '…thank the Lord that is all over now!'

Inside his head Marc heard the very last of his lifelong warnings to himself—heard it and dismissed it. He had not come this far, endured this much, to listen to it any more. Hans and Celine were gone—but Tara… Oh, Tara was here—and here was exactly where he wanted her…

And whatever else he wanted of her—well, he was damn well going to yield to it. Resisting it any longer, resisting *her*, was just beyond him now. Totally beyond him. Yes, she was a woman he would never usually have allowed himself to get this close to physically, but fate had brought them this far and he was not going to deny any longer what was between them.

Up till now it had been playacting—but from this morning onwards, he would make it searingly, blazingly *real.* It was all he wanted—all that consumed him.

She was gazing at him now, with uncertainty in her face—and something more than that. Something that told him he was not going to be the only one giving in to what had flamed between them right from the very start.

He smiled a smile warm with anticipation. With the relief he felt not just at Celine's departure but at the thought of his own yielding to what he so wanted.

He poured himself some more coffee, helped himself to a brioche. 'Now,' he went on, 'we just have to decide how we're going to celebrate the routing of the unspeakable Celine.'

Tara looked at him. Part of her was still reeling from the news that Hans was finally going to get rid of his dreadful wife, but that was paling into insignificance because she was reeling from the total change in Marc.

It was as if a different person sat there at the head of the table. Gone was the tight-faced, ill-humoured, short-fused man who could barely hide his constant displeasure and exasperation. Just gone. Now an air of total relaxation radiated from him, with good humour and satisfaction all round…

The difference could not be greater.

Nor the impact it was having on her.

She watched him sit back in his chair, one long leg crossed over the other, completely at his ease.

Was this really Marc Derenz of the frowning brows, the steel jaw, the constant darkling expression in his eyes?

'So,' he said, buttering his brioche, 'what would you like to do now that we have the day to ourselves?'

Tara started. 'What do you mean?' She tried to gather her thoughts. 'Um…if Celine and Hans have gone, I ought to go back to London.'

Suddenly the frown was back again on his face. 'Why?' he demanded.

'Well, I mean… I've done what you brought me out here to do, so there's no point me being here any longer.'

He cut across her. 'Oh, for God's sake—there's no

need to rush off!' He took a breath, his stance altering subtly, as did the expression in his eyes. 'Look, let's just chill, shall we? We damn well deserve it, that's for sure! So, like I say, what would you like to do today?' His eyes rested on her. 'How well do you know the South of France—I mean apart from trailing around the damn shops with Celine and seeing those dire houses she dragged us to? Why don't I show you the South of France that's actually worth seeing?'

He seemed to want an answer, but she could not give one. How could she? This was a Marc Derenz she had never known existed. One who could smile—really smile. One who radiated good humour. Who seemed to be wanting her company for *herself*, not for keeping Celine Neuberger at bay.

She felt something flutter inside her. Something she ought to pay attention to.

'Um… I don't know. I mean…' She looked across at him. His expression was bland and she tried to make it out. 'Why?' she said bluntly. 'As in why do you want me to stay? As what?'

That strange feeling inside her was fluttering again, more strongly now.

'What do you mean, "As what?",' he countered.

'Am I still in your employ, or what? Am I supposed to have some sort of role? Am I—?'

He cut across her questions. 'Tara, don't make this complicated. Stay because you're here…because Celine and Hans have gone…because I want to celebrate their impending divorce. Stay for any damn reason you like!'

He was getting irritated, she could see. For some reason, it made her laugh. 'Oh, that's better,' she said dulcetly. 'I thought the new, improved Marc Derenz was too good to be true!'

For a second he seemed to glower at her. Then his face relaxed. 'You wind me up like no other woman,' he told her.

'You're so easy to wind up,' she said limpidly.

She could feel that flutter inside her getting stronger. Changing her mood. Filling her, suddenly, with a sense of freedom. Of adventure.

He shook his head, that rueful laugh coming again. 'I'm not used to being disagreed with,' he admitted.

Tara's eyes widened. 'No? I'd never have guessed.'

He threw her a look, then lifted both his hands in a gesture of submission. 'Truce time,' he said. He looked at her. 'You know, I'm not really a bear with a sore head most of the time. You've seen me at my worst because of Celine. And,' he admitted, 'you've caught the sharp edge of my ill-humour because of that. But I *can* be nice, you know. Why don't you stick around and find out just how nice, hmm…?'

She felt a hollow inside her, into which a million of the little flutters that had been butterflying inside her suddenly swooped.

Oh, Lord, this was a bad, *bad* idea! To 'stick around', as he'd put it! Yet she wanted to—oh, she wanted to! But on what terms? With what assumptions? That was what she had to get clear. Because otherwise…

She took a breath. 'Marc, these past days have

been…' She tried to find a word to describe them and failed. 'Well, you know—the role-playing. It was…' she swallowed '…confusing.'

She didn't want to recount all the incidents, the memories she couldn't cope with, the times when all self-control had been ripped from her.

He nodded slowly. His dark eyes rested on her with something behind them she did not need a code-breaker to decipher.

'Yes,' he said. 'And it's time—way beyond time—to end that confusion.'

He did not spell it out—he did not have to. She knew that as he went on.

'So let's put the confusion behind us, shall we? And the acting and the role-playing? We'll just take it from here. See what happens.' He paused, those dark eyes unreadable—and yet oh-so-readable. 'What do you say?'

He was waiting for her answer.

She could feel those butterflies swooping around in that hollow space inside her, knew that she'd stopped breathing. Knew why. Knew, as she very slowly exhaled, that whatever she'd said to herself while being so 'confused'—dear God, that word was an understatement!—about the way this man could make her feel, that now, with just the two of them here, like this, finally free to make their own choices, that she was making a decision that was going to take her to a place with Marc Derenz that she did not know. Had never yet been.

But she wanted to go there with a part of her that

she could not resist. She heard words frame themselves in her mind. Knew them to be true.

It's too late to say no to this—way too late.

As he'd said—no more role-play, no more acting. No more 'confusion'. Just her and Marc…seeing what happened…

And if 'what happened' was her yielding to that oh-so-powerful, never before experienced desire for him, would that really be so bad?

She glanced about her at this beautiful place, at the devastating man sitting there, drawing her so ineluctably. Would it be so bad to experience all that she might with this man? Whatever it brought her?

I've never known a man like this—a man who makes me feel this way. So why should I say no to it? Why not say yes instead...?

She could feel the answer forming in her head, knowing it was the answer she would give him now. A tremor seemed to go through her as slowly she nodded her head.

She saw him smile a smile of satisfaction. Pleased…

His smile widened and he pushed a bowl of pastries towards her. 'Have a croissant,' he invited. 'While we plan our day.'

CHAPTER SEVEN

'So, WHAT DO you think?'

Marc slewed the car to a juddering halt at the viewpoint and killed the engine. This was the car he liked to drive when he was at the villa—a low-slung, high-powered beast that snaked up the *corniches*, ate up the road as they gained elevation way up here in the foothills of the Alpes-Maritimes.

He turned to look at the woman sitting beside him in the deep bucket passenger seat as the engine died. Satisfaction filled him. Yes, he had made the right decision. He knew he had—he was definite about it.

The discovery from a clearly upset Hans that morning that he had accepted his marriage was over, and that Celine was not happy with him, had been like a release from prison for Marc. He'd said what needed to be said, organised Hans's flight, then seen him off with a warm handshake.

Celine's departure he had left to his staff while he himself had gone off to phone a jubilant Bernhardt.

And after that there'd only been himself to think about. Basking in heartfelt relief, he'd gone to breakfast in peace, his glance automatically going to the upper balcony. To Tara's bedroom.

Tara.

He had known a decision had to be made.

What am I going to do? Pack her off back to London or...?

Even as he'd framed the question he'd felt the answer blazing in his head. For days now she'd haunted him…that amazing beauty of hers taunting him. His but only in illusion. His only reality, punching through every moment of his time with her, was that he wanted to say to hell with the role he'd hired her to play. He wanted *more.*

And when she'd walked out onto the terrace he'd taken one look at her and made his decision.

No, she wasn't from his world. And, had it not been for the insufferable Celine and his need to keep her away from him, he'd never have let Tara get anywhere near him. Yes, he was breaking all his rules never to get involved with someone like her.

And he just did not care.

Not any more.

I want her—and for whatever time we have together it will be good. I know that for absolute sure—

It was good already. Good to have had that relaxed, leisurely breakfast, deciding how to spend their day—a day to themselves, a day to enjoy. Good to have her sitting beside him now, her sandaled feet stretched out in the capacious footwell, wearing a casual top and skinny cotton leggings that hugged those fantastic legs of hers. Her hair was caught back with a barrette and her make-up was minimal. But her beauty didn't need make-up.

His eyes rested on her now, drinking her in.

'The view is fabulous,' she was exclaiming. Then she frowned. 'It's just a pity it's so built up all along the coastline.'

Marc nodded. 'Yes, it's a victim of overdevelopment. Which is why I like being out on the Cap—it's more like the Riviera was before the war, when the villa was built.'

He gunned the engine again, to start their descent, telling her how the villa had been party central in the days of his great-grandfather.

It was a subject he continued over lunch, stopping off at a little *auberge* that he liked to go to when he wanted to get away from his usual plush lifestyle.

'He invited everyone who was anyone—painters, ex-pat Americans, film-makers, novelists.'

'It sounds very glamorous.' Tara smiled as he regaled her with stories.

'My grandfather was much quieter in temperament—and my father too. When I was a boy we spent the summers here. Hans and his first wife and their children were often visitors, before my parents were killed—'

He broke off, aware that he was touching on something he did not usually talk about to the women in his life. But Tara was looking at him, the light of sympathy in her eyes.

'Killed?' she echoed.

'They both died in a helicopter crash when I was twenty-three,' he said starkly.

Her expression of sympathy deepened. 'That must have been so hard for you.'

His mouth tightened. 'Yes,' was all he said. All he could say.

He watched her take a slow forkful of food, then she looked at him again. 'It can't compare, I know, but I have some idea of what you went through.' She paused. 'My parents are both in the army, and part of me is always waiting to hear that…well, that they aren't going to come home again. That kind of fear is always there, at some level.'

It came to him that he knew very little about this woman. He only knew the surface, that fabulous beauty of hers that so took his breath away.

'Did you—what is that old-fashioned phrase in English?—"follow the drum"?' he heard himself asking.

She shook her head. 'No, I was sent to boarding school at eight, and spent most of my holidays with my grandparents. Oh, I flew out to see my parents from time to time, and they came home on leave sometimes, but I didn't see a great deal of them when I was growing up. I still don't, really. We get on perfectly well, but I guess we're quite remote from one another in a way.'

He took a mouthful of wine. It was only a *vin de table*, made from the landlord's own grapes, but it went well with the simple fare they were eating. He found himself wondering whether Tara would have preferred a more expensive restaurant, but she seemed content enough.

She was relaxing more all the time, he could tell. It was strange to be with her on her own, without Celine and Hans to distort things. Strange and…

Good. It's good to be here with her. Getting to know her.

And why not? She came from a different world, and that was refreshing in itself. But it was about himself that he heard himself speaking next.

'I was very close to my parents,' he said. 'Which made it so hard when—' He broke off. Took another mouthful of wine. 'Hans was very kind—he stepped in, got me through it. He stood by me and his wife did too. I was…shell-shocked.' He frowned, not looking at her, but back into that nightmare time all those years ago. 'Hans helped me with the bank too. Not everyone on the board thought I could cope at so young an age. He guided me, advised me—made sure I took control of everything.'

'No wonder,' she said carefully, 'you're so loyal to him now.'

His eyes went to hers. 'Yes,' he said simply.

She smiled. 'Well, I hope his life will soon be a lot happier.' Her expression changed, softened. 'He's such a lovely man—it's so sad that he was widowed. Do you think he'll marry again eventually? I mean, someone *not* like Celine!'

'It would be good for him, I think,' Marc agreed. 'But, as I said to you, the trouble is he can be too kind-hearted for his own good—easy for him to be taken advantage of by an ambitious female.'

'Yes…' She nodded. 'He needs someone *much* nicer than Celine! Someone,' she mused, 'who really values him. And…' she gave a wry smile '…who enjoys German romantic poetry!'

Marc pushed his empty plate aside, wanting to change the subject. Of course he was glad for Hans that he'd freed himself from Celine's talons, but right now the only person he wanted to think about was Tara.

She had already finished her *plat du jour*, and she smiled at him as she reached for a crusty slice of baguette from the woven basket sitting on the chequered tablecloth.

'You've no idea how good it is to simply eat French bread!' she told him feelingly. 'Or that croissant I had at breakfast! So many models are on starvation diets—it's horrendous!'

He watched her busy herself, mopping up the last of the delicious homemade sauce on her empty plate, disposing of it with relish.

'Won't you have to starve extra to atone for this now?' he posed, a smile in his voice.

She shook her head. 'Nope. I'm going to be chucking in the modelling lark. It's been good to me, I can't deny that, but I haven't done anything since university that qualifies me for any other particular career—not that I want to work nine-to-five anyway. I've got other plans. In fact,' she added, 'it's thanks to being out here that I can make them real now.'

He started to ask what they were, but the owner of the *auberge* was approaching, asking what else they might like. They ordered cheese and coffee, changing the subject to what they would do in the afternoon. It was an easy conversation, relaxed and convivial.

Marc's eyes rested on her as they discussed what she might like to see. She was so different, he observed. That all too familiar argumentative antagonism was gone, that back-talking that had irritated him so much. Oh, from time to time there was a wicked gleam in her eye when she said something he knew was designed to try and wind him up, but his own mood was now so totally different it had no effect except to make him laugh.

She's easy to be with.

It was a strange thing to think about her after all the aggro, all the tension that had been between them.

We've both lightened up, he mused.

Only one area was generating any tension between them now. But it was at a low level, like a current of electricity running constantly between them, visible only in sudden veiled glances, in the casual brush of hands, in body contact that was not intentional or was simply necessary, such as handing her a menu, helping her back into the low-slung car as they set off again, catching the light floral fragrance of her scent.

His eyes wanted to linger on her rather than on the road twisting ahead. On their constant mutual awareness of each other. He let it run—low voltage, but there. This was not the time or the occasion to do anything about it. That was for later…for this evening. And then… Ah, then… He smiled inwardly, feeling sensual anticipation ease through him. Then he would give it free rein. And discover, to the full, all that he burned to find in her.

There would be no more drawing back—no more hauling himself away, castigating himself for his loss of self-control, no more anger at himself for wanting her so much…

I am simply not going to fight it any more.

He had not deliberately sought her out, or selected her for a relationship. She had come into his life almost accidentally, certainly unintentionally, because of his urgent need to protect himself from Hans's amoral wife—but she was here now. And after all he'd had to put up with over Celine, damn it, he deserved a reward!

He glanced sideways at her as they drove back down towards the coast. And she deserved something good too, didn't she? She'd done the job he'd set her—triumphantly!—so why shouldn't he make sure that now she had as enjoyable a time remaining as he could ensure?

He would do his best, his very best, to ensure that. It was impossible for her to deny the desire that flared between them, and now there was no more aggravation, no more frustration, no more confusion, no more role-playing and no more barriers.

As his eyes went back to the twisting road ahead, and he steered his powerful car round the hairpin bends, he felt his blood heat pleasurably in his veins.

Whatever the risks of breaking the rules he lived his life by—Tara would be worth it.

Most definitely worth it…

Tara sat at the silvered Art Deco dressing table, carefully applying minimal eye make-up—just a touch of mascara tonight was all that was needed—and a sheen of lip gloss. Her mood was strange. Everything was so similar to the previous night, when she'd been making up her face and getting dressed for that yacht party with Celine's awful friends, and yet everything was totally different.

Marc was different.

That was the key to it, she knew. That 'bear with a sore head', as he had called himself with total accuracy, was simply gone. She couldn't help but make a face at how he'd railed at her. This time yesterday he'd laid into her furiously in this very room for daring to take matters into her own hands, and to damn well lay off him! But her ploy had worked—and he'd had to admit it had worked even better than either of them could have imagined!

And now, mission more than accomplished, they could both have their reward for freeing poor Hans from his ghastly wife.

Reward...

The word hovered in Tara's head. Beguiling, tempting.

She knew just what that reward was going to be…

Impossible not to know…

And to know with a certainty that had been building up in her hour after hour, all day.

Marc was right—whatever was happening between them, it was powerful and irresistible. They wanted each other—had done since first seeing each other, and had gone on wanting each other all through those torturous days when they'd both been forced to pretend in public what they had tried so hopelessly to deny in private.

They wanted each other. It was the one undeniable truth between them.

It was as simple as that.

Her eyes flickered around the beautiful room and she looked out through the windows to the darkening view beyond, over the gardens and the sea. Her very first thought on arrival here had been how gorgeous it all was, and how she should make the most of it.

Well…a half-smile played around her mouth…now she *was* going to make the most of it. And of the man who came with it.

The man who, even when he was at his most overbearing, his most obnoxious, his most short-tempered, possessed the ability to set her pulse racing, her blood surging, her heart-rate quickening…

She could feel it now, and with another little flutter inside her, she got to her feet.

I can't resist him and there's no reason to. He wants me—I want him. I know it won't last—can't last—but I must simply enjoy this time with him.

He wasn't a man she'd ever have got involved with had it not been for him hiring her, but since he had, and she was—well, why not accept what was happening between them?

Why not—as she was doing now—slip into an ankle-length, fine cotton sundress in a vivid floral print of vibrant blues and crimsons that was nothing like the formal evening gowns and cocktail dresses she'd worn when the Neubergers were there. She was 'off duty' now, and she wanted only to feel comfortable.

It was a look that Marc had echoed, she saw as she joined him out on the terrace. He wore a plain white open-necked shirt with the cuffs turned back and dark blue chinos. Still devastatingly attractive, but relaxed.

The two of them were all set, ready for a comfortable and relaxed evening together…

She felt that little flutter inside her again.

But that was for later. For now there was just the warmth in Marc's eyes—a warmth that wasn't only male appreciation of her, but a side of him she hadn't seen in him before, except for when he had greeted Hans. A side of him that had so taken her aback as he'd dropped that perpetual ill-humour of his.

He was walking towards her, an open bottle of champagne and two flutes in his hands. He set the flutes on a table laid for dinner, with candles glowing in protective glass cases, and started to pour the champagne. Silently he handed her a softly effervescing glass, keeping the other for himself.

'It's a champagne evening,' he announced, a smile playing at his mouth. He raised his glass. 'To us,' he said softly, his eyes never leaving her. 'To our champagne evening. *Salut!*'

And it *was* a salute, Tara knew. It was a recognition of what was happening between them—what had been happening ever since their first encounter. An acknowledgement that neither of them could walk away now from the other...from this champagne evening.

I want this—I want everything about it. Even for the short while that it will be mine...

The words were in her head—unstoppable. And she didn't want to stop them, to silence them. All she wanted, on this evening of all evenings, was what there was and what was to come.

'Salut...' she said in soft reply, and took a mouthful of the delicate drink, her eyes still holding his. There was a glow in her body, a sweetness in her veins, a low pulse at her throat.

He drank as well, and then, with a smile, said, 'Walk with me.'

She did, and they strolled across the darkening garden to the edge of the lawn, where the manicured grass gave way to rougher land, and then a rocky shore tumbled down to the lapping sea below.

There was a little jetty, and steps cut into the rocky outcrop to take them there, and he led her down. They stood on the jetty awhile, looking out across the night-filled sea. From this point at the tip of the Cap there was no line of sight to the shoreline with all its bright lights. Even the villa behind them was not visible this low below the shoreline.

'We might be on a desert island…' Tara breathed, her voice still soft. 'All on our own.'

At her side, Marc gave a low laugh. 'The world vanished away,' he said.

He turned to her. Lifted the hand that was not holding his flute to trail a finger along the contours of her mouth.

'I want this time with you,' he said, and she could hear the husk in his voice now, feel the frisson in her veins that it engendered. 'We are free to have it—and I very much wish to share it with you.'

There was a question in his voice—and yet an answer too. For how could she refuse him? She knew she would not be here, standing with him out on the jetty, beneath the gathering night, if she did not want what he wanted too.

Marc felt desire creaming inside him, yet he knew he must not be precipitate. He had considered her out of bounds, was breaking all his rules by indulging himself with her, and as that was so he wanted to take from this forbidden *liaison d'amour* all that it could offer him.

And it will be worth it! She is promising everything I want—everything I have already so tantalisingly tasted.

Tara made no reply to what he had said, but she did not need to, she knew. Perhaps, it was unwise, letting herself be drawn into a world that was not hers, to a man who could never be hers for that reason, and she knew it must be brief, but she accepted it. Accepted all of it. This beautiful villa, this beautiful place, and the man whose domain it was.

She took another slow mouthful of her champagne, feeling its potency ease into her bloodstream, committing her to what she was doing.

They stood awhile, as the sky darkened to absolute night and one by one the stars began to shine. The low lapping of the water was seductive…as seductive as the warm, caressing breeze that lifted off the sea. Then, the sky dark, the champagne drunk, they made their way back to the terrace to dine together.

What they ate Tara would not afterwards remember. She knew only that it was delicious, and that the conversation flowed between them as effortlessly now as it had been fraught before. Had they really been so…so intemperate towards each other? So antagonistic, so irritated and exasperated by each other? It seemed impossible. Impossible to think of Marc as the man he had been when now his ready smile, his low laugh, his lambent eyes were warm upon her.

What they talked about she would not remember either. She only knew that another conversation was taking place as well—a conversation that, as the meal ended and liqueurs were consumed, the coffee pot drained, he suddenly brought to vivid life as he reached for her hand, drew her to her feet.

The staff were long gone, and they were here alone on the candlelit terrace. He stood in front of her, so dark against the night beyond. She caught his scent, felt herself sway and smile…

He said her name—a caress—and lifted his hand to her hair to draw her closer to him. But there was no need. With a little sigh, closing her eyelids, she let her body fold against his, let it rest, as it wanted so much to do, against the strong column of his. He took her weight against him effortlessly and her hand slid around his waist, resting on the cool leather of his belt, the tips of her fingers feeling the hard heat of his flesh beneath the thin fabric of his shirt.

She gave a soft, almost inaudible sigh in her throat. And then his mouth was silencing her. Moving with the velvet softness that had caused her sleepless nights, and which now sent a drowning bliss through her with every feathering touch.

She gave herself to it. This time… Ah, this time there was no barrier, no regret, no resistance to what was happening between them. She was giving herself utterly to it…

Their kiss was long, unhurried, for they had all the night before them… Then, as her breasts engorged, their peaks cresting against the hard wall of his muscled chest, she heard him growl, felt his mouth releasing hers. His eyes poured down into hers, and she felt with a frisson of arousal that he was responding as strongly as was she.

Was it wickedness that made her loop her hands around his neck and whisper, 'Shall we slow dance?'

For tonight they could—oh, yes, they could indeed—and with that came the knowledge that now there need be no more play-acting, that they could finally accept and revel in the desire that flamed between them. No more being thwarted, no more pulling away… At last they could give in to what they had wanted from the very first.

The growl came again—a low rasp—and instead of an answer she was suddenly, breathlessly, swept up into his arms.

'We can do better than that,' he told her, and the deep husk in his voice was telling her just what that 'better' was going to be.

She gave a half-cry, half-laugh, and then he was striding indoors, across the marble hall, up the marble stairs. She clung to him, and she was held fast in his powerful grip as he carried her along the landing, to head inside a room she had never yet stepped into.

It was dark, but he knew the way. Knew the way to the wide bed waiting for them. And as he lowered her to its surface, coming down beside her, he knew there were no more questions to ask, no more answers. Their bodies had asked and answered all that was needed.

Desire—that was the question *and* the answer. And it flamed between them, powerful and unquenchable. They were to be aroused by all that it could offer, to savour it…to enjoy. In a sharing of slow, caressing pleasure, a banquet of the senses.

He leant over, dark against the dimness of the room, smoothing the tumbled mass of her glorious hair, spearing his fingers through the lush tresses as she gazed up at him, starlight from the undrawn drapes shining in her dilated eyes. Waiting for his possession. For her possession of him.

He kissed her again slowly, tasting, drawing from her every drop of nectar. Again he felt his body fill with desire, with wanting.

For a moment he held back, as if to give himself one last chance to draw away completely, but she caught his mouth again, arching her neck, her spine, putting her hands around his back, drawing him down to her to feel the swell of her breasts, to hear the soft moan of desire in her throat.

He gave a low, husky laugh, cut short as his kiss deepened, his arousal surged. His palm closed over one peak and her soft moan came again as she pressed against his caressing hand, wanting only what he could arouse in her. Heat filled her body—her limbs…the soft vee of her thighs.

Her dress was in the way, and restlessly she sought to free herself. But he was there before her. His hands slipped the material from her, cast it aside even as he cast aside his own clothing, freeing them both to come together now, as their bodies longed to do, with a will they could not stop, nor wanted to.

They wanted only to do as they were doing—to wind themselves around each other, pinioning and clasping. His mouth was gliding down the satin contours of her slender body, and again low moans came from her.

Her head twisted helplessly on the pillow as she gave herself to his silken touch. Desire soared within her and she wanted more—oh, she wanted all of him! She felt her thighs slacken, her body's heat flare, and her fingers clawed over his strong, muscled shoulders.

She drew him into her and he surged in full possession. She cried out, gasping at the power of him, the potency. Her hands clutched him tighter, and more tightly yet, as he moved on her, within her, releasing with every surge more and more of what was rising within her, unstoppable, unquenchable. A glory of sensation, a gasping of delight, of mounting urgency…

And then it broke within her, flooding out into every vein, every portion of her body, racing out from her pulsing core to the furthest extremity, her whole body burning in this furnace of ecstasy.

As she cried out he surged within her again, his body thrashing, fusing with hers like metal melting into metal, white-hot and searing.

And she was everything he desired—everything he wanted. She was fulfilling all her promise, pulsing around his body, her own body afire, until the fire consumed itself and he felt her hands at his shoulders slacken, felt her whole body slacken.

He felt his do so too, heavy now upon her, and he rolled her, with the last of his strength, so that she was beside him and he could fold her to him, feel her shuddering body calm, her racing heartbeat slow, her hectic breathing quieten. He held her as his own slugging heart steadied, his limbs heavy, inert.

Slowly he felt the lassitude of her body's repletion ease through her as he stroked her hair, murmuring to her he knew not what. He knew only that his soft caressing, his softer murmurs, brought her to stillness in his cradling arms.

He felt his eyelids droop, sleep rushing upon him. He knew he must yield to it—for now. But as consciousness slipped from him, and the warmth and the silken length of her body pressed against his, something told him his sleep would not be long…

Nor hers…

CHAPTER EIGHT

MORNING LIGHT WAS bathing them. Tara could feel it warm upon her back, which was partly covered by a single sheet. Her arm was flung across the bare torso of the man beside her, still asleep.

She herself was still drowsy and somnolent from the night that had passed. A night like no other she had ever known.

Memory drenched through her and she hugged her naked body more closely against the one she was entwined with. Had she ever imagined a night like that was possible?

Time and time again he had possessed her—each time a consummation of bliss that had caused her to cry out over and over again as her body had burned with his, in a heat that had been a consuming fire, bathing their straining muscles and sated flesh, her spine arched like a bowstring, his body plunging into hers, her hands clutching at the twisting contours of his shoulders, her head thrashing on the pillow as they reached their peaks together.

And then peace had blanketed down upon her,

upon them both—an exhaustion, a sweeping sigh of exhalation as their bodies had closed upon each other, no space between them, pressed to each other in heated fastness, hers turned into his, folded against him, her limbs heavy, his yet heavier. And then, dazed and dazzled, she had sought the rest that had come—instant and obliterating.

Only for him to rouse her yet again…and for her to wake in an instant, to overpowering desire again…

Memories indeed…

She felt her mouth smile against his throat, her eyelids flutter, felt him stir in answer, his hand easing across her flank with soft caress.

For a while they simply lay there, letting the sun from the windows warm their entwined bodies, dozing and then waking slowly to full awareness of the day. Saying nothing, for there was no need.

Not until Marc, with a stretching of his limbs, turned his head to smile across at her. 'Breakfast? Or—?'

She laid a finger across his mouth. 'Breakfast!' she said, shaking her head. 'One night with you lasts a long, *long* time…'

He gave a laugh, pleased with her answer. Pleased with the entire universe. He had known women before—many women. But this one…

His mind sheered away. It wasn't necessary to think, to examine or analyse. It was only necessary to enjoy this gloriously sunny morning, here in the place he loved where he never seemed to have enough time to spend. It was only necessary to get himself up from his bed, reach for a grey silk robe and knot it around his waist.

His muscles felt stretched, fully used…

He reached a hand down to her. 'If you want breakfast,' he said, and there was a husk in his voice with which Tara had become very familiar with in the long, sensual reaches of the night, 'you had better use your own shower.'

He nodded towards the communicating door, then headed for his own en suite bathroom. At the door to it he turned. She was starting to stand up, and the sight of her fabulous racehorse body, full in the sunlight now, almost made him change his mind and carry her through to his own shower, where washing was *not* going to be a priority…

But his stomach gave a low grumble. He had expended a great deal of energy last night and it needed to be replenished.

So he said only, 'See you downstairs. And think about what you would like to do today—because if you can't come up with anything I have a very enticing idea of my own…'

He let his voice trail off and raised a hand in half-salute, leaving her to her own rising.

When they regrouped, out on the terrace, he threw himself into a chair. He was wearing shorts, and a striped top.

Tara, settling herself down opposite him, gave a laugh. 'You look like a *matelot*!' She smiled.

Marc's eyes glinted. 'The very thing,' he said. He

sat back. 'It's a beautiful day and the wind is just right—let's take to the water.'

She laughed. 'Is *that* your enticing idea?' she returned. 'I was assuming something far more...*physical*...' she said wickedly.

'Depends where we drop anchor,' Marc returned, his expression deadpan.

She laughed again. She could have laughed at anything this morning—this glorious, *glorious* morning. The morning after the night before...and the night before had been like no other night had ever been...

Could ever be...

For just a moment she felt a dart pierce her. Would anything in all her life ever compare to the night she'd spent in the arms of this man she had so rashly committed herself to? A man she knew she should never have given herself to but had simply not been able to resist?

What if nothing could?

She pushed the question aside. This was not a morning for questions—for doubts of any kind. She was having this time with Marc, and if he was a million miles from her own normality—well, so be it. Too late for regrets now, even if she wanted to have them—which, right now, she did *not*.

She reached for a croissant, revelling in its yeasty temptation, in yielding to *all* temptations. 'That sounds fun.' She smiled. 'I didn't see a boat moored at the jetty, though.'

'It's kept at the dock in Pierre-les-Pins, at the head of the bay. I'm having it sailed to the jetty now.'

He said it casually, but the remark lingered in Tara's head as she busied herself with her breakfast. It was another reminder of just how hugely wealthy he was. Just as much as this villa was a reminder, with its manicured lawn and pool, and its complement of attentive staff, and the top-marque car he'd driven her about in yesterday, and the chauffeur-driven limo, the gourmet restaurants, and the designer wardrobe he'd snapped his fingers for, and every other element of his life.

Unease filtered through her. Before, while she'd been working for him, it hadn't bothered her, his vast wealth. But now… Was she wise to get personally involved with him in any way? Even for what must inevitably be only a brief time, in this mutually self-indulgent 'reward' for their torturous past week? With a man from a world so entirely different from her own?

It was difficult to remember that—to believe in all that fabulous wealth of his, in the bank that bore his name and was the source of all that wealth—when she was skimming over the azure waters of the Mediterranean, the breeze filling the billowing sails.

But the huge disparity in their wealth was harder to ignore that evening when, gowned once more in one of the fabulous couture evening dresses supplied for her by him for the role that was no longer a role, but real, for whatever short duration it would prove, he whisked her off in the sleek, chauffeured car, to dine out in another fearsomely expensive Michelin-starred restaurant, where every dish cost a fortune and the wines ten times as much.

She put it aside. For this evening, this time they would have together, it was just the two of them, lovers for real now. She felt a little shimmer of wonder at the transformation. She could actually enjoy it. She had Marc to herself, and it was 'new Marc'—Marc with his ready smile, his air of absolute relaxation, total well-being.

He raised his glass to her and she did likewise, taking a sip of the formidably pricey vintage wine, savouring it even as she savoured all the wonderful delicacies on offer from the menu.

'This is beyond heaven!' She sighed blissfully as whatever concoction he'd ordered for her slipped down her throat. 'I could really get used to this! How on earth am I going to go back to my usual humble fare after this?'

She expected to hear his low laugh, which she was getting used to hearing now, but it didn't come. Instead there was a flickering in his eyes, as if his thoughts were suddenly elsewhere. And in a place he did not care for.

She wondered at it, then set it aside. Nothing was going to spoil this evening. She gazed around the restaurant, taking it in, knowing that this was an experience she must make the most of. Once she was in her little cottage in Dorset, places like this would be a distant memory only.

A little pang went through her and her eyes moved back to the man sitting opposite her. He, too, one day, would be only a distant memory…

There was a tiny catch in her throat and she reached

for her wine glass, made some deliberately light remark, to which Marc responded this time—as if he, too, had set aside something there was no point thinking about. Not now…not tonight. Not with the night ahead of them…

Anticipation thrummed through her, and a sudden sensual awareness. Her eyes went to him across the table, caught his, saw in them what she knew was in hers… What remained in them all through their long, leisurely and exquisite meal, as conversation flowed between them—easy now, when it had been impossible before.

It was nearly midnight before they left—but when they returned to the villa Tara discovered that the night was still young…

Their night lasted till dawn crept over the edge of the world, and brought with its first light the sleep her body was too exhausted to deny… The sleep that overtook their bodies, all passion finally spent, folded around each other as if parting could never come.

It was a false illusion…

Marc was in his office, attempting to catch up with work. But his mind wasn't on it. He gave a rueful grimace. Where his mind was right now was out by the pool—the pool beside which Tara would be sunning herself, turning her silken skin a deeper shade of delectable gold, all the more enticing to caress…

With a groan, he tore the seductive vision from his head and focussed on the computer screen, on the myriad complexities of his normal working life making their usual round-the-clock demands on him. Demands that he had no inclination to meet at the moment but that were piling up nevertheless.

He knew he could not postpone them indefinitely. That at some point he'd have to knuckle down and deal with them. The truth was, he wasn't used to taking so much time out from work.

Work had dominated his life ever since he'd had to shoulder all the responsibilities of his inheritance at a painfully early age. Even when he set aside his workload for social engagements, or for his carefully considered forays into highly selective affairs, as was his habit, they never interfered with his primary task in life—to see Banc Derenz through to the next era of its survival in an ever-changing financial landscape. So why, he pondered now frowningly, the figures on the screen ignored still, was he being so careless of his responsibilities at this time?

At first he'd put his indulgence at giving in to his inconveniently overpowering attraction to Tara simply as relief at getting the wretched Celine off his case once and for all. But that had been two weeks ago—two weeks of pure self-indulgence, as he was well aware. Of indulging himself with Tara—giving himself to a sensual feast and to a time out of his customary highly disciplined and demanding lifestyle to simply…simply what?

To have a holiday.

That was what he was doing. Simply having a holiday with this irresistible woman! A holiday that was an endless drift of golden days here in the balmy weather of the Riviera. Lounging by the pool, taking out the sailboat, driving along the coast or up into the hills, making a foray across the border into Italy one day to explore San Remo, strolling around the perfumeries of Grasse another day, heading further still to St Raphael, with its ochre-red cliffs, and then St Tropez, with all the nostalgia of its fashionable heyday in the sixties. They had explored the villages and landscapes that had so beguiled the Impressionists, wandered around the narrow streets of the old town in Nice, strolled along the seafront in Cannes, lunched on one of the many private beaches, or out on the jetty over the water…

A procession of easy-going days, relaxed and carefree, before returning home to the villa…and all the sensual delights of the nights they shared.

He shifted in his seat. When would he tire of Tara? When would her allure grow stale? When would he not want to trouble himself with making conversation with her, engaging in repartee as she presumed to tease him and he returned as good as he got, volleying with her until they both were laughing…or kissing…

I must tire of her soon. Surely I must?

She wasn't from his world, so how could he think of her as anything other than a passing *amour*? Oh, she'd adapted to it easily enough—but then, what woman *wouldn't* find it easy to adapt to the wealthy ease of his highly privileged life.

Has she adapted too well? Got too used to it?

The thought was in his head before he could stop it. Reminding him of all the reasons why he never took up with women who did not share his own lifestyle in their own financial right.

His eyes went to his screen. No sum of money there was without a whole string of zeroes after it—it was the realm he worked in, that encompassed the accounts of his extremely rich clients. Sums of money that the likes of Tara would never see in her lifetime…

Memory scraped in his head. Unwelcome, but intruding all the same. How Tara had sat with Celine on that ultra-tedious afternoon in Monte Carlo, and made that casual comment that 'marrying money' was still a sure-fire way to help oneself to riches. He'd considered it a snipe at Celine, but now, his frown came again. But maybe it was something she believed herself?

More memories came…uglier and more intrusive, forcing their way in. Marianne…making up to him… enticing him and luring him, the young heir to Banc Derenz, only to callously abandon him for a much safer financial bet—a man with his own wealth already safely in his pockets.

Another image formed in his mind. Sitting in that restaurant with Tara—one of the most exclusive and expensive on the Riviera—the day after their first night together. *'I could really get used to this!'* she'd said, and sighed pleasurably…

More thoughts came to him—disturbing and uneasy. He had declared to Celine that Tara was his fiancée, and the sole purpose of the announcement had been to try and get Hans's wife's clutching claws off him. But had that impulsive proposal set thoughts running in Tara's head? Was she remembering them when they were together now? When they kissed…embraced…made love?

Does she think I might propose for real? Make her my wife?

Roughly, he pushed his chair away from his desk. He would not let such thoughts in. He glanced at his watch. She'd been sunning herself far too long—she must not burn her skin…her oh-so-delectable skin.

Again memory skimmed in his mind—of how irritated he'd been that first day here, to arrive and find the woman he had hired to keep Celine at bay behaving as if she were here on a free luxury holiday.

Well, now she really is here on a free luxury holiday...

Again the unwelcome thought was in his head. Again he dismissed it. For she could enjoy this time with him with his blessing—enjoy all the luxury he took for granted himself. His expression changed. After all, *she* was a luxury herself—to him. An indulgence like none he'd ever experienced. And he wanted to indulge himself…

An anticipatory smile played about his mouth. Her heated skin would need cooling down—and a shower together was the very thing to achieve that. He would lather her body all over with his own hands…every beautiful centimetre of her…

His mood much improved, he abandoned any fruitless attempt to work and strode impatiently from the room to make his anticipation reality.

* * *

Tara stretched languorously and rolled over so that it was her back—bare from neck to hip—that received the blessing of the sun's rays.

This really was *gorgeous.* To be basking here in the sun, after a late, leisurely breakfast, with nothing more strenuous to do than maybe take a cooling dip in the pool beside her and then, later on, drape herself in her chiffon sarong and drift across to where the staff were setting out their customary al fresco lunch.

She and Marc would make their *déjeuner* of the finest delicacies, all freshly prepared by hands other than theirs, and whisked away at the end of their meal by those other hands, leaving them nothing to do but laze the afternoon away or take the sailboat out, or swim off the jetty in the calm seas lapping the shore. Or maybe, if they were feeling energetic, head off in that powerful black beast of a car, purring like a contented tiger, to see yet more of the fabled Côte d'Azur.

And then they'd return as the sun was lowering, to sip sundowners by the pool and wait for yet another gourmet meal to be served to them by others' labour.

A pampered lifestyle indeed…

Idly she flexed her toes, eased the arms cushioning her head, utterly at ease. *I could get used to this...*

Oh, she could indeed! she thought, half-ruefully, half-languorously. No wonder the rich liked being rich…

But, for all the luxury of her surroundings and the ease of her days, she knew that not a single glass of vintage champagne, not a moment spent lounging like this beside the pool, would count for anything at all were she not here with Marc.

It was Marc and Marc alone who was turning this luxury into paradise for her. Marc—who only had to glance at her with those dark, knowing eyes of his and she would feel her whole body flicker as if with unseen electricity. All he had to do was touch her…

A shadow fell over her, and as if she'd conjured him from her thoughts he was hunkering down beside her, letting his index finger stroke sensuously down the long curve of her spine, arousing every bit of that flickering electricity.

She gave a little moan in her throat at the sensation and heard his low laugh. Then, suddenly, she was being caught in his arms, dizzyingly swept up. Her moan of sensuous pleasure turned into a squeal, and he laughed again.

'Time for a cool-down,' he informed her.

For a second she thought he was going to toss her into the pool, but he was striding indoors with her, heading upstairs. Suddenly mindful of her abandoned bikini top, she pressed herself hurriedly against his torso, lest they encounter one of the staff. She felt her breasts crest, and knew there was only one way that this was going to end…

Lunch was going to have to wait…

'What's the plan for this afternoon?' Tara enquired casually as, quite some time later, they settled down to the delicious *al fresco* lunch awaiting them on the vine-shaded terrace.

'What would you like to do?' Marc asked indulgently.

His mood was good—very good. Their refreshing shower had done a lot more than refresh him…

Have I ever known a woman like her?

The question played in his mind and he let it. So did the answer. But the answer was one that, unlike the question, he suddenly did not care to consider. Did he really want to accept that no other woman in his life had come anywhere close to how Tara made him feel? Accept how she could elicit his desire for her simply by glancing at him with those amazing blue-green eyes?

How long had this idyll here at the villa been so far? A fortnight? Longer still? The days were slipping by like pearls on a necklace…he'd given up counting them. He did not wish to count them. Did not wish to remember time, the days, the month progressing. He liked this timeless drift of day after day after day…

'You choose,' Tara said lazily, helping herself to some oozing Camembert, lavishing it on fresh crusty bread.

She must have put on pounds, she thought idly, but the thought did not trouble her. She didn't care. Didn't even want to think about going back to London, picking up on the last of her modelling assignments, giving notice on the flat-share, clearing her things and heading west to move into her thatched cottage and start the life she had planned for so long.

It seemed a long, long way away from here. From now.

Her eyes went to Marc, her gaze softening, just

drinking him in as he helped himself to salad, poured mineral water for them both…

He caught her looking at him and his expression changed. 'Don't look at me like that…' There was the familiar husk in his voice.

She gave a small laugh. 'I haven't the strength for anything else but looking,' she said. Her voice lowered. 'And looking at you is all I want to do…just to gaze and gaze upon your manly perfection!'

There was a lazy teasing in her voice and his mouth twitched. He let his own gaze rest on her—on her feminine perfection…

Dimly, he became aware that his phone was ringing. Usually he put it on to silent, but he must have flicked it on when he'd attempted—so uselessly—to knuckle down to some work.

He glanced at it irately. He didn't want to be disturbed. When he saw the identity of the caller his irritation mounted. He picked up the phone. He might as well answer and get it over and done with…

Nodding his apologies to Tara, he went indoors. Disappeared inside his study. Behind him, at the table, Tara tucked in, unconcerned, turning her mind to how they might amuse themselves that afternoon.

But into her head came threads of thoughts she didn't want to let in. She might not want the time to pass, but it was passing all the same. How long ago had she flown out here from London? It plucked at her mind that she should check her diary—see when she had to be back there, get in touch with her booker. Show her face again…

I don't want to!

The protest was in her head, and it was nothing to do with her wanting to quit modelling and escape to her cottage. It was deeper than that—stronger. More disturbing.

I don't want this time with Marc to end.

That was the blunt truth of it. But end it must—how could it not? How could it *possibly* not? How could anything come of this beyond what they had here and now—this lotus-eating idyll of lazy days and sensual nights…?

She shifted restlessly in her chair, wanting Marc to come back. Wanting her eyes to light upon him and him to smile, to resume their discussion about how to spend a lazy afternoon together…

But when he did walk out, only a handful of moments later, it was not relief that she felt when her eyes went to him. Not relief at all…

She'd wondered when this idyll would end. Well, she had her answer now, in the grim expression on Marc's face—an expression she had not seen since before the routing of Celine. It could presage nothing but ill.

She heard him speak, his voice terse.

'I'm sorry, I'm going to have to leave for New York. Something's come up that I can't avoid.' He took a breath, throwing himself into his chair. 'One of my clients—one of the bank's very wealthiest—wants to bring forward the date of his annual review. I always attend in person, and it's impossible for me to get out of it. Damned nuisance though it is!'

Tara looked at him. She kept her face carefully blank. 'When…when do you have to leave?' she asked.

'Tomorrow. I should really leave today, but…'

'Oh,' she said. It seemed, she thought, an inadequate thing to say. But the words she wanted to say, to cry out to him, she could not. *Should* not.

I don't want this time to end! Not yet!

Even as she heard the cry inside her head she knew it should not be there. Knew she should not be feeling what she was feeling now—as if she were being hollowed out from the inside. She had no right to feel that way.

Right from the start she had known that whatever it was she was going to indulge herself in with Marc, it was only that—an indulgence. They had come together only by circumstance, nothing more. Nothing had ever been intended to happen between them.

He never meant to have this time with me. Would never have chosen it freely. It was simply because of his need to use me to keep Celine away from him! He'd never have looked twice at me otherwise—not with any intent of making something of it.

Memory, harsh and undeniable, sprang into her head. Of the way Marc had stood there, that first day she'd arrived, telling her that her presence was just a job, that he was out of bounds to her, that she was there only to play-act and she was not to think otherwise. He could not have spelt out more clearly, more brutally, that she wasn't a woman he would choose for a romance, an affair, any relationship at all…

She knew it. Accepted it. Had no choice but to accept it. But even as she told herself she could hear other words crying out in her head.

He might ask me to go with him! He might—he could! He could say to me just casually, easily, Come to New York with me—let me show you the sights. Be with me there.

She looked at him now. His expression was remote. He was thinking about things other than her. Not asking her to go with him.

Then, abruptly, his eyes met hers. Veiled. He picked up his discarded napkin, resumed his meal. 'So,' he said, and his voice was nothing different from what it always was, 'if this is to be our last day, how would you like to spend it?'

She felt that hollow widening inside her. But she knew that all she could do was echo his light tone, though she could feel her fingers clenching on her knife and fork as she, too, resumed eating.

'Can we just stay here, at the villa?' she asked.

One last day. And one last night.

There was a pain inside her that she should not be feeling. Must not let herself feel.

But she felt it all the same.

Marc executed a fast, hard tack and brought the yacht about. His eyes went to Tara, ducking under the boom and then straightening. Her windblown hair was a halo around her face as she pushed it back with long fingers, refastening the loosened tendrils into a knot.

How beautiful she looked! Her face was alight, her

fabulous body gracefully leaning back, and her eyes were the colour of the green-blue sea.

One thought and one thought alone burned in his head. *I don't want this time with her to end.*

How could he? How could he want it to end when it had been so good? All the promise that she had held for him, all that instant powerful allure she'd held for him from the very first moment he'd set eyes on her, had been fulfilled.

He knew, with the rational part of him, that had he never had to resort to employing her to keep Hans's wife at bay he would never have chosen to follow through on that initial rush of desire. He'd have quenched it, turned aside from it, walked away. Hell, he wouldn't even have known she existed, would he? He'd never have gone to that fashion show had it not been for Celine…

But he had gone, he had seen her, and he had used her to thwart Hans's wife…

He had brought her into his life.

Had rewarded himself with her.

His grip on the tiller tightened. *It's been good. Better than good. Like nothing else in my life has ever been.*

From the first he'd known he wanted her—but these days together had been so much more than he'd thought they could be! He watched as she leant back, elbows on the gunwale, lifting her face to the sun, eyes closed, face in repose as they skimmed over the water, her hair billowing in the wind, surrounding her face again.

He felt something move within him.

I don't want this to end.

Those words came again—stronger now. And bringing more with them.

So don't end it. Take her with you to New York.

His thoughts flickered. Why shouldn't he? She could be with him in New York as easily as she was here. It could be just as good as it was here.

So take her with you.

The thought stayed in his head, haunting him, for the rest of the day. As he moored the yacht at the villa's jetty, phoned for it to be taken back to harbour. As they washed off the salt spray in the pool, then showered and dressed for dinner. As they met on the terrace for their customary cocktails.

It was with him all the time, hovering like a background thought, always present. Always tempting.

It was there all through dinner—ordered by him to be the absolute best his chef could conjure up—and all through the night they spent together…the long, long night in each other's arms. It was there as he brought her time and time again to the ecstasy that burned within her like a living flame, and it seemed to him that it burned more fiercely than it ever had, that his own possession of her was more urgent than it ever had been, their passion more searing than he could bear…

Yet afterwards, as she lay trembling in his arms, as he soothed her, stroked her dampened hair, held her silk-soft body to his, his unseeing gaze was troubled. And later still, when in the chill before the dawn he rose from their bed, winding a towel around his hips and walking out onto the balcony, closing his hands over the cold metal rail, and looking out over the dark sea beyond, his thoughts were uncertain.

If he took her with him to New York, what then? Would he take her back to France? To Paris? To stay with him at his hotel? Make her part of his life? His normal, working life?

And then what? What more would he want? And what more would *she* want…?

Again that same disturbing thought came to him—that she, too, might be remembering his impulsive declaration that afternoon, casting her as his intended wife, his fiancée, the future Madame Derenz.

Foreboding filled him. Unease. He did not know what she might want—could not know. All he knew was how he lived his life—and why. Just to have this time with her he'd already broken all the rules he lived by—rules that he'd had every reason to keep and none to break.

It had been good, this time he'd had with Tara—oh, so much more than good! But would it stay good? Or would danger start to lap at him…? Destroying what had been good?

Was it better simply to have this time—the memory of this time—and be content with that? Lest he live to regret a choice he should not have made…? Their time here had been idyllic—but could idylls last? *Should* they last?

He moved restlessly, unquiet in his mind.

He heard a sound behind him—bare feet—and

turned. She was naked, her wanton hair half covering her breasts, half revealing them.

'Come back to bed,' she said, her voice low, full with desire.

She held out a hand to him—a hand he took—and he went with her.

To possess her one last time…

Their bodies lay entwined, enmeshed. He stroked back the tumbled mass of her hair, eased his body from hers. Tara reached out her hand, her fingertips grazing the contours of his face. The ecstasy he'd given her was ebbing, and in its place another emotion was flowing.

She felt her heart squeeze and longing fill her. A silent cry breaking from her. *Don't let this be the last time! Oh, let it not be the last time for ever!*

A longing not to lose him, to lose *this*, flooded through her. Her eyes searched his in the dim light. When she spoke her throat was tight, her words hesitant, infused with longing. 'I could come to New York with you…' she said.

The hand stroking her hair stilled. In the dim light she saw his expression change. Close. Felt a coldness go through her.

'That wouldn't work,' he answered her.

She heard the change in his voice. The note of withdrawal. She dropped her eyes, unable to bear seeing him now. Seeing his face close against her, shutting her out.

She took a narrowed breath and closed her eyes,

saying no more. And as he drew her back against him, cradling her body, and she felt his breath warm on her bare shoulder, he knew that what they'd had, they had no longer. And never could again.

Behind her, with her long, slender back drawn against his chest, his arm thrown around her hips, Marc looked out over the darkened room. He had answered as he'd had to. With the only safe answer to give her. The answer that he had known must be his only answer from the very first.

CHAPTER NINE

TARA WOKE, STIRRING slowly to a consciousness she did not want. And as she roused herself from sleep and the world took shape around her she knew that it was already too late.

Marc was gone.

Cold filled her, like iced water flooding through her veins. A cry almost broke from her, but she suppressed it. What use to cry out? What use to cry at all?

This had always been going to happen—always!

But it was one thing to know that and another to feel it. To feel the empty place where he had been. To know that he would never come back to her. Never hold her in his arms again…

She felt her throat constrict, her face convulse. Slowly, with limbs like lead, she sat up, pushing her tangled hair from her face, shivering slightly, though the mid-morning sunlight poured into the room.

She looked around her blankly, as if Marc might suddenly materialise. But he never would again—and she knew that from the heaviness that was weighing her down. Knew it in the echo of his voice, telling her he did not want to take her with him. Knew it with even greater certainty as her eyes went to an envelope propped against the bedside lamp…and worse—oh, far worse—to the slim box propping it up.

She read the card first, the words blurring, then coming into focus.

You were asleep so I did not wake you. All is arranged for your flight to London. I wish you well—our time together has been good.

It was simply signed *Marc*. Nothing more.

Nothing except the cheque for ten thousand pounds at which she could only stare blankly, before replacing numbly into the envelope with the brief note.

Nothing except the ribbon of glittering emeralds in the jewellery case, catching the sunlight in a dazzle of gems. She let it slide through her fingers, knowing she should replace it in its velvet bed, leave it there on the bedside table. It was a gift far too valuable to accept. Impossible to accept.

But it was also impossible not to clutch it to her breast, to feel the precious gems indent her skin. To treasure it all her life.

How can I spurn his only gift to me? It's all that I will have to remember him by.

For a while she sat alone in the wide bed, as if making her farewells to it and all that had been there for her, with him. Then, at length, she knew she must move—must get up, must go back to her own bedroom, shower and dress, pack and leave. Go back to her own life. To her own reality.

The reality that did not have Marc in it. That *could* not have him in it.

I knew this moment would come. And now it has.

But what she had not known was how unbearable it would be… She had not been prepared for that. For the tearing ache in her throat. For the sense of loss. Of parting for ever.

It wasn't supposed to be like this! To feel like this!

The cry came from deep within her. From a place that should not exist, but did.

No, it was *not* supposed to be like this. It was supposed to have been nothing more than an indulgence of the senses…a yielding to her overpowering attraction to him…a time to be enjoyed, relished and revelled in, no more than that.

She should be leaving now, heading back to her own life, with a smile of fond remembrance on her face, with a friendly farewell and a little glow inside her after having had such a wonderful break from her reality!

That was what she was supposed to be feeling now. Not this crushing weight on her lungs…this constricted throat that choked her breath…this desperate sense of loss…

With a heavy heart she slipped through the connecting door. She had to go—leave. However hard, it had to be done.

Two maids were already in her room, carefully

packing the expensive clothes Marc had provided for her—an eternity ago, it seemed to her. She frowned at the sight. She must not take them with her. They were couture numbers, worth a fortune, and they were not hers to take.

She said as much to the maids, who looked confused.

'Monsieur Derenz has instructed for them to go with you, *mademoiselle*,' one said.

Tara shook her head. She had the emerald necklace—that was the only memory of Marc she would take, and only because it was his gift to her. That was its value—nothing else.

On sudden impulse, she said to the two young girls, '*You* have the clothes! Share them between you! They can be altered to fit you… Or maybe you could sell them?'

Their faces lit up disbelievingly, and Tara knew she could not take back her words. She was glad to have said them.

It was the only gladness she felt that day. What else had she to be glad about? That tearing feeling seemed to be clawing at her, ripping her apart, her throat was still choked, and that heaviness in her lungs, in her limbs weighing her down, was still there as she sat back in the chauffeured car, as she was whisked to the airport, as she boarded her flight.

He had booked her first-class.

The realisation made her throat clutch, telling her how much things had changed since her arrival.

My whole life has changed—because of Marc...

It was not until a fortnight later, as she checked her calendar with sudden, hollowing realisation, that she knew just how much…

Marc stood on the terrace of his penthouse residence in one of Manhattan's most luxurious hotels, staring out over the glittering city. His meeting was over, and the client was pleased and satisfied with what Bank Derenz had achieved for him. Now, with the evening ahead of him, Marc shifted restlessly.

There was something else he wanted.

Someone.

I want Tara—I want her here with me now. To enjoy the evening with me. I want to take her to dinner, to see her smile lighting up her eyes—sometimes dazzling, sometimes teasing, sometimes warm with laughter. I want to talk about whatever it was we used to talk about, in that conversation that seemed to flow so freely and naturally. And, yes, sometimes I want to spar with her, to hear her sometimes deadpan irony and those sardonic quips that draw a smile from me even now as I remember them...

And after dinner we'd come back here, and she'd be standing beside me, my arm around her, all of Manhattan glittering just for us. And she'd lift her face to mine, her eyes aglow, and I would catch her lips with mine and sweep her up, take her to my bed...

He could feel his body ache with desire for her, the blood heating in his veins.

With an effort of sheer will he tore his mind away from that beguiling scene so vivid in his head. He must not dwell on the woman he had left sleeping that morning, her oh-so-beautiful body naked in his bed, her glorious hair swathed across the pillow, her high, rounded breasts rising and falling with the gentle sound of her breathing.

It had been hard to leave her. Hard to reject her plea to come with him. Harder than he'd wanted it to be. Harder than it should have been. Harder than it was safe to have been—

But the safe thing for him to do had been to leave her. He knew that—knew it for all the reasons that had made him so wary of yielding as he had…yielding to his desire for her.

And the fact that he wanted to yield to it again, that his body so longed to do so, that he wanted to phone her now, tell her a flight was booked for her and that she should join him in New York, must make him even more wary.

It isn't safe to want her. It isn't safe because it's what she wants too. She asked outright—asked to come with me, wanted more than what we had in France. How much more would she have asked of me? Expected of me?

That was the truth of it. The harsh, necessary truth he'd always had to live his life by.

His eyes shadowed, thoughts turbid. He was making himself face what he did not want to face, but must—as he always had.

If I bring her here...keep her with me...how can I know if it's me she's choosing or Banc Derenz?

That was the reason he now turned away from the plate-glass window overlooking the city far below.

His thoughts went back to when he had last set eyes on her, sleeping so peacefully in his bed. He had slipped past her, to the bedside table, where he had placed the farewell note he had scrawled. And his gift for her.

The gift that would part him from her for ever. The gift that he'd left, quite deliberately, to tell her that what they'd had was over.

To tell *himself…*

Tara leant against the window frame of her bedroom at the cottage, breathing in the night air of the countryside. So sweet and fresh after the polluted traffic fumes of London. An owl hooted in the distance, and that was the only sound.

No ceaseless murmurings of cicadas, no sound of the sea lapping at the rocky shore, no scent of flowers too delicate for England...

No Marc beside her, gazing out over the wine-dark sea with her, listening to the soft Mediterranean night, his arm warm around her, drawing her against his body, before he turned her to him, lowered his mouth to hers, led her indoors to his bed, to his embrace...

She felt her heart twist, her body fill with longing.

But to what purpose?

Marc was gone from her life and she from his. She must accept it—accept what had happened and accept everything about the life she faced now.

Accept that what I feel for him, for the loss of him,

is not what I thought I would feel. Accept that there is nothing I can do about it but what I am doing now. Accept that what I'm doing is all that I can do. All that can happen now.

Her expression changed as she gazed out over the shadowy garden edged by trees and the fields beyond.

How utterly her life had changed! How totally. All because of Marc…

She felt emotion crush within her. Should she regret what she had done? Wish that it had not happened? That it had not changed her so absolutely?

How *could* she regret it?

She gave a sigh—but not one of happiness. Nor of unhappiness. It was an exquisitely painful mix of both.

I can think of neither—feel neither. Not together.

Separately, yes, each one could fill her being. They were contradictory to one another. But they never cancelled each other out. Only…bewildered her. Tormented her.

She felt emotion buckling her. Oh, to have such joy and such pain combined!

She felt her hand clutch what she was holding, then made herself open her palm, gaze down at what was within. In the darkness the vivid colour of the precious gems was not visible, yet it still seemed to glow with a light of its own.

It was a complication she must shed.

I should never have taken it! Never kept it to remember him by!

She felt the emotion that was so unbearable, buckle

her again. For one long moment she continued to gaze at what she held. Then slowly, very slowly, she closed her hand again.

She had kept it long enough—far too long. It must be returned. She must not keep it. Could not. Not now. *Especially not now.*

The emotion came again, convulsing her, stronger than ever. Oh, sense and rational thought and every other worldly consideration might cry out against what she was set on—but they could not prevail. *Must* not.

I know what I must do and I will do it.

With a slow, heavy movement she withdrew from the window, crossed over to the little old-fashioned dressing table that had once been her grandmother's and let fall what she held in her hand.

The noise of its fall was muffled by the piece of paper onto which it slithered. That, too, must be returned. And when it had been the last link with Marc would be severed. *Almost* the last...

She turned away, her empty hand slipping across her body. There was one thing that would always bind them, however much he no longer wanted her. But she must never tell him. For one overwhelming reason.

Because he does not want me. He is done with me. He has made that crystal-clear. His rejection of me is absolute.

So it did not matter, did it? Anything else could not matter.

However good it was, it was only ever meant to be for that brief time. I knew that, and so did he, and that is what we both intended. That is what I must hold in my head now. And what he gave me to show me that he had done with me, so that I understood and accepted it, must go back to him. Because it is the right and the only thing to do.

And when it was gone she would get on with the life that awaited her now. With all its pain and joy. Joy and pain. Mingling for ever now.

Marc was back in Paris. After New York he'd had the sudden urge to catch up with all his affairs in the Americas, making an extensive tour of branches of Banc Derenz from Quebec to Buenos Aires, which had taken several weeks. There had been no pressing need—at least not from a business perspective—but it had seemed a good idea to him, all the same, for reasons he'd had no wish to examine further.

The tour had served its purpose—putting space and time between those heady, carefree days at the villa and the rest of his life.

Now, once more in Paris, he was burying himself in work and an endless round of socialising in which he had no interest at all, but knew it was necessary.

And yet neither the tour of the Americas, nor his current punishing workload, nor the endless round of social engagements he was busying himself with were having the slightest effect.

He still wanted Tara. Wanted her back in his life. The one woman he wanted but should not want.

With the same restlessness that had dominated him since he'd flown to New York a few months ago he looked out over the Parisian cityscape, wanting Tara there with him.

He glanced at his watch without enthusiasm. His car would be waiting for him, ready to take him to the Paris Opera, where he was entertaining two of his clients and their daughter. His mouth tightened. The daughter was making it clear that she would be more than happy for him to pay her attention for reasons other than the fact that her parents banked at Banc Derenz. And she was not alone in her designs and hopes.

He gave an angry sigh. The whole damn circus was starting up again. Women in whom he had no interest at all, seeking his attention.

Women who were not Tara.

He shut his eyes. *I'll get over her. In time I'll forget her. I have to.*

He knew it must happen one day, but it was proving harder than he had thought it would. *Damnably* harder.

It was showing too, and he was grimly aware of that. Aware that, just as he'd been when Celine had plagued him, he was more short-tempered, having little patience either for demanding clients or fellow directors.

A bear with a sore head.

That was the expression he'd used to Tara.

Who was no longer in his life. And could never be again. However much he wanted her. *Because* he wanted her.

That was the danger, he knew. The danger that

his desire for her would make him weak…make him ready to believe—want to believe—that his wealth was not the reason at all for her to be with him.

He'd believed that once before in his life—and it had been the biggest mistake he'd ever made. Thinking he was important to Marianne. When all along it had only been the Derenz money.

And the fact that Tara valued the Derenz money was evident. Right from the start she'd been keen on it—from that paltry five hundred pounds for chaperoning Celine back to her hotel to the ten thousand pounds she'd demanded for going to France.

And she had taken those emeralds he'd left for her. Helped herself to them as her due—just as readily as she'd helped herself to the couture wardrobe he'd supplied.

Oh, she might not be a gold-digger—nothing so repellent—but it was undeniable that she had enjoyed the luxury of his lifestyle, the valuable gifts he'd given her. And that was a danger sign—surely it was?

If I take her back she'll get used to that luxury lifestyle...start taking it for granted. Not wanting to lose it. It will become important to her. More important to her than I am. And soon would it be me she wanted—or just the lifestyle I could provide for her?

He felt that old, familiar wariness filling him. Restlessly, he shifted again, tugging at the cuffs of his tuxedo.

What point was there in going over and over the reasons he must resist the urge to get back in touch with her, to resume what they had had, seek to extend it? However powerful that urge, he had to resist it. He must. Anything else was just too risky.

The doors of the elegant salon were opening and a staff member stood there, presumably to inform Marc that his car was awaiting him. But the man had a silver salver in his hand, upon which Marc could see an envelope.

With a murmur of thanks he took it, then stilled. Staring down at it. It had a UK stamp. And it was handwritten in a hand he had come to recognise.

He felt a clenching of his stomach, a tightening of his muscles. A sudden rush of blood.

What had Tara written? *Why?*

His face expressionless, belying a melee of thoughts behind its impassive mask, he opened it. Unfolded the single sheet of paper within and forced his eyes to read the contents.

The words leapt at him.

Marc,

I am not going to cash your cheque. What started out as a job did not end that way, and it would be very wrong of me to expect you to be bound by that original agreement.

Also, but for different reasons, I cannot keep the beautiful necklace you left for me. I am sure you only meant to be generous, but you must see how impossible it is for me to accept so very expensive a gift. Please do not be offended by this. I shall have it couriered back to you.

By the same token, nor can I accept the gift

of all the couture clothes you provided for me. I hope you do not mind, but I gave them to the maids—they were so thrilled. Please do not be angry with them for accepting.

I'm sorry this has taken me so long, but I've been very busy working. My life is about to take me in a quite different direction and I shall be leaving London, and modelling, far behind.

It was simply signed with her name. Nothing more.

The words on the page seemed to blur and shift and come again into focus. Slowly, very slowly, the hand holding the letter dropped to his side.

His heart seemed to be thumping in his chest as if he'd just done a strenuous workout. As if a crushing weight had been lifted off him. An impenetrable barrier just…dissolved. Gone.

He stared out across the room. The member of staff was standing in the doorway again.

'Your car is ready, Monsieur Derenz,' he intoned.

Marc frowned. He wasn't going to the opera. Not tonight. It was out of the question. A quite different destination beckoned.

The thud of his heartbeat was getting stronger. Deafening him. The letter in his hand seemed to be burning his fingers. He looked across at the man, nodded at him. Gave him his instructions. New instructions.

An overnight bag to prepare, a car to take him to Le Bourget, not the Paris Opéra. Regrets to be sent to his guests. And a flight to London to organise.

As the man departed only one word burned in Marc's head, seared in his body. *Tara!*

She had taken nothing from him—absolutely nothing. Not the money she'd earned, nor the couture wardrobe, nor the emerald necklace. Nothing at all! So what did that say about her?

Emotion held in check for so many punishing weeks, so many self-denying days and nights, exploded within him. Distilled into one single realisation. One overpowering impulse.

I can have her back.

Tara, the woman he wanted—*still* wanted!—and now he could have her again.

Nothing he had ever felt before had felt so good…

CHAPTER TEN

TARA WAS WALKING along the hard London pavements as briskly as she could in the heat. Summer had arrived with a vengeance, and the city was sticky and airless after the fresh country air. She was tired, and the changes in her body were starting to make themselves felt.

She'd travelled up from Dorset by train that morning and gone straight to her appointments. The first had been with a modelling agency specialising in the only shoots she'd be able to do soon, to see if they would take her on when that became necessary. The other, which she'd just come from, had been with her bank, to go through her finances.

Now that she could no longer count on the ten thousand pounds from Marc, it was going to be hard to move to Dorset immediately. Yet doing so was imperative—she had to settle into her new life as quickly as she could, while she was still unencumbered. She would need to buy a car, for a start—a second-hand one—for she would not be able to manage without one, and she still hadn't renovated the kitchen and the bathroom as planned.

She'd hoped that her bank might let her raise a small mortgage to tide her over, but the answer had not been encouraging—her future income to service the debt was going to be uncertain, to say the least. She was not a good risk.

It would have been so much easier if I could have kept that ten thousand pounds...

The thought hovered in her head and she had to dismiss it sharply. Yes, keeping it would have been the prudent thing to do—even if Marc would never know why—but as he *could* never know, she could not possibly keep it.

It was the same stricture that applied to her destination now, and her reason for going there. Yes, the prudent thing to do now would be to sell the necklace, realise its financial value, and bank that for all that she would need in the years ahead. But she had resisted that temptation, knowing what she must do. It was impossible for her to keep his parting gift!

Her letter to him, which he must have received now, for she had posted it from Dorset several days ago, had made that clear. Perhaps he was accustomed to gifting expensive jewellery to the women he had affairs with—but to such women, coming as they did from his über-rich world, something like that emerald necklace would be a mere bagatelle! To her, however, it was utterly beyond her horizon.

If he had only given me a token gift—of little monetary value. I could have kept that willingly, oh, so willingly, as a keepsake!

Her expression changed. More than a keepsake. A legacy…

She shied her mind away. She could see her destination—only a little way away now. The exclusive Mayfair jeweller she was going to ask to courier the necklace back to Marc. They would know how to do it—how to ensure the valuable item reached him securely, as she had written to him that it would.

Once it was gone she would feel easier in her mind. The temptation to keep it, against all her conscience, would be gone from her, no longer to be wrestled with. Her eyes shadowed, as they did so often now. And she need no longer wrestle with a temptation so much greater than merely keeping the emeralds.

She heard it echo now in her head—what had called to her so longingly… *Tell him—just tell him!*

Oh, how she wanted to! So much!

But she knew she was clutching at dreams—dreams she must not have. Dreams Marc had made *clear* she must not have.

Wearily, she put her thoughts aside. She had been through them, gone round and round, and there was no other conclusion to be drawn. Marc had finished with her and she must not hope for anything else.

Not even now.

Especially not now.

Deliberately she quickened her pace, walking up to the wide, imposing doors. A security guard stood there, very visibly, and as she approached moved to open the electronically controlled doors for her. But just as they opened, someone walked out.

'Fraulein Tara! *Was fur eine Uberraschung!*'

She halted, totally taken aback. Hans Neuberger came up to her, pleasure on his kindly face, as well as the surprise he'd just exclaimed over seeing her.

'How very good to see you again!' he said in his punctilious manner. 'And how glad I am to do so.' He smiled. 'This unexpected but delightful encounter provides me with an excellent opportunity! I wonder,' he went on, his voice politely enquiring, 'whether you would care to join me for lunch? I hope that you will say yes. Unless, of course,' he added, 'you have another engagement perhaps?'

'Um—no. I mean, that is…' Tara floundered, not really knowing what to say. She was trying to get her head around seeing Hans again, since the last time she'd seen him had been just after that party on the yacht in Cannes, with Celine's dreadful friends…

'Oh, then, please, it would be so very kind of you to indulge me in this request.'

His kindly face was smiling and expectant. It would be hard to say no, and she did not wish to hurt his feelings, however tumultuous hers were at seeing him again, which had plunged her head back to the time she'd spent in France. So, numbly, she let him guide her across the street where she saw, with a little frisson of recognition, the side entrance to a hotel that stung in her memory.

This was the hotel where Marc had deposited Celine that first fateful evening…

Emotion wove through her, but Hans was ushering her inside. His mood seemed buoyant, and he was far less crushed than he'd been at Marc's villa. Getting Celine out of his life clearly suited him.

And so he informed her—though far more generously than Celine deserved. 'I was not able to make her happy,' he said sadly as they took their places in the hotel restaurant. 'So it is good, I think, that she has now met another man who can. A Russian, this time! They are currently sailing the Black Sea on his new yacht. I am glad for her…'

Tactfully, Tara forbore to express her views on how the self-serving Celine had latched on to yet another rich man. Hans's face had brightened, and he was changing the subject.

'But that is quite enough about myself! Tell me, if you please, a little of what is happening with *you*?' His expression changed. 'I have, alas, been preoccupied with—well, all the business of setting Celine free, as she wishes to be. But I very much hope all is still well with you and Marc.'

There was only polite enquiry in his question, yet Tara froze. Floundering, she struggled for something to say. Anything…

'No—that is to say Marc and I— Well, we are no longer together.'

She saw Hans's face fall. 'I am sorry to hear that,' he said. His eyes rested on her and there was more than his habitual kindness in them. 'You were, I think, very good for Marc.' He paused, as if finding the right words. 'He is possessed of a character that can be very…*forceful*, perhaps is the way to describe him. You were—how can I express this?—a good match for him.'

'Yes,' Tara said ruefully. 'I did stand up to him—it's not my nature to back down.'

Hans gave a little laugh. 'Two equal forces meeting,' he said.

She looked at him. 'Yes, and then parting. As we have. Whatever there was,' she said firmly, 'is now finished.'

Hans's eyes were on her still, and she wished they weren't.

'That is a pity,' he said. 'I wish it were otherwise,'

She took a breath. 'Yes, well, there it is. Marc and I had a…a lovely time together… But, well, it ran its course and that is that.'

She wanted to change the subject—any way she could. Her throat had tightened, and she didn't want it to. Seeing Hans again had brought everything back in vivid memory. And she didn't want that. Couldn't bear it. It just hurt too much.

'So,' she said, with determined brightness as the waiters brought over the menus, 'what brings you to London? Have you been here long?'

Thankfully, Hans took her lead. 'I arrived only this morning,' he said. 'My son Bernhardt will be joining me this evening with his fiancée. They are making a little holiday here. His mother-in-law-to-be is accompanying them. She was a close friend of my wife—my *late* wife—and, like me, was most sadly widowed a few years ago. We have always got on very well, both sharing the loss of our spouses, and now, with the engagement of our children, we have much in common. So much so that—well,' he went on in a little rush of open emotion, 'once my divorce from Celine is finalised, Ilse and I plan to make our future together. Our children could not be more delighted!'

A smile warmed Tara's expression. 'Oh, that's wonderful!' she exclaimed.

Just as she'd hoped, the kindly Hans would be marrying again—happily this time, surely? Such a match sounded ideal.

He leant forward. 'You may have wondered,' he said, 'why I was emerging from that so very elegant jeweller's when I encountered you—'

Tara hadn't wondered—had been too taken aback to do anything of the sort—but she didn't say so. Anyway, Hans was busy slipping a hand inside his jacket, removing from it a small cube of a box. Tara did not need X-ray vision to know what it would contain.

He held it towards her, opening it. 'Do you think she will like this?' he asked.

There was such warmth, such hope in his voice, that Tara could not help but let a smile of equal warmth light up her own face.

'It's *beautiful*!' she exclaimed, unable to resist touching the exquisite diamond engagement ring within. 'She will *adore* it!' Spontaneously, she reached her hand to his sleeve. 'She's a lucky, *lucky* woman!' she told him.

And then, because she was glad for him—glad for anyone who had found a happiness that for herself could never be—her expression softened.

'Let me be the very first to congratulate you,' she said. And she kissed him on the cheek, an expression of open delight on her face.

Marc sat in his chauffeured car, frustration etched into his expression. He was burning to find Tara—the imperative was driving him like an unstoppable tide, flooding over him.

He was free. Free to take her back. Free to claim her, to make her his again. There was nothing to stop him, to block him—not any more. Had she been anything like he'd feared she would never have written that letter to him—never have said what she had.

He took it out of his jacket pocket again now, read it again, as he had read it over and over, his eyes alight.

Their expression changed back to frustration. To know that he was free to take her back, to renew what had been between them and yet not to be able to find her…! It was intolerable—unbearable.

But she was not to be found.

He had gone to her flat last night, heading there the moment the private jet from Le Bourget had landed at City Airport, after urging the car through the traffic, to be told in an offhand fashion by a flatmate that she was away, and they had no idea where.

Thwarted, he had had to repair to his hotel, to kick his heels, and thence to interrogate her modelling agency first thing that morning—only to be informed that she had no modelling engagements that day and that they had no idea where she was and did not care. For reasons of confidentiality they would not give him her mobile number—which he, for reasons now utterly incomprehensible to him, had never known. They would let him know he was trying to contact her, and that was all.

He glowered, face dark, eyes flashing with frustration, as the car moved off into the London traffic. He had occupied himself by calling in on the branch of Banc Derenz in Mayfair, but now he was hungry.

He did not want the manager's company for lunch. He didn't want anyone's company. *Only one person.*

It burned within him…his sense of urgency, his mounting sense of frustration that he had come to London to find her—claim her. To throw lifelong caution to the winds and to ride the instinct that was driving him now, that her letter had let loose, like a tidal wave carrying him forward…

His car pulled up at his hotel. The very same hotel where he'd deposited Celine the first night that Tara had come into his life.

He'd wanted her then—had felt that kick of desire from the first moment of seeing her, so unwillingly responding to his impatient summons at that benighted fashion show, had felt it kick again when she'd sat beside him in the limo, and yet again creaming in his veins as, with a deliberate gesture, he'd taken her hand to kiss her wrist…to show her that she might be as hostile, as back-talking as she liked, but she was not immune to him, to what was flaring like marsh fire between them…

A smile played at his mouth, as his mind revolved those memories and so many more since then…

And all those yet to come.

Immediately his imagination leapt to the challenge. Their first night together again… The sensual bliss would burn between them as it always had, every time!

His mind ran on, leaping from image to image. And afterwards a holiday—only the two of them. Wherever she wanted to go. The Caribbean, or maybe the Maldives, the Seychelles? The South Seas? Wherever in the world she wanted. Wherever they could have a tropical island entirely to themselves…

Nights under the stars...days on silver beaches... disporting ourselves in turquoise lagoons...lazing beneath palm fronds waving gently in the tropical breeze...

Anticipation filled him, surging in his blood…

The chauffeur was opening his door and he vaulted out. He would grab lunch, and then interrogate that damn agency of hers again. He'd already sent one of his staff from the London branch of Derenz to doorstep her flat, lest she arrive there unexpectedly.

She's here somewhere. I just have to find her.

Find her and get her back. Back into his life—where she belonged.

He strode into the hotel, fuelled with the urgency now driving him…consuming him. Filled with elation—with an impatience to find her again that was burning in his veins. To have her unforgettable beauty before him once again…

'Mr Derenz, good afternoon. Will you be lunching with us today?'

The polite enquiry at the entrance to the restaurant interrupted his vision.

'Yes,' he said distractedly, impatiently.

His glance needled around the restaurant.

And froze.

The image in his head—the one his eyes had frozen on—solidified.

Tara—it was *Tara*. Here. Right in front of him. Across the dining room. Sitting at one of the tables.

There was someone with her—someone with his back to him.

Someone that Tara was looking at. Gazing at.

Smiling at, her face alight with pleasure and delight.

He saw the man she was smiling at offer something to her, saw the flash as it caught the sunlight. Saw her lean forward a little, reach out a long, slender forearm. Saw what it was that she touched with her index finger, how the delight in her eyes lit her whole face.

Saw her lean closer now, across the table, saw her bestow a kiss upon the cheek of the man he now recognised.

Saw blackness fill his vision. Blinding him…

Memory seared into his blinded sight.

Marianne across that restaurant, sitting with another man, his diamond glittering on her finger, holding up her hand for Marc to see...

Still blinded, he lurched away.

There was blackness in his soul…

* * *

Just as she brushed her soft kiss of congratulation on Hans's lined cheek, Tara's gaze slipped past him.

And widened disbelievingly.

Marc?

For a second emotion leapt in her, soaring upwards. Then a fraction of a section later it crashed.

In that minute space of time she had registered two things. That he had seen her. And that he had turned on his heel and was walking out of the restaurant again as rapidly as the mesh of tables would allow him.

That told her one thing, and one thing only. He had not wanted to see her. Or acknowledge her presence there.

She felt a vice crushing her as she sat back in her seat, unable to breathe. She urgently had to regain control of herself. If Hans noticed her reaction he might wonder why. If he turned he might see Marc leaving the restaurant. Might go after him...drag him back to their table. She would have to encounter Marc again—Marc who had turned and bolted rather than speak to her.

If she'd ever wanted proof that he was over her—that he wanted *nothing* more to do with her—she had it now. Brutally and incontrovertibly!

The vice around her lungs squeezed more tightly. *I've got to get out of here!*

She didn't dare risk it! Didn't dare risk an encounter with him that he so obviously did not want! It would be mortifying.

'Hans, I'm so sorry, but I'm afraid I don't have time for lunch after all.' The excuse sounded impolite, but she had to give it. 'Do please forgive me!'

She got to her feet; Hans promptly did the same.

'I'm so very pleased for you—you and Ilse.' She tried to infuse warmth into her voice but she was keeping an eye on the exit to the hotel lobby. Was it clear of Marc yet? If she could just get to the corridor leading to the side entrance Hans had brought her in by she could escape…

She got away from Hans. He looked slightly bewildered by her sudden departure, but it could not be helped. At the door to the restaurant she glanced towards the revolving doors at the main entrance, leading to the street, then whirled around to head towards the side entrance.

Just as a tall, immovable figure turned abruptly away from the reception desk, out of her eyeline.

She cannoned into it.

It was Marc.

CHAPTER ELEVEN

SHE GAVE AN audible cry—she couldn't stop it—and lurched backwards as quickly as she could. He automatically reached up his hands to steady her, then dropped them, as if he might scald himself on her.

She couldn't think straight—couldn't do anything at all except stumble another step backwards and blurt out, 'Marc—I… I thought you had left the hotel.'

Marc's face hardened. The livid emotion that had flashed through him as she'd bumped into him turning away from the reception desk was being hammered down inside him. He would not let it show. *Would not.* He'd been cancelling his reservation for that night. What point and what purpose to stay now? he thought savagely.

He knew he had to say something, but how could he? The only words he wanted to hurl at her were… pointless. So all he said, his voice as hard and as expressionless as his face was, 'I am just leaving.'

Had she come running after him?

But why should she? She has no need of me now!

The words seared across his naked synapses as

if they were red-hot. No, Tara had no need of him now—no need at all!

Savage fury bit like a wolf.

Hans! God in heaven—Hans, of all men! Beaming like a lovesick idiot, offering her that ring...that glittering, iridescent diamond ring! For her to reach for. To take for herself. Just as Marianne had.

Fury bit again, but its savagery was not just rage. It was worse than rage. Oh, *so* much worse…

Yet he would not let her see it. That, at least, he would deny her!

She was looking up at him, consternation in her face. Was she going to try and explain herself—justify herself? It sickened him even to think about it.

But she made no reference to the scene he knew she had seen him witness. Instead she seemed to be intent on attempting some kind of mockery of a conversation.

'So am I,' he heard her say. 'Just leaving the hotel.'

Tara heard her own words and paled. *Oh, God, don't let him think I'm angling for a lift! Please, please, no!*

Memory, hot and humiliating, came to her, of how she had asked to go to New York with him—and the unhesitating rejection she had received. She felt that same mortification burning in her again, that he might think she had come racing after him.

This whole encounter was a nightmare, an ordeal so excruciating she couldn't bear it. He was radiating on every frequency the fact that seeing her again was the last thing he wanted. His stance was stiff and tense, his expression closed and forbidding. He could not have made it plainer to her that he did not want to talk to her. Did not want to have anything at all to do with her any more.

He wants nothing to do with me! He didn't even want to come over and say hello—not even to his friend Hans!

Could anything have rammed home to her just how much Marc Derenz did *not* want her any longer? That all he wanted was to be shot of her?

Her chin came up—it cost her all her strength, but she did it. 'I must be on my way,' she said. She made her voice bright, but it was like squeezing it through a wringer inset with vicious spikes.

She paused. Swallowed. Thoughts and emotions tumbled violently within her, a feeling akin to panic. There was something she had to say to him. To make things clear to him. As crystal-clear as he was making them to her. That she, too, had moved on with her life. That she would make no claim on him at all. Not even as a casual acquaintance…

She felt emotion choke her, but forced herself to say what she had to. Reassure him that she knew, and accepted, that she was nothing to him any longer.

She had said as much in her letter to him and now she would say it again, to make sure he knew.

'I'll be moving away from London very soon. I'm getting out of modelling completely. I can't wait!' She forced enthusiasm into her voice, though every word was torn from her.

His stony expression did not change.

'I'm sure you will enjoy your future life,' he replied.

He spoke with absolute indifference, and it was like a blow.

'Thank you—yes, I shall. I have every intention of doing so!' she returned.

Pride came to her rescue. Ragged shreds of it, which she clutched around her for the pathetic protection she could get from it.

'Hans is still in the restaurant.' She made herself smile, forcing it across her face as if she were posing for a camera—putting it on, faking it, clinging to it as if it were a life raft. 'I'm sure that he will want to see you! He has such exciting news! Best you hear it from him…'

She was speaking almost at random, in staccato ramblings. She could not bear to see his face, his indifferent expression, as he so clearly waited for her to leave him alone, to take himself off. She shifted her handbag from one hand to the other, and as she did so she jolted. Remembering something.

Something she might as well do here and now. To make an end to what had been between them and was now nothing more than him waiting impatiently for her to leave him be.

She raised her bag, snapping open the fastener.

'Marc—this is most opportune!' The words were still staccato. 'I was going to ask the jeweller across the road to courier this to you, as I promised, but you might as well take it yourself.'

She delved into her bag, extracted the jewellery case. Held it out to him expectantly.

His eyes lanced the box, then wordlessly he took it. His mouth seemed to tighten and she wondered why. Expressionlessly, he slid it into his inside jacket pocket.

For a second—just a second—she went on staring up at him. As if she would imprint his face on her memory with indelible ink.

Words formed in her head, etching like acid. *This is the last time I shall see him...*

The knowledge was drowning her, draining the blood from her.

'Goodbye, Marc,' she said. Her voice was faint.

She turned, plunging down the corridor. Eyes blind. Fleeing the man who did not want her any longer. Who would never want her again.

Whom she would never see again.

Anguish crushed her heart, and hot, burning tears started to roll silently down her cheeks. Such useless tears...

Marc stood, nailing a smile of greeting to his face as his guests arrived. It was the bank's autumn party, for its most valued clients, held at one of Paris's most famous hotels, and he had no choice but to host it. But there was one client whose presence here this evening he dreaded the most. Hans Neuberger.

Would he show up? He was one of the bank's most long-standing clients and had never missed this annual occasion. But now...?

Marc felt his mind slide sideways, not wanting to articulate his thoughts. All he knew was that he could not face seeing Hans again.

Will he bring her here?

That was the question that burned in him now, as he greeted his guests. What he said to them he didn't know. All that was in his head—all there had been all these weeks, since that unbearable day in London—was the scene he had witnessed. That nightmare scene that was blazoned inside his skull in livid, sickening neon.

Ineradicable—indelible.

Tara, leaning forward, her face alight. Hans offering that tell-tale box, its lid showing the exclusive logo of a world-famous jeweller, revealing the flash of the diamond ring within. And Tara reaching for it. Tara bestowing a kiss of gratitude on Hans's cheek with that glow in her face, her eyes...

Bitter acid flooded his veins. Just as it had all those years ago as he'd watched Marianne declare her faithlessness to the world. Declare to the world what she wanted. A rich, older man to pamper her...shower her with jewellery.

His face twisted. To think he had *rejoiced* that Tara had declined to cash the cheque he'd left for her! Had returned his emeralds.

Well, why wouldn't she? Now she has all Hans's wealth to squander on herself!

He stoked the savage anger within him. Thanks to *his* indulgence of her, she had got a taste for the high life! Had realised, when he'd left her, that she could not get that permanently from himself! So she'd targeted someone who could supply it permanently! Plying Hans with sympathy, with friendliness...

It was the very opposite of Celine's open scorn, but with the same end in mind. To get what she wanted—Hans's ring on her finger and his fortune hers to enjoy…

With a smothered oath he tore his mind away. What use to feel such fury? Such betrayal?

He had survived what Marianne had done to him. He would survive what Tara had inflicted upon him too.

Yet as the endless receiving line finally dwindled, with only a few late guests still arriving, he found his eyes going past the doors of the ornate function room to the head of the stairs leading up from the lobby.

Would she come here tonight with Hans?

He felt emotion churn within him.

But it was not anger. And with a sudden hollowing within him, he knew what the emotion was.

Longing.

He stilled. Closing his eyes momentarily. He knew that feeling. Knew its unbearable strength, its agony. Had felt it once before in his life.

After his parents had been killed.

The longing…the unbearable, agonising longing to see again those who were lost to him for ever.

As Tara was.

Tara who could never be his again…

'Marc—I am so sorry to arrive late!'

His eyes flashed open. It was Hans—alone.

He froze. Unable to say anything, anything at all. Unable to process any thoughts at all.

Hans was speaking again. 'We have been a little

delayed. Bernhardt is with me, and I hope you will not object but I have brought two other guests as well. Karin—Bernhardt's fiancée—and…' He smiled self-consciously as Marc stood, frozen. 'And one more.' And now Hans's smile broadened. 'One who has become very dear to me.'

Marc heard the words, saw Hans take a breath and then continue on, his eyes bright.

'Of course until my divorce is finalised no formal announcement can be made, and it has been necessary, therefore, to be discreet, so perhaps my news will be a surprise to you?'

Marc's expression darkened. 'No—I've known for weeks.' His voice was hard—as hard as tempered steel. His eyes flashed, vehemence filling his voice now, unable to stay silent. 'Hans, this is *madness*—to be caught again! Did you not learn enough from Celine? How can you possibly repeat the same disastrous mistake! For God's sake, man, however besotted you are, have the sense not to do this!'

He saw Hans's expression change from bewilderment to astonishment, and then to rejection. 'Marc,' he said stiffly, 'I am perfectly aware that Celine was, indeed, a very grave error of my judgement, but—'

'And so is *Tara*!' Marc's voice slashed across the other man's.

There was silence—complete silence. Around him Marc could hear the background chatter of voices, the clinking of glasses. And inside the thundering of his heartbeat, drowning out everything. Even his own voice.

'Did you think I hadn't seen you both, in London? You and Tara—' His voice twisted over her name. Choking on it. 'Did you think I didn't see the ring you were giving her? See how her face lit up? How she couldn't wait to take it from you? How eager she was to kiss you?'

Hans stared. Then spoke. *'Bist Du verukt?'*

Fury lashed across Marc's face. Insane? No, he was *not* insane! Filled with any number of violent emotions, but not that!

Then suddenly Hans's hand was closing over his sleeve with surprising force for a man his age. 'Marc—you could not *possibly* have thought—' He broke off, then spoke again. His tone brooked no contradiction. 'What you saw—whatever it is you *feared* you saw, Marc—was Tara's very kind reaction to the news I had just told her. Of my intention to remarry, yes, indeed. But if you think, for an instant, that *she* was the object of my intentions—'

Marc felt his arm released. Hans was turning aside, allowing three more people who had just entered the room to come up to them. Marc's eyes went to them. Bernhardt, a younger version of Hans, well-known to him, with a young, attractive woman on one arm. And on the other arm an older woman with similar looks to the younger one. A woman who was smiling at Hans with a fond, affectionate look on her face. And on the third finger of the hand tucked into Bernhardt's arm was a diamond ring…

Hans turned back to Marc and his tone was formal

now. 'You will permit me to introduce to you Frau Ilse Holz and her daughter Karin?'

His eyes rested on Marc.

'Ilse,' Marc heard him say, as if from a long way away, 'has done me the very great honour of agreeing, when the time is right, to make me the happiest of men. I know,' he added, 'that you will wish us well.'

Marc might have acknowledged the introduction. He might have said whatever was required of him. Might have been aware of Hans's gaze becoming speculative.

But of all of those things he had absolutely no awareness at all. Only one thought was in his head. One blinding thought. One absolute realisation. Burning in him.

And then Bernhardt was leading away his fiancée, and the woman who was to be both his mother-in-law and his stepmother, into the throng.

Hans paused. His eyes were not speculative now. They were filled with compassion. 'Go,' he said quietly, to Marc alone. 'This…here…' he gestured to the party all around them '…is not important. You have others to see to it. So—go, my friend.'

And Marc went. Needing no further telling…

CHAPTER TWELVE

A BLACKBIRD WAS hopping about on the lawn, picking at the birdseed which Tara had started to scatter each day now that autumn was arriving. A few late bees could be heard buzzing on what was left of the lavender. There was a mild, drowsy feel to the day, as if summer were disinclined to pack its bags completely and leave the garden, preferring to make a graceful handover to its successive season.

Tara was glad of it. Sitting out here in the still warm sunshine, wearing only a light sweater and cotton trousers, her feet in canvas shoes, was really very pleasant. The trees bordering the large garden backing on to the fields beyond were flushed with rich autumnal copper, but still shot through with summer's green. A time of transition, indeed.

It echoed her own mood. *A time of transition*. She might have finally made the move from London to Dorset some weeks ago, but it was only now that she was really feeling her move was permanent. As was so much else.

She flexed her body, already less ultra-slim than

she'd had to keep it during her modelling career. It was filling out, softening her features, rounding her abdomen, ripening her breasts.

Her mind seemed to be hovering, as the seasons were, between her old life and the one she was now embarked upon. She knew she must look ahead to the future—what else was there to do? She must embrace it—just as she must embrace the coming winter. Enjoy what it would offer her.

Her expression changed, her fingers tracing over her midriff absently. She must not regret the time that had gone and passed for ever—the brief, precious time she'd had during that summer idyll so long ago, so far away, beside that azure coast. No, she must never regret that time—even though she must accept that it was gone from her, never to return. That Marc was gone from her for ever.

A cry was stifled in her throat. Anguish bit deep within her.

I'll never see him again—never hear his voice again—never feel his mouth on mine, his hand in mine. Never see him smile, or laugh, or his eyes pool with desire... Never feel his body over mine, or hold him to me, or wind my arms around him...

Her eyes gazed out, wide and unseeing, over the autumnal garden. How had it happened that what she had entered into with Marc—something that had never been intended to be anything other than an indulgence of her overpowering physical response to him—had become what she now knew, with a clutching of her heart, to be what it would be for ever?

How had she come to fall in love with him?

She felt that silent cry in her throat again.

I fell in love with him and never knew it—not until he left me. Not until I knew I would never see him again. Never be part of his life...

Her hands spasmed over the arms of the padded garden chair and she felt that deep stab of anguish again.

But what point was there in feeling it? She had a future to make for herself—a future she *must* make. And not merely for her own sake. For the sake of the most precious gift Marc could have given her. Not the vast treasures of his wealth—that was dust and ashes to her! A gift so much more precious…

A gift he must never know he had given her…

Her grip on the arms of the chair slackened and she moved her hands across her body in a gesture as old as time…

She would never see Marc again, and the pain of that loss would never leave her. But his gift to her would be with her all her life… The only balm to the endless anguish of her heart.

In the branches of the gnarled apple tree a robin was singing. Far off she could hear a tractor ploughing a field. The hazy buzz of late bees seeking the last nectar of the year. All of them lulled her…

She felt her eyelids grow heavy, and the garden faded from sight and sound as sleep slipped over her like a soft veil.

Soon another garden filled her dreamscape…with verdant foliage, vivid bougainvillea, a glittering sunlit pool. And Marc was striding towards her. Tall, and strong, and outlined against the cloudless sky. She felt her heart leap with joy…

Her eyes flashed open. Something had woken her. An alien sound. The engine of a car, low and powerful. For a second—a fraction of a second—she remembered the throaty roar of Marc's low-slung monster…the car he'd loved to drive. Then another emotion speared her.

Alarm.

The cottage was down a dead-end lane, leading only to a gate to the fields at the far end. No traffic passed by. So who was it? She was expecting no visitors…

She twisted round to look at the path leading around the side of the cottage to the lane beyond. There was a sudden dizziness in her head…a swirl of vertigo.

Had she turned too fast? Or was it that she had not woken at all, was still dreaming?

Because someone was walking towards her—*striding* towards her. Someone tall and strong, outlined against the cloudless sky. Someone who could not be here—someone she'd thought she would never see again.

But he was in her vision now—searing her retinas, the synapses of her stunned and disbelieving brain. She lurched to her feet and the vertigo hit again.

Or was it shock?

Or waking from the dream?

Or still being within the dream?

She swayed and Marc was there in an instant, steadying her. Then his hands dropped away.

Memory stabbed at her—how he'd made the same gesture in that nightmare encounter at the hotel, dropping his hands from her as if he could not bear to touch her. She clutched at the back of her chair, staring at him, hearing her heart pounding in her veins, feeling disbelief still in her head. And emotion—unbearable emotion—leaping in her heart.

She crushed it down. Whatever he was here for he would tell her and then he would leave.

For one unbearable moment dread knifed in her.

Does he know?

Oh, dear God, she prayed, please do not let him know! That would be the worst thing of all—the very worst! Because if he did…

She sheared her mind away, forced herself to speak. Heard words fall from her, uncomprehending. 'What…what are you doing here?'

He was standing there and she could see tension in every line of his body. His face was carved as if from tempered steel. As closed as she had ever seen it.

Yet something was different about him—something she had never seen before. Something in the veiling of his eyes that had never been there before.

'I have something to give you,' he said.

His voice was remote. Dispassionate. But, as with the look on his face, she had never heard his voice sound like that.

She stared, confused. 'Wh-what?' she got out.

'This,' he said.

His hand was slipping inside his jacket pocket. He was wearing yet another of his killer suits, she registered abstractedly through the shattering of her mind. Registered, too, the quickening of her pulse, the weakening of her limbs that she always felt with him. Felt the power he had to make her feel like that… Felt the longing that went with it.

Longing she must not let herself feel. No matter that he was standing here, so real, so close…

He was drawing something out from his inner pocket and she caught the silken gleam of the grey lining, the brief flash of the gold fountain pen in the pocket. Then her eyes were only on what he was holding out to her. What she recognised only too well—the slim, elegant jewel case she had returned to him that dreadful day in London that had killed all the last remnants of her hope that he might ever want her again…

She shook her head. Automatically negating.

'Marc—I told you. I can't take it. I know…' She swallowed. 'I know you…you mean well…but you must see that I can't accept it!'

Consternation was filling her. Why was he here? To insist she take those emeralds? She stared at him. His face was still as shuttered as ever, his eyes veiled, unreadable. But a nerve was ticking just below his cheekbone and there were deep lines around his mouth, as though his jaw were steel, filled with tension.

She didn't understand it. All she understood—all that was searing through her like red-hot lava in her veins—was that seeing him again was agony… An agony that had leapt out of the deepest recesses of her being, escaping like a deranged monster to devour her whole.

Through the physical pain rocking her, from holding leashed every muscle in her body, as if she could hold in the anguish blinding her, she heard him speak.

'That is a pity.' He set the case with the emerald necklace in it down on the table beside her chair.

There was still that something different in his voice—that something she'd never heard before. She'd heard ill-humour, short temper, impatience and displeasure. She'd heard desire and passion and warmth and laughter.

But she'd never heard this before.

She stared at him.

He spoke again. 'A pity,' he said, 'because, you see, emeralds would suit you so much better than mere diamonds.'

'I don't understand…' The words fell from her. Bewildered. Hollow.

The very faintest ghost of what surely could not be a twisted smile curved the whipped line of his mouth for an instant. As if he was mocking himself with a savagery that made her take a breath.

'They would suit you so much better than the diamond ring which Hans presented to you.'

Tara struggled to speak. '*Presented?* He *showed* it to me! Dear God, Marc—you could not…? You could not have thought…?'

Disbelief rang in every word that fell from her. He

could *not* have thought that! How *could* he? Shock—more than shock—made her speechless.

A rasp sounded in his throat. It seemed to her that it was torn from somewhere very deep inside him.

'We see what we want to see,' he replied. The mockery was there again, in the twist of his mouth, but the target was only himself. And then there was another emotion in his face. His eyes. 'We see what we *fear* to see.'

She gazed at him, searching his face. Her heart was pounding within her, deafening her. 'I don't understand,' she said again. Her voice was fainter than ever.

'No more did I,' he said. 'I didn't understand at all. Did not understand how I was being made a fool of again. But this time by *myself*.'

She frowned. '"Again"?'

He moved suddenly, restlessly. Not answering her.

Here he was, standing and facing her in this place that had been almost impossible to find—hard to discover even by relentless enquiry.

It had taken him from a ruthless interrogation of her former flatmates, in which he had discovered that she had moved out...had hired a van to transport her belongings, to the tracking down of the hire company, finding out where they had delivered to, and then, finally, to hiring a car of his own and speeding down to that same destination.

All with the devil driving him.

The devil he was purging from himself now, after so many years of its malign possession. So much depended on it. *All* depended on it.

He took a breath—a ragged breath. 'When you look at me, Tara, what do you see?'

What do you see?

His words echoed in her skull. Crying out for an answer she must not give.

I see the man I love, who has never loved me! I see the man who did not want me, though I still want him—and always will, for all my days! That is the man I see—and I cannot tell you that! I cannot tell you because you don't want me as I want you, and I will not burden you with my wanting you. I will not burden you with the love you do not want from me... Nor with the gift you gave me.

But silence held her—as it must. Whatever he had come here for, it was not to hear her break the stricken silence that she must keep.

He spoke again, in that same low, demanding tone.

'Do you see a man rich and powerful in his own realm of worldly wealth? A man who can command the luxuries of life? Who has others to do his bidding, whatever he wants of them? Whose purpose is to protect the heritage he was born to—to protect the wealth he possesses, to guard it from all who might want to seize it from him?' His voice changed now. 'To guard it from all who might want to make a fool of him?'

He shifted again, restless still, then his voice continued. Eyes flashing back to her.

'You saw Celine with Hans—you saw how she took ruthless advantage of him, wanted him only for his wealth. You saw what she did to him—' He made a noise of scorn and disgust in his throat. 'I am richer than Hans—considerably so, if all our accounts were pitted one against the other! But…' He took a savage breath. 'I am as vulnerable as he is.' A twisted, self-mocking smile taunted his mouth. 'The only difference is that I know it. Know it and guard endlessly against it.' He shook his head. 'I guard myself against every woman I encounter.'

His expression changed.

'And the way I do it is very simple—I keep to women from my own world. Women who have wealth of their own…who therefore will not covet mine. It was a strategy that worked until—' he took a ravaged breath, his eyes boring into hers, to make her understand '—until I encountered you.'

A raw breath incised his lungs.

'I broke a lifetime's rules for you, Tara! I knew it was rash, unwise, but I could not resist it! Could not resist *you*. You taunted me with your beauty, with that mouthy lip of yours, daring to prick my *amour propre*! Answering me back…defying me! And your worst crime of all…' His voice was changing too, and he could not stop it doing so. It was softening into a sensual tone that was echoing the quickening of his pulse, the sweep of his lashes over his eyes. 'You denied me what I wanted—pushing me away, telling me it was only play-acting, tormenting me with it.'

His breath was ragged again, his eyes burning into hers.

'And so when we were *finally* alone together, free of that damnable role-play, I could only think that I should not make it real with you—that I should not break my lifetime's rules…'

He saw her face work, her eyes shadow.

'Not all women are like Celine, Marc.'

Her voice was sad. Almost pitying. It was a pity he could not bear.

He gave a harsh laugh. 'But they *could* be! And how am I to *tell*? How would I *know*?' He paused, and then with a hardening of his face continued. 'I thought I knew once. I was young, and arrogant and so, so sure of myself—and of the woman I wanted. Who seemed to want me too. Until…' He could not look at her, could see only the past, indelible in his memory, a warning throughout his life, 'Until the day I saw her across a restaurant, wearing the engagement ring of a man far older than I. Far richer—'

He tore his voice away and he forced his eyes to go back to the woman who stood in his present, not in his past.

'How could I *know*?' he repeated. His eyes rested on her, impassive, veiling what he would not show. 'That last night you asked to come with me to New York…'

She blenched, he could see the colour draining from her skin, but he could not stop now.

'But if you came to New York with me then where next? Back to Paris? To move in with me perhaps? For how long? What would you want? What would you start to take for granted?' His voice changed, and there was a coldness in it he could not keep out. 'What would you start to expect as your due?'

He drew breath again.

'That's why I ended it between us,' he said. 'That's why,' he went on, and he knew there was a deadness in his voice, 'I left you the emerald necklace. Sent you that cheque. To…to draw a line under whatever had been. What you might have thought there was—or could be.'

He fell silent.

Tara could hear his breathing, hear her own. Had heard the truth he'd spoken. She pulled her shoulders back, straightening her spine, letting her hands fall to her side. Lifted her chin. Looked him in the eye. She was not the daughter of soldiers for nothing.

'I never thought it, Marc.' Her voice was blank. Remote. 'I never thought there was anything more between us than what we had.'

She had said it. And it was not a lie. It was simply not all the truth. Between 'thought' and 'hope' was a distance so vast it shrank the universe to an atom.

'But I did,' he said. His jaw clenched. 'I did think it.' His expression changed. 'I didn't want to end it, Tara. I didn't want *us* to end. But…' Something flashed in his face. 'But I was afraid.'

She saw a frown crease his forehead, as if he had encountered a problem he had not envisaged. As if he were seeing it for the first time in his life.

'But what is the point of fear,' he asked, as if to the universe itself, 'if it destroys our only chance of happiness?'

His eyes went to her now, and in them, yet again, was something she had never seen before. She could not name it, yet it called to her from across a chasm as wide as all the world. And as narrow as the space between them.

She saw his hand go to the jewel case, flick it open. Green fire glittered within.

'Emeralds would suit you,' he said again, 'so much better than mere diamonds. Which is why—'

There was a constriction in his voice—she could hear it…could feel her heart start to slug within her. Hard and heavy beats, like a tattoo inside her body.

She saw him replace the necklace on the table, saw his hand slide once again within his breast pocket, draw out another object. A cube this time, with the same crest on it that the emerald necklace case held. She saw him flick it open. Saw what was within.

He extended his hand towards her, the ring in its box resting in his palm. 'It's yours if you want it,' he said. The casualness of the words belied the tautness of his jaw, the nerve flickering in his cheekbone, the sudden veiling of his eyes as if to protect himself. 'Along with one other item, should it be of any value to you.'

The drumming of her heartbeat was rising up inside her, deafening in volume. Her throat thickened so she could not breathe.

He glanced at her again, and there was a sudden tensing in his expression that hollowed his face, made it gaunt with strain. 'It's my heart, Tara. It comes with the ring if you want it—'

A hand flew to her mouth, stifling a cry in her tearing throat. 'Marc! No! Don't say it—oh, don't say it! Not if…not if you don't mean it!' Fear was in her face, terror. 'I couldn't bear it—'

Her fingers pressed against her mouth, making her words almost inaudible, but he could hear them all the same.

'It's too late,' he said. 'I've said it now. I can't take it back. I can't take back anything—anything at all! Not a single thing I've ever said to you—not a single kiss, a single heartbeat.' Emotion scythed across his face. 'It's too late for everything,' he said. 'Too late for fear.'

He lifted his free hand, gently drew back the fingers pressing against her mouth, folding his own around her, strong and warm.

'What good would it do me? Fear? I can gather all the proof I want—the fact that you returned my cheque, refused my emeralds, gave away a couture wardrobe! That my insane presumption that you had helped me dispose of Celine only to clear the path for your own attempt on Hans was nothing more than the absurd creation of my fears. But there *is* no proof! No proof that can withstand the one sure truth of all.'

He pressed her fingers, turning them over in his hand, exposing the delicate skin of her wrist. He dipped his head to let his lips graze like silken velvet, with sensuous softness… Then he lifted his head, poured his gaze into hers.

Her eyes glimmered with tears, emotion swelling within her like a wondrous wave. Could this be true? Really true?

'Will you take my heart?' he was saying now. 'For it holds the one sure truth of all.'

His eyes moved on her face, as if searching…finding.

'It's *love*, Tara. That's the only one sure truth. All that I can rely on—all that I need to rely on. For if you should love me then I am safe. Safe from all my fear.'

His eyes were filled with all she had longed to see in them.

'And if my love for you should be of any value to you—'

Another choking cry came from her and her arm flung itself around his neck, clutching him to her. Words flew from her. 'I've tried so hard—so desperately hard—to let you go! Oh, not from my life—I knew that you were over in my life—but in my heart. Oh, dear God, I could not tear you from my heart…'

The truth that she would have silenced all her life, never burdening him with it, broke from her now, and sobs—endless sobs that seemed to last for ever—discharged all that she had forced herself to keep buried deep within her, unacknowledged, silent and smothered.

As he wrapped her arm around her waist, pressing it tightly to him, something tumbled from his palm. But he did not notice. It was not important. Only this had any meaning…only this was precious.

To have Tara in his arms again. Tara whom he'd thrown away, let go, lost.

He had let fear possess him. Destroy his only chance of happiness in life.

He soothed her now, murmuring soft words, until her weeping eased and ebbed and she took a trembling step back from him. He gazed down at her. Her eyes were red from crying, tear runnels stained her cheeks, her mouth was wobbly and uneven, her features contorted still…

The most beautiful woman in the world.

'I once took it upon myself to announce that you were my fiancée,' he said, his voice wry and his eyes with a dark glint in them. 'But now…' His voice changed again, and with a little rush of emotion she heard uncertainty in his voice, saw a questioning doubt in his eyes about her answer to what he was saying. 'Now I take nothing upon myself at all.' He paused, searching her eyes. 'So tell me—I beg you… implore you—if I proposed to you now, properly, as a suitor should, would you say yes?'

She burst into tears once more. He drew her to him again, muffled her cries in his shoulder, and then he was soothing her yet again, murmuring more words to her, until once again she eased her tears and drew tremblingly back.

'Dare I keep talking?' he put to her.

She gave another choke, but it was of laughter as well as tears. Her gaze was misty, but in it he saw all that he had hoped beyond hope to see.

He bent to kiss her mouth—a soft, tender kiss, that calmed all the violent emotion that had been shaken from her, leaving her a peace inside her that was vast and wondrous. Could this be true and real? Or only the figment of her longings?

But it *was* real! Oh, so real. And he was here, and kissing her…kissing her for ever and ever…

And then he was drawing back, frowning, looking around him.

'What is it?' Tara asked, her voice still trembling, her whole body swaying with the emotion consuming her.

He frowned. 'I had a ring here somewhere,' he said. 'I need it—'

She glanced down, past where the emerald necklace lay on the garden table in its box, into the grass beneath. Something glinted greener than the grass. She gave a little cry of discovery and he swooped to pick it up from where it had fallen.

He possessed himself of her hand, which trembled like the rest of her. Slid the ring over her finger. Then he raised her hand to his lips, turned it over in his palm. Lowered his mouth to kiss the tender skin over the veins in her wrist. A kiss of tenderness, of homage.

Then he folded her hand within his own. 'I knew that I had gone way past mere desire for you,' he said, his voice low, intense, his eyes holding hers with a gaze that made her heart turn over, 'when on the evening of the bank's autumn client party—which Hans always comes to—I realised that for all the blackness in my heart over what I thought you had done, there was only one emotion in me.'

He paused, and she felt his hands clench over hers.

'It was an unbearable longing for you,' he said, and there was a catch in his voice that made Tara press his hands with hers, placing her free hand over his.

'As unbearable as my longing to see my parents again after their deaths—'

He broke off and she slipped her hands from his, slid them around him, drawing her to him. She held him close and tight and for ever. Moved beyond all things by what he had said.

Then, suddenly, he was pulling away from her.

'Tara…' His voice was hollow. Hollow with shock.

Her expression changed as she realised what he had discovered. And she knew she must tell him why she had made the agonising decision that she had.

'You didn't want me, Marc,' she said quietly. Sadly. 'So I would never, *never* have forced this on you.'

He let his hands drop, stepped back a moment. His face was troubled.

'Are you angry?'

He heard the note of fear in her voice. 'Only at myself,' he said. 'My fears nearly cost me my life's happiness,' he said. His voice was sombre, grave. Self-accusing. 'And they nearly cost me even more.' His face worked, and then in the same sombre voice he spoke again. 'I tried to find proof—proof that you did not value my wealth above myself.' He took a ragged breath. 'But if I wanted the greatest proof of all it is this. That you were prepared to raise my baby by yourself…never telling me, never claiming a single *sou* from me—'

Her voice was full as she answered him. 'I could not have borne it if you had felt any…any *obligation*. Of any kind.' She drew breath. 'But now…'

She smiled and took his hand in hers again. Slowly,

carefully, she placed it across her gently swelling waistline. She saw wonder fill his face, light in his eyes, and her heart lifted to soar.

French words broke from him, raw and heartfelt. She leant to kiss his mouth. There was a glint in her eye now. 'I'm going to lose my figure, you know… Turn into a barrage balloon. You won't desire me any more—not for months and months and months!'

The familiar look was in his eyes—that oh-so-familiar look that melted the bones of her body.

'I will *always* desire you!' he promised, and he laughed. Joy was soaring in him, like eagles taking flight. And desire too—heating him from within.

She gave a laugh of pure happiness that lifted her from her feet—or was it Marc, sweeping her up into his arms?

She gave a choke, felt emotion wringing her. 'Marc, is this real? *Is* it? Tell me it is! Because I can't be this happy—how *can* I?'

The future that had loomed before her—empty of all but the most precious memento of her brief time with him—now flowed and merged with the past she had lost…becoming an endless present that she knew she would never lose!

His arms tightened around her, his eyes pouring into hers. 'As real as it is for me,' he said.

Happiness such as he had never known since the carefree days of his youth overflowed in him. Tara was his for ever, and she was bringing to him a gift that was a wonder and a joy to him: the baby that was to be born.

He was striding with her now, towards the cottage. He glanced around, as if seeing it for the first time. 'Is this the new life you said you were making for yourself?'

She smiled, tightening her grip around his neck with the hook of her arm. 'A new life—and an old one,' she said. 'The cottage belonged to my grandparents, and they left it to me. It's always been my haven…'

'And it will be ours, too, if you will permit me to share it with you,' he said, his voice warm. 'In fact it seems to me that it would be the ideal place for a honeymoon…'

The glint in his eyes was melting her bones as he negotiated the narrow doorway, sweeping her indoors and ducking his tall frame beneath the beamed lintel. Purposefully, he headed for the stairs. There must be bedrooms upstairs, and beds…

He dropped a kiss on her mouth as he carried her aloft, following her hurried directions to her bedroom, lowering her down upon the old-fashioned brass bed which creaked under their combined weight, sinking them deep into the feather mattress.

'Starting right now.'

'Now, that…' Tara sighed blissfully '…is a *wonderful* idea!'

Marc gave a growl of satisfaction at her answer and began to remove their entirely unnecessary clothing, covering her face in kisses that would last their lifetimes—and beyond.

EPILOGUE

MARC STOOD ON the terrace of the Villa Derenz, his infant son cradled in his arms. Out on the manicured lawn, under the shade of a huge parasol beside the pool, Tara dozed on a lounger.

His eyes went to her, soft with love-light. Here she had first beguiled him and entranced him, lighting a flame within him that his own fears had so nearly extinguished but which now burnt with everlasting fire.

He walked up to her, feeling the warmth of late summer lapping him. At his approach she roused herself and smiled, holding out her arms expectantly.

'Afternoon tea is served, young Master Derenz!' she said, and laughed, busying herself settling him to feed.

Marc dropped a lingering kiss on her forehead, then turned as two figures of military bearing emerged from the villa, coming towards him and Tara.

'Feeding him up? Good, good…' Major Mackenzie nodded approvingly at his grandson's nursing.

'Latched on properly?' the other Major Mackenzie asked her daughter.

'Mum, I'm not one of your subalterns,' Tara remonstrated good-humouredly, with a laugh, patting the lounger for her mother to sit down beside her.

Her parents had welcomed the news of their daughter's marriage with open delight, and her mother had organised the wedding at the little parish church near the cottage with military precision. Her father had even summoned a guard of honour for the bride and groom, formed by the men of his regiment.

And if a tear had moistened her mother's eyes, only Tara had seen it, and only she had heard her mother say, with more emotion in her voice than her daughter was used to hearing, 'He can't take his eyes off you, that utterly gorgeous man of yours! And he is lucky—*so lucky*—to have you!' Then she had hugged her daughter closely.

The arrival of their grandson had also persuaded her parents to return to Civvy Street, and they would soon buy a house on the Dorset coast, near enough to for them to keep an eye on the cottage. Tara was glad for them and glad for herself—she would be seeing more of them, and they were safe from future military deployment.

She was also glad that Marc's son would have grandparents on her side to grow up with. But there would be happy memories in the making here, too, at the villa on Cap Pierre, just as Marc had from his own boyhood with his parents and their friends.

The Neubergers, with Hans's new grandchild on

the way, would soon be here to spend a fortnight, after her parents had returned to the UK. Hans had not been slow to express his gladness that Marc and she were so happy together.

She looked up lovingly at her husband and he met her gaze, his dark eyes softening, his heart catching.

How can I love her so much? How is it possible?

All he knew was that he did, and that theirs was a love that would never end. And to have found it made him the most fortunate man in the world.

There was the sound of a throat clearing and he glanced across at his father-in-law.

'If it's all right with you, old chap,' said Major Mackenzie, 'we'd like to take out that very neat little boat of yours! Wind's rising, and we're keen to try out the spinnaker.'

Marc smiled broadly. 'An excellent idea,' he said warmly, and Tara added her own encouragement.

Her mother rose briskly to her feet and she and Marc watched them stride across the lawn to the path leading to the jetty, where the boat was moored.

'You could go out with them too, you know,' she said to Marc.

He shook his head. 'I was thinking, actually, of a quite different activity. When, that is, young Master Derenz requires his afternoon nap…'

Tara's eyes glinted knowingly. 'And what might that be, Monsieur Derenz?' she enquired limpidly.

He gave a low laugh. 'Well, Madame Derenz, I was thinking,' he said, returning the glint in her eye with a deeper one of his own, 'that perhaps it is time to consider the addition of a Mademoiselle Derenz to the family…'

She caught his hand and kissed it. 'An *excellent* idea,' she agreed. 'Happy families…' She sighed. 'It just doesn't get better.'

And Marc could not help but agree—with all his heart.

* * * * *

Heiress's Pregnancy Scandal

MILLS & BOON

DEDICATION

For WSW—my cosmology adviser!

CHAPTER ONE

Nic Falcone stepped through the service door into the casino, glancing around with a deeply satisfied sweep. Yes, this had been a good idea, acquiring and restoring this fading *hacienda*-style hotel deep in the western desert, yet still within reach of both Las Vegas and the West Coast. Another prestigious money-spinner for the global Falcone chain of luxury hotels. More glittering proof of just how far he'd come in his thirty-odd years—from the backstreets of Rome to being one of the richest men in Italy.

The fatherless slum kid who'd started his first job at barely sixteen in the basement—literally—of the fabled Viscari Roma hotel had, by his own gruelling efforts, climbed as high as that dilettante playboy Vito Viscari, who'd had a legendary hotel chain handed to him on a plate by his family.

Nic's expression shadowed as he remembered. Through dogged hard work he'd worked his way up through the ranks at the Viscari Roma, every promotion striven for, until he had finally been in line for the big move into management that he had *known* he was totally qualified for.

But Vito's uncle, the chairman of the company, had instead preferred that his inexperienced nephew—fresh out of university, with none of the hard-earned, hands-on track record that Nic had under his belt—should get a taste of his future inheritance.

Nic had been passed over—and from that moment he'd known that from now on he would work only for himself. The seeds of the Falcone hotel chain had been sown. Falcone would be the rival that would outsoar Viscari once and for all.

And through a level of hard work that had absorbed his whole life Nic had succeeded—fantastically. So much so that last year he had been able to swoop, like his namesake the predatory falcon, to take ruthless advantage of an internal power struggle within the divided Viscari family and snap up an entire half of the Viscari portfolio of hotels in a blatantly hostile acquisition.

It had proved, though, to be a triumph that had turned to ashes. Yet again Nic had felt the pampering hand of nepotism thwarting him. This time it had been, of all things, Vito's mother-in-law, persuading Nic's own investors, who'd funded his acquisition, to sell the hotels back to her so she could hand them over to her son-in-law, Vito.

Yet again Vito had prospered without lifting a finger for himself—thanks to help from his family.

But the determination that had lifted Nic from the

backstreets had kicked in again, and in the months since losing his grip on the Viscari portfolio he had reacted by lining up a string of potential new Falcone properties, including this, the newly opened Falcone Nevada, with its oh-so-lucrative on-site casino.

His keen eyes swept the crowded gaming floor as he strolled forward, noting that a good few of the gamblers had likely come over from the conference wing of the hotel, where a gathering of astrophysics academics were holding their annual shindig. Including the cluster of young hopefuls now quitting the bar area to head to the gaming floor. Leaving behind a woman who was now raising a hand to them in a casual goodnight.

A woman who halted him in his tracks. Tall, graceful and dazzlingly blonde.

Every sense went on high alert. In his time he'd seen—and sampled—many, many beautiful women. But none like this. He felt his stomach muscles clench, held his breath. His eyes fastened on her. And desire—hot, intense and instant—quickened…

Fran watched the post-grad students go off to buy their chips and hoped they wouldn't lose their shirts at the tables. They were clearly in demob happy mood and making the most of this, the final night of the conference. As for herself, she should head off, for she still had a poster session to give the following morning, before the plenary session, and it wouldn't hurt to run through her presentation again.

But as she turned back towards the barman to call for her bill a voice behind her spoke.

'No temptation to try your luck at the tables?'

It was a deep voice, with an American accent that did not sound western, and it held a gravelled timbre that made her turn.

And as she did so her eyes widened.

Oh, wow...

The silent exclamation, as instinctive as it was unstoppable, resonated in her consciousness.

The man who stood there, his pose deceptively relaxed, was tall—easily topping her own willowy figure—with broad shoulders, lean hips and a muscled chest that looked as if it could take a punch without even noticing.

In fact, she registered, in her subliminal sweep of his features, it looked as if his nose, set in a face that was hard-planed and strong-jawed, had been on the receiving end of a slug at some stage.

The slight bump was a flaw that only added to his powerful appeal. The man might be in a tux, but everything about him said *tough*.

Part of the security team here? she wondered, a mind still reeling from the visceral impact he'd made on her. It had been like walking into a wall—a wall she'd never seen coming.

For a second—a sub-second—she was frozen, taking him in, reacting to him on a level at which she never, just *never*, reacted to men. Not even the formidably good-looking Cesare, the man she had so nearly married, had had the overpowering instantaneous impact the man standing here now was having on her.

He's nothing like the men I usually find attractive!

With the exception of Cesare, with his hawkish, aristocratic demeanour, she'd always only gone for men with studious looks—not the muscled type that she'd always regarded as…well, *brutish.*

But there was nothing brutish about this man. Not with eyes like that. Glinting with sharp intelligence.

And blue—piercing blue—which is really weird, because the tan of his skin tone and the sable of his hair indicates Hispanic, probably…

Yet even as she made that reasonable assumption she realised she needed to do something other than just gaze dumbstruck at him. Should she acknowledge his remark? Without vanity, she knew from experience that her blonde looks drew male eyes—and more—and if she was chatted up she normally kept her reaction vague to the point of evasive until she could get away or the man gave up. If absolutely necessary she froze them out.

For the moment, though, she went for option one, and gave a brief, impersonal flicker of a smile and a demurring shake of her head.

'Not my thing…gambling,' she replied, glad to accept the leather-bound drinks bill, and jot her room number on it.

'You're part of the conference?'

Again, the deep, slightly gravelled voice made her glance up as she pushed the folder back to the barman.

'Yes,' she acknowledged.

She moved to slip off the high stool, and immediately the man's hand was there, guiding her. She glanced at him, murmuring her thanks, but wished that she could retain the air of impersonal indifference that she knew she should be displaying at this time.

Only it was impossible to do so. Impossible to do anything but feel the extraordinary visceral impact on her that he was having.

An impact that suddenly increased exponentially.

He was smiling—and the smile was like the smile of a desert wolf.

Fran felt her lungs squeeze, her breath catch. The smile was swift—a sudden indentation of the firm mouth, a brief flash of teeth, a lightening of his tough features as if the sun had just come out and then disappeared again.

'Forgive me for sounding clichéd, but you don't look the least like an astrophysicist!'

Amusement played around his firm mouth, as if he knew perfectly well that it was, indeed, a clichéd observation, but didn't give a damn. Because the light in those blue, blue eyes of his was telling her just why he'd said what he had.

He wanted to do anything to keep the conversation going.

Fran lifted an eyebrow. Whatever was going on here, it was unlikely to be anything to do with the man's role as a member of the hotel's security team, if that was who he was, given the air of toughness radiating from him. And if he wasn't—if he was just another guest—then that made it no better. He was still chatting her up. So maybe she should just call time and walk.

Except that she didn't want to. The sudden fizzing in her veins, the catch in her heart rate, was telling her that she was reacting to this man as she had never reacted to any man before—that something was happening to her that had never happened to her before.

So, instead of whatever she might have been planning to reply to him with, she could hear her own voice, with a clear hint of answering amusement in it, saying, 'And you've encountered many astrophysicists in your time, have you?'

She was conscious that her eyebrow had lifted, just as her mouth had twitched in amusement, conscious too of how that flashing smile had come again. Her sense was that here was a man totally at ease with himself. Even if he was a security guy, chatting up one of the guests in the hotel he worked in, he didn't care—and he was inviting her not to care either. He was a man who knew he was blatantly accosting a woman who had caught his eye…

She was conscious that long, dark lashes had swept down over those brilliant blue eyes as he answered her in turn.

'Enough,' he said laconically.

Fran's eyes narrowed deliberately. 'Name three,' she challenged.

He laughed—a low, attractive sound that went with the flashing smile, and the brilliant blue eyes and the tough face and the tougher body. All of which were doing incredible things to her.

She felt herself reel inwardly.

What is happening to me? I get chatted up by some guy strolling up to me in a bar at a casino hotel and suddenly I feel like I'm eighteen again. Not a sober-minded post-doc on the far side of twenty-five, who writes abstruse scientific papers on cosmology at a prestigious West Coast university.

Hard-working research academics didn't go doolally because some muscled hunk smiled at them. And nor, came the even more sobering thought, did the woman who was her identity as well as Dr Fran Ristori.

Donna Francesca di Ristori. Offspring of two noble houses—one Italian, one English—both centuries old, with bloodlines that could be traced back to the Middle Ages, and estates and lands, castles and *palazzos*. She was the daughter of Il Marchese d'Arromento, and granddaughter of one of the peers of the British realm, the Duke of Revinscourt.

Not that anyone here in the USA knew that—or cared. In academia only the quality of your research counted, nothing else. It was something that her mother—born Lady Emma, now Marchesa d'Arromento—had never really understood. But then her mother had never really understood why Fran had turned away from the life she'd been born to in order to follow her deep love of learning to the halls of academia.

It had caused, Fran knew, something of a rift between them, and it was only because Fran had agreed to marry into the Italian aristocracy that her mother had been reconciled to her research career.

But last year Fran had broken up with Cesare, Il Conte di Mantegna, whom she had long been expected to marry, and now her mother was barely speaking to her.

'But he was *perfect* for you!' her mother had cried protestingly. 'You've known each other all your lives and he would have let you continue with all this star-gazing you insist on as well as being his Contessa!'

'I got a better offer,' was all Fran had been able to say.

It had been an offer her mother could never have appreciated—the exciting invitation to join the research team of a Nobel Laureate out in California.

Fran had been relieved to take the offer, and not just for herself. Cesare was a friend—a good friend—and he would always be a friend, but it had turned out that he was actually in love with someone else and had since married her.

Fran was glad for Cesare, and for Carla, his new bride, and the baby that had been born to them, and wished them every happiness.

She had moved out to the West Coast, rented an apartment, and was revelling in the heady atmosphere of one of the world's most advanced cosmology research centres. Although it was strange not to have Cesare in her life any longer—even long-distance, across the Atlantic—she had joyfully immersed herself in her work, thrilled to be assisting the famous Nobel Laureate.

Except that this last semester her revered professor had suffered a heart attack and retired prematurely, and his successor wasn't a patch on him. Already Fran had resolved to seek another post, another university. She would see out this conference and then start actively looking.

'OK—I fold.' The man blatantly chatting her up held up a large, square-palmed hand to indicate defeat. 'You called my bluff.'

The flashing smile came again, and yet again Fran felt her heart give a kick. Tomorrow's plenary session, the poster session she was giving—both vanished.

She gave a laugh. She couldn't help it. The guy was so sure of himself. Usually that put her right off, but somehow, in this man, it was simply one more part of his appeal. As to *why* he had that appeal to her—she just could not analyse that. It was beyond rational thought.

'Well, we had the conference dinner tonight, so we're all togged up in our best bib and tucker,' she answered him. 'None of us are looking like nerdy scientists right now!'

Blue, blue eyes swept over her. Open in their admiration for her.

'Sicuramente no.' Definitely not.

The murmured syllables were audible, and Fran's expression changed automatically. He wasn't Hispanic after all...

'Sei Italiano?'

The question came from her before she could stop himself. The man's expression changed as she asked it. Slight surprise and then clear satisfaction.

Fran realised she'd just given him a whole new avenue to chat her up with. And she found she didn't mind at all.

She didn't notice the slight flicker in his expression as he answered her, nor the very slight air of evasion in his voice.

'Many Americans are,' he said, speaking English now. *'E sei?'* And you?

'Italian on my father's side. English on my mother's,' answered Fran.

With every passing exchange she could feel herself simply giving in to this—whatever it was—and still not really knowing *why* it was happening. Why she should be giving the time of day—make that the time of nearly midnight!—to a muscled hunk who was blazingly sure of himself, blatantly chatting her up, when she really ought to be heading back to her room to go through her presentation for tomorrow.

She only knew a sense of heady breathlessness that had come from nowhere the moment he'd spoken to her. Knew that he was suddenly making her feel so, so different from the sober-minded research academic she knew herself to be—so, so different from the stately Donna Francesca she had been born to be.

He was speaking again. 'English, huh? I thought you were from the East Coast.'

'I lived there for a while,' she allowed. 'Studying for my doctorate.'

A sudden whoop coming from the direction of the post-grads gathered at one of the blackjack tables distracted her and she glanced towards them.

She frowned suddenly. 'I hope they're not trying to beat the dealer by counting in cahoots!' she exclaimed. 'They're all maths hotshots, so they probably could if they tried, but I know casinos don't like that…'

'Don't worry—the croupiers know not to let that happen.'

The words were reassuring, the tone laconic, but Fran glanced at him all the same.

'You sound like you *know* that,' she said.

He nodded, the blue eyes on her. 'I do,' he answered.

She looked at him. So that sounded as if he was definitely part of hotel security, didn't it? But she still wasn't sure.

Then she realised she didn't care either way. He was speaking again, in that deep, laconic and oh-so-attractive voice of his.

'So, has it been a good conference for you?' he was asking.

She nodded. He was keeping her in conversation. She knew he was, he knew she knew he was, and she was OK with it. She didn't know *why* she was OK with it, but she was. And right now she would give him an answer to his question.

'Yes—it's been mentally stimulating. Full-on, but good. And this hotel…' she gestured with her hand '…is fantastic. I don't really know the Falcone chain, but they've pulled out the stops here. My only regret is that I haven't made enough use of the facilities—I haven't even had a chance to try out the pool. I definitely will tomorrow, though, before we leave. It's just a shame I won't have time to take any of the tours on offer—not even the one to the Grand Canyon!'

The minute she'd said that she regretted it. Oh, Lord, did he think she was angling for an invitation? She hoped not.

To her relief he let it pass and simply said, 'I'm glad you like the hotel—a lot of work went into it.'

There was professional pride in his voice—she could hear it. It confirmed to her that he must, indeed, be part of the security team that any hotel—let alone one that included a casino—would surely need.

'I'd prefer it without the casino, but there you go. When in Nevada…' she finished insouciantly.

'Casinos make a lot of money,' came the laconic reply, and there was another sweep of those long dark lashes over those blue, blue eyes.

Another whoop of triumph came from the post-grads at the blackjack table.

Fran laughed. 'Maybe a little less tonight,' she observed dryly.

'Maybe,' he allowed, with a glint of amusement in his face, his eyes, around his mouth.

The amusement didn't leave his face, but suddenly there was something else there in his expression—a question. A question that told her, with a quiver of reassurance, that maybe he was not so absolutely sure of himself as he was giving out. And she liked him the more for it.

'And maybe…' he went on, and there was a speculative look in his eyes now that went with the question, that went with the sense that he was in no way taking her answer for granted. 'Maybe,' he continued, the change in his tone of voice matching the change in his expression, 'if I asked if I might buy you a drink to celebrate your fellow astrophysicists' obvious win over there, you might say yes?'

Fran looked at him, glanced back over towards the blackjack table, then looked back at the man who had been chatting her up and was now clearly intent on getting to second base.

Should she co-operate? Did she want to? Or should she say no politely and head to her room to mug up on her presentation?

Even as she cogitated, in the milliseconds it took for her brain's synapses to flash their signals to each other, she felt another emotion stab through her. A sense of restlessness, of wanting something more than to give a fluent presentation the next day. Something more than the hard year of non-stop slog she'd put in since breaking up with Cesare, taking up her research post with the world-famous Nobel Laureate, producing a clutch of published papers with him and his team.

Whoever this blue-eyed, tough-faced, muscled hunk was, and why it was that, for reasons she could not yet figure out, he was capable of drawing her into conversation the way he so effortlessly had, only one thought was dominating her consciousness right now.

No, she didn't want to retire meekly to her room. She wanted, instead, to keep this conversation going, keep this encounter going—keep the rush of fizzing blood in her veins from falling flat.

A smile parted her lips and she climbed back on to the high bar stool. He let her this time, without trying to help. She looked straight at him. Liking what she saw. Going for broke.

'Why not?' she said.

Nic's gaze swept over her with distinct appreciation as she resettled herself on the bar stool. And with gratification too. He hadn't been entirely sure she would accept his move on her. But that, he knew, was part of her appeal. He was bored with women being over-keen on him, and maybe that was why he was being evasive about who he was—Nicolo Falcone, billionaire founder and owner of the Falcone hotel chain.

For that very reason he threw a warning glance at the barman as he glided up to them, and received an infinitesimal nod of acknowledgement in return.

They gave their orders—a Campari and soda for her, a bourbon for him—and Nic lowered himself to sit beside her on the next bar stool.

'So,' he opened, 'are you giving any papers yourself at the conference?'

'Yes, a post—that's a small presentation—about

where I've got to in my current research. It's for tomorrow, before the final plenary session.'

'What's it about—and would I even understand the title?' he added with good-humoured self-deprecation.

For all that her incandescent beauty lit up the room for him, she lived in a world that was far, far distant from the cut and thrust of his.

He watched her take a sip from her drink, admiring her delicate fingers, the elegant air she had about her. She was wearing a mid-price-range cocktail dress, with a square neckline and cap sleeves, which, although it was fitting for the purpose of a formal conference dinner, had little pizzazz about it. Her hair was dressed in a neat pleat, and her make-up was subdued. She looked what she was—an academic dressed up for the evening.

Desire curled in him, focussed and demanding.

She was answering him now, and he paid attention, subduing his primitive response to her.

Her voice, light and crisp in the English style, had warmed with an enthusiasm that came, he knew instinctively, from the intellectual passion in her that lit up in her eyes, animating her fine-boned face.

'My research field is cosmology—understanding the origins and eventual fate of the universe. This poster is just one small aspect of that. I'm running observational data through a computer model, testing various options for the geometry and density of space which might indicate whether, to put it at its simplest, the universe is open or closed.'

Nic frowned in concentration. 'What does that mean?'

Her voice warmed yet more as she explained. 'Well, if it's open, the expansion that started with the Big Bang will cause all the matter in the universe to be dissipated, so there will be no stars, no planets, no galaxies and no energy. It's called heat death and it would be really boring,' she said with a moue of dislike. 'So I'm rooting for a closed universe, which could cause everything to eventually collapse back in a Big Crunch and trigger another Big Bang—and the universe will be reborn. Far more fun!'

Nic took a mouthful of bourbon, feeling the strong liquid ease pleasantly down his throat.

'So, which is it?' he asked in his laconic fashion.

She gave another moue. 'No one knows for sure—though it's tending towards open at the moment, alas. Whichever it is we have to accept it—even if I don't like it.'

Nic felt himself shake his head. 'No. I don't buy that.'

She was looking at him questioningly, her eyes beautiful and wide.

He elaborated, his voice decisive. 'We should never accept what we don't like. It's defeatist.' His jaw set. 'OK, maybe it applies to the universe—but it doesn't apply to humanity. We can change things, and it's up to us. We don't have to accept the status quo.'

She was still looking at him, but her expression was one of curiosity now. 'That sounds like it runs very deep in you,' she said. Her eyes rested on him a moment, as if reading him.

He gave a half-shrug of one shoulder, as if impatient. 'We can't just accept things as they are.'

She frowned slightly. 'Some things we have to, though. Some things we can't change. Who we are, for example. Who we were born as—'

Like I was born Donna Francesca—that's in me whether I want it to be or not. It's part of my heritage—an indelible part. For all the changes I've made to my life, I can't change my birth.

'That's *exactly* what we can change!' There was vehemence in his reply, and he took another slug of bourbon. Memories were pressing in on him suddenly—*bad* memories. His hapless mother, abandoned by the man who'd fathered her son, abandoned by all of the other men who'd taken up with her—or worse. His memory darkened. Like the brute who had inflicted beatings on her until the day had come when Nic had reached his teenage years and had been strong enough to protect her from thugs like that….

I had to change my life! I had to do it for myself—by myself. There was no one to help me. And I did *change it.*

She was looking at him, a slightly curious look in her eyes at the vehemence of his expression, her beautiful grey eyes clear in her fine-boned face.

She gave a slow nod. 'Then perhaps,' she said, in an equally slow voice, 'we have to bear in mind that old prayer, don't we? The one that asks that we be granted the courage to change what we can, but the patience to accept what we can't, and the wisdom to know the difference.'

Nic thought about it. Then, 'Nope,' he said decisively. 'I want to change everything I don't like.'

She gave a laugh—a deliberately light one. 'Well, you wouldn't make a scientist, that's for sure,' she said.

He gave an echoing laugh, realising with a sense of shock that he had spoken more about his deepest feelings to this woman than he had ever done to anyone. It struck him that to have touched on matters that ran so very deep within him with a woman he hadn't known existed twenty minutes earlier was….

Significant?

I don't have conversations like this with women—never. So why this one?

It had to be because of her being a scientist—that had to be it. It was just that, nothing more.

She's a fantastically beautiful woman—and I want to know her more. But there have been a lot of beautiful women in my life, when I've had time for them. She's just one more.

She was different, yes, because of her being an incredibly talented astrophysicist when the women he was usually interested in were party girls, prioritising good times and carefree enjoyment, which allowed him time out from his obsession with building his personal empire. Females who didn't ask for commitment. For more than he could give them.

But thinking about the assorted women who'd been and gone in his life was not what he was here to do. He was here to make the most of this one.

He flexed his shoulders, feeling himself relax again, his eyes focussed on drinking in her extraordinary entrancing beauty.

She had finished her drink, and so had he. With every instinct in his body, long honed by experience, he knew it was time to call time on the evening. He'd set the wheels in motion, but tonight was not going to get them further to the destination he wanted for them both. She was not, he knew, the kind of woman who could be rushed. He'd followed through on the impulse that had brought him across the casino floor to her, and for now that was enough.

He signalled the barman, signed the chit as presented, making sure his scrawling *'Falcone'* was visible only to his employee, and got to his feet with a smile.

Fran did likewise. Her emotions were strange—new to her—but she smiled politely. 'Thank you for the drink,' she said.

The long dark lashes swept over the blue, blue eyes. 'My pleasure,' came the laconic reply. 'And thank you for the science tutorial,' he added, the smile warm in his gaze.

'You're welcome,' Fran replied, her smile just as warm, but briefer, more circumspect.

She headed towards the bank of elevators across the lobby, conscious of his gaze upon her. Was she regretting the fact that he was calling time on their encounter? Surely not? Surely anything more was out of the question?

And yet even as with her head she knew it must

be, with quite a different part of her body she knew—from the heady buzz in her bloodstream and the quickened heart rate—that she was regretful that she must retire to her solitary bedroom.

That sense of restlessness she'd felt earlier filled her again. Cesare had been a long time ago—over a year ago now—and anyway, theirs had never been a physical relationship. That, she knew, would have waited until well into their engagement, or even their actual wedding night, for Cesare was a traditionally-minded Italian male.

Not many would have understood their relationship—understood that, having known each other all their lives, it had made perfect sense for them to marry one day. In the meantime, they had both been single agents, and she was well aware that Cesare—an extremely attractive male, blessed with a high social position and great wealth to boot—had indulged in many a romantic liaison.

He had accepted that such tolerance was two-way, and until they had become formally engaged she had been as free as he to indulge in affairs. She'd had only two what might be called 'full affairs' in her life—one with another undergrad at Cambridge, a very boy-girl romance, and one brief liaison with a visiting academic while on her PhD course on the East Coast—and that had amply sufficed.

Her dating had nearly always been with fellow academics, and usually based around concerts, films or theatre outings. Searing passion had not played a role, and its absence had not troubled her. One day, after all, she would be marrying Cesare…

Except that now she wouldn't, after all.

She was footloose and fancy-free. If she chose to be. Free to move on from Cesare, to seek romance—free to take a break, if she wanted, from the demands of academia.

Free to be chatted up by a muscled hunk with the bluest eyes she'd ever seen in a man, let alone one of Italian origin. A man whose smile was lazy, his speech laconic, and whose expression and long-lashed deep blue eyes were telling her just how very much he appreciated her.

She jabbed at the elevator button, her feeling of restlessness increasing as she stepped inside, feeling it swoop her the couple of floors upwards in this low-rise hotel that blended so gracefully into the desert landscape.

Inside her room, she glanced at the folder with her notes, but did not open it. Instead she stripped off for bed, taking off her make-up, brushing out her hair. Wondering why her heart rate still was not back to normal.

Her dreams, when they came, were full—and unsettling.

CHAPTER TWO

THE CONFERENCE WAS wrapping up, with the panel of plenary speakers paying courteous tribute to each other.

Fran flexed her tired fingers, having taken copious notes throughout. Her thoughts were uncertain. She was scheduled to fly back to the West Coast with her colleagues that afternoon, but was conscious that she was reluctant to do so. She'd meant what she'd said about wanting to take advantage of the hotel's amenities, and why shouldn't she? She hadn't taken any holiday time for a year—she was overdue for a break. So why not here and now?

And whether that hunky security guy chatting her up last night had anything to do with her decision, she would not consider. He'd been a catalyst for it, that was all.

The sense of restlessness that had started to well up in her again subsided, her decision made. She said as much to her colleagues, telling them that she would be staying on for a few days at the hotel.

Grinning, they informed her they were off to hit

Vegas and see if their luck at the tables was holding out. Fran wished them well and waved them off. Las Vegas was one place she did *not* want to go to.

No, if she went anywhere it would be to see something of the western desert—maybe even, she pondered, as she headed for the reception desk to keep her room on, take one of the hotel's tours to the Grand Canyon.

She made enquiries, took away the tour brochure, and headed into the poolside bistro to have a light lunch and go through her notes. Her mind felt wiped out from all the heavy-duty presentations, and she realised she was looking forward to a few days off.

As she tucked into her salad she found herself wondering if she would see that hunky security guy again. But if he'd been on duty the night before maybe he wasn't around in the daytime? Or if he was maybe he wouldn't show any further interest in her anyway? Or maybe—

'Hi—so, conference all finished?'

The deep, gravelled voice sounded behind her, and Fran turned her head. Felt something quiver inside her as she set her eyes on his powerful body again. This time he was not in a tux, but in a dark burgundy polo shirt bearing the hotel's logo—the words Falcone, Nevada, with a golden falcon, wings outstretched, above—that stretched across his broad, muscled chest in a way that made her want to study the contours minutely.

That internal quiver came again, and a quickening of her heart rate. She felt something lift inside her…a sense of lightness.

'All done,' she acknowledged. 'Just the notes to go through.' She gestured at the pile of papers in the folder.

He glanced at them, and then at her. 'May I?' He indicated the free seat at her table.

He was asking her—courteously—if he could continue their slight acquaintance. Fran saw it and registered the courtesy, the request.

She knew she was entirely free to say something like, *Oh, I'm sorry, but I really do need to go through my notes straight away while they're fresh in my head*, and he would simply accept it, give her a regretful smile and stroll away. Accept her rejection.

But those words of polite rejection never came. Instead she heard her voice say, just as courteously, 'Of course,' and she smiled.

She felt that lift again inside her—in her body, in her spirits. Seeing him again was reinforcing the extraordinary reaction she'd had to him last night—confirming it for her. Whatever was going on, something different was happening to her.

And she would let it happen. Mentally, the decision had been made. And as he lowered his powerful frame on to the chair, with a grace and ease that she found pleasing to the eye, she knew she would let him continue with his move on her.

For a move it was—that was obvious. Inexperienced she might be, compared with many of her contemporaries, but she knew when a man was making a play for her. And this one was. Quite decidedly.

So his next words came as no surprise.

'You've decided not to check out yet—I'm glad.'

She threw him an old-fashioned look. Clearly he'd had a word with the staff at the reception desk, discovered she'd extended her booking.

Nic returned her look with a bland expression. He was deliberately wearing the staff polo shirt today, to confirm the impression he guessed she had that he was one of his own employees. That suited him fine.

'Glad?' she queried. *Challenged.*

The bland expression did not falter. 'Glad you'll have a chance to enjoy the hotel's leisure amenities—and maybe take one of the tours as well?'

His glance now went to the hotel tour brochure. It was extensive—part of the offering the resort made to visitors. It included personalised tours to anywhere in the US West they might want to visit. Far or near.

'Maybe,' he went on, his expression still bland, but belied by a glint in those incredibly blue dark-lashed eyes that was telling Fran something not bland in the slightest, 'you might like to start with the Sunset Drive this evening?'

Fran's heart gave a little unconscious skip but she frowned slightly—her first glance at the brochure hadn't listed such a tour.

'It's one of the personalised ones.' On cue came the answer to her unspoken question. His voice was as bland as his expression. 'It sets off from here late afternoon, going to a viewing spot for the sunset. It's only a couple of hours. You'll be back in time for dinner.'

He smiled. Not the desert wolf smile, but a bland smile, his long dark lashes dipping over his blue, blue eyes.

Fran considered it. Carefully analysed it for all the pros and cons for all of five seconds. Then gave her answer.

'Sounds good,' she said, and smiled a bland smile in return.

'Great,' he said.

Satisfaction was in his voice. Mission accomplished. Fran heard it, and it amused her. Nothing about this man was putting her off. He was being open about his intentions—conspiratorial, even. And yet she realised she still didn't actually know whether this Sunset Drive was really part of the hotel's offering to guests or was a particularly personalised tour, customised for herself alone.

That he would turn out to be the driver for this Sunset Drive, and she the sole passenger, she had little doubt at all.

And no reservations either.

He got to his feet—again, remarkably smoothly and easily for a man with his powerful frame—and smiled down at her again. His expression was just a touch less bland. A touch more openly appreciative.

'I'll fix it,' he said, and lifted a hand in casual farewell and strolled away.

As he went Fran's eyes went after him, saw how he

paused to say something to one of the waitresses—a young woman whose expression as he talked to her told Fran that she was not the only female susceptible to that unforced, laid-back charm, those powerful good looks. Whatever the man had to draw women to him he had it in spades.

She gave a little sigh that turned into a good-humoured wry smile. She'd felt restless, mentally wiped from the conference—as if she were surfacing after a long, intensely focussed cerebral engagement that had lasted a whole year since she'd realised that making her life with Cesare was not what she wanted to do after all.

And now suddenly, out of nowhere, the future was beckoning to her. A future that was her own—that held more than her career. That held adventure—

And if that adventure, for now, happened to include a man who was making it very clear that she was pleasing to his eye—a man who was pleasing *her* eye in a way that was as totally unexpected as it was unpredicted—well, she would go for that.

She felt that lift inside her come again, that heady quickening of her pulse.

And welcomed it.

'Hi, let me help you up.'

Nic handed Fran up into the SUV he'd commandeered and parked on the hotel forecourt, before vaulting into the driver's seat. He'd changed into a western shirt, jeans and boots, and saw that for her part she'd sensibly put on firmer footwear, a loose shirt and long cotton trousers.

'One Sunset Drive coming up,' he said, casting his wolf-like smile at her, making Fran glad she was wearing sunglasses. Making her glad she was taking a chance for a change.

He fired the engine, easing the SUV down the hotel drive on to the main highway, then turning to her as he settled into a cruising speed. 'So, did you enjoy your leisurely afternoon, Dr Ristori?'

It was an amiable, courteous enquiry, and she answered in kind, accepting that he must know her name from the hotel register. 'Yes, I wrote up my notes then got in a swim and flopped on a lounger poolside. Totally lazy.'

'Well, why not?' he answered easily. 'Your vacation—your choice.'

He glanced at her—a throwaway glance that was hidden by his aviator sunglasses, accompanied by a smile indenting around his mouth. It was a friendly, open smile, yet one that acknowledged that behind the word 'choice' there was more than whether or not she had had a lazy afternoon.

A lot more might be hers to choose.

She answered with a flickering smile and looked away, down the dusty road stretching through the desert landscape like something out of a Western movie.

He didn't talk any more as he drove, and after some miles he turned off up an unmade track, along the edge of a bluff that terminated in a rocky col overlooking a valley beyond, where he parked.

As they got out the heat and the silence enveloped them. Nic jammed a wide-brimmed hat on his head, offering her one for herself, which she dutifully donned against the glare of the lowering sun. He then helped himself to a backpack holding twin water bottles and the mandatory emergency kit.

'It's about a ten-minute hike now,' Nic said, and set off up a trail that led higher among the rugged outcrops.

Fran followed nimbly, and as they gained height saw the valley beyond fill with deep golden light, the azure sky arching above. It seemed very far from anywhere, with only the wind keening in her ears. Eventually they reached a flat outcrop affording a ringside view of the sight they had come to see and they settled down, backs against the warm rock behind them.

'Now we wait,' Nic said.

He passed her a water bottle and Fran drank thirstily. So did he. Before their eyes the sun was starting to lower into the horizon, turning deep bronze as it did so. Fran gazed, mesmerised, glad of her sunglasses as the sun seemed to fuse with the earth, flushing the azure sky with a halo of deep crimson until finally it slipped beyond the rim of the ever-turning globe and the sky began to darken.

She slid the dark glasses from her face, and saw him do likewise. Then he turned to her.

'Worth it?' he asked laconically.

She nodded. 'Oh, yes,' she breathed.

Her eyes met his, held, and for a moment—just a moment—something was exchanged between them. Something that seemed to go with this slow, unhurried landscape, desolate but with a beauty of its own, lonely but intensely special.

A thought occurred to her, and she heard herself give voice to it.

'I don't know your name,' she said. She said it with a little frown, as if it were strange to have shared this moment with him not knowing it.

He gave her his slow smile, holding out his strong, large hand.

'Nic,' he said. 'Nic Rossi.'

He gave his birth name quite deliberately. He didn't want complications—he wanted things to be very, very simple.

She took his hand, felt its strength and warmth. Felt more than its strength and warmth.

'Fran,' she said. Her smile met his. Her eyes met his. Acknowledging something that needed to be acknowledged between them. The fact that, whatever was going on, from this moment she was no longer a hotel guest and he was not part of the security team, or whatever his role was.

That this was something between them—only between them.

'Doc Fran,' Nic murmured contemplatively, his eyes working over her. He nodded. 'It suits you.'

He didn't release her hand, only drew her upright as he climbed to his feet as well.

'We need to head down before the light goes,' he told her, and carefully they made their way back to the SUV. 'Hungry?' Nic asked. He kept his question studiedly casual. 'Because if you don't want to head back to the hotel yet I know a diner nearby...'

He let the suggestion hang, let her choose to answer it as she wanted.

She gave her flickering smile—the one that told him she was hovering between holding back and not holding back.

'That sounds good,' she answered. 'A change from the hotel.'

He gunned the engine and they headed off, headlights cutting through the desert dusk that had turned to night by the time they drew up in the car park of a roadside diner.

It was a typical western diner, with a friendly, laid-back atmosphere and staff in the customary western outfits that went with the setting.

They ate at a table overlooking the desert, making themselves comfortable on the padded banquettes. Fran stuck to iced tea, but Nic had a beer, and they both ordered steak.

Hers was so massive she cut off a third, placing it on Nic's plate. 'You need to feed your muscles,' she told him with a smile, refusing to let herself think that it was a strangely intimate gesture.

He laughed. 'I'll trade you my salad,' he said, and pushed the bowl towards her.

'Salad's good for you!' she protested, and pushed it back.

His hand was still on the bowl. Did her fingers brush against his hand? She didn't know. Knew only that she pulled her hand away and that as she did so she felt it tingle, as though, maybe, she had made contact. Electrical contact…

She started to eat her steak. Made some remark about its tenderness. Any remark.

What am I doing?

The question framed itself. Rhetorical. Unnecessary. She knew what she was doing—knew perfectly well.

I'm on a date. Not official. Not announced. Not planned. But a date, all the same. We've watched the sun go down together, and now we're eating together.

And what would they do next together?

She didn't answer that one. Didn't want to. Not yet. Not now.

Instead she asked a question—something about the desert. After all, he worked in this region—he must know more about it than she did. And, whatever Italian-American locality he came from originally, right now he was way more a native here than she was.

He answered the question readily, and all her other questions, but sometimes he shrugged and said he didn't know. So they asked the diners at another table, obviously locals, who assumed they were tourists.

Fran did not enlighten them.

They also assumed they were a couple.

Fran did not enlighten them on that either.

Supposing we were.

The thought was in her head. Tantalising. Making her wonder. Speculate. Was that why she was sharing dinner with him now? Because she was accepting that she was willing to take things further between them?

But just how far?

She felt her mind thinking ahead. An affair? No, maybe not even that. A—a fling. That was more like it. Something out of the ordinary in her life…something that wouldn't happen twice—because he was from a world different from her, as she was from him.

But that doesn't matter.

Her eyes went to his face again, slid down over his strong, muscled body. The flicker of electricity came again—a kind of current flowing between them, strengthening, or so it seemed to her, with every circuit that it made. She didn't know why… knew only that it was powerful and enticing.

Why not? Why not take this opportunity if it comes? I need to move on from Cesare. I need something...different. It would be good for me—mark a new chapter in my life.

Would Nic Rossi—so entirely different from any man she'd known before, so rawly, powerfully attractive to her—be it?

The question circled in her head. They'd finished eating—steaks demolished, side orders too—and now Nic was leaning back in his chair, letting his weight tilt it back, easing his broad shoulders. Relaxed, leonine, powerful.

Sexy as hell.

The phrase forced its way into her head. It was not one she'd ever used about a man. Not a phrase that had fitted any man she'd ever known. Not even Cesare. Her lips twisted. Cesare would have loathed any woman calling him that. Nic, she suspected, with another twist of her lips, but this time with humour in it, would simply take it as his due.

He knows he can pull. It's in him, in every cell of his body. It's part of him. It isn't arrogance or conceit—it's just... Well, it just is, that's all. And he'd be glad I'm thinking it.

She didn't need to spell it out. Didn't need to think about it. Didn't need to analyse it or wonder about it or speculate about it. All she needed to do right now was answer the question he was asking her as he picked up the menu, flicked it over to the dessert list.

'Ice cream?' he asked.

Fran smiled. That was one decision that was easy to make.

'Oh, yes,' she said. 'Definitely.'

They drove back to the hotel, the moon rising to the east, the night ablaze with stars. Nic had seen Fran glance upwards as they got back into the SUV and an idea had struck him. As they drove he gave voice to it.

'Would you have any interest,' he opened, glancing at her briefly, then back to the ink-dark road, 'in maybe taking off to see the South-West Array tomorrow?'

She turned her head. 'Could we do it in a day?' she asked. Unconsciously, she had used the word 'we', and it registered a moment later. But she didn't mind that she had. It seemed right that she had.

'If we make an early start,' Nic said. He paused. 'So, how about it?'

'Oh, yes!' Fran answered, enthusiasm in her voice. 'You know,' she mused, 'as a theoretical physicist I simply use the data that the observational physicists provide for me, to test my theories—but to actually see *where* they get that data is always a privilege. The South-West Array is only just coming on-stream—'

She fished in her bag for her phone, looked it up. Her face brightened.

'Nic, *could* we? I can message them tonight, see if I can get in touch with one of the onsite guys tomorrow…' She paused. 'It might be boring for you, though,' she warned.

Then she wondered whether she should have said that. Maybe this was just another tour laid on by the hotel, with her own personal chauffeur? But she didn't think that—not now. Not any longer. Not after sharing steak and ice-cream at a roadside diner.

This isn't about his job, or even mine. This is about us.

She felt the now familiar skip of her heart rate, telling her she was glad—glad that that was what it was about. Then she realised Nic was speaking again.

'You can give me another physics tutorial on the way there,' he said. 'The elementary version, that is.'

There was a smile in his voice, and in hers as she answered: 'Physics is usually simple—it's just the maths that's hard!'

He laughed, that low, gravelly sound that she was getting used to sending a little frisson through her—a frisson that she felt again as, gaining the hotel's rear car park, he helped her step down, retaining her hand just a fraction longer than was necessary. Then he was opening a side door and they were heading down a deserted corridor towards the lobby.

As they did, a service door opened and someone emerged. He glanced at Nic as they headed past.

'Evening, boss.'

Nic acknowledged him with a brief nod, and as the staff member passed by, Fran murmured, 'Boss?'

'He's on my team,' Nic answered smoothly.

They arrived at the elevators. Nic was glad that no other members of his staff were around, and without waiting to be invited he stepped inside the lift with her.

'I'll see you to your room,' he said.

Fran made no demur, but suddenly, out of nowhere, she was supremely conscious of the confined space of the elevator, of Nic's closeness to her, of her own heightened sense of the moment. Would he try and kiss her? She tensed, not knowing whether she wanted him to or not.

He made no move on her, however, just waited until she had opened her room door and was turning to bid him goodnight, finding it hard to take her eyes from him when she was this close to him.

His hand splayed against the doorjamb, enclosing her. 'Thank you for tonight,' he said. 'It's been good.'

There was a low note in his voice, a huskiness, and a smile— she could hear it, see the slight curve of his mouth, the dip of his long, long lashes over those blue, blue eyes. And then, while she was still gazing up at him, his mouth was lowering to hers.

It was a kiss like none she'd known. Slow, deliberate, and for one purpose only. To tell her what she could have if she chose to.

She gave herself to it, her eyelids fluttering closed, feeling her shoulders sag against the door, her hands slacken as her whole being became focussed on the sensation he was drawing from her.

It was like a kind of silken velvet, moving over her leisurely, tasting, exploring, taking his time. And then, without her even realising, he was deepening the kiss, easing her lips apart. Letting her taste, enjoy his tasting, enjoy what there was between them. What more there could be.

She felt arousal flare within her, more powerful than she had ever felt, more intense, more sensuous, and she yielded her willing mouth to his, feeling the pleasure of it until, it seemed like an age later, he was drawing back from her, gliding his mouth over her, skimming leisurely over her parted lips, a velvet withdrawal.

He lifted his head and her eyes fluttered open, looked into his gaze. So close…so very close to hers. She felt dazed, dizzy. He smiled, seeing her reaction to his kiss, liking it.

He stepped away, giving her a little space. 'Goodnight, Doc Fran,' he said, but there was intimacy in the way he said it. 'Sleep well.'

She gave a reply, and then he was turning away, heading back down the corridor. She watched him reach the elevators. Felt dizziness inside her still.

Knew that whatever this man wanted of her she wanted it too.

Nic did not sleep well that night in the suite he'd reserved for himself at this, his latest multi-million-dollar acquisition. He lay sleepless, gazing at the shadowed ceiling, one arm crooked behind his head, feeling a mix of restlessness, satisfaction and anticipation.

Dio, but how he'd wanted to stay with her! That kiss had been like dipping his finger into a pot of honey to taste the sweetness, and it had told him she had found it just as pleasurable as he had. But it had also told him, just as every instinct since he'd first set eyes on her had told him, that she was not a woman to be hurried. She was no hedonistic party girl. She was a mature, highly intelligent woman, who would make her decision in her own time, in her own way, about indulging in a romance with him.

And if she did, as he burningly hoped she would, it would not be conducted here at the hotel. He liked it that to her he was not Nicolo Falcone, and if they stayed here it was bound to come out at some point. That encounter in the corridor had been a warning of that inevitability. No, better that they took off to somewhere he was not known, so that he was still simply Nic Rossi to her.

Nic Rossi—his birth name, abandoned so long ago, when he'd first set out to forge his glittering empire, echoed in his mind. It had been strange to use it again. As strange as remembering the way he'd revealed so much of his own deep feelings and his passionate beliefs to her in that very first conversation he'd had with her the previous night. His belief never to accept what life had dumped you with—to make someone new of yourself by effort and dedication and determination.

His thoughts moved on. Back to the familiar territory of his empire-building. He ran through his latest ambitions to launch a flagship hotel in Manhattan. It wouldn't be easy, let alone cheap to achieve, but he'd do it in the end. He always did. Always. The determination to succeed in business never left him.

And to succeed on more pleasurable fronts too.

His thoughts went back to the breathtakingly beautiful, entrancing blonde, the oh-so-lovely Doc Fran, alone in her lonely bed—alone for one last night.

He smiled, anticipation filling him again.

'Oh, wow!' Fran breathed, her eyes widening at the sight appearing before them as the SUV gained the low brow of a hill, revealing what was beyond.

It was like something out of a sci-fi film—otherworldly—with a vast matrix of huge dish antennae, angled upwards to catch the faintest radio whisper of distant stars, each one set on rails for moving into precise position.

The whole place was perimeter-fenced, but they drove up to the visitor centre, where Fran identified herself as from her university and promptly got the attention of one of the technical staff to show them around.

Nic was as impressed as anyone would be by the engineering feats achieved, but understood scarcely a word of their erudite exchanges. He was content just to see how the animation in her face, the interest in her keen, intelligent eyes, only enhanced her beauty, her appeal to him.

As they finally left the array she was fulsome in her thanks. He gave her his slashing smile. 'This morning was your treat—this afternoon is mine. But you'll enjoy it, I promise you.'

She did, too—though she gasped breathlessly as Nic showed her just why it was *his* treat.

They drove on another forty miles or so to a reservoir lake with a water resort, where they lunched at a waterfront café. Then Nic led her out along the jetty and hired the leanest, meanest motorboat available.

And hit the accelerator.

Fran's breath and speech were blown far behind her, her hair streaming, her hands clutching at the rails as the boat flew across the lake, the bow hitting the water's surface as if it was concrete. Italian words broke from her—and she heard Nic laugh, realised he could understand her expletives, and her description of him as a certifiable maniac who would kill them both.

'No way! You're safe as a baby!' he yelled at her, in the same language, his face alight with laughter.

He bombed across the width of the lake, slewing around in a huge arcing curve of water that caught the sun's rays in a million rainbows before racing back towards the jetty again.

Within reach of it he slowed and turned to Fran. Her hair was a wild tangle, her eyes alight with laughter. Nic let his arm slide around her shoulder and pulled her against him.

'Fun?' he asked.

He didn't really have to ask. It was visible in her face.

She let her head rest on his shoulder, feeling it strong beneath her cheek. 'Most fun ever,' she said.

'Happy to please you,' he said, and dropped a kiss on her forehead.

Such a slight gesture, such a slight tightening of his arm around her... They sat beside each other, his other hand on the wheel, guiding the boat lightly on the water as if he were Cesare on one of his thoroughbreds.

Fran's eyes flickered slightly, and she wondered why, of all things, she was thinking of Cesare now.

Nic saw it, saw her expression change. 'What is it?' he asked quietly.

She looked at him, easing away a little, but not freeing herself. 'I'm thinking of the man I nearly married,' she said.

Nic stilled. It was impossible to think of her married, or even engaged—taken by another man. Not when he wanted her himself so much.

'What happened?' he heard his voice asking. He heard the tension in it, but didn't know why it was there.

'I broke it off,' she said. 'I'd just been offered a research post out on the West Coast, working with a Nobel Laureate, and I couldn't resist it. And I was pretty sure,' she added slowly, 'that Cesare was involved with someone else anyway.'

'Then he was nuts,' said Nic bluntly. 'Nuts to prefer someone else to you.'

She gave a little laugh. 'Thank you,' she said. 'But he and I…we never—well, you know. It wasn't an affair that we had. It was a— Well, I guess a kind of *expectation*. We'd known each other all our lives. It would have worked, him and me.'

'Cesare?' mused Nic, registering the Italian name, which she'd pronounced in the Italian way. 'So—back in the old country?'

'Very much so,' she said dryly, thinking of just how sizeable a chunk of 'the old country' Cesare's estates covered.

Nic eased the throttle again. He didn't want to know any more about the guy that she'd nearly married and hadn't. Right now he wanted to be the only male in her vision, her thoughts.

Her desires.

At a much slower pace he nosed the boat forward again, keeping his arm around Fran, where he wanted it to be.

'Let's see what's at the far end of the lake,' he said.

The sun was lowering by the time they handed the boat in. Nic turned to her. Her hair was still windblown, her skin sun-kissed even with sun-block. She looked effortlessly lovely.

'What next?' he asked.

His eyes were light on her, the question in his voice putting the decision in her hands. The choice of what was to happen—or not—between them now.

Fran's expression flickered. 'It's a long way back to the Falcone,' she observed. 'Maybe too far?' Her glance went to the resort motel that was set back on a low bluff.

'Not in the Falcone league,' Nic said, 'but it looks passable.'

He kept his voice neutral, not wanting to show his satisfaction that she was indicating they should stay there together. As he so wanted.

Fran gave a wry smile. 'There speaks a loyal employee of the famous Falcone chain!' she answered lightly.

Then she nodded, as if making a silent decision for herself. Maybe thinking about Cesare, talking about him, had confirmed her feelings. Told her that whatever it was that was happening between her and Nic, she wanted it to happen.

'OK…' She took a breath. 'Let's go for it.'

Even so, she booked separate rooms at Reception—and not just because anything else might have seemed too…obvious. She definitely needed a bathroom and a bedroom entirely to herself—her wind-tangled hair and water-splashed day-worn clothes were a disaster.

Gratefully spotting a small retail outlet, inset into the lobby, she plunged in.

It was a good hour before she was ready to meet Nic in the motel's bar. As he rose to greet her, she laughed.

'Snap!'

They had both, it seemed, availed themselves of the retail outlet's offerings—and not just shampoo and toiletries for her, and a razor for him. They were both now wearing tee shirts bearing the name of the lake, Fran's in pink and Nic's in blue.

But where Nic was making do with the chinos he'd been wearing all day, Fran had found a wraparound cotton skirt in white seersucker that floated gracefully to mid-calf to replace her water-stained Bermuda shorts. Her newly washed hair tumbled over her shoulders, and her only make-up was a touch of mascara and lip gloss.

She knew Nic's eyes were warm upon her.

But then, hers were warm on him, too. He was cleanly shaven, damp hair feathering at the nape of his neck, and the deep blue tee shirt matched his eyes and lovingly moulded his torso. But he was no muscle-bound Adonis. That innate air of Italian style he possessed was overwhelming—the kind of automatic male display that she was used to seeing in her countrymen. It was not vanity, or showing off, but it came instinctively to them.

'You look *so* Italian,' she heard herself say as they took their happy hour cocktails over to a table looking out across the darkening lake. She studied his face consideringly. 'I wonder where the blue eyes come from? Some Norman ancestor way back...rampaging through the peninsula to make a kingdom for themselves?'

Nic thought about it and liked the idea. He'd made his own kingdom—the Falcone kingdom—deliberately choosing that new name for himself because it made him want to fly high, swoop down on his prey, fly ever higher.

'What about your grey eyes and blonde hair?' he asked in return. 'Are they from your English mother?'

She nodded, not wishing to elaborate about her parentage, aware that she did not want to bring that side of her into what was happening now. Here, with Nic, she was 'Doc Fran'—she smiled inwardly at his amusedly bestowed moniker—and that was all she wanted to be.

The fact that her mother, Lady Emma, would consider it incomprehensible that her daughter might want to take off as she had with someone who worked in hotel security was irrelevant to her. Her whole other identity, as Donna Francesca, was also irrelevant, as it always was when she was here in the USA, whether it was in her university department, or now, here, with Nic.

And Nic was—well, just Nic. And she didn't want him any other way. He had a strength to him, a quality to his character that was as evident as his physical strength. It lay beneath the casual, laid-back attitude—a sure knowledge of his own worth, but without any need to display it. She liked him all the more for it.

He was asking her, now, how she had become an astrophysicist, and she answered readily.

'I fell in love with science at school, because it explained everything about the world. And physics and astronomy just captivated me,' she said. She paused, then heard herself add, 'My family was less enthusiastic.' She frowned, her mouth setting. 'My father came round, because he's always been very indulgent with me, but my mother—'

She broke off. She was saying more than she wanted to. More than she ever said to people, admitted…

'Wanted you to marry and settle down to be a wife and home-maker?' Nic finished for her. The name of the rejected former fiancé hovered in his head but he pushed it aside.

Fran nodded heavily, taking a mouthful of her strawberry daiquiri. 'Yes,' she said briefly.

For all that her home would have been a vast medieval *castello*, and she would have been a *contessa*, Nic had nailed it.

She took a breath. 'Oh, they're proud of me now, but my mother hasn't forgiven me for ditching Cesare—'

She broke off, and Nic did not pick her up on it again. He didn't want her remembering the man she hadn't married.

She was speaking again, and he realised she'd turned the conversation to him. That was something he didn't want either. But it was too late to halt her.

'What about you, Nic? How did you come to be where you are in life now?'

He paused, his tequila mid-way to his mouth. He lowered it again slowly, his eyes veiled.

'Well, it wasn't thanks to my schooldays,' he heard himself saying.

His voice sounded grim. Bleak, even to his own ears.

'What I learnt at school was how not to get beaten up or corralled into running drugs for the gangs.' His mouth tightened and he looked across at Fran. 'I left as soon as I could and went to work. It was a fancy hotel and I was way down in the basement!'

His expression changed now, his eyes clearing.

'But it changed everything for me,' he said. 'I was earning money—not much, but it was my own, through my own efforts. And I could see, for the first time, a future for me. Something I could make for myself, *of* myself. Out of the nothing I'd been handed at birth, despite all the expectations that I'd amount to nothing!'

She heard the vehemence in his voice and it resonated with her—their defiance of what had been expected of them, each in their very different ways.

'What about your parents?' she asked. Her voice was sympathetic, admiring of the way he'd fought and won his grim battles.

Nic's mouth twisted, and he reached for his tequila, taking a deep draught. 'My father wasn't there—I never knew him. He cleared out before I was born. And my poor mother—'

He broke off again. Took another mouthful of tequila.

'Well, let's just say that she had a bad time with men. The final man landed her in hospital.' His eyes darkened. 'I put *him* in hospital too—and never regretted it!' His expression changed again, the darkness lessening. 'Although she was an invalid she lived long enough to see me make good, and I'll always be grateful for that.'

He took a final slug of his tequila, finishing it and getting to his feet. The air of grim darkness had dropped from him and he wanted it gone. Wanted only to focus on the now. He held his hand out to Fran, the woman he wanted for this very enticing *now*.

'Time to eat,' he announced.

She took the outstretched hand, liking the way he was wanting to join the present again.

She smiled at him as she stood up. 'Sounds good,' she said.

Without conscious realisation she walked with him into the restaurant, not having dropped his hand. His strong fingers closed around hers, warm and reassuring.

The 'now' of their being together seemed very good.

Yet across her consciousness slid the thought that they had exchanged more about themselves, about what drove them, what they'd overcome, in their brief time together than so casual an acquaintance would usually expect.

Maybe, she mused as they took their places at the table in the motel's restaurant, casting a pondering look across at Nic picking up the menu, it was *because* they were so new to each other that they could speak like this? Or was it because they seemed to resonate with each other, despite their very different backgrounds?

Maybe we share the same resonant frequency, she thought with flickering amusement. Was that it?

She let the thought slip away, focussing only on the immediate present. On the present that was beckoning her. And on what, she was now thrillingly aware, was yet to come.

She felt her heart rate give that now familiar little skip, a flush of warmth going through her. Life seemed good—an adventure, and different, headily so, but very good.

Thanks to her being here with Nic.

CHAPTER THREE

'OK, Doc Fran, tell me about the stars.'

Nic's invitation was just that—inviting, and Fran could not resist it. They had come out into the night, after a leisurely, easy-going Tex-Mex dinner, and taken a paved path that led up to the top of the bluff, where the lights from the resort did not reach. The low level lighting for the path showed where several benches were, and they had settled down on one. Nic's arm was around her shoulders and it felt warm, the right place for it to be.

He was lifting his face up to the heavens and so was she, and her breath caught. The night sky was ablaze, the moon not yet risen, and the stars were putting on a show that was unmatched in this clear, unpolluted air.

An exuberance filled her, fuelled by the night and the stars and the desert and their distance from her everyday life. The world she'd been born to—of castles and *palazzos* and titles and estates—and the world she now lived in—of arcane academia and erudite research—seemed very far away.

And it wasn't the daiquiri running in her veins that was making her feel elated. It had everything to do with the warm, heavy arm around her shoulders, the solid mass of Nic at her side as she leant against him and gazed upwards into the blazing glory of the heavens.

'Where do I begin?' she breathed, wondering how to convey to Nic all that she knew, knowing it was impossible.

She knew she must start with opening his eyes to the searing power of the universe itself.

'So—stars.' She took another breath, her eyes lighting with her eagerness to share with him what she knew, what she felt, what filled her life. She waved a hand upwards. 'Fiery, burning balls of gas, each one a powerhouse of energy, nuclear fusion, born in stellar nurseries deep in the galaxy, blazing their time, then burning away. Some stars are small, some huge, and how big they are, and how hot, tells us their fate. Some—the largest—will explode in fantastic supernovae that collapse into black holes, while smaller ones become red giants, as our sun will one day—'

She was away, and he let her talk. She regaled him with Main Sequence and Hertzsprung-Russell and Chandrasekhar Limits and every variety of dwarf star, and neutron star and pulsars and quasars, star clusters and nebulae, until his head was spinning. And in the end he heard not her words but the passion in her voice for the subject she loved. It warmed him to do so, for passion was passion, and it could be expressed in more than cerebral enthusiasm…

His could—oh, his could, indeed!

He felt the slender weight of her body against him as they gazed upwards, so soft. The scent of her freshly washed hair caught at him, the silken fall of its lush tresses beneath his bare forearm inflaming all his senses.

Desire was kindled in him, and all of a sudden he wanted no more of stars. His free hand came to her face and he laid one finger across her lips, silencing her.

She paused, her eyes lowering to his, meeting his. Seeing in his, under the starlight, a blaze that was nothing to do with the heavens above. A blaze that lit up in her own eyes.

Her breath caught in her throat. Her gaze worked over his face. 'Enough with the stars?' she asked, and her voice was husky suddenly.

Long lashes dipped over blue eyes turned inky in the dim light. 'For now,' he answered, and the huskiness was in his voice too. His strong fingers cupped her cheek as if it were the rarest porcelain, his gaze pouring into hers. 'You love your subject so much…'

'I adore it,' she whispered.

But her hand was lifting to his face now, exploring its rough contours with the delicate tips of her fingers, tracing the planes and edges, the outline of his mouth.

'The stars will burn for aeons, for a time we cannot grasp or fathom…' her voice was still husky, a whisper, and her eyes were clinging to his, his to hers '…but this night, now, is ours.'

Slowly, sensuously, she reached her mouth to his, feeling its familiarity, its acceptance as he let her explore, slowly and sensuously, taking her time, all the time she needed, as her fingertips slid into his sable hair, cupping the nape of his sinewy neck, as his muscles flexed minutely—as, slowly and sensuously, he began to kiss her back.

How long they kissed she did not know—only knew that at some point she was drawn against his body, that strong, powerful body, folded to him as if she were silver tissue paper.

She could feel her breasts crushed, then engorged, peaking, and she gloried in it, gloried in the way his hand around her shoulder was pulling her to him, the way his mouth was foraging deep within hers, and she gloried in her answering response, eager, quickening the desire that was filling her, overwhelming her.

She heard her own voice, low in her throat, heard a kind of primitive growl in his, and then with a sudden movement he had swept her to her feet, then into his arms, as if she were a feather.

She gave a cry of laughter, exhilarated, enchanted. 'You can't carry me all the way back to the motel!'

He only laughed, carrying her down the path to the motel while she clung to him, setting her down outside the door. His hand clasping hers, he led her inside, down the corridor to his room, opening the door with a rapid swipe of the key card.

Then his arms were around her again, and he was yielding to all the overpowering impulses of his heated desire for her, setting it ablaze in her as a heady exhilaration filled her. Whatever it was that was happening between them, she was giving herself to it totally, consumingly.

A bedside lamp was all that illuminated the room, softening its contours as he drew her towards the waiting bed. A sense of rightness filled him that they were coming together now, like this. Whatever it was about this beautiful, breathtaking woman, she was right for him.

And *this* was right, what he was doing, sliding his hands on either side of her face, feeling the softness of her hair, her skin, gazing down at her with desire in his eyes, and warmth, and something more than both.

For one long moment he just gazed at her, into those clear grey eyes which showed she had made the decision to be here with him, now.

For this.

For his mouth slowly moving down to hers, kissing her slowly, carefully, to start the union that they would make together.

She answered his kiss, gave herself to it, and he folded her to him. Her arms moved around the strong column of his body. She felt him surge against her, and whilst a little ripple of shock went through her in its wake came a shiver of excitement. His desire for her was blatant, and she welcomed it. She felt her breasts cresting against his hard-muscled chest and knew he felt her reaction to him. Heard the low laugh of pleasure in her pleasure.

Slowly, sensuously, he peeled her clothes from her, never taking his eyes from hers, letting her delicate hands perform the same intimate office for him.

He let her do what she realised she had been aching to do—run the palms of her hands over his bare, smooth, taut-muscled torso, glorying in its muscled strength. And for answer he cupped the small weight of her swelling breasts with his hands, thumbs lifting to their cresting peaks.

She gave a moan in her throat, dropping back her head at the arousal of the sensation. Desire quickened in her, a sense of urgency, and in that same harmony that united them he was pressing her back down upon the coverlet of the bed, drawing it back so they lay upon the sheets.

Italian words broke from him as he gazed down at her perfect body, expressing his desire for her, telling her how beautiful she was, and she answered with a sensuous smile, for of course she understood his husky praise, answered it with her own for him. She lifted her hands to run them once more over that glorious torso, to glide them downwards over his taut, muscled abs and then, with a little gasp, realised just how very, very ready for her he was.

He laughed, collapsing down beside her, rolling her on to him so that she gasped again, then quickened, heat surging in her. His hand was around her nape, drawing her eager mouth to his, feasting on its sweet delights. She moved upon him, and with another groan he flipped her back on to the sheets, coming over her. His hands clasped hers, high on the pillow, and her hair was like a flag, blazoning her welcome of what was to come.

His eyes poured into hers. 'Fran…' He said her name, nothing more. And in it was a question—he wanted her to be sure, so very sure, that this was what she wanted.

She could sense his absolute self-control, his absolute assurance that nothing would happen that she did not want, did not want to share, totally and consumingly, with him.

She lifted her mouth to his. Kissed him softly, sensuously. Then she let her head fall back upon the pillow. Still gazing up at him. Knowing what she wanted. Knowing absolutely.

It was all the answer he needed.

Slowly, with infinite precision, he lowered himself to her, and with a response as old as time her thighs slackened, letting him find what he so urgently sought. She opened to him, feeling her body flower, all her blood surge in a swelling tide. Her heated flesh fitted around his strength, enclosing him within her, feeling the power of him, the desire of him for her, for her body, for her answering desire of him.

She felt her spine lift, arching towards his body as it reared over hers. Her crested nipples grazed his torso so that he gave a groan, his fingers meshing with hers yet more tightly. The strong cords of his neck, the tensed line of his jaw—all told her how very, very near release he was.

Yet he waited for her. Waited for her to make slow,

exploratory movements of her hips, to feel him full and engorged within her, to feel the rightness of him being so, the sensual pleasure of it. With every slow, deliberate movement she made she could feel the tide of her desire mounting within her, heat rising within her, dissolving her into him until, in a vast upwelling of unstoppable sensation, they ran together, flooding out into the wholeness of her body, sweeping through her, consuming her, possessing her…

She heard her voice cry out, felt her neck arching, and heard his own roar of release, felt the spasming of his hands on hers, the surging pulse of his body within hers, carrying them forward, onward, into the vast unknown, into what bound them, body to body, to blaze and burn together.

Time stopped. Everything stopped. There was only this now, this possession, this fusion, this glory of desire fulfilled, passion sated upon passion, binding them together, making them one…

Until slowly, infinitely slowly, time began again, and now she could feel the pounding of her heart, of his, as their bodies slackened. And now he was cradling her trembling body, moving away from her only to draw her back against him, his strong hands tender on her, his breath warm on her shoulder as he held her until her body lay still and quiet with his.

Softly he eased the tangled tendrils of her hair back from her face, kissing her cheekbone gently, murmuring low words she could not hear for the ebbing drumming in her ears, the heartbeat that was quietening finally.

Peace, a wondrous peace, filled her. The peace of fulfilment, of a contentment that seemed to be in every atom of her being, body and mind and soul. She could feel his powerful body, relaxed, exhausted in the aftermath of the overpowering intensity of their union.

A slow, tender smile eased her lips and then her eyelids were fluttering closed and sleep, so necessary, was sweeping up over her like the softest cashmere, embracing her as sweetly as did his slackening arms around her.

In the cradle of the night they slept…in the cradle of their embrace of each other.

'OK,' said Nic, 'all set for the Grand Canyon?'

They were having brunch at the buffet bar of the motel—late, for theirs had been a long, *long* lie-in. Fran's thoughts skittered away from just what that lie-in had entailed, lest it make her want to rebook the room.

A kind of wonder filled her—wonder that the night that had passed had been like *nothing* she had ever experienced. Her eyes fastened on the man sitting opposite her, his lithe, powerful frame relaxed, indolent, even. But then *he* was like no other man ever could be.

He was relaxing back with an air of well-being about him, and she knew perfectly well what the cause of that was. Because she shared it with him—as they had shared their passion, their fulfilment, and now would share the day that was to come.

And what would come after? Her mind sheered away from that question. There was no point thinking about what might happen 'after'—they would take it a day at a time, a night at a time. That was all she wanted right now. And it was more than enough.

She felt delight flood through her—a sense of carefree happiness that came from what she was doing, indulging in this adventure with a man whose lazy glance could make her heart beat faster even before he reached for her.

She felt again that lift that came whenever she looked at him, thought about him, felt a smile play on her lips, her gaze soften. Her pulse quickened. She didn't know, could not tell just why it was like this with him, knew only that it was what she wanted.

Nic had swept her away, and here she was, at his side, on the road trip of a lifetime—an adventure she would embrace with all her will. She hadn't sought it, but it was here and now—with Nic.

That lift came again, the rush of happiness.

'North Rim or South?' Nic was saying now. 'South means we could take in Vegas if you wanted?'

Fran shook her head vigorously in rejection. Nic was glad. He'd prefer to avoid Vegas himself. Though he had no property there, there was always a chance he might be recognised if they stayed at one of the major hotels.

A thought struck him—one that intruded into his good mood.

'Is it somewhere your ex-fiancé would have taken you?' he heard himself ask.

Hell, why had he said that? It made him sound possessive—and he was never possessive about women. Nor did he let them get possessive about *him*, either.

There was no point. No point in a woman wanting commitment from him.

No point in a woman wanting commitment from any man.

Hadn't his poor mother hammered that home to him, her own sorry life story grim proof of that? Men let women down…they didn't stick around. They cut and ran when it suited them, when the woman tried to get possessive, wanted commitment from them.

With a jolt out of his dark reverie he realised that Fran had given a choked laugh in response. *'Cesare?'* she said, again giving his name the Italian pronunciation. 'Las Vegas would have been the *last* place he'd have visited!'

Cesare would loathe Las Vegas—*far* too vulgar and touristy for his aristocratic tastes.

'Is he an astrophysicist too?' Nic heard himself ask. He wondered why he was going on about the man.

'Oh, heavens no! Cesare is…' Fran paused, trying to find a way to describe him to Nic. 'Well, I guess you could say he works on the land.'

That was true enough. Cesare ran his vast estates with businesslike efficiency, as well as a proprietorial stewardship that took responsibility for his ancient heritage.

Nic gave a satisfied laugh. 'A hick? A—what's that particular English term? Oh, yes—a country bumpkin!' It was good to think of the unknown Cesare as some kind of plodding farm boy.

'Mmm…' murmured Fran equivocally.

She really needed to change the subject. La Donna Francesca, once engaged to Cesare, Il Conte di Mantegna, had no place here in this egalitarian country. Here, she was only Doc Fran Ristori.

And Nic was Nic Rossi, who ran the security team at the Falcone Nevada.

And that's what I want—here and now. Nothing else. Just him and me—for while it lasts.

'OK, we'll skip Vegas,' Nic said now, his laid-back, laconic style already so endearingly familiar to her.

He drank some coffee and made a face. Fran smiled sympathetically. 'Your Italian genes are showing again,' she said, amused. 'I've lived Stateside a few years now, and still the coffee is grim!'

He laughed, lines indenting around his mouth. This was tricky territory—she was taking him for Italian-American, and he wanted to keep it that way. Wanted to stay as simple Nic Rossi, who had worked his way up from a deadbeat childhood to a respectable career in hotel security.

He stretched out his legs and returned to the subject of the Grand Canyon. 'How about West Rim?' he suggested. 'The Hualapai Reservation does helicopter flights, a skywalk and a river ride. Plus we can stay in one of the cabins there tonight if we want.'

Fran's face lit. 'Sounds wonderful!' Then she paused. 'But pricey… I'll go halves with you.'

Nic was touched. Just as he had been when she'd

asked him, before they'd set out for the Array, to charge the SUV hire against her room. He'd waved it away, said he'd fix it, and left it at that. She hadn't pressed and he was glad.

'Deal,' he answered, and they busied themselves making their reservations before getting on the road.

It was an unforgettable experience when they got there, reducing them both to awed silence. They stood at the canyon's edge, in the heat and the silence, looking across to the far North Rim, seemingly so close, but actually ten miles away across the great chasm in the earth, the dramatic formations of rocks and cliffs, the narrow ribbon of river far, far below, the great arching sky above.

They did not speak, only found each other's hands and stood, fingers meshed, together, side by side. Then another group of tourists came up behind them and Fran stepped aside, slipped her hand from Nic's to let them by.

Nic found himself glancing down at his hand. It felt empty without Fran's in it.

He shook his head to clear it. It was the effect of this place, that was all.

They headed back to eat lunch under an airy awning before their flight down into the canyon, then a boat trip, gliding sedately along the Colorado river, deceptively calm in this stretch, gazing up at the towering cliffs above slowly passing them by.

'Fancy white water rafting next?' Nic asked wickedly.

'No, thank you!' Fran said primly. 'This is quite fast enough for me.'

He laughed, relaxing with her. Resting his arm around her shoulder in a gesture that seemed to come naturally to them as she leaned into him companionably.

Back up on the rim again, they made their way to their SUV, which was looking decidedly dusty by now. It had come a long way.

And so have I, she thought.

Her mind skittered away, not wanting to ponder or analyse. She just wanted to enjoy this adventure and wherever it took her.

'OK,' she said as they strapped themselves in, turning on the air-con with relief, 'where to now?'

'Shall we aim for the North Rim?' Nic said. 'It's a long drive, but we could give it a go.'

'Let's do it!' she said, settling back happily.

The sense of exhilaration that she was getting used to filled her again. Crazy this might be, but she wanted it! She was not thinking beyond it—just going along for the ride. With Nic at her side.

In the end they didn't head straight for the North Rim. Instead they diverted to meander into the vast Canyonlands of Utah, making their way along the well-trodden tourist trail, taking in the Grand Staircase, Zion and Bryce, stopping over at lodges, hotels and motels along the way.

They were taking it easy, each day a new adventure, for now putting aside their own lives, their existence beyond this road trip romance.

They did some short, easy-access hiking trails, nothing strenuous, buying the kit they needed as they went, and they did a lot of driving through the awe-inspiring, breathtaking scenery all around, stopping as and when they felt like it. Unpressured, leisurely…

Days slipped by, each one bringing its own delights. And each night was as burningly passionate as the first had been. As if by silent mutual consent neither of them counted the days, wanting nothing more than to reach the next awe-inspiring destination. Never looking further ahead than the next day. Never thinking about what would happen when, finally, they ran out of road. Ran out of time.

It was at a small, cabin-style café, where they'd stopped for leisurely coffee and donuts one mid-morning, as they were finally heading back south towards the North Rim, where both the road and their time together finally ended.

Fran had been deliberately keeping her phone off except to look ahead to their next impromptu destination, which she was doing now, to see what accommodation they might book before finishing their drive to the National Park north of the Grand Canyon the next day.

Usually there were no messages, but today, as she switched on the phone, a flurry of texts, missed calls and voicemails greeted her. She would have ignored them but she could see the identity of the sender. It was her brother, Tonio.

She frowned, starting to read his texts with growing anxiety. Not noticing that Nic, like her, was checking his phone as well, and his expression was changing too.

The message on his screen demanded his attention. But it was bad timing. Bad timing to get a heads-up from his business development manager that a potential prime site was likely to become available in Manhattan. He would need to check it out personally and move fast. Immediately.

But protest reared in him. He didn't want to call time on being with Fran.

I don't want this to end! Not yet.

Even as the protest sounded in his head he felt hard, cold rational thought pour down on it.

So how long do you want it to last? How long before it ends? Just how much more do you want of this—of her, of Fran? Another week? Two weeks? How long? How long to put your life on hold while you drive around the American West?

His eyes bored into the screen, willing the message to disappear. But it was still there. His real life was summoning him back. This hedonistic R&R, unscheduled, snatched out of his life, this instinctive, overriding diversion with this incredible woman who had blazed across his path was over.

Dimly, he realised that Fran was speaking, and he switched his attention to her. Her voice was hollow, her eyes filled with fearful emotion. For a second, just a split second, he thought it must be because he'd said out loud that their time was over.

But it was not that.

'Nic…' The strain was naked in her words. 'Nic, my grandfather…he's had a heart attack. They—they don't think he's going to pull through.' Her voice wobbled at the end, choking.

Instantly, instinctively, he reached across the table to take her hand. She looked at him, her fingers clutching at his.

'I have to go to England,' she said. 'My mother is there already, and my brother and sister. My father is on his way too. I—I have to be there.'

He nodded. The decision was made. The only decision to make. He beckoned to the server, wanting to pay and go.

In minutes they were back in the SUV, heading south.

'We can make McCarran in Vegas in just over three hours, I think. Can you sort a plane ticket while we drive?'

Fran nodded numbly. It was unreal, surely, what was happening? Her grandfather, who had seemed to be as indestructible as the ancient ducal castle that was his principal seat, was dying. By the time she got there it might be too late.

Guilt smote her. She'd kept her distance from her family ever since breaking up with Cesare, not wanting to hear any more of her mother's recriminations for doing so, burying herself in her work, devoting herself to her research.

Her guilt was exacerbated by realising that the last thing she wanted her mother to know was that she had taken off on a crazy road trip with a guy who worked in security at a hotel.

She felt emotion twist inside her. This adventure with Nic had been a mad, impetuous break out of time—away from all that she knew. It had been heady, and fantastic, and wonderful.

But it had nothing to do with her real life, did it? Neither the sober life she lived as a scientist in the halls of academe, nor the life she had been born to as Donna Francesca.

The life she was being summoned back to now, to what might be the deathbed of her grandfather, the centre of her mother's family, who even now might be passing his ducal coronet to his successor—her uncle—while his son-in-law—her father the Marchese—would be paying the respects due from one nobleman to another.

And she must be there too—she *must*. Whatever the friction with her mother, it counted for nothing at a time like this.

Blindly, she stared out of the tinted windows of the SUV at the wild, rugged landscape they were passing through. It had become so familiar in the past amazing, unforgettable days she had spent there, spent with the man who was now at the wheel, driving her to Las Vegas airport with all the speed the law allowed.

I don't want to leave this—to lose this.

It was a cry that came from within, from a place she hadn't known existed until that moment. But it was a cry she must silence.

And if not now, then when?

That was the knowledge that pressed upon her. Had her brother's messages not summoned her away, what would it have gained her? Another few days with Nic? Maybe another week at most? How could it have lasted longer than that? Her other real life would have called her back. She had things to do. Papers to write. Another research post to find, maybe a move to another city—another country, even.

So maybe this sudden ending of her time with Nic was for the best. Wasn't it? Yet something seemed to twist inside her, like a heavy stone turning over…

Nic was talking and she made herself listen. He was telling her not to worry about her suitcase, left at the Falcone Nevada, that he would ensure it reached her office.

She thanked him absently, her hands clenched in her lap. She urged the SUV onwards, towards the airport, anxiety filling her lest she arrive in London too late. But even as she urged it onward she knew that the last of her time with Nic was ticking away.

Their parting, when they arrived at McCarran, was swift. She was cutting it fine for the flight she'd booked, and there was no time for anything more than for her to take Nic's hands as he helped her to the concourse at Departures and press them tightly.

'Thank you!'

Her words were vehement, her kiss swift, pressing his mouth so fleetingly he had no time to do what he wanted, to yank her into his arms and crush her to him one last time.

But the last time had been and gone, without either of them knowing it. So she slipped her hands from his, slung on the backpack she'd acquired on their road trip, gripped her passport. She had already checked in online, had no luggage to drop, and she needed to make her flight now—right *now*.

Unable to bear to look back at him, she forged forward through the opening doors, was swallowed up inside.

For one endless moment he stared after her, not believing she was gone.

Then, making his muscles work, feeling a sudden clenching in his stomach, he swung away, back to the SUV, gunned the engine. He drove off. Heading back to the Falcone Nevada.

It was over. His time with Fran was done. His expression tightened, and he wondered why he felt as if he'd just been punched in the guts…

CHAPTER FOUR

BY THE TIME she arrived at Beaucourt Castle, her grandfather's principal seat, it was late morning.

Her young sister Adrietta ran up to Fran as she climbed wearily out of the Rolls-Royce sent to collect her from Heathrow, hugging her and exclaiming, 'He's rallying! He told the doctor to take himself off and he wanted lobster for lunch! Washed down with claret!'

Fran gave a tired, relieved smile. 'He's a tough old boot,' she said fondly.

They made their way to her grandfather's bedroom where, somewhere in the huge, crimson tester bed, her grandfather was propped upright, looking frail, testy, but blessedly alive—even though he was wired up to all kinds of medical kit and a nurse was hovering.

'So they got you here too, did they?' the Duke barked as he saw her, but his voice was hoarse and his face had aged and, despite the defiance of his attitude, Fran knew she'd done the right thing in hastening here.

However wrenched away from Nic she felt.

No, she must not think of that. Must not think, as she had for the ten-hour duration of her flight, of Nic making his way back to the Falcone, sorting her things to be sent on to the West Coast. Must not think of him doing his job, putting on his tuxedo for the evening, resuming his duties. Must not think of him at all.

She felt a strange tearing inside her—a hollowing out. But she knew she must set it aside. Now she must focus on her family, on her indomitable grandfather who had pulled through, and who, even if lobster and claret were most certainly *not* on the menu today, nor for some weeks to come, was still very much here.

He was commanding the scene, as he always did, ordering her mother to stop fussing and fretting, telling her uncle the Marquess he must make do with his courtesy title yet awhile, that the ducal coronet was going nowhere for now.

And there was relief for Fran for another reason too. Her mother, her face tear-stained, had swept her into a clinging embrace.

'Darling, I'm so, *so* glad you came! Thank you… *thank you*!'

'Of *course* I came.' Fran had hugged her mother back.

It was all that had been said, but Fran knew that her estrangement from her mother was over. It had been helped, she soon realised, not just by her grandfather's close call with death, but also by the news that was clearly serving to divert her mother from endlessly bewailing Fran's decision not to marry Cesare.

Adrietta was getting engaged to a highly suitable *parti*, heir to a *visconti*—which gave the Marchesa the enjoyable prospect of organising a lavish engagement party and an even more lavish wedding the following year.

Fran was relieved, glad both for her mother and her sister. But her mood was strange. She was being absorbed back into her family, into the world, she'd been born into. Yet it jarred—the contrast between her days now at Beaucourt and how her days so short a time ago with Nic, cruising the American West, could not have been greater.

She told none of her family about him. Tried not to think about him. They had had a road trip romance—brief, impulsive and carefree. It had never been intended to be anything more. Their time together must become a precious memory.

Yet, in the long reaches of the night she could feel her body ache for his as she lay in her bed in the room that was always hers whenever she visited Beaucourt Castle.

As the days passed, and her grandfather gradually regained his strength, her time with Nic receded more and more. She was absorbed into her existence as Donna Francesca, with her parents, her siblings, her aunt, uncle and her cousins, all accepting her presence again easily—just one more member of the close-knit family spread between England and Italy.

With her grandfather robustly on the mend, her parents and siblings decided to head back to Italy. Fran went with them, to spend a week at the eighteenth-century *palazzo* in Lombardy that was her childhood home, before returning to her university, now that both her vacation and her compassionate leave were over.

She told her parents she would be looking for another research post, and this drew from her mother the hope that she would find one in Europe this time. And, even better, find a replacement for the fiancé she had discarded so cavalierly.

'I just want you to be *happy*, darling!' her mother exclaimed.

'I *am* happy. I'm happy in my work,' Fran replied.

'Oh, it's not the *same*,' her mother protested. 'Look how happy Adrietta is! She's radiant! I want that for you, too, my darling girl. I want there to be that special man in your life who is like no other that you have known!'

Fran did not answer. Thoughts flickered in her head, memories flashing…

Her mother pounced. 'You're thinking of Cesare, aren't you?'

'No!' Fran's refutation was instant. Instinctive. It had not been Cesare in her head. In her memory. It had been a quite different man.

No. The admonition to herself came swiftly. She had taken off with Nic because it had confirmed that Cesare was in the past and she was free to indulge herself. But the point about indulgence, she had to remind herself sternly, was that that was *all* it was. The easy companionship and casual camaraderie that had been between her and Nic from the off, and all that hot desire for his strong, tough body that had melted her in his searing embrace, had passed.

It's been and gone. It was good, but it's over.

It made sense to tell herself that, to remind herself of that when she was back in her department, working on her next paper, teaching her assigned batch of undergrads, looking out for new research posts. Made sense to tell herself that just as she had accepted that Cesare was no longer in her life, so she would accept the same of Nic—she had let Cesare go easily enough, so it would be the same with Nic.

Yes, it made sense. But it had caused a pang, all the same, to find her suitcase from the Falcone Nevada beside her desk, delivered as promised by Nic. Suddenly vivid in her head was that last farewell to him, in the hectic anxiety of her departure from the airport at Las Vegas. Even more vivid was the sensation of that last farewell kiss, so hurried and fleeting.

But maybe it was good that it had ended so abruptly. Road trips could not go on for ever. In time, the vivid memories would fade. She would move on with her life. She must.

Yet as she called up on her screen a complex set of graphs depicting the interactions of the data she was examining her mind went momentarily blank.

A stray, random thought drifted across it. *We never did get to North Rim, did we?*

Their road trip had stopped before that. And for a moment, before she bent her mind to focus on the graphs again, that seemed a cause for regret.

As if something remained unfinished…

* * *

Nic picked up the thirty-thousand-euro gold pen that lay on his fifty-thousand-euro eighteenth-century desk in his office and scrawled his strong, incisive signature—*Falcone*—onto the purchase contract in front of him.

The prime Manhattan site was his. It had cost him top dollar, as would the refurb and the launch, but he didn't care. It would be worth it. For a few brief months last year he'd enjoyed rebranding the Viscari Manhattan, but that had been ripped from him. Now he had a flagship property of his own, and no one could take it from him.

Setting down the pen, he waited for a sense of satisfaction at such a signal acquisition to fill him.

Instead, memory flickered in his head, of how he'd signed that bar chit in the Falcone Nevada in the summer, keeping his name from the sight of the woman beside him.

Instantly the view before him, overlooking the ancient city of Rome which had spawned him in its slums and now housed him in a High Renaissance former papal *palazzo*, the headquarters of Falcone, vanished. In its place, as vivid as if he were there, was a wild landscape, rocky and bare, sun-scorched, parched and desolate, or darkly forested land, pine trees towering all around him, and he and Fran driving through it, day after day, the road ahead always stretching endlessly, taking them wherever they wanted, over the next horizon, and the next—as if their journey together would never end.

Except that it had—the road had forked, and they had gone their separate ways. She to study the arcane mysteries of the universe, he to soar ever higher with Falcone.

More memory pierced—of that feeling of having been punched in the guts, winded, as he'd watched Fran hurry through into Departures at McCarran. He felt it again now, and in his head he heard his own thoughts coming in its wake.

Should I get in touch? Arrange to see her again?

Because they had been good together.

The anodyne description flared like a struck match in his body's memory, flaming into heat, instantly recalling all their days and their nights, making him shift restlessly. It would be easy to make contact again, to track her down at her university. All he had to do was pick up the phone.

But his hand stayed where it was. He made it stay.

Let it go—let her *go. There is no purpose in making contact. What there was, was good—but it has gone. Its course has run. Move on.*

He always moved on. All his affairs were transient. He would not risk anything else. In his head he heard his mother, scarred by what life had done to her, lamenting the infidelity of men. Of the man who had seduced her then left her pregnant and alone, a prey to other men.

'You'll be the same,' she would say to him sorrowfully. *'You look so like him...so handsome! But so faithless—'*

His mouth thinned. Well, he would *not* be like

his unknown father—because he would never let a woman expect anything of him.

And Fran—would she have expected anything more of me, more than what we had?

He did not know, but it was best not to ask the question. Best not to ask how she would be once she knew he was not Nic Rossi, who worked in security at the Falcone Nevada, but Nicolo Falcone. It would inevitably come out if he contacted her again. It would mean explanations, complications…

No, best to let their brief time together fade into the past, where it belonged. The best place for it to be. The best place for *her* to be.

Fran gazed at the packed-up boxes of her possessions in her West Coast rental apartment, ready for freighting back to the UK, her emotions mixed. She had finally taken another research post—a temporary position at her old Cambridge college, which had delighted her mother. Fran's own feelings were less certain—ultra-prestigious though Cambridge would always be, it seemed to be a step back into her past, into the life, the world, she'd come from.

In America she felt freer—free to be only Dr Fran Ristori, not La Donna Francesca as well… Free to take off on an impulsive road trip with a guy she'd met at a hotel—one of the staff there.

In her head sounded the affectionate nickname Nic had bestowed upon her—Doc Fran. Yes, with him she had been that, too, and it had endeared him to her. She felt her lips twitch in a fond smile at the memory.

Emotion swirled again inside her, disquieting. Leaving America would set the final seal on that impetuous romance. Was that truly what she wanted? In the months that had passed since her time with Nic she knew that for all her admonitions to herself she'd never quite been able to let go entirely of wondering about him—wondering whether she should, after all, attempt to get in touch.

The question had hovered at the edges of her mind, however many times she'd told herself it was best to accept it had been a fling, nothing more than that. Wonderful, memorable, joyous—but only for the duration of their road trip. It couldn't be anything more.

Yet the question came again, and her hand, she realised, was hovering over her phone.

Maybe I just want to say goodbye. To let him know I'm leaving the States. To reach closure. Closure? Or...?

Was that the reason? She didn't know. Didn't want to hear the voice inside her head telling her that if Nic had wanted to get in touch with her, if *he* had not wanted to accept it was over, then he'd had plenty of opportunity to do so. He could have found her through her university, easily.

But he hasn't, has he? He's moved on—clearly and obviously moved on.

But something plucked at her all the same…that flickering emotion she knew she should quell.

As if of its own accord, her hand picked up her phone. She found the hotel's number, dialled it…

Two minutes later she was disconnecting again, emotions twisting inside her. The receptionist, polite as she had been, had been adamant that there was no Nic Rossi working at the Nevada hotel, nor at any Falcone hotel.

Fran stared blankly into space. A hollow feeling was forming inside her. Nic had left the Falcone with no trace.

He could be anywhere.

And 'anywhere' was the same as 'nowhere'. She felt the hollow inside her increasing. In practical terms she had no idea where he was, or how to find him.

She stared at her empty living room, filled only with sealed boxes. Just as sealed as, she realised, the time she had spent all those weeks ago with Nic.

Sealed into the past.

Where it would have to stay.

Nic was in London, at his residence in the Falcone Mayfair.

The hotel was an elegant, double-fronted Georgian town mansion, occupying the south side of a fashionable square, and its possession had meant he had been content to leave the rival Viscari property in nearby St James's in the Viscari portfolio during the brief period of daggers-drawn co-ownership last year.

As it happened, though, he would be visiting the

Viscari St James's this very evening, attending as the plus-one of the up-and-coming designer responsible for the Viscari's lavish new roof garden, the launch of which was the occasion for a glitzy party.

Nic, obviously, given the acrimony between himself and Vito Viscari over Falcone's short-lived corporate raid last year, was not on the extensive and exclusive guest list, but that did not trouble him. He merely wanted to evaluate Lorna Linhurst's horticultural design skills with a possible view to using them on his own hotels—as he had already intimated to her.

What he had *not* yet intimated to her was the fact that he was considering taking a more than professional interest in her.

He shifted restlessly, tugging on the cuffs of his tuxedo, his mood just as restless. Maybe it was time he had another affair. The months since his road trip with Fran had been intense and full on, his priority focussed on opening the brand new Falcone Manhattan. It had absorbed him completely, along with his already ongoing programme of acquisitions, and R&R had taken a back seat. But now, surely, it was time to finally move on from Fran.

Lorna Linhurst could be just the woman to move on with. Divorced, in her late twenties, highly attractive, a good figure—what was not to like? Not to desire?

He told himself that again as they made their way into the Viscari St James's a short while later. Lorna was appealingly dressed in a dark red evening gown, her chestnut hair carefully styled. She seemed a little tense this evening, but that was to be expected. She was showing off her abilities to a potentially highly valuable client.

Yes, there was nothing to object to in her—she was intelligent and very attractive. Except she wasn't Fran.

Nic was well aware that his presence as Lorna's plus one had not gone unnoticed, and it gave him a stab of satisfaction.

But he blandly ignored the staff member who had admitted them to the elevator that was to sweep them up to the roof garden as he promptly got on his mobile phone—presumably to alert his boss that Nicolo Falcone had just strolled in. He wasn't here to see that pampered playboy Vito Viscari holding court, he was here to see what his rival had achieved, and whether to poach his garden designer from him if he sufficiently liked what she'd done.

As they emerged on to the roof garden Nic could see in an instant that it was a triumph of design—a green haven high above the London traffic on this mild autumnal evening. He let Lorna take him around, let her explain how she'd coped with the inherent difficulties of creating a garden on a functioning roof, making trickling rivulets out of drainage channels and disguising ventilation shafts with skilful plantings.

They reached the far side of the garden and Nic paused, glancing down at her. 'Draw up some initial ideas for refreshing the gardens at the Falcone Firenze,' he said. He made his voice warm, less businesslike. 'We'll discuss them over lunch sometime.'

He saw her face light with pleasure at the potential commission—and at such a prestigious property. It confirmed his decision. Florence would be an ideal location to pursue an R&R interest in her as well as a professional one. It might be just what he needed to cure his restlessness.

His eyes rested on her a moment. On the rich chestnut hair, deep-set eyes, generous mouth. She would be very easy to take to bed. But was that what he really wanted?

Being with Lorna would do the job of finally moving him on. Put that brief fleeting time with Fran out of his head and close the door on it firmly, decisively. Fran had been different—his time with her had been different—but that changed nothing. He didn't *do* relationships. He did R&R, and kept it to that. Fran, however memorable, had been just one more round.

And now, surely, it was time to start another. Potentially with the woman at his side this evening.

Nic's gaze lifted from Lorna, moved out across the expanse of the rooftop garden to the throng of guests, most of whom were gathered on the wide white-paved area in front of the long conservatory that housed the rooftop restaurant, softly lit, with concealed lighting creating a stage effect from where he stood on the less lit edge of the garden.

His eyes panned across the chattering guests, over the waiters circulating with silver trays of champagne flutes and canapés. He could see Vito Viscari, busy circulating, meeting and greeting his guests, distinctive with his slim elegance and height, letting the female guests bestow effusive air kisses on him, effortlessly charming them with his matinee idol looks.

An expression of casual contempt for how easy the cossetted handsome heir to the Viscari dynasty had had it all his gilded life crossed Nic's hardening face.

He shifted position restlessly. He had seen what he'd come to see and now he'd take his leave. Lorna, doubtless, would want to stay on, enjoy her creative triumph.

Then, just as he was about to tell her he was leaving, the shifting pattern of the throng changed. Nic's gaze froze.

Out of the mass of guests one distilled into focus.

A tall, slender woman in a long deep blue gown, her hair in elaborate coils on her head, an embroidered silk shawl over her elbows, was talking to two other people. A woman he had last seen disappearing into the Departures hall of McCarran airport in Las Vegas. A woman he had not thought to ever see again.

And immediately, piercingly, two thoughts plunged into his brain.

He had not moved on at all.

And Lorna Linhurst had ceased to exist for him.

Fran smiled, listening to Cesare's wife Carla telling her something amusing about her infant son. Beside them, Cesare was looking down at his wife, with an expression in his eyes that had never come Fran's way in all the time she'd known him—not even in their brief engagement.

She shifted position, feeling restless suddenly, confined by the close-fitting haute couture evening gown from one of her favourite Milan designers. Her sapphire necklace—also a favourite, bestowed upon her by her father for her twenty-first birthday from the di Ristori vaults—was heavy around her throat. She was in full make-up, her hair professionally styled in an ornate fashion. It felt strange to be so dressed up once more, disporting herself at opulent affairs like this party tonight.

Even though she was now back at Cambridge, she was keeping her social life to a minimum. She went to visit her grandfather from time to time at Beaucourt, glad that he was steadily getting back to his old, irascible self, and before Christmas she would be flying out to Italy for her sister's engagement party—a huge bash that her mother and Adrietta were revelling in.

But she'd come back to England to go to Cambridge and work, not to party. Tonight was an exception.

She was here with Cesare and Carla at this lavish do at the Viscari St James's because it was owned by Carla's step-cousin, Vito. Fran's own cousin, Harry, the young Earl of Cranleigh, was here as well, as her partner, and all of them were adding an aristocratic cachet to the glittering, high-society evening at Carla's request.

Now Carla was thanking her for coming.

'I always do what I can to support Vito,' Carla said frankly to her.

'Well, that's what families are for.' Fran smiled.

'And friends,' she added, throwing an affectionate glance towards Cesare.

She would always count him as a friend, and only felt relief to discover how much in love he was with Carla, so that she knew breaking her engagement to him had been a welcome release.

That sense of restlessness came again. She had given up Cesare easily, eager to plunge into the excitement of working with a Nobel Laureate. Thinking no more of him. A frown creased her brows. She had thought more about Nic than she ever had about Cesare.

Nic, with his searing blue eyes that crinkled when he smiled his wolf smile at her, laughed with her, and swept her into his strong arms to kiss her until she was breathless with desire for him.

She tore her mind away. Since accepting that he was gone from her life, that he belonged only in the past and that her life had moved on, she had tried not to think of him, not to remember their time together. She had sought to ignore the flickering emotions that came from time to time, uninvited—little eddies that swirled like dust devils, stirring up her memories.

Cesare was asking about her new research post, and Carla was mentioning something about the Fitzwilliam Museum in Cambridge and its artworks of the High Renaissance—the subject she wrote about in her professional life.

Fran listened with only half an ear, distracted by the dust devils of memory she had just stirred up, seeking to still them. She swept her eyes out and around, determined to divert her thoughts away from pointless memories of Nic. She was here, in London, and Nic was thousands of miles away and in the past. Where he must stay.

Her gaze threaded through the mass of guests, past the paved terrace with its tables and benches, the stone-rimmed pools and trickling rivulets, along the little pathways lined with topiary, onward towards the fenced perimeter at the roof's edge.

And stopped dead.

Two people were standing there at the intersection of two pathways. One, a woman in a dark red evening gown, was half turned towards the man beside her—a man in a tuxedo, like all the other men present. A man who was like no other man present. A man who should not be here. Could not be here—not in London, not here, a few dozen metres away from her.

But he *was*.

And in the bare handful of seconds it took Fran to see him, for her brain to recognise him, she knew with a rush of emotion that was a sudden whirlwind inside her that should not be there, even as *he* should not be here, that something had leapt within her.

Joy.

Nic started forward—then halted. She had seen him. He'd seen it in her face, the sudden recognition in her gaze.

He felt his stomach clench, his mind blank. He wasn't prepared for this. He felt numbed, as if someone had just slugged him in the solar plexus, knocking the wind from him. For a second he could not move. Then, like an automaton, he turned to the woman at his side.

'Excuse me a moment.' His voice came from very far away.

He started forward again. Fran was walking towards him, making her way down a path bordered by a low box hedge either side, her stride quickening on her high heels. She came up to him as he stepped towards her, closing the distance between them.

'*Nic!* What on *earth* are you doing here!' The exclamation in her voice matched the astonishment in her face, in her widened eyes.

Was there more than astonishment in them? Nic thought, feeling again that slug to the solar plexus as his eyes met hers, seeing that sudden leap of expression in them. For a second, nothing else existed.

Then, like another slug, realisation hit him—that seeing her again, here, like this, was going to mean an instant revealing of himself. There was no time for anything else. No time to do anything but fasten his eyes on her, feel the rush of adrenaline in his body, catch the scent of her hair, all so familiar, crowding back into his consciousness as if it had been only yesterday that he'd parted with her. As if the months between had simply vanished.

Dimly, he realised she was speaking again.

'Are you working *here* now?' she was asking. 'At Viscari?'

Her mind was tumbling over itself, incoherence in her jangling thoughts. Was that why she hadn't been able to trace him at Falcone? Because he had swapped employers? But the reasons for his vanishing weren't what was preoccupying her—it was the soaring of her emotions like fireworks going off inside her.

Nic! Oh, Nic! His name sang in her head as her eyes fastened on him, clung almost tangibly to his form, his real, solid frame. He was here, here right in front of her! And it was *good*—oh, more than good to see him again! It was *wonderful*!

All her endless telling herself that it had been just a fleeting romance, that that was all it *should* be, that she had to let him slip away into the past, all melted like ice on a hot stove, evaporating instantly.

That was the truth filling her now, pushing out all the arguments to herself that she'd marshalled to justify why their road trip had had to end. Now, seeing him so tall, so solid, so *real*—so close…

Blood was rushing to her cheeks, leaping in her veins. She felt that same immediate, primitive response she'd given when she'd first set eyes on him, that instinctive, instant *Wow!* as she'd felt the hit of his physical impact on her. She could feel it again now, as unstoppable as the hot, surging memories that assailed her.

Nic, his mouth velvet on hers, melting her bones.

Nic, his arms strong about her, sweeping her off to bed.

Nic, his body arching over hers, caressing hers, possessing her, taking her to places that had made her cry out with ecstasy…

It was all vivid in her head, her consciousness. The searing reality of his presence in front of her was so absolutely, totally unexpected—so absolutely, totally wonderful!

It took her a moment, in the rush to her brain, the leap in her blood, to realise that he wasn't answering her, and her expression faltered for a moment. She dragged herself back to the present, to what was happening now.

Nic knew he had to speak. Had no choice but to do so. He tried to think what to say and failed. Failed to do anything but let his eyes cling to her hungrily. If even a fragment of his mind was registering that she was gowned in haute couture, her hair dressed high on her head in convoluted coils and her throat emblazoned with an ornate sapphire necklace—a look utterly at odds with the casually styled way she'd been in the USA—he shook it aside. Only her beauty mattered, and in that she was radiant. As beautiful as ever.

How could I have let her go? I must have been crazy to let her go!

The words leapt in his head, knocking down all the principles he lived his life by. His mind was ragged, but he had to force himself to find words to answer her.

'I—it's—complicated.' His voice sounded terse as he urgently pulled a mask over his expression, trying to pull together his thoughts, trying to work out how to handle this, how to cope with what was inevitably going to happen.

She was going to discover that, no, he was *not* working here at the Viscari St James's…

He saw her react to his blank expression, saw the withdrawal in her face as she backed away slightly.

'Oh, I'm sorry.' Fran halted. The leap that her heart had taken collapsed.

Belatedly she realised that if Nic were indeed working here at the Viscari in London, then maybe he shouldn't be mingling with the guests. Maybe the easy-going atmosphere at the Falcone Nevada did not prevail here at the Viscari. Maybe he was still on approval only, had to be cautious. Maybe he was supposed to be low-profile, here to keep an eye out for the security of guests who, like her, glittered with jewels at this gala event. Maybe—

Maybe you are the last person he wants to see—maybe that's why he's not exactly opening his arms to you.

Brutally, she reminded herself of what she'd said to herself often enough in the months since their road trip.

He's had every chance to get back in touch if he wanted to. He knows where you worked, where you lived, and could easily have found out you'd moved to Cambridge. He could easily have looked you up now that he's come over to the UK. But he didn't. So what does that tell you?

The answer was stark. It told her that he wasn't interested in her any more.

With that same hollowing inside her she watched the woman in the red evening dress come up to them.

The woman was beautiful, and Fran felt it like a blow. Nic had moved on.

She felt emotion churn within her, shocking her with its power—a power it should not have, but did. Then, out of nowhere, the emotion was wiped away. Another took its place.

The beautiful brunette was lightly touching Nic's sleeve, her voice diffident. 'Would you excuse me for a few moments, Mr Falcone? I've just seen someone I should speak to…'

Her words wiped everything from Fran's hectic brain. She heard her own intake of breath sharply.

Then, the word *'What?'* broke from her like a gunshot.

What had that woman just called him? Mr *Falcone?* She couldn't have.

CHAPTER FIVE

FRAN'S FEATURES FROZE, her eyes widening in disbelief.

As if in slow motion, Nic moved. Took Lorna's arm from his sleeve. Nodded in dismissal, his face thunderous.

For a second longer Fran's eyes stayed blankly on the woman as she smiled her thanks uncertainly and then hurried away, as if sensing some untoward incident had just occurred and she wanted to be out of it.

Then Fran's eyes slewed back to Nic. There was a drumming in her ears, a blankness in her head. She stared at Nic. His face was masked, as if a steel screen had been slammed down over it. The face that was as familiar to her as her own. Nic's face.

Nic. Nic Rossi. Who worked in Security at the Falcone Nevada.

Mr Falcone.

It can't be—I misheard. I must have misheard.

'Tell me I misheard.' She spoke aloud, her voice as hollow as the gaping hole inside her.

She saw him give a quick, unmistakable, unarguable shake of his head, felt that wash of disbelief go through her again as he did so.

'No, you didn't,' he said. His voice sounded curt. 'I'm Nicolo Falcone.'

She stared, not taking it in. 'You said your name was Nic Rossi.' Her voice was hollow.

'It is,' he said. 'That's my birth name. I took the name Falcone when I decided to make something of myself.'

She took a step backwards, not realising that she had. It was an instinctive gesture—a withdrawal. Emotion was pounding within her, drumming in her ears.

'Why lie to me?' Her voice was a blade, accusing him.

Emotion flashed in his eyes. Those blue, blue eyes she had gazed into so often, for so long—eyes that crinkled at the corners when he laughed, that changed from laughter to desire, to hot, burning passion.

'I didn't lie. I just didn't tell you.'

His voice seemed to be coming from very far away. As if the man she knew was receding from her. Because the man she'd thought she knew didn't exist.

I thought he was one person, but he's another.

The hollowness was spreading. It was as if her whole being were now nothing but a shell, surrounding an emptiness that was yawning inside her. Then, suddenly, she saw his expression change, his eyes snap past her. She heard footsteps, then a voice. Deep. Commanding. Speaking in Italian.

'Francesca, are you all right?'

It was Cesare. Cesare was moving to her side, being very much the imperious Il Conte, throwing the aura of his protection around her, casting an inquisitorial look towards the man opposite her that kept him at a distance, that wanted to know why he was importuning her.

Instinctively—because Cesare was an old friend, because she'd known him all her life, because once she'd thought to live her life with him—Fran clutched at his arm, leaning her weight on it, which he supported instantly.

She said his name, faintly. 'Cesare…'

She saw that Nic heard it—Nic, the fabulously rich billionaire who owned the hotel she'd stayed in for the conference—owned that hotel, owned dozens more.

But not, as it happened, this one. For right now someone else was approaching them. Vito Viscari was stepping up beside her on her other side, flanking her just as Cesare was, throwing his protection around her as well. But the focus of his attention was on Nic.

'Falcone.' The voice was tight, borderline hostile.

She saw Nic's head turn. Nod. His mouth was set, his eyes steeled suddenly, acknowledging the presence of the man whose hotel this was. She heard Vito Viscari continue, in that same chill, tight tone of voice.

'I don't recall your name being on the invitation

list, Falcone.' He, too, spoke in Italian—the language they all shared.

Fran saw Nic's mouth curl. 'That didn't prove necessary.'

'With you, what else should I expect?' There was a twist in Vito's voice. Then, with studied coolness, he challenged, 'So, have you come to admire? Or dismiss?'

'To assess,' came Nic's answer, his voice deeper than Vito's but just as clipped.

'And what is your assessment, Falcone?' Vito's eyes were unreadable. But Fran was dimly aware it was a taunt.

Nic gave a slow nod. 'Impressive,' he said—as if he begrudged the compliment but would not demean himself by denying it.

Vito tilted an eyebrow. 'Good of you,' he said sardonically.

The stand-off between them was palpable, and then dimly, through the frozen blankness that was the inside of her head, Fran became aware that someone else was joining them. Harry, her cousin, was sauntering up to them with all the casual self-assurance of someone who had been born an earl and would one day be a marquess and then a duke—a youth who had an entrée everywhere, however exclusive. The kind of inherent self-assurance that came with five hundred years of being bred to it.

'Hi,' he said cheerfully, in his upper-class public schoolboy accent, speaking English, utterly oblivious of the net of tension in the frozen tableau. 'Fantastic bash, this, Vito,' he said with a grin, raising his glass to his host. Then his gaze widened to throw an enquiring glance at the man opposite.

Stiffly, as if jolted into social niceties, Vito spoke. 'Falcone, allow me to introduce you to my guests…' There was a slightest emphasis on the word 'guests', as if to indicate that his rival was not one.

'Lord Cranleigh…' He nodded towards Harry, who waved his champagne glass airily as Vito continued, in English, his voice as tight as his expression. 'Il Conte di Mantegna you will obviously know of—have you met before? Perhaps not…' he said dismissively.

His expression changed very slightly, his eyes suddenly speculative, and he threw the briefest glance towards Fran, in the same protective manner Cesare had used.

'Though it would seem you have already made the acquaintance of Lord Cranleigh's cousin—Il Marchese d'Arromento's daughter, Donna Francesca di Ristori.'

It was as if slow motion had stilled to nothing. Most of all in Fran's hollowed brain. Then, as if motion had started again, she saw Nic's expression change. Saw it drain, stiffen. The steel mask dropped down over it again. Yet behind it she could see the glitter of his eyes.

She heard him speak.

'Donna… Francesca.'

The simple repetition. Two words. Like stones dropped from a great height, one after another. Then his eyes went past her to the man she was clinging to as if for dear life. The man she had called Cesare.

Cesare the hick...the country bumpkin. The farm boy. The dismissive names he'd given to the man who'd been in Fran's past paraded through his head with mocking brutality.

Cesare was the Count of Mantegna. Polished, cosmopolitan, a man of the world, owner of vast ancestral estates, moving in the very highest echelons of Roman society, holder of a title that stretched back a thousand years.

This...*this* was the man she'd spoken of that day, in another world, another life, when she'd sat beside him in that speedboat on the desert lake... The woman he'd romanced across the Canyonlands and deserts, in the wild, wide-open spaces of America, who'd laughed with him, travelled with him, made love with him...

His mouth twisted. His guts twisted.

I thought I knew who she was! Doc Fran, who gazed up at the stars and told me all about them. Who fell into my arms and held me close. Doc Fran, who didn't care that she was romancing a guy she took to be a security guard at a hotel.

But she wasn't that person at all. She came from a world that was nowhere like the free and easy democratic society of the States. Her world—her *true* world—was one of stiff formality and ancient titles, of blood that had been blue for centuries. A world of *palazzos* and *castellos*, of ancestors reaching back into the annals of history. A world of those born to privilege and possessions. A world that had nothing, *nothing* to do with him.

That never could. Nor anyone who belonged to it.

For one endless moment his gaze rested on her, then on the men standing in a protective rank beside her, flanking her, guarding her, keeping him at bay, keeping him away from her. The men she belonged to, in the world she came from, as she stood there in her couture gown, antique sapphires glittering in her priceless necklace… Donna Francesca…

Not the woman he knew. Had thought he knew…

But he hadn't. Not at all.

He turned away, feeling skewered, eviscerated. Walked off. Not caring that he was doing so. His stride was rapid, mechanical, and he almost pushed past other guests to reach the conservatory, march up to the elevator, jab at the button to open the doors, walk inside.

His face was a steel mask, his eyes glittering with an emotion he would not name.

But he knew what it was, and why it was scything through him like a knife in his guts.

'Nic, wait!'

A hand had seized the closing doors, forcing them open again. Fran stumbled inside, the tightness of her gown constricting her, her high heels twisting her ankles in her desperate haste. She grabbed the handrail to steady herself, hearing the doors slice shut again, felt the lift begin to descend.

'Nic—' She started again, but he cut across her. His voice hard.

'We have nothing to say to each other.' The words fell into the yawning space between them. Then, with a savage punctiliousness, he added, *'Donna Francesca.'*

Her face contorted. 'Don't call me that!'

The glitter in his eyes flashed, as coruscating as the priceless antique sapphires around her throat.

'But it is who you are,' he said. His voice was still harsh, biting out the words.

'So *what*?' she shot back.

Emotion was storming inside her. What had happened back there had been horrendous: Cesare at his most pompous and lordly, Harry being a Hooray Henry to a T, Vito barely civil and deliberately, she was sure, hammering home her family and her title. It was the very worst way she could have imagined Nic learning who she really was.

But he isn't 'just' Nic Rossi, either!

That fact seared across her.

'And Nicolo Falcone is who *you* are!' She took a shuddering breath. 'You never mentioned that, did you? And I never mentioned a title that means absolutely *nothing* in America!'

She saw his mouth tighten. 'But we are in Europe now, and you are Donna Francesca—as Viscari so *kindly* pointed out to me.'

Fran's eyes flashed. 'Well, that's what Vito knows me as! His step-cousin married Cesare—the man I turned down!'

'Ah, yes.' Nic's voice was tightly vicious, but the target was himself, for having once written off one of the leaders of Italian high society as a rustic farm boy. 'His Excellency the Count of Mantegna, no less!'

'Yes, and what of it?' she demanded. 'He's a family friend. I've known him since I was a child!'

Nic's eyes hardened. Of *course* the illustrious Count was a family friend. And a childhood one at that. What else should he be? They all knew each other, these aristos—knew each other and stuck together, protecting their privileges, protecting each other.

Memory daggered him. Just as the likes of Vito Viscari all protected their privileges—privileges they hadn't had to work for, had had handed to them on a plate. Effortlessly taking it as nothing more than their due, their God-given right. Not caring if it shut out those who'd actually had to *work* for everything they'd achieved.

Well, he wanted nothing to do with such people. Nothing to do with a woman who turned out to be part of all that.

She's not the woman I thought she was.

The knowledge seared across him like a burning brand.

'Donna Francesca, your family and your friends are no concern of mine!' he ground out. Savage anger was still scything across his brain, rage at himself, at her…

Something contorted in her face. 'Nic, don't be like this!'

Her hand reached towards him, as if to touch him as she had touched him so often in their time together. But now it faltered, unsure, uncertain. He was holding her at bay. Repelling and repudiating her. And all that they had once been to each other—

Memory scythed across her mind of how they had stood together in an elevator that evening after the Sunset Drive and she had wondered whether he would kiss her, whether she would kiss him back. That had been the very start of their time together, their coming together in shared desire, becoming friends, then lovers.

How could this stone-faced, harsh-featured man holding her so coldly at bay be that same man?

She almost cried out with the anguish of it, of the clash of worlds between then and now.

He wasn't answering her impassioned plea, was shutting her out. His face was shuttered and closed. Blanking her. The elevator had stopped, had reached the lobby, and the doors were starting to open. He was ignoring her, turning towards them to exit the lift.

She would not chase him across the hotel. Before he moved she impulsively jabbed at the control buttons and the doors juddered shut again, the lift soaring upwards once more.

Nic gave what seemed to be a snarl of anger at her high-handedness. He turned on her. He wanted an end to this. Emotions were knifing through him, out of his control.

'Enough!'

A hand slashed into the air and suddenly, as Fran stared at him, consternation at what was happening, why it was happening, filling her, she saw him change. She had known right from the first moment of their encounter that he was tough, but it had been a toughness that had never been directed at her. Now, suddenly, it was.

And it was a toughness that went way beyond that required of a guy who worked in security at a luxury casino hotel.

A hard, arctic gaze pinioned her. Suddenly this was not Nic Rossi the man she knew, the man she had spent such an easy-going, passionate, unforgettable time with. It was Nicolo Falcone, billionaire owner of a global hotel chain, with thousands of staff at his command, a property portfolio that stretched around the world, revenues that dwarfed anything her father possessed. Nicolo Falcone, who'd made his immense fortune by his own efforts, starting from nothing, clawing his way to wealth by strength of will.

And men like that were ruthless, single-minded and not to be messed with.

Nor was he.

His hand lowered to the control panel, pressing the halt button, staying the elevator where it was. Then he spoke.

'Donna Francesca,' he began, with an icy formality that chilled her to the quick as she stood staring at him, skewered by the arctic gaze of this man who was nothing like the man she'd thought she knew. 'You will oblige me by not attempting to delay my departure. You will also oblige me—' his mouth hardened even more as he issued not a request but an order, a warning '—by not attempting any further contact with me.'

The hand at the control panel pressed another button and the doors slid open on an intermediate floor.

'Goodnight, Donna Francesca.'

He stood, pointedly waiting for her to step out. She was staring at him, her face pinched. Defeated. Emotion bit in him, like acid, but he blanked it. Then, with a sudden sweep of her skirts, she walked out, holding herself as stiffly as if she were made of marble.

For a second—an endless second that seemed to stretch like the distance of the deserted corridor—Nic went on holding the door open. Then, numbly, he released the button, pressed for the lobby again, felt the elevator start its plummeting descent with a lurch. Leaving his guts somewhere way above.

Gaining the lobby, he walked out of the hotel, out on to the pavement. He didn't want to summon his car. Striding blindly, he headed towards Mayfair, his face still a steel mask. That same emotion still acid in his mouth.

Blindly, Fran reached the end of the corridor, pushed open the doors leading to the stairwell. She had to return to the party—a lifetime of training that told her one could not indulge one's feelings at the expense of social demands impelled her. Yet emotions were tumbling through her, jarring and clashing. To see Nic again…to learn who he really was without warning, so abruptly…and he to learn her other identity, equally without warning—

Was it just shock? Mutual shock on both their parts?

But he'd seemed so *angry* to discover she was Donna Francesca.

I'm not angry that he's really Nicolo Falcone! In fact—

She stopped, as she was climbing the stairs to the roof level. If Nic really was Nicolo Falcone then surely that was *good*, wasn't it? Wasn't it good that she was Donna Francesca as well as Doc Fran? Wasn't it *better* that Nic was Nicolo Falcone? Not Nic Rossi working in Security in a hotel in Nevada?

Because if she were Donna Francesca, and he was Nicolo Falcone, then—

Her thoughts raced through her head as she painstakingly climbed upwards. Whatever the shock that had followed after that brunette had disclosed his real identify, nothing could take away from her that rush of emotion she'd felt, overpowering her when she had seen him.

Joy.

She felt it again—felt that surge of pleasure and delight at seeing him once more. Felt the rush that came with it, the lift of her spirits.

Telling herself that Nic was in the past, that her

time with him was over, was totally useless. She felt emotion sweep within her yet again—and hit a wall.

She jerked to a halt, lungs tightening. That brunette…

Her insides hollowed. Nic—whether he was Nic Rossi or Nicolo Falcone didn't matter—had moved on. That was why he was repudiating her, rejecting her.

Bleakness filled her. Slowly she resumed her heavy climb. That was the reason—the obvious, glaring reason—Nic would have nothing to do with her.

He had someone else, and whether she was Doc Fran or Donna Francesca made no difference at all to him.

It was the only explanation.

And it devastated her.

'Vito!' Eloise Viscari exclaimed, coming up to her husband. 'Is it true? Did Nicolo Falcone really have the nerve to turn up here tonight?'

Instantly Fran tensed at the name. The rooftop party had finally ended, but she and Harry, together with Cesare and Carla, had been invited by Vito to join him and Eloise, who was heavily pregnant with their second child, and so hadn't attended the garden launch, for an informal supper in their private suite at the hotel.

Fran would have preferred not to go, but social obligations could not be avoided, however much her personal preference would have been otherwise.

As she heard Vito answer his wife, Fran was aware of Cesare glancing at her. Since rejoining the roof party she'd been aware of his watchful eyes on her. He knew her well enough to know when she was upset, however much she strove to conceal it. She did not want him asking questions why.

Not when she scarcely knew the answer herself.

'Yes, he came as Lorna Linhurst's plus-one,' Vito was confirming. His voice and mouth were tight.

'Well, she's either his latest squeeze in a long, long line of squeezes or she's touting for work at Falcone,' Eloise said caustically. 'Whichever, she won't get any more work from *you*, Vito!'

'Falcone?' Harry joined the conversation, strolling towards them from the buffet table where he'd been helping himself liberally. 'Is that the guy built like a forward you introduced to us? Guy with the broken nose? *Is* he a rugby player?' he asked casually.

'No,' Cesare corrected him. 'He owns the Falcone chain of hotels.'

'No way!' Harry commented cheerfully, putting away the last of a large slice of quiche. 'Looks a bit of a bruiser to me!'

'A good description in many ways,' Vito observed grimly. 'Especially in business.'

Harry looked questioningly at Vito, but it was Carla who answered. 'Last year he briefly acquired half the entire Viscari portfolio in a highly hostile corporate raid. It came to nothing in the end, but it was pretty nasty at the time.' Her tone changed, sounding chastened. 'It was all my fault—I should have stopped my mother, Vito's step-aunt, selling her shares to him.'

Eloise reached a hand across to her. 'Carla—no. Don't go there. It's all sorted now.' Her voice was sympathetic.

'Only because *your* mother bought the hotels back for Vito from Falcone's investors!' Carla exclaimed.

'Well, that's one of the plus points of having a mum who runs her very own hedge fund,' Eloise riposted lightly. 'And Falcone's talons are out of us now. We've seen him off! He's furious—but who cares?'

Fran was staring at them, totally focussed. *What* had they just been saying?

Then Eloise was continuing. 'Anyway, he's gone off on an acquisition spree instead. The most recent was in Nevada—not in Vegas, but some desert resort.'

Harry glanced to Fran. 'Sounds like where you went for that conference last summer. Tonio had to yank you back when Gramps had his heart attack.'

All eyes turned to Fran. With effort, though her thoughts were suddenly hectic, she kept her voice calm. 'Yes. It had only recently opened, I believe.'

'Any good?' Eloise asked enquiringly. She smiled. 'Just casing the opposition!'

'It was very luxurious,' Fran answered. 'Beautifully situated—right out in the desert. Amazing scenery.' Her voice was stilted, but she knew she had to sound as normal as possible. Yet in her head flashed the memory of her and Nic, on that first outing, watching the sun set in a blaze of gold.

She blinked, and the memory was gone.

Carla was speaking again. 'His latest venture is New York. He's finally found a Manhattan site of his own now that he can't have Vito's,' she said.

Eloise held up her hand. 'No more talk about Falcone—the wretched man or his hotels! Not a patch on Viscari!'

She raised her glass of orange juice, then glanced to where her husband was talking in a low, preoccupied voice to Cesare.

'Darling, we're just about to toast your success tonight! Do pay attention!'

There was laughter, and they all raised their glasses to Vito. But as Fran lowered hers and the conversation turned general, she realised Cesare had come to stand beside her, where she sat on one of the sofas, trying to conceal her suddenly hectic thoughts.

He inclined his head to hers. 'Is that why Falcone approached you this evening? Had you encountered him in Nevada while you were there?' His voice was low, and he was speaking in Italian.

Fran swallowed. 'Briefly,' she acknowledged, her tone constrained. She did *not* want Cesare probing.

She saw Cesare's expression tighten. 'Then I hope, Francesca, that you will take this in the spirit with which I offer it. I was concerned when I saw you with him—which is why I came up. It is a concern shared by Vito, who knows his reputation—as he was just telling me.' He paused a moment. 'Nicolo Falcone is well known as a womaniser, so—'

Fran cut across him repressively. 'Cesare, I appreciate what you're saying, but—'

He smiled faintly. 'Yes, I know—it's none of my business. But we go back a long way, you and I, so I will claim the privilege of speaking now in a fraternal way. I would not like to see you misled by someone of...let us say, an unscrupulous disposition. So, if Falcone was importuning you tonight—'

She shook her head decisively. Any 'importuning' had come from her, she thought bleakly, when she had demanded he speak to her...talk to her...

'I was surprised to see him here, that was all,' she said constrainedly. 'As, apparently, was everyone else.' She frowned, putting into words what was uppermost in her head right now. 'I hadn't realised he'd tried to take over Viscari and lost.'

'It was headline news in the financial press in Italy, but you were in the States at the time,' Cesare said. 'There's huge friction between Falcone and Viscari.'

She was relieved she had no opportunity to reply. Harry had sauntered over to them, demolishing a chicken leg as he did so.

'Fran, old bean, I'm off clubbing. You've got keys for the flat, haven't you?'

She nodded. Most of the family made use of Harry's father's flat in Chelsea when they were in town. Restlessly, she got to her feet. Her thoughts were still hectic, emotions racing. What had been disclosed just now was fuelling them. She wanted to be gone.

Using the excuse of Harry's departure, she took

her leave. It seemed ages before she was in the chauffeured hotel car Vito had ordered for her, dropping Harry off to meet up with his friends. Alone at last, she felt her mind race, replaying everything she'd heard said in Vito's suite.

Was *that* why Nic had been so icily hostile to her? Because she'd been Vito Viscari's guest? Because he'd aligned her with the man who was his bitter rival in business? Add to that the fact that she was the last person he'd wanted to meet up with again, that he'd thought her safely tucked away back on the West Coast, never to be encountered again now that he had moved on to another woman in his life…

Something knotted inside her, and with a smothered cry she released the pent-up emotions that she had bottled up inside her all evening since that disastrous encounter on the rooftop—that wretched, icy exchange when she'd run after him. How could it have come to this? That Nic—*Nic*—who'd swept her up into his arms, laughed with her, made love to her, driven across deserts with her, should be so harsh towards her now?

Oh, their affair might be over, and he might have moved on, but everything in her—every feeling—was rebelling at letting that cold, callous scene between them be all that was left between them now.

We parted as friends. I don't want to remember him like this, now, the way he was this evening.

Hands twisting in her lap, she stared blindly out of the car's front window as it made the turn into a large square in Mayfair, en route for Chelsea. She suddenly started. Above the white pillared entrance to the building that dominated one side of the square a blue flag hung, illuminated by skilful lighting. A gold falcon on a blue field—

'Stop the car!'

The driver pulled up at the kerb. From there she could see the gold lettering above the grand doorway. *Falcone Mayfair.*

She swallowed, aware the driver was waiting for further instructions. Aware of much more than that. Of an urge she could not stop. An urge that was pressing on her like a sudden impulse she must obey.

To be passing the Falcone hotel just like this, unexpectedly… It was a sign, surely? A sign to do what was leaping in her head.

I have to do this. I can't leave it the way he left it. I won't let him spoil my memories of that time we had.

With fast-beating heart she dismissed the car, went into the hotel. Though she had no idea if Nic were here at the moment, she could but ask. Try and find out where he was if he wasn't here.

Straightening her spine, she sailed up to Reception as if she owned the world. Sometimes being Donna Francesca, granddaughter of the Duke of Revinscourt, resplendent in her couture gown and her antique sapphires, could come in useful. It would now—she would make sure of it.

'Good evening,' she said, her smile polite but supremely expectant of being paid attention to. 'Can you tell me if Mr Falcone is back yet? We were together earlier this evening and arranged to meet here later.'

The receptionist was co-operative, but cautious. 'I believe so, madam, but let me check.'

She picked up a phone. 'Ah, Mr Falcone, there is someone in Reception for you.' The woman glanced expectantly at Fran, waiting for a name.

Fran smiled. Her heart was thumping in agitation, but she did not let it show.

'Lorna Linhurst,' she said serenely.

CHAPTER SIX

NIC SAT AT his desk in his residence, trying to concentrate on the latest occupancy figures on his screen and failing. There was only one focus for his thoughts—one he did not want to have but which burned in his head, flaring on his retinas as if she stood there still in front of him the way she had that evening, suddenly reappearing in his life. Vividly real and as beautiful as ever.

With an oath, he pushed his chair back, gazed grimly across the sitting room. His residence was on the topmost floor, with slanting eaves, set into what had once been the servants' quarters of the Georgian mansion. Maybe there were those who thought it a fitting place for him.

His mouth twisted. Well, now he owned the whole damn mansion—and dozens more multi-million-dollar properties. Not bad for a slum kid! A slum kid who'd somehow 'made the acquaintance'—Viscari's supercilious words seemed to mock him savagely—of the daughter of a *marchese*.

Donna Francesca.

The name, her courtesy title, was hardly used any more, but still it was redolent of centuries of fine breeding, of titles and lands and privileges, and coats of arms and ancient houses and historic *palazzos* filled with priceless artworks—all related to each other, all marrying each other, all closing ranks against outsiders, all helping each other to keep their privileges for themselves.

Oh, Italy might be a republic these days—most European countries were—but that didn't mean a thing to those born to the aristocracy. Maybe they didn't call the shots politically any longer, but they had the rest of the world handed to them on a plate.

They'd worked for none of it—had simply sat back and inherited it. Just the way Vito Viscari had sat back and waited for his plush inheritance to fall into his lap, courtesy of his father and uncle, who'd ensured he'd had his path to the top smoothed and eased, had never had to strive for anything. Brushing aside as irrelevant anyone who got in the way—as he had been brushed aside in favour of the pampered young Viscari heir.

Scorn filled him—a familiar scorn that reached to the woman who'd stood in front of him this evening, a woman from that gilded world of privilege and aristocracy. And another emotion was shafting through it—anger. Anger that she wasn't who he'd thought she was.

I thought she was Dr Fran Ristori—with her golden hair and a smile to take the breath out of my body. And a body to fuse to mine like it was part of me.

Memory, hot and searing, tore at him.

To think he'd even contemplated breaking his rule of a lifetime to get back in touch with her. To seek to capture again that time he'd had with her. His expression hardened. Thank God he hadn't! Thank God he'd done what he'd done all his life—moved on.

Whoever the hell she really was, he was done with her. So why should he care that she was the daughter of a *marchese*?

The phone on his desk was ringing and he snatched it up.

'Yes?'

His voice was curt. Who wanted him at this late hour of the evening? He was in no mood to be hospitable. Then, as the receptionist gave the name of his unexpected visitor, his frown cleared. Unexpected she might be, but he should make the most of it.

Hadn't he been telling himself he'd moved on? Well... His expression changed again. Now he really could. This very evening. Right away. Whatever had brought Lorna here, he would take advantage of it. He would open champagne, make it clear to her that he was interested in more than her skills in garden design and see where it took them.

He wanted her to say yes.

Memory, unwanted but piercing, arrowed through him. Once it had been another woman, with golden hair and a beauty to inflame him, he'd wanted to say yes.

Enough! The same word that he'd silenced her with sliced through his brain now.

'Tell Ms Linhurst,' he said to the receptionist, making his voice far less curt, 'that she is most welcome.'

He hung up. Strode to the climate-controlled drinks cabinet, drawing out a suitable bottle of champagne, setting out two flutes beside it, checking that the lighting created the right ambience for the message he wished to convey to the woman who was going to be his way to move on from the woman he needed to move on from…

There was a soft rap at the door. He crossed towards it, opened it with a welcoming smile.

'Lorna, this is a most pleasant surprise—' he began warmly.

Then the welcoming smile was wiped from his face.

Fran was inside the door before Nic could register it or stop her.

'What the hell…?'

There was nothing welcoming in his voice now, nothing warm.

She strode past him, the long silk skirts of her gown swishing. 'Nic, I have to talk to you!' She slewed round to face him, and as she did so she was burningly conscious of his raw physical presence all over again.

He was still in his tuxedo, but his top shirt button was undone, the black bow tie hanging open either side. In the hours since she'd set eyes on him his jaw had shadowed with the beginning of regrowth, and it gave him a rough, piratical edge that hollowed something out inside her.

How often in their time together, lolling in bed together late at night, or early in the morning, had she run her fingers along that roughened edge, glorying in the sheer masculinity of it until he caught her fingers, hauled her mouth to his and started all over again in his urgent, demanding possession of her?

A word in Italian escaped from him, a crudity that broke on the air, and she blenched. Nic didn't care that she could understand it—all that was in him now was an open anger that was instantaneous. There was shock too—and more than shock.

Her image had been burning in his head and now it was more than just that. It was *her*—her presence—just as it had been on the rooftop of the Viscari. As resplendent as it had been then. And he realised there was no way he could move on with Lorna.

His eyes honed in on the couture gown in blue silk, the sapphires snaked around her pale throat, the golden hair piled high on her head. La Donna Francesca in all her aristocratic grandeur.

Then her words registered with him. *I have to talk to you!*

Anger slashed across his consciousness. No, she did *not* have to talk to him! He wanted none of it.

His expression closed. Hardened. The way it had in the elevator. 'There is nothing I wish to hear, Donna Francesca—' he began, his voice cold.

Something flashed in her eyes, and he realised with a start that it was anger too.

'Well, tough, Nic—because you're going to hear it! I will *not* be treated like this by you!'

It was the wrong thing to say. Immediately his eyes narrowed, his voice icing. 'Do *not* throw your aristocratic privileges at *me*, because they don't impress me! God knows how you blagged your way in here. But you can leave right now!'

He made to go and open the door, but Fran was there before him.

'Nic, *no!*' Her voice changed and she took a heaving breath. Emotion was storming in her, threatening to overwhelm her. She'd nerved herself for this and she would see it through. She *must*.

'Nic, *listen* to me. You've got no business stonewalling me like this. It's *me*, Fran. You owe me some courtesy, at least. I've not done any harm to you. Listen…' She took another shuddering breath. 'Don't take your anger out on me! I am not anything to do with whatever the hell is going on between you and Vito. I didn't even *know* you'd tried to take over half his company, let alone that it was ripped back from you. Why should I? I didn't even damn well know you were Nicolo Falcone. You made sure I didn't know.'

Nic's voice stayed icy. 'And *you* made sure I didn't know who *you* really were!'

'Because it wasn't relevant!' she shot back vehemently. 'It wasn't relevant then, and it isn't now.' She took another shuddering breath. Held out her hand towards him. 'Nic, please, don't be like this.' Her voice changed, dropped. 'There was something good between us…don't spoil it now! Don't spoil those memories—'

She broke off, feeling emotion rising in her, her hand still outstretched towards him, where he stood rigid and unmoving.

But behind the mask of his face something was moving. Something was building like an unstoppable tide. She was standing there, breasts heaving, the jewels around her throat catching the low lamplight. The woman he was finally going to put behind him. Into the past, where she needed to be. Needed to stay. The past that was reaching forward now, reaching towards him as she was reaching her hand towards him, her eyes huge, lips parted, as if imploring him. As if tempting him beyond endurance.

'There was something *good*, Nic, and it doesn't deserve your hostility to me!'

Something changed in his eyes. Something that glittered with memory and was fuelled by the heat suddenly rising in his body, the heat *she* was engendering, with her slender body moulded by that gown that showed every curve, every contour, the body he knew with all the intimacy of possession.

As if of their own volition his feet took a step towards her. He did not touch her outstretched hand. Instead his fingers reached to touch her cheek. Lightly…the slightest brush.

'Shall I tell you what there was between us? Shall I show you?'

The fingers trailed to her lips, grazed their outline. The husk in his voice was low, sensual…

She stilled. 'Nic, *no*! I didn't come here because—' She broke off, stricken. Lifted her hand to push his fingers away. 'Nic, I know you have someone else in your life now—another woman! I *know* what we had is over.'

A rasp broke from him and there was a glitter in his eyes now, like the glitter of light on the sapphires around her throat.

'There *is* no other woman…' The words fell from his lips, hoarse.

How could there be any other woman when *this* woman had reappeared in his life, out of nowhere, taking his senses by storm? As she had the very first time he'd laid eyes on her.

As she always would…every time…

The truth seared through him like a burning brand. He would *always* want her, this woman he could not resist. He would be foolish to think otherwise.

He saw her expression change at what he'd said, heard the intake of her breath, saw her pupils start to dilate, a flush rise in her cheeks, her breasts rise and fall. Her hand fell to her side, too weak to ward him off as he lifted his fingers to her cheek again, slid his hand around the delicate line of her jaw to cup the nape of her neck, drawing her towards him.

She faltered, and yielded, exhaling his name in a breath, on a soft, helpless sigh, as his other hand reached forward towards her straining breasts, curved openly around one lush mound, felt it crest through the silk.

Desire shot through him. Hot, urgent. The world receded, ceased to exist. He heard her gasp—a gasp he knew, recognised. It was a gasp of pleasure, of arousal.

'Nic…' Her voice was a low moan, an exhalation of desire.

He moved towards her. 'Shall I show you what there was between us?' he said again, and his voice was that low husk still, his lashes dropping over his eyes, mouth lowering to hers.

His kiss was velvet. Slow, deliberate, controlled, opening her mouth to his with practised ease. A moan broke from her. A cry inside her head. This should not be happening—it was not why she had come.

But she was beyond stopping him. Beyond anything except letting her clutch bag tumble to the floor to free both her hands, sliding them around the strong column of his body, feeling a release inside her as she did so, as she felt the warmth of his body beneath her sliding palms.

She said his name again and it was a sigh, a plea. A yielding.

She could not stand against it—against what was happening. She hadn't come here for this… She had come for understanding, for making peace, for—

I came for this.

The truth—the truth she'd blinded herself to—seared across her brain.

'Oh, God, Nic… *Nic!*' It was half a sob, half a

sigh, and then she was kissing him back, kissing him with a fervour, an urgency that was like a flame lit within her, a flame that was becoming a fire—hot, unstoppable, consuming everything, consuming all the world.

Everything ceased to exist. There was only this, only Nic, only his mouth on hers, his hands on her, and hers crushing him to her, his stance shifting so that she was cradled against his hard, lean hips. He wanted her. He wanted her with all the urgency with which she wanted him.

Hunger leapt in her. Her mind was a daze, a jumble of naked, desperate desire.

Nic—only Nic! Nic, who was sweeping her up into his arms as if she weighed as much as a feather, who was striding with her to another room, lowering her down upon a bed, coming down beside her. His mouth fusing with hers again.

Words came from him as he drew breath, but he did not know what. Knew only that he could not draw back. That all he wanted was here, now. With her. With Fran. Clothes were in the way—impossible, unnecessary. Must be cast aside somehow, anyhow.

Urgency filled him, drove him onwards. Somewhere in the last recesses of his sanity he knew that this was mad, insane. That this was the last thing he should be doing. But rational thought was gone, burned away completely as he found her naked body waiting for him, her eyes wide, pupils dilated, gaze blind with passion and desire.

A passion and desire that was blinding him too…

He could not resist her, and nor did he want to. He wanted only to sink himself within her, to have her body opening to his, claiming him, taking him in.

And with a cry of triumph she was his possession and he was hers. She cried out too, her legs wrapping herself around him so he could not escape.

Not until the great tide sweeping up in him—overpowering, unstoppable, gaining power as it swept, taking him over—broke in a shuddering, low-throated roar that went on and on.

He could hear the echo in her voice crying out, felt her whole body clenching around him, convulsing with cry after cry, endless and infinite, it seemed, until, after an eternity he felt his body start to slacken, and hers, the tide ebbing from him, from her, her limbs falling exhausted to the sheets, his shoulders lowering, meeting hers, folding her into him so that the frantic pounding of their hearts was pressed, one to the other, their sweating bodies fused together, collapsing into each other, breaths ragged, exhausted.

He said her name. Slurred, inchoate. Then wrapped her to him, feeling a sweeping lassitude taking him over, impossible to halt. Impossible to do anything other than say her name again and let his eyes fall shut, let sleep—post-coital, exhausted—consume him.

With Fran in his arms. The only place he wanted her…

Fran stirred. Her limbs were heavy. She moved them slowly across the fine cotton sheets. Seeking… Seeking Nic's warm, embracing body.

But he wasn't there.

Her eyes sprang open, blind for a second, then they adapted. Letting her see the bright outline of the doorway and Nic framed within it. He was wearing a white towelling robe and was quite motionless. Then he spoke.

'You need to go,' he said. He reached out with his hand, flicked a switch on the wall so that twin bedside lights came on. 'You need to go,' he said again.

She stared. There was something wrong with his face. It was as if it was carved in stone. Hands plunged into the pockets of the towelling robe, he stood four-square—immobile. She saw him take a breath, steel himself visibly.

'What just happened should not have,' he said. 'It was...' he breathed out '...a mistake.'

She could feel her heart start to beat faster within her body, with heavy slugs. It was all she could feel. Nothing else...nothing at all. There seemed to be a wall inside her, somewhere around her skull. Keeping her together. It was all that was keeping her together.

He took another breath. 'I'll leave you to dress. A car will take you wherever you need to go.'

He turned away. In her head, a cry came—his name, just his name. But she did not give it voice. Could not. Would not. She would do nothing except ease her body from the bed, find her underwear, scattered somewhere, her dress, and even her necklace, on the side table...

Somehow she dressed. Somehow she pinned up

her hair, which had tumbled wantonly over her shoulders. Her hands were shaking, and still there was the same wall around her mind. Still the hideous thumping of her heartbeat. Marching her forward, into the sitting room.

Nic turned, his eyes on her. Eyes that were blank. He bent to pick up her fallen evening bag, handed it to her wordlessly. His face was set, a nerve ticking at his jaw.

She took the bag, not letting her fingers touch his, slithered her sapphire necklace into it. Murmured a low 'thank you', not meeting his eyes. She walked towards the door and he opened it for her. Only there did she turn her head briefly, so briefly. Her throat was as tight as if barbed wire were around it.

'Goodbye, Nic.' There was no emotion in her voice. She would not permit it. 'I won't trouble you again. You have my word.'

Then she turned away, crossed to the elevator, its doors standing open, stepped inside. The doors closed, and Nic was gone from sight.

Gone from her life.

Finally gone.

Behind her, Nic went on standing, motionless, staring at the closed doors of the elevator. He had sent her away. It was what he'd wanted to do. Needed to do. Surfacing from that post-coital slumber to the realisation of what had happened had been like waking up with a punch to his guts. Slamming home to him just what he had done. The impossibility of it.

You need to go.

Go back to the world she came from, to the person she was—Donna Francesca, the person he wanted nothing to do with.

Nothing.

It was the only thing that made sense. Because sure as hell emotion scythed through him now, knifing in his eyes. Nothing else made sense. And not, above all, the sudden yawning emptiness inside him. That least of all.

CHAPTER SEVEN

FRAN WAS HURRYING past the majestic elevation of King's College Chapel, shivering in the chill east wind blowing up from the Backs. Was it the cold, or was she sickening for something? She hadn't felt right for over a week now.

Her thoughts hollowed. A bug was the last thing she cared about assailing her. Far, far worse was the desolation inside her.

How could I have let it happen? How could I have let myself? Let Nic?

Her thoughts sheered away, but their echo hung in her head like a weight she could not move. The clutch of nausea came again. She should have cancelled this luncheon engagement she was hurrying to, but it was too late now. Cesare would be waiting for her.

Still in the UK, he'd driven up to Cambridge with Carla, who was at the Fitzwilliam, interviewing an art specialist there, and had suggested he and Fran meet for lunch. Fran had found it hard to say no, yet she was deeply reluctant.

She was in no mood for socialising. No mood for

anything except burying herself in her work, wanting only to immerse herself in it, block out everything else. Block every memory, especially the one that was trying to seek entrance—the one she must not allow entrance to.

Her mind sheered away again. She glanced across at the imposing frontage of the colleges, all so familiar. A sense of claustrophobia assailed her. Cambridge seemed to be closing in around her, and apart from her work she had no time for it any more. She no longer found the antiquity, the archaic traditions—from the meticulous formality of High Table to the endless rivalries between the colleges—as appealing as she had once found them, as an undergrad thrilled to be accepted into this ancient seat of learning, these hallowed halls. Since then she had spent too long in the USA, enjoying the freedom there.

Memory clutched at her again—of just what freedoms she had found in the States—and sheered away again. It had not been academic freedom she'd been remembering.

No, don't go there! Don't go anywhere at all except the present—today, now. Meeting Cesare for lunch, even though she didn't want to. Didn't want his shrewd gaze on her, seeing her agitation, wondering at the cause of it. Coming up with a reason for it.

Cesare was not an easy person to hide things from, and the last thing on earth she wanted was any replay of his warning to her about Nicolo Falcone.

The nausea came again, putting Cesare and her reluctance to meet him out of her mind, making her take a steadying breath that did not steady her. Her breasts felt tender, her abdomen distended. As if she were pre-menstrual…

She frowned, confused. Her cycle was regular, and PMS usually hit only a couple of days before her period, which wasn't due for a week. So why—?

She stopped dead. Her hand flew to her mouth, eyes widening in horror. No—no, it couldn't be! It just couldn't! Memory racked her—a memory she didn't want to have, but had to make herself have. That night that should never have happened!

He used protection! Dear God, he must have used protection! He must have!

But she could remember nothing—nothing except the white-out passion that had blinded her, consumed her.

A smothered cry broke from her. With a gasp, she started forward again, changing direction, plunging into the shopping area of Cambridge. Desperate to find a chemist.

How she got through the next two hours she didn't know. Somehow she coped with lunch. Cesare must have seen how distracted she was, but thankfully he made no observations on it, was his usual urbane self.

Only once, when she answered him at random, did he pause and ask if she was all right. She made a face, said she was coming down with a bug and changed the subject to something about how her mother and sister were in the throes of preparations for Adrietta's lavish engagement party—to which, of course, Cesare and Carla had been invited as family friends.

Then, at the end of the meal, as she was getting to her feet, Cesare drew back her chair for her. Her nerves totally on edge, she fumbled for her handbag, managing to knock it to the floor. It spilled open, and instantly she bent to retrieve the disgorged contents, exclaiming about her clumsiness, urgently stashing away the tell-tale item she'd purchased from the chemist on the way here, desperate to head home and use it.

Desperate to discover whether she was panicking unnecessarily.

'Francesca!' Cesare's voice was shocked.

She wheeled about, clutching her handbag to her chest as if to hide it from X-ray vision. But one look at Cesare's expression told her it was too late.

She threw her head up. 'It's none of your business, Ces!' she said furiously.

His face tautened, and she was sorry she had spoken so sharply.

She took a ragged breath. 'Yes, I know you're protective of me! You've said so before! And I've told you it isn't necessary!'

His dark eyes rested on her. 'If the test is positive are you going to tell him?'

He did not say *Falcone*, but she heard it all the same. She bit her lip, unable to reply, and into the silence Cesare spoke again.

'A father has a right to know, Francesca.'

She shut her eyes, anguished. 'Ces, *please*, I can't talk about this! I don't even know what the test will show.' There was a weariness in her now, that dragged her features into misery. 'All I know, believe me, is that if it is positive, it will not be welcome news to him.'

He did not reply, but his expression was grim as they left the restaurant. On the pavement he turned to her. 'A father,' he said, and there was a sternness in his voice that steeled his expression, 'also has an *obligation* to know—'

She cut across him, agitated, wanting only to stop this ordeal. 'There may not be anything *to* know! And this is *my* situation, for *me* to deal with. *If* there is anything to deal with at all.'

But within the hour, as she stared at the blue line forming on the small white stick, she knew, along with the numbness that was filling her whole body, her whole disbelieving mind, that there was, indeed, a situation for her to deal with.

Nic was back in Rome. The Manhattan launch had been a triumph, putting the latest, most glittering addition to the Falcone portfolio on the map. New money attracted new money. And if the Falcone Manhattan proved to be the last place old money wanted to be seen at—well, he wasn't interested in old money.

Or in those who had it.

His mouth tightened. No, not in anyone who had old money. Or titles just as old. Even if they came with blonde hair down to the waist and a beauty to light the night sky with.

No. The guillotine sliced down. Fran was out of his life. She had to stay out. Anything else was impossible.

I want nothing to do with anyone from her world—nothing.

He swore, pushing back his chair, striding to the window, gazing out at Rome blindly.

You have to forget her. You have to. You have to want *to forget her...*

The phone on his desk rang and he snatched it up. It was his PA.

'You have a visitor, Signor Falcone.' She spoke diffidently. 'He has no appointment, but…' her voice became even more diffident '…it is Il Conte di Mantegna…'

She trailed off.

Nic stilled.

'Show him in,' he said. He dropped the phone, thoughts racing. None of them good.

As the door opened, and his PA admitted his totally uninvited and unexpected visitor, Nic stood poised on the balls of his feet, perfectly balanced. With part of his mind he realised he was in a ready pose—the stance that every fighter took on just before the first blows lashed out.

Cesare di Mondave, Il Conte di Mantegna, who enjoyed an entrée everywhere in Rome—including, so it seemed, the HQ of Falcone International—walked in. The very way he walked put Nic's back up—as if the whole world belonged to him and always had.

'Falcone,' said Cesare, his eyes resting on Nic.

They were unreadable, and Nic kept his likewise.

'Signor Il Conte,' he returned. His voice was neutrally impassive. Eyes veiled. Watchful. Senses on high alert. Muscles primed.

A flicker of what might have passed for humour showed in the Conte's face. 'I'm not here to fight with you, Falcone,' he murmured. His eyes skimmed over Nic's face, as if trying to read him. 'You might want to sit down,' he said.

'Might I?' replied Nic, doing no such thing. Adrenaline, the kind before a fight, was sharp-set in him.

'Yes,' said Cesare and, uninvited, took possession of the chair in front of Nic's desk. Nic threw himself into his own chair, swinging it back to stare at Il Conte, his hands gripped over the arms. Muscles still tensed. What the hell *was* this?

He soon found out.

'I'm doing you the courtesy, Falcone,' he heard Cesare di Mondave say in cool, clipped tones, 'of assuming that you have absolutely no knowledge of what I am going to tell you.'

Nic's eyes narrowed. They were very blue. Very hard. 'Which is...?'

Dark, unreadable eyes rested on him, and Nic realised the man was steeling himself to speak.

A second later, he knew why.

'Are you aware, Falcone,' he heard Cesare di Mondave ask, with sudden tension in the cool, clipped tones, 'that Francesca—' he took an intake of breath '—may be pregnant?'

The breath left Nic's lungs as if a vacuum had sucked it out of him in one gigantic inhalation.

'What?' The word shot from him, propelling his body forward so that he was pressing down on the arms of his chair.

'You don't deny the possibility?'

There was something in Cesare di Mondave's voice that registered in Nic and told him that he hadn't been sure of what he'd announced.

Nic's face hardened. Inside his head chaos had taken over. But his voice, as he spoke, was edged like a blade. 'Do you really imagine it is any of your business?'

Now it was Cesare's eyes that narrowed. 'Donna Francesca will *always* have my protection,' he bit out. 'Which is why I'm here.' His expression changed. 'So, now that you know, you can do what you are required to do.'

Chaos was still raging in Nic's head. But he couldn't pay it any attention—not right now. Right now his adrenaline was running and his opponent was in his sights.

'And what, Signor Il Conte di Mantegna, do you think that is?' His hands had tightened over the chair arms—tightened with a deadly grip.

Then suddenly, moving with a lightning speed that Nic had not expected, Cesare was on his feet, the palms of his hands slammed down on the desk in front of Nic. Eyeballing him.

'If you need me to tell you, Falcone, then I'd sooner throw you out of the window right now! Leave you to the street dogs to eat!' He straightened. Looked down at Nic. 'You've got twenty-four hours before I tell her I've told you. She's in Rome today. At her parents' apartment.'

He walked out of the room. Behind him, at his desk, Nic very slowly sat back in his chair. The adrenaline had drained out of him. He hadn't the strength to move—not a muscle. In his head, the seething chaos suddenly was not there any more. In its place was only one thing. One emotion. One urgency.

He snapped his hand forward. Reached for his phone. 'I need an address immediately!' he bit out to his PA. 'The Rome residence of the Marchese d'Arromento. Right now!'

Fran was on her laptop, drafting her resignation to her professor. She could not continue at Cambridge, nor even stay in Europe at all. Urgency impelled her. Her mind was too distracted to think about work, which was why she'd come here, to her parents' Rome apartment, after the ordeal of attending Adrietta's lavish engagement party, where she'd forced herself to appear carefree for her sister and parents' sake.

But Cesare had been there too, with Carla, and grimly Fran had known that because she had not told him the pregnancy test had been negative he had realised that the opposite was true.

Instinctively, her hand glided to her stomach. There was nothing to indicate the profound, irreversible change that was happening in her. On the surface she looked just as she always had. It would take weeks for her pregnancy to show.

It's like starlight...taking light years to reach us. So long that some stars have burnt out by the time their light reaches us.

Her pregnancy would be like that—she would be long gone before it showed.

Emotion rippled through her. But eventually, like starlight, the baby would arrive. Arrive and have to be coped with, with all the implications thereof. And the first, overwhelming implication was the one that she had known right from the very beginning.

I can't tell him. I can't. It doesn't matter what Cesare said. Nic couldn't have made it clearer that he wants nothing to do with me.

No, she could not tell him.

Heaviness, as if there were a weight crushing her, pressed down upon her. All she could do was what she was doing. What she was going to *have* to do. To go as far away as she could, make a new life for herself and her baby. Because there was no alternative.

The heaviness pressed down even more. She shut her eyes, trying to bear it.

The doorbell was ringing. She heard it. Wanted it to stop. Ignored it. But it went on. Insistent. Intrusive.

She hauled herself to her feet and walked out into

the hallway of the lofty high-ceilinged apartment. Her parents had a maid, but Fran had given her the day off, wanting only to be alone.

She reached to open the security locks of the double front door, then opened one side of it.

And slumped against the other side.

It was Nic.

He strode in, shutting the door behind him with a snap as she backed away. His eyes swept over her.

'Is it true?' he asked.

She stared, blinking at him. 'Is what true?' she said dimly. Faintness was drumming in her, a deluge of emotion swamping her.

His voice was terse. 'That you're pregnant.'

She stilled, turned to stone except for her eyes, which were dilating. 'How—?'

'Mantegna—he's just been to see me!' He bit out the words.

To tell me what I need to do—which he did not have to tell me. Which I knew from the very instant he said those words.

He could feel his guts twisting, feel so much more. A storm of emotion he could not deal with, like a tempest in his head. And then, slicing through him, came the sight of her swaying.

Fran felt the blood drain from her, dizziness pumping over her. She heard Nic give an oath, and then he'd closed the space between them, taken her arms, her weight against his shoulder.

He was guiding her through into her parents' opulent drawing room, with its gilded furniture, hand-blocked wallpaper, oil paintings on the walls. Was setting her down on a silk-upholstered eighteenth-century sofa. Standing in front her. Tall, overpowering. Demanding the truth.

The truth she had kept from him. Concealed. Because what would be the point in telling a man who did not want her that she carried his child? A child he would not want.

Through the stab of emotion she cursed Cesare for his interference.

Nic was speaking again, towering over her, demanding an answer.

'Tell me!' Something flashed across his face. 'I need to know!'

She took a breath like a razor in her lungs. A razor that cut through the emotions storming inside her—emotions that weren't relevant. That got in the way of what she must say.

She lifted her eyes to his, making herself meet that demanding gaze. Steeling herself to speak.

'No, Nic, you don't need to know. And I didn't *want* you to know—what would be the point?'

She got to her feet. She would do this standing. Say what needed to be said. Keep all emotion out of it. For what use was emotion in such an impossible situation?

With a strength she called upon from a place she had not known she possessed, she spoke, making her voice clear.

'Nic, what happened in the States was a passing

romance for both of us. We both knew that. And what happened in London was a mistake.' Her lips pressed together. 'We both know that too—you said as much to me, and I agree.'

She said the words calmly, as if calm was what she was feeling. She saw his face close.

'A mistake that has had consequences—' His voice was terse, clamping down on any other possibility.

She cut across him. 'Consequences that *I* shall cope with.' She lifted her chin, meeting his eyes head-on. Not flinching or floundering. Saying it straight out. 'Nic, I'll be living in America. You won't be troubled by me. I give you my word.'

With biting mockery she heard herself say what she had said to him that nightmare morning when he'd thrown her out of his bed, his life.

She took a breath, ploughing on. 'I'll be a single mother, and that will be fine. I'll probably work part time. I don't need a salary to live on. I have income enough of my own—a trust fund that was set up by my father when I was born. So you see—'

A hand slashed down through the air, silencing her.

'No. That will not be happening.' Nic's eyes were like sapphires, blue and hard. 'What will happen is that we shall marry.'

Fran stared, stopped in her tracks. 'You can't be serious…' The words fell from her, hollow and disbelieving.

'And *you* cannot think that I would say otherwise!' He shifted his stance, taking a breath. Emotion was churning in him—emotion he could make no sense of.

She was still staring at him as if he were mad. As if he'd said the last thing she had expected him to say.

With an effort, she spoke. 'Nic, you made it clear you wanted nothing more to do with me. And now you speak of *marriage*?'

'Of course I do! Did you think I *wouldn't*?'

She shook her head. Dazed and confused and so much more. Abruptly, her legs weak, she sat down.

Nic went on standing, looking down at her. 'We'll marry and that is all there is to it. We'll have to sort out where we'll be living—if necessary I can move my base to the West Coast, if you intend to keep working, but if not then Rome would be best for me, if that suits you. We'll need to buy somewhere—a house or apartment suitable for us both, of course—but that won't be a problem, so—'

She held up a hand, consternation in her face. 'Nic, stop! *Stop!* You're making assumptions, taking it for granted that I— That we—'

His face hardened. 'Nothing else is possible,' he said tightly.

Emotion seared in him. *Because no child of mine will be born a bastard, as I was, even if it means I have to marry a woman I would never want to. A woman who represents everything I detest.*

He could hear the words in his head, hear himself incise them into his brain.

She was speaking again, and he made himself listen through the emotions searing through him.

'Nic, give me *time*.'

He slashed a hand through the air. 'We don't *have* time. You need to accept that we must marry as soon as possible.' His eyes flashed darkly. 'Make whatever arrangements you require.'

Whatever those were, he did not want anything other than a quick, private wedding, to get them legally married. His face set. At some point he would have to meet the precious Marchese and his Marchesa—her parents. His expression hardened. Not to mention all her aristocratic English relatives as well—like that gilded *ragazzo*…the young lordling knocking back champagne at Viscari's damned party. How many more of them were there? Dozens, probably. All those aristos were related to each other, so Italy would be crawling with them as well.

Her voice cut off his vicious thoughts. She was standing up again. Facing him off.

'Nic, listen to me. *Listen*.'

Fran's voice was like a knife, cutting through him.

'I am not going to marry you. There is no *need* for it.'

He stared at her. 'There is *every* need,' he ground out.

For one long, endless moment they stared at each other, the tension between them palpable. Then, out of nowhere, he felt his emotions change.

She carries my child. It grows within her. Invis-

ible—but there. Binding me to her. And her to me. Beyond all that separates us.

He felt another wave of that emotion he could not explain except by thinking of the child, *his* child, growing within her, silently and invisibly.

He took her shoulders suddenly and felt her flinch, as if she had not expected it. Through the fine wool of her sweater she was warm beneath his touch. He caught the scent she was wearing and it lingered in his senses. Everything about her had *always* lingered in his senses.

His eyes held hers, lifted to his with confusion in them…uncertainty. Well, he would be certain for both of them.

'Fran…' It was the first time he'd said her name since their time together, all those long months ago—months during which he'd wanted to put her behind him, into the past where she needed to be.

But she wasn't in the past any longer. Because of his own madness that night when she'd come to him, his madness and his weakness, she was in his present and in his future.

He said her name again. Without the honorific. The honorific he did not want her to have. Then took a breath, his hands still closed over her shoulders.

'We can make this work. We can and we must.' He said what had to be said, in spite of what she had indicated with everything she had done since she had discovered she was pregnant with his child: the decision she had made to keep it from him, making assumptions about him that were not hers to make.

And now she was indicating with every proviso she put to him how little she wanted what she was going to have to do. What they were *both* going to have to do.

'I know it won't be easy, or straightforward. But it must be done.'

She looked at him sadly. Something seemed to have gone out of her, and there was defeat in her eyes now. 'Neither of us want this, do we?'

He didn't answer, and he didn't have to. She knew his answer. Knew it from his veiled eyes, from the sudden pressure of his hands over her shoulders. Those strong hands that had once caressed her body to ecstasy…

She tore her mind away. This was not the time or the place to think of that. She felt her heart start to hammer and stepped aside from him, making his hands fall away. She felt unsteady on her feet without them, but she ignored it.

'I think you should go now, Nic,' she said tiredly. 'We both need time to…to come to terms with this.'

He did not move. 'But you accept that we have no option but to marry?'

She heard that word again, floating in the gaping space between them—unreal, so unreal, impossible to contemplate, whatever he said.

But face it she must.

He saw her tense her jaw, swallow. 'I—I suppose so.'

Defeat was still in her voice. It cut at him—just as it had when she had walked out of the elevator, as if turned to marble, after he had ordered her to leave him alone.

And now he was back at her side, and neither of them had a choice about it. Both had to accept what neither of them wanted to. Because there was nothing else to be done *but* accept it.

She ran a hand wearily over her forehead. 'I don't know what to think...what to do.'

'For now, nothing. Rest. We'll talk more this evening...make plans.' His voice was brisk, businesslike.

Her expression changed. 'Nic, not tonight. I can't. I'm meeting Cesare and his wife for dinner. It's all arranged.'

The blue eyes flashed. The word *Cancel!* hovered on Nic's lips, but then his expression changed.

'Then I'll come too,' he announced.

There was an edge in his voice. That damned Cesare could put up with his company. And it would declare to Il Conte—and the world—that he and Fran were a couple now. Whatever her aristocratic friends and relations thought about her marrying a jumped-up *nouveau riche* billionaire, bred in the backstreets of Rome.

Fran was staring at him, her thoughts jangled. Maybe Nic *should* come tonight—maybe they needed to behave like an engaged couple, if that was what they were, what they would have to be now. And who better to start with than Carla and Cesare? Her mouth twisted. After all, it had been

Cesare who'd sent Nic here, so he must have wanted this outcome to his interference.

And is this what I want? Nic forcing himself to marry me? Me forcing myself to marry him? Is this really what I want?

She felt emotion churn within her with a sickening sensation. Felt herself steel herself in response. Maybe it didn't matter what she felt about it—maybe Nic was right—maybe marrying each other was the only thing to be done…

'So, what time do you want me to collect you tonight?'

She focussed her thoughts away from the enormity of even contemplating marrying the man in front of her—the man who had thrown her out of his bed, told her he wanted nothing more to do with her, and yet was now telling her they should marry.

'Um…about eight, if that's convenient? I'm meeting them at eight-thirty, and the traffic is always fiendish.' A thought suddenly struck her. 'Nic, it's at the Viscari. Carla always patronises it. But surely you won't want—?'

He gave a grim smile. 'I'll cope,' he said tightly. He slipped his hand inside his jacket pocket, drew out a card. 'This has my mobile number on it. Or my PA will put you through wherever I am.'

She took the card with nerveless fingers. 'I'd better give you mine as well,' she said.

We don't even know each other's phone numbers but we're going to marry each other.

A bead of hysteria at the enormity of what she

was agreeing to formed in her throat. But then he was handing her another card to write on, and a pen to use. She recognised the make—custom-designed and exorbitantly expensive. Like nothing that Nic Rossi, who worked in security at a hotel in Nevada, could ever have aspired to.

She felt something rip inside her—a memory being torn up, its ragged shreds to be whipped away by the desert wind, lost for ever…

Handing back his pen with the card she'd written her phone number on, and taking his in exchange, she made herself look at him.

He isn't Nic Rossi. He never was. He's Nicolo Falcone, a billionaire who's forcing himself to marry a woman he doesn't want to marry just because she mistakenly got pregnant by him.

She felt her throat tighten and forced it open. What good was it to think of that? To remember the man she'd thought he was…the man he'd never been?

'Until tonight, then,' she said.

Donna Francesca speaking to Nicolo Falcone.

He took a visible breath as he stashed his pen, and the card she'd written on.

'Until tonight,' he said.

Then he strode from the room, from the apartment, and was gone.

Leaving behind the woman he was going to marry for the sake of the child she was carrying. For no other reason.

The words seared across his brain, etching their truth into his consciousness.

CHAPTER EIGHT

'THE VISCARI.' NIC'S instruction as the car pulled away from the kerb outside the Marchese d'Arromento's Rome apartment was curt.

His driver glanced round at him, as if questioning the instruction.

'You heard me,' Nic said, his tone grim.

He hadn't set foot in the Viscari Roma since walking out all those years ago, refusing to kowtow to the pampered stripling who'd been handed on a gilded plate the managerial post Nic had worked so hard to merit.

Beside him sat the reason he was now going to walk back in.

She'd slid into the back seat, murmuring a stilted, low-voiced greeting, but since then had said nothing. As the car moved into the infamous Rome traffic Nic looked across at her, taking in the chic but understated cocktail frock—a couture number, he saw at a glance—the elegant coil of her chignon at the nape of her neck, a double row of antique pearls looped over her bodice, matching pearl drops at her ears. Every inch La Donna Francesca.

Memory pierced him of how he'd critiqued the dress she'd been wearing that first evening he'd set eyes on her as suitable for an academic dinner, but not doing full justice to her breathtaking beauty.

Well, the dress she wore now certainly did do her justice, but he would have given a fortune to have her back as the woman she'd been then.

But she never was that woman. She was always La Donna Francesca, whatever she told you.

He cleared his mind. No point thinking about that...no point remembering what had been, or never been. No point doing anything but addressing the situation they both faced now: Nicolo Falcone marrying Donna Francesca di Ristori.

'Have you thought any more about our wedding?' he said abruptly.

Fran's eyes flickered to him. 'Not really,' she said.

It had been impossible to think about anything coherently. She'd spent the day in a kind of daze, still trying to come to terms with what she had agreed to do. It still seemed impossible, unreal—as unreal as going to dine at the Viscari with Nicolo Falcone.

She'd texted Carla to tell her that Nic would be with her that evening. She had added nothing more. Presumably Cesare would have informed his wife of his high-handed interference in her life. Now they could cope with the results. Starting with having dinner with both herself and the man she had, so it seemed, agreed to marry.

Her dazed thoughts whirled confusedly in her head. Finding no rest.

'Obviously you have the pick of any of my hotels,' Nic was saying now. 'Unless you want to be married from your home?'

He realised he had no idea where that was. Some *palazzo* or *castello* somewhere—but where? He would have to look it up. There would be plenty of information on her family if he consulted the genealogies of the Italian nobility. It was a world he didn't know and wasn't interested in. Had no sympathy with.

'No.' She shook her head. 'My sister's getting married there next year—a huge affair. I think one of your hotels sounds better. Maybe abroad?'

She shouldn't have said 'abroad'. Instantly in her mind's eye was the Falcone Nevada, an oasis of luxury, lapped by the desert, where she had taken Nic to be one of his own employees, taken off with him for the road trip that would change her life for ever. That had brought her to this destination now.

The tearing feeling assailed her again.

'What about the Caribbean?' Nic was continuing. 'I've got a good few there you can choose from.'

'I'm sure any one of them will be fine,' she answered.

She didn't mean to sound dismissive. It was just that the very thought of standing beside Nic, becoming his wife, seemed beyond unreal.

'I'll…um… I'll look them up on the internet,' she went on, trying to sound less blitzed.

The car was gliding up to the imposing frontage of the Viscari Roma. Nic climbed out, opening the passenger door for Fran, who got out gracefully.

Nic's eyes went to her. He felt his stomach clench, as it always did whenever he looked at her. *Per Dio*, how beautiful she was.

He crushed the reaction down. He was not marrying her for her beauty, but for the baby she carried.

The doorman was coming forward, his eyes registering exactly who it was walking into his employer's flagship hotel. A caustic smile tightened Nic's mouth. Fran seemed unaware, turning towards him.

'We're meeting Cesare and Carla in the cocktail lounge,' she said.

Nic's eyes were sweeping around the lobby, going to the service door behind Reception that led down to the basement where he had first worked—the lowest of the low, the humblest employee of all. As he went forward towards the cocktail lounge, which opened off the lobby, his face was set.

It stayed set as they approached the Conte and his Contessa. The former got to his feet, greeting Fran with a kiss on her cheek, and then turned to Nic.

'Falcone,' he said, and held out a hand to him.

For a moment Nic was motionless. Then, wordlessly, he took the outstretched hand. After all, had the illustrious Conte not wanted him to be here with his ex-fiancée he would not have deigned to inform Nic that there was any requirement to call upon Fran that morning.

'Signor Il Conte,' he acknowledged.

The handshake was brief. Cesare's hand was slim,

but strong for all that, in Nic's larger hand. Then the Conte was introducing his wife, whom Fran was already greeting cordially.

'Contessa,' offered Nic dutifully.

He could see the Contessa's eyes were alive with curiosity. A dramatic brunette, her looks were a striking foil to Fran's pale blondeness, and her dress in dark cerise was a vivid contrast to Fran's eau de Nil. He wondered in passing whether he had ever seen her here at the hotel when he'd worked here, for she was, after all, Vito Viscari's late uncle's stepdaughter.

Nic and Fran took their seats and the Conte resumed his. For a moment there was silence, as if the full impact of just why he was there with his host's former fiancée was pressing upon them all. Then a waiter was there, the Viscari emblem blazoned on his shirt.

'Campari and soda, please,' Nic heard Fran say.

And as he heard it memory thrust into his head. It was the very drink she'd ordered that night he'd homed in on her. Was she remembering it too? He thought she was, for she suddenly paled.

He ordered a martini for himself and then sat back, crossing one leg confidently over the other. He was here in the Viscari Roma—enemy territory—and he was socialising with Il Conte di Mantegna, who had once thought to marry the woman that he, Nic, was in fact going to marry.

And no way—no way on God's earth—was Nicolo Falcone, who had dragged himself from slum kid to billionaire by his own efforts and had had *nothing* handed to him on a plate, going to do anything but own the evening.

'Francesca and I are trying to decide where to have our wedding,' he said, addressing his hosts, taking control of the conversation from the off, wanting nothing unspoken about why he was there. 'At the moment the Caribbean is the front runner. I have several properties there to choose from.'

'That sounds very romantic,' the Contessa said brightly, sipping at her drink.

It wasn't the best word to choose, and it hung awkwardly in the air.

Fran stepped into the gap. All the long-learned habits of social correctness slipping into gear. 'I don't really know the Caribbean,' she mused. 'How different are the islands?'

It started, as she'd hoped, a conversation—very civil, very anodyne, and completely masking the inherent strain of the situation—about the variety of islands to be found in the Caribbean. All seemed perfectly fine places to get married. Perfectly lovely. Perfectly acceptable. Perfectly—

Fran ran out of words to describe the place where she and Nic were likely to join their lives together. Unexpectedly. The word was utterly inadequate to describe the situation, as the prospect had only become real that morning.

Emotion jolted through her, but she pushed it aside. Not the time, not the place.

However, the subject of the Caribbean served its

purpose and got them to the point of having menus discreetly handed to them. A discussion about food then followed, which got them through some more of the evening and was in turn followed by a discussion about which wines to choose.

A sommelier glided up to help them select the best from the extensive cellars the Viscari Roma had to offer its guests.

Nic glanced at the sommelier and recognised him. He raised a brief hand in casual greeting. 'Pietro—*ciao*.'

The other man's eyes flickered slightly, but all he said was, 'Good evening, Signor Falcone.'

Nic knew why, and acknowledged his professionalism. But there was no way he was going to blank this man he'd worked with when both of them had been juniors. Pietro in the kitchens and Nic as general dogsbody, his strong physique making him ideal for shifting furniture, unloading delivery lorries, and doing any other heavy lifting that was required.

He smiled. 'How are Maria and the children?'

Pietro had married his sweetheart—one of the chambermaids—and babies had swiftly followed.

Pietro nodded, but only as any member of staff might do to a guest. 'They are all very well, Signor Falcone.'

Nic's smile widened. 'I'm glad to hear it.'

He could see that Fran was looking at him, her gaze questioning. The Conte was looking as if the conversation were not taking place. His Contessa was observing with a look of lively curiosity on her face.

'Remember,' Nic went on addressing his erstwhile fellow staffer, 'if you ever want a change of scene from Viscari let me know—'

Tactfully, Pietro said nothing.

Nic's gaze swept back to his hosts. 'Pietro and I go back a long way. We both started work here at the same time, as teenagers,' he said.

The questioning look on Fran's face deepened. She was about to speak, but a voice behind Nic pre-empted her.

'Here to poach my staff now, Falcone, as well as my garden designer?'

Nic turned, not rushing the movement. He'd half expected this approach. His eyes glinted sapphire. 'Only if they want to improve their prospects—as I did,' he returned with pointed acerbity.

Vito Viscari did not deign to reply to that. Instead he simply went on, his cultured voice cool, his eyes watchful. 'And *is* headhunting the purpose of your patronage tonight?' he probed.

His body's stance radiated whatever the opposite of welcome was. Nic was only too aware of that. But before he could reply, he heard the Contessa interject.

'Vito, I left a message for you. Obviously you never picked it up.' She spoke casually, but there was a determined brightness to her voice. 'Signor Falcone is here with Francesca.'

Vito's cool gaze was suddenly sharp. 'Is he?'

'Yes,' corroborated Fran, knowing it was time to defuse the situation. She lifted her chin. 'I do hope that won't cause any problems, Vito?' Her question was as pointed as Nic's comment had been.

Vito smiled—a tight smile, but a smile nevertheless. It was a professional smile, Nic could tell instantly—one to use with an influential and favoured guest as, of course, was Donna Francesca di Ristori.

His own hackles were rising, just as they always did when he encountered Vito Viscari. The only time they had not done so had been during those heady days a year ago when, armed with half the Viscari shares in his back pocket, he'd been able to stride into Viscari board meetings, and throw down a list of prime properties he intended to move to the Falcone brand.

A familiar stab of anger flared in him. Thanks to Vito's mother-in-law his triumph had turned to ashes. Nepotism had struck again, balking him of his due.

'Not at all,' Vito was saying now, in reply to Fran.

As if belatedly aware that one of his sommeliers was waiting to discuss their wine for the evening, he nodded across at Pietro.

'I'm interrupting—my apologies,' he said. His eyes went back to his guests. 'Enjoy your evening,' he said, his smile warmer now as it encompassed the three people whose presence in his hotel he did *not* begrudge.

He walked away and Nic heard the Conte putting a question about a certain wine to Pietro, who immediately got involved. Nic left him to his discussion, aware that Fran wanted to speak to him.

'I didn't know you once worked *here*,' she said.

That air of puzzled questioning was still in her tone of voice, her eyes, and Nic knew she was remembering that conversation they'd had in the motel by the desert lake, and him telling her how he'd got his start in life. He felt more memories push at him, seeking entrance—memories of everything else that had happened at that humble lakeside motel.

He crushed them from him. Returned to the moment in hand. Pietro had left them, to find the wines selected for their evening.

'Yes, my first job was here, at sixteen. Right after the police made it clear it was either get work or be charged for assault for beating up the man beating up my mother.'

He was addressing the Conte and his Contessa now, not caring if he shocked them.

It didn't shock Fran, hearing me tell her that.

The thought was in his head even as he saw Il Conte's features tighten and the Contessa looking taken aback.

Then she rallied. 'So you came to work here? I'm glad,' she said. 'My stepfather, Guido Viscari, was always keen on giving disadvantaged youngsters a start in life.'

'Oh, yes,' said Nic dryly, 'he certainly was happy to give us a *start*—providing we knew our place and kept to it.' *Like never aspiring to race up the management ladder ahead of his precious nephew.*

'Evidently he did not succeed in your case,' Cesare murmured dryly.

Nic's eyes flashed to his. 'Evidently not,' he agreed, with a tightness that was acerbic.

Then the maître d' was coming up to them, murmuring to Il Conte that their table was ready for them. Dutifully, they all got to their feet.

Fran, Nic could see, had an introspective air about her. He held out his arm. 'Shall we?' he said.

With a little start she rested her hand on his arm, and they followed behind the Conte and Contessa into the opulent dining room beyond the bar. It was the lightest of touches but he still caught her scent, a delicate, expensive fragrance, and felt it pluck at him.

He almost turned to look down at her and smile, but then his attention was caught by another diner, whom he recognised as a society journalist who ran a diary column in one of the upmarket dailies. The Contessa had clearly spotted him too, and Nic recalled that she was some kind of journalist as well.

He watched as the Contessa murmured something *sotto voce* to her husband, resulting in a brief nod from him.

'It was inevitable.'

He caught Il Conte's reply, and knew what he was referring to.

He bent his head slightly towards Fran. 'It seems we may make a news item tomorrow morning,' he warned her.

Fran gave a little start again, and the Contessa explained. 'He won't be waspish. I know his style. But he will,' she went on, 'definitely speculate.'

'He may also feed the news to his colleague on the

finance pages, given that it is Nicolo Falcone dining at the Viscari,' Cesare contributed.

Fran shut her eyes for a moment. She did not relish reading about herself and Nic in the morning papers.

I should have foreseen this.

Rome was such a hive of gossip, with everyone buzzing about what everyone else was doing, and who they were doing it with. Since living in the USA she'd forgotten just what a fishbowl it was. Belatedly, it dawned on her that the other diners here might well see her too, and speculate as to why she was here with Nicolo Falcone. And that might reach her parents.

I don't want them to find out like that. I have to tell them myself.

She gave a sigh, opening her eyes again. Letting her gaze go to Nic.

But he isn't Nic, is he? He's Nicolo Falcone, a man rich and powerful enough to provoke the interest of journalists.

'He's welcome to do so,' she heard him say, and there was a coldness in his voice that belonged to the billionaire hotelier, not to the man she had once known.

The arrival of their first course was a welcome diversion, and conversation returned to innocuous topics. Fran was grateful. Cesare, she could see, was exerting himself, though there was inevitably an air about him of what could only be deemed unconscious hauteur. Beside him, Carla was being her usual incisive and forthright self.

But it wasn't her hosts who drew her attention. It was the man at her side.

Nic.

No, not Nic—Nicolo Falcone.

Her eyes flickered to him. That same overpowering impression she'd got of him in that disastrous exchange in the elevator at the Viscari St James's slammed into her. The laid-back, easy-going man she'd spent those glorious days with in America was gone. This was a man of formidable achievement, of huge wealth, of the power and self-assertion that went with that. A man who scarcely smiled…

Memory flashed through her of that slashing smile like a desert wolf, crinkling the vivid blue eyes, warming them on her…

She blinked and it vanished, and there was Nicolo Falcone once more, making some impatiently scathing comment about the latest government delays in respect of the topic they seemed to have moved on to—Italy's earthquake warning system. It was a subject Fran knew was of keen interest to Cesare, whose medieval *castello* was deep in the Apennine fastness, much prone to earthquakes.

'I considered opening a mountain resort there at some point, but it's just too risky,' Nic was saying.

'A pity—the area needs inward investment,' Cesare replied.

Nic's eyes flickered. Had that been intended as a criticism of him?

'Something that surely is the responsibility of the landowners?' he asserted.

Did aristocrats like Il Conte assume their effortlessly inherited wealth was there to spend on their own pleasures, not on the vast patrimony they possessed?

'Indeed,' acknowledged Cesare, and Fran could see his air of unconscious hauteur heightening. 'And I make considerable investment in the local economy of my estates,' he replied. 'My family has done so for centuries.'

He reached for his wine, the candlelight catching the gold of a signet ring incised with his family crest—a crouching lion, ready to attack. Nic felt his hackles bristle in response, just as they had when Vito had strolled over to challenge his presence on his territory.

It was Vito's step-cousin who spoke now. 'I hope you will visit Castello Mantegna one day with Francesca,' Carla said brightly. 'It's absolutely magnificent! For me, of course, the particular appeal is the artworks.'

She launched into a catalogue of her husband's collection and Fran joined in, making some remark about how she had enjoyed seeing them when she had last been there.

Then she halted. The last time she'd been to Cesare's *castello* had been when she had just become his fiancée. She had visited with her parents and siblings to celebrate their forthcoming union.

And now it's a completely different man I'm going to marry. Going to have *to marry.*

She felt emotions pulling inside her, tugging in

different directions like ropes knotted inside her. Unconsciously she ran a hand over her abdomen. Unbelievable to think that silently, invisibly, a child was growing there—a child that would be both hers and the man's beside her… Uniting them.

Can anything unite us, though?

The question was unanswerable, impossible, and it hung silent in the space between them.

'Are you all right?' Nic's voice was suddenly low in her ear.

There was concern in his voice. But it was not for her, she knew. It was for the baby she carried—his son or daughter.

Impulsively she seized at the opportunity he'd presented with his enquiry. 'I do feel tired,' she admitted. 'It's been a long day…'

She let the sentence trail. 'Long' had not been the problem. Weariness washed over her.

'Perhaps I could just have coffee and skip dessert,' she said.

It was what they all did, and Fran was grateful. Grateful too for the desultory conversation that limped on, with Carla doing her best to be bright and Cesare still exerting himself. And Nic… She gave an inward sigh. Nic was still broadcasting on all frequencies that he was no longer the man she'd known.

At last the evening came to an end. It had been an ordeal—she could only call it that. Weariness assailed her, but it was a weariness of the spirit.

As she climbed into Nic's car she gave a sigh.

'What is it?' Nic's voice was taut as he sank heavily down beside her. His mood was grim.

Fran looked at him. 'I'm just not used to you being—well, who you really are.'

'Do you imagine it isn't the same for me?' he answered, and she could hear the edge in his voice that she had heard there for most of the evening.

She did not reply—what could she say?

'So, having got through an evening with the illustrious Conte di Mantegna and his Contessa,' Nic was saying now, that edge still in his voice, 'at what point will you be presenting me to your parents?'

Her expression flickered in the streetlights as the car made its way back to her parents' apartment.

'I'll need to tell them first,' she said. 'And I must make sure they don't hear it from any wretched gossip columnist!' She gave another sigh. It was all so complicated. So difficult. So—

Impossible—that's what it is.

But it didn't matter that it was impossible. It had to be done.

She took a breath. 'I don't know when. Sometime this week I must head back to Cambridge. But maybe I can go via Milan and stop off at home first. Or maybe—'

'I could drive you.' Nic cut across her. 'And you can tell them with me there. There's no point prevaricating. The sooner the better. It has to be done.'

She shut her eyes. Yes, it had to be done—it *all* had to be done. She had to tell her parents, arrange a wedding somewhere, anywhere—it didn't matter—and Nicolo Falcone had to become her husband and—

Her thoughts cut out. It was impossible to think any further ahead.

They reached her parents' apartment and Nic helped her out. To her relief, he merely saw her to the door.

'Come for lunch with me tomorrow,' he said. 'I'll send a car to collect you.'

She shook her head. 'I don't want to eat out, Nic. Tonight was bad enough.'

His face tightened as they stood on the pavement. 'We need to talk. There are arrangements to be made.'

'Then come here for lunch,' she said.

He nodded, and they agreed a time. Then he was climbing back into his car, nodding at the chauffeur, and the car was heading off again.

Wearily, Fran went upstairs. This time last night she had thought she was to be a single mother, and now…

'Come through into the dining room. It's just cold meat, bread and salad—I hope you don't mind. I always give the maid time off when I'm here. I don't need her.'

Fran led the way from the wide entrance hall into a room Nic had not seen the previous day, but it was similar to the one that he had seen. The same antique furniture—inherited, of course, not purchased, as his was at his headquarters and at his hotels—oil paintings on the wall, an abundance of silverware and porcelain. All the accoutrements of an aristocrat's town apartment.

His mouth twisted unconsciously.

A simple meal was set out on a long mahogany table. White wine was chilling in a cooler, and there was fruit on the sideboard.

He took the place Fran indicated. She was not wearing couture clothes today, just a pair of elegantly cut trousers and a pale green shirt with a white stripe running through it. Her hair was caught back in a switch, and she wore no make-up. It was impossible to tell that she was pregnant.

For a moment—just a moment—Nic found himself wondering whether he should ask for confirmation of her pregnancy. He frowned.

Maybe it was a false alarm...maybe I don't have to go through with this after all.

'What is it?' Fran's voice was cool as she directed the question to him, sitting down opposite him at the table and reaching for a linen napkin.

Nic started. Had she read his mind? No, for she was continuing in the same cool, challenging voice.

'Do you disapprove of something?' She lifted her hand to indicate their surroundings.

Nic heard the challenge in her voice—a coolness that had never been there with him before.

Into his head came a moment from their very first encounter at the bar in the Falcone Nevada—the way she had challenged him to name three astrophysicists to corroborate his blatant hook-up line that she did not look like the stereotypical image of one.

There had been humour in that challenge. Amusement. Engagement with him.

There was none of that now. Now she was simply Donna Francesca, expressing her displeasure at any criticism of her father the Marchese's choice of décor.

He shook his head, his expression shuttered. 'It's very elegant,' he said.

'It's old-fashioned,' she admitted, 'but I like it. It hasn't changed much since my grandparents' time. Or even before theirs, I suspect,' she added, trying to make her voice lighter.

But it was an effort to do so. Yet again into her mind shafted memories of how she had once been able to chat effortlessly with Nic, yet now she was conscious of the awkward restraint between them, making all conversation stilted. Laborious.

She indicated the spread on the table. 'Help yourself,' she said.

Memory shafted in her yet again—they'd had picnics en route several times on their road trip, stocking up at small town supermarkets, pulling over at viewpoints, eating out of paper bags…

She crushed the memories back. Those carefree days were gone. Now there were grimmer things to sort out.

'I think you're right about the Caribbean,' she said, watching him help himself to freshly bought rolls and multiple slices of ham and salami, remembering how hearty his appetite had always been, to feed that powerful frame of his.

She dragged her mind away from such memories, away from how his smooth-muscled torso had felt beneath her gliding fingertips.

'We should marry there, at one of your resorts.' She paused. 'But on our own.' She paused again, made herself look at him. 'It would be easier for my parents and…' she swallowed '…since you don't have any family—'

She broke off. That had been tactless. His glance at her was mordant, shuttered.

'Suits me,' he said, beginning to eat.

It was a laconic reply, but nothing like the laid-back way he'd spoken to her in America. This registered…*indifference*. A verbal shrug indicating how unimportant it was to him.

She blenched. Struggled on. Pushed a helping of salad around her plate. She wasn't hungry in the slightest. Just nauseous.

And not because of her pregnancy.

'It's going to be difficult for them, Nic. I can't help that. A shotgun wedding is never what parents want for their children.' She gave a heavy sigh. 'And an unintentional pregnancy is never ideal in the first place,' she finished.

Blue eyes lifted, skewered her. Anger was suddenly spearing through him.

'Did I *ask* you to come to me that night in London?'

The words stabbed from him and found their

target. Fran blenched again as they impacted. He stabbed again.

'Don't blame *me* for your predicament. You're as responsible for this as I am. I made it clear to you that I did not want to continue our...*acquaintance*—' his mouth twisted on the word '—yet you persisted.'

His voice was icy—as icy as it had been in that elevator, telling her to make no further contact with him. She gave a cry, dropping her fork. Crested silver, he noticed absently.

'I'm *not* trying to blame you. I'm simply saying that no one should *have* to marry for the sake of a baby that wasn't planned.' She shut her eyes. Misery filled her suddenly.

Dear God, however were they to make this marriage he was insisting on work? It was impossible.

'Nic, it's *you* going on about getting married—not me!' Her eyes flew open again. 'I *told* you I was OK with being a single mother—'

'Well, I am *not* OK with that.'

His voice was grim and tight. He pushed his plate away. All appetite had left him. Hell, what a damnable mess this was. He stared across at the woman opposite him, his eyes hard. The woman he did not want to *have* to marry. The woman who came from a world he rejected and despised. The woman who so screamingly obviously considered it a massive problem for her, and for her precious aristocratic family, for her to be marrying *him*, a jumped-up slum kid.

His eyes targeted hers. She had paled, her face whitening, and for a moment—just a moment—it cut him to the quick. But then words were being spoken, and he could not call them back.

'You *will* marry me, Donna Francesca.' He deliberately used her title, incising each word so she could not mistake them. 'Because I will accept nothing else. I will hear no more about single motherhood.' His eyes were narrow shards of hardest sapphire. 'Tell your parents whatever you want—it's no concern of mine.'

He got to his feet, tossing aside his unused napkin—white damask, monogrammed.

'My only concern—my only *possible* concern—is for the baby you carry. Nothing else.'

He strode from the room, heart pounding. Emotion thundered in his ears. Deafening him to everything else in the universe.

Behind him Fran sat shaking, staring blindly at the abandoned meal. It had been a disaster.

Emotion wrenched in her, crushing and tearing. This was never going to work.

CHAPTER NINE

NIC THREW HIMSELF back into the chair behind his desk in his office, his face still thunderous. But his anger was at himself now. How had he lost it like that? What help was that? To let rip as he had?

He swore, descriptively and crudely, and was glad no one could hear him.

Yet for all the anger targeted at himself for losing his rag like that, and the guilt that he had done so to a pregnant woman, he knew that his hackles were still up. And he could find no way to lower them.

He didn't want to marry her.

Correction, I don't want to marry the woman she is—Donna Francesca di Ristori! Who comes with a whole baggage train of relatives I want nothing to do with, who'll be appalled and dismayed at her marriage to me.

His face tautened. It was who she was that was the problem. The very person she was….

In his head, fleetingly, like smoke from a campfire, memory caught. Once she had not been that person. Once she had been someone quite, quite different.

He pushed it away. She had never been that person—*never.* She had only ever been the person she was. The person he deplored, wished with all his being she was not.

Grimly, he stared out into the emptiness of his office, at the papal splendour he'd acquired second-hand, with money. In his mind's eye he saw the Marchese's grand apartment, resplendent with historic inherited possessions, each one ramming home to him the difference between them—between the Marchese's daughter and the self-made billionaire from the back streets of Rome.

Privilege—the privilege of birth and an effortlessly inherited right of wealth and nobility and social prominence, taking it all for granted.

That was *her* world. Not his.

Roughly, he reached for his computer, flicking it on. What point was there in dwelling on what could not be changed? He had work to do.

His mouth twisted and he started to bury himself in the day's business.

How long he worked he was not aware. He was aware only that his PA was coughing nervously at his office doorway.

'Signor Falcone, there is a visitor.'

His head lifted from his focus on his screen, brows beetling. A sense of *déjà vu* hit him—how his PA had a mere forty-eight hours ago announced the illustrious Conte di Mantegna, who had come strolling in to blow his world apart.

'Who?' he demanded tersely.

'Dottore Ristori,' his PA said cautiously, reading his grim mood.

Nic stilled. OK, so she wanted to play it that way, did she? Pretend she wasn't who she was.

He sat back in his chair, curtly indicating that she be shown in.

Fran walked in, still in the same outfit she'd had on when he'd arrived at the Marchese's apartment. But her face was set and strained.

'I need to talk to you,' she said without preamble.

He'd risen to his feet automatically and now came around his desk, indicating the pair of gilded *fauteuils* that flanked a small ormolu table where he received his informal appointments. He became conscious that he was feeling as warily constrained as he had been when her ex-fiancé had walked in as if he owned the place.

His expression closed, guarded, he waited to hear what she had to say. Giving nothing away until she had spoken.

She sat herself down on one of the chairs, set her handbag on the delicate table. He took the other chair. For a moment, a measurable passage of time, she said nothing. But her face was still drawn.

Something moved in Nic, but he quelled it. He wanted to know what she had to say.

A moment later she had said it—and it silenced him.

'Why do you hate me so much now, Nic?'

The words fell into the space between them.

He stiffened, and frowned. Whatever he had been expecting, it had not been that.

'I don't hate you.' His voice was clipped and tight.

She shook her head, rejecting his denial. 'Nic, your hostility to me is radiating off you like a star going supernova. I might think it's just because I'm pregnant, and the news is as unwelcome to you as I always knew it was going to be. Which is why I'm cursing Cesare for interfering, telling you what I knew you would not want to know. But it's not just that, is it? It's been like that ever since Cesare and Vito did their *Begone, lowly peasant!* routine on you at that wretched roof party.'

She took a razored breath. It had taken all her nerve to come here and confront Nic like this, but she was making herself do it. If their marriage—*if* it ever happened!—was to have *any* chance at all, she had to confront him now, not let it fester.

I won't have that! I won't have him bristling at me, blaming me, resenting me.

'So tell me, Nic. Tell me to my face. Why are you so damn *angry* with me?' She took another shuddering breath, leaning forward now. 'That night you blame *me* for—I *wasn't* damn well throwing myself at you. All I wanted, Nic, was to make peace with you. Because, like I said to you at the time, we had parted friends. So I don't see why discovering that *both* of us have other identities has made everything so damn difficult between us. I want you to explain that, Nic, I really do.'

She fell back, breathless, lungs heaving.

He'd heard her out, but she could see in the tense, taut features of his face that a nerve was ticking at his cheekbone, indicating the self-control he was exerting. She didn't care—she was beyond caring. She'd forced herself here and now she wanted answers. Answers she hadn't got that night at his hotel. She wanted to give a hysterical laugh. The night that had resulted in her presence here now.

He looked at her. Looked with those blue, blue eyes that had once poured all his hot desire into hers, but now which were as chill as Arctic ice, as remote as the upper layers of the atmosphere before it dissipated into black frozen space.

'It's very simple,' he said. 'I don't like who you are.'

She stared at him. 'I don't understand...' she said faintly.

He gave a rasp in his throat. 'I don't like everything you stand for!' he spelt out. 'I don't like the world you come from. I don't like the world *any* of you come from. I don't like your precious ex-fiancé, the illustrious Conte di Mantegna, and I don't like the man his wife is related to—that pampered playboy Vito Viscari, who had *everything* handed to him on a plate without working for it, without effort, without anything other than being born to it. I don't like anything about that world and I want nothing to do with it. But I'm going to have to.' His voice hardened. 'Because I have to marry *you*.'

She was silent, hearing him out. Then, in a low,

emotional voice she said, 'I can't help who I am, Nic, any more than you can.' Her gaze flickered. 'And if you want my reply, I can tell you something as well.' She took a breath. 'I don't like the man *you* are, Nicolo Falcone. I don't like him at all, and I don't want to marry him.'

She got up, her hand splayed over her abdomen in an instinctive protective gesture. She could feel her blood surging in her veins, feel adrenaline pushing it around, and there was a tightness in her lungs, a sickness in her very being.

She looked at him. He hadn't stood up when she had, and he seemed to be frozen in his seat. Her eyes rested on him. It was strange… He looked so like Nic, the man she had known long ago. Nic Rossi, with his easy laugh and his laid-back charm and the teasing humour in his smile. But he wasn't that man at all.

'We're strangers,' she said quietly. 'And strangers should never marry.' She took a breath. 'Goodbye, Nic.'

Her hand pressed on her body, where their baby, secret and silent, lived and grew. She would have to sort something out eventually, but not now.

'We'll share custody, Nic—somehow, when the time comes. But I can't cope with that right now. I can't cope with anything.'

She looked at him, and something like a shard of glass pierced her. She did not let herself feel it.

'I'm going now,' she said. 'Please don't try and stop me.'

He didn't. He let her go. Let her walk out of his office, his space, his life.

Taking their child with her.

And he could not move. Not a muscle.

CHAPTER TEN

FRAN CLIMBED INTO the hotel shuttle bus at San Francisco airport. It had been a long flight, and it had come after a gruelling few days. She had flown out of Rome the very afternoon after confronting Nic, not able to bear to stay longer, then landed at Stanstead, taken the bus to Cambridge.

She had spoken to her professor the next morning, telling him she had to leave as soon as possible for urgent personal reasons. Replied to the email sitting in her inbox, accepting an invitation to an interview for a research position at a university in Southern California that she'd applied for when she'd discovered she was pregnant by a man who did not want her.

Her throat tightened unbearably. Now it was *she* who did not want *him*. Not the man he was.

And now, it seemed, with bitter irony, it was *he* who wanted *her*—or rather the baby she carried.

He was still determined on them marrying. And to that end there had come a slew of emails from him, and text messages, and voicemails, and calls she had ignored just as she'd ignored all his other attempts to communicate with her.

Because she knew what he was saying. The first message from him had said it all.

You're emotional—I understand that. But we can't leave it like this. When you've calmed down we can talk. For now, I'll leave you in peace. Then I'll come and see you in Cambridge and we can sort things out. We have no choice but to sort things out.

She'd deleted the message. And all the others. Only as she'd sat in Departures at Heathrow had she texted him. One final text before boarding.

She had flown quite deliberately to San Francisco. She had somewhere to go before she headed for LA. Somewhere she *had* to go.

As she checked in to her hotel, hearing the familiar American accents all around her, hearing herself being called Dr Ristori in the way she was used to here, she felt a sense of familiarity, of ease.

It comforted her.

But it brought memories too. Memories that she could not keep out. Memories that came of their own volition. That brought their own pain with them. It was a pain she would have to bear now. Memories of a tall, powerfully built, sable-haired guy with blue, blue eyes and a smile like a desert wolf.

Who was lost to her for ever.

And there was only one place to bear that. The place where she was going now.

* * *

Nic stared at the words on the phone screen as if they made no sense. But then, they didn't. They didn't make sense at all.

Nic, I'm not going to marry you. It would be a disaster for both of us. Neither of us is who we once thought we were. You aren't the man I remember, and I am not the woman you remember. We are better off without each other. Please don't try and make me change my mind, because I won't. I can't. We have well over half a year to sort out things like access rights. I'm sure we can come to a civilised arrangement. For now, I can't cope with that.

He kept reading the words, re-reading them. But still they made no sense. How could they? The imperative of their marriage was paramount. Except... His eyes rested on the words on the screen. For her, that imperative was absent.

We are better off without each other.

He read the words, read them again. Something was building in him. Something he didn't know, didn't recognise. But it was powerful. As if pressure were building up inside a volcano—a volcano that had been consigned to dormancy. Mistakenly.

His eyes moved back to the sentence that came before.

You aren't the man I remember.

He felt the pressure mount within him. His phone was ringing—his PA—but he lifted it only to slam the receiver down again. His focus was on the words, only on the words. And on the sense of pressure building in him. On the words that came next.

I am not the woman you remember.

And the pressure inside his head burst, flowing through his consciousness like lava racing down a mountainside, consuming everything in its path. He was remembering the woman he had once thought her to be. Remembering in absolute coruscating detail every single moment of their time together.

And with that came a realisation, blasting through everything else.

His phone rang again, and this time he snatched it up. 'Charter a plane to Cambridge, England—*now*!'

Fran was deplaning again, this time in Las Vegas. To walk out of McCarran had been to feel her throat spasm, as if she could see herself there in the summer heat, backpack on one shoulder, that last hurried kiss with Nic…

The rental car she picked up was no luxury SUV. Thoughts flashed through her of how she'd been so concerned that Nic had blithely helped himself to a hotel vehicle to take off in—and how that other security guy had greeted him on their return from the desert sunset.

'Evening, boss.'

'He's on my team,' Nic had explained casually.

Yes, you might say that—you might also say that your team ran to thousands of people all around the world.

And all the time he was Nicolo Falcone, and I never noticed...

Getting out of Vegas occupied her mind, and she was glad to hit Route 15, out of the city, heading north-east. She would need to break her journey, stop off overnight, but that should be no problem. The problem would come later—closer to her destination.

Winter was closing in, and though she'd checked the forecast, and it had been sufficiently clement, snow would stop her in her tracks.

She drove on, determined to make her destination. Expression set.

Nic was throwing his weight around. He knew it and didn't care. That was what it was for. He was shamelessly using a mixture of arrogant imperiousness and calculated charm to get the information he wanted. *Needed.*

His eyes flashed blue fire. *Where the hell was she?*

Because she wasn't in Cambridge. Her departmental secretary was looking at him apologetically. 'You've just missed her, I'm afraid. She's gone to California—for an interview I believe.'

He strode off, claws clenching inside him. Then his phone was in his hand, and he was straight through to his own security team at his Mayfair property.

'I need you to trace someone,' was his terse command.

It was a simple order, but it took a frustratingly long time for the answer to get back to him. And when it did it stopped him in his tracks. Then galvanised him with the very first emotion he'd felt since he'd opened her email, in which she had refused to marry him.

Something that he could clutch at.

Hope.

Fran heaved a sigh of relief. The snow had not come, the road was still open, and day tickets were still available. She drove on between the dark conifers, all signs of habitation long gone, and then finally she was there, leaving the car in the almost deserted car park, making her way to where she wanted to be.

To remember what had never happened. What now never could.

She sat on one of the many benches, huddled into the ski-jacket she'd bought en route, her feet warm in the solid boots she'd also bought. The cold nipped at her, and she glanced at some of the few hikers, even more warmly clad than her, ready to go backpacking even at this time of year.

The sky above was leaden, but that did not spoil the view.

Ten miles across. Ten miles to where she had stood in the summer heat. She sat and gazed across the unbridgeable distance from there to here, to where she was now. Here at this point in her life.

We can't go back. We can't get back to what has gone. That time has past.

Wasn't that what she'd told herself in all those months since then? She told it to herself again—because she must. Because there was no alternative. This journey here, now, had been for one reason only. To finally say goodbye to that time. To finally let it go.

To let Nic go—the man she had come to say goodbye to.

Silently her hand went to her abdomen and she spoke to her unborn child, who still seemed so unreal, but who was there, secret inside her. Her voice was low, but clear in the cold air, here where there was no one else but the hikers starting their descent. So she spoke aloud the words she needed to say. To the child she needed to say them to. About the man she needed to say them for.

'I've brought you here so I can tell you, in years to come, that I made it here. But only on my own—only with you. And I want you to know that on that far side of here, ten miles away, I once stood—but not with you. I want you to know, my son or my daughter, that it was the most important time of my life. But I didn't know it then.'

She had thought herself alone, unheard by anyone but the tiny being growing within her.

But she was wrong.

A voice behind her spoke.

'And no more did I know it.'

A gasp broke from her. Instant recognition of that deep, gravelled voice, charged with so much.

She slewed around. Felt faint suddenly with shock. With so much more than shock.

It was Nic.

CHAPTER ELEVEN

FRAN'S EYES LEAPT WIDE. She got to her feet, impelled upwards. 'How—?' The most banal of questions. The most irrelevant.

He walked towards her. Like her, he was enveloped in a ski-jacket, thick boots on his feet, crunching on the stony path.

'My security team found you,' he told her. 'They're good at their job.' He took a breath. 'I was always glad you assumed I was one of them.'

'You *let* me think that,' she countered.

Her mind was reeling, but it was impossible to say anything else. Nic—*Nic,* here? It made no *sense.*

'Just as you let me think things about you.'

She gave a sigh. 'It was what we both wanted at the time.'

'Ah, yes,' said Nic. His hands were plunged into the pockets of his jacket. 'At the time.' He paused, his eyes resting on her. 'And now? Now what is it that we want?'

She let her gaze slip away, and there was sadness in her voice. 'Different things. Impossible to reconcile. You're forcing yourself to marry me, and I don't want that. I don't want to marry a man who hates everything about me. A man I don't like for that very reason.'

'Is that so?' A studied neutrality filled his words. As if he were balanced on the point of a sword so sharp it could slice away his life with the merest slip.

'Yes!' There was vehemence in her voice—there had to be. How could she be standing here, thousands of miles from Rome, and Nic be standing here too? Having this conversation. A conversation that was a waste of time, of effort.

A waste of so much.

Emotion burned in her throat. Made her words sound as if they were wrung from her. 'Oh, Nic, you shouldn't have come here. It serves no purpose. It changes nothing. You're still Nicolo Falcone and I'm still Donna Francesca. We're strangers to each other. Strangers who deplore what the other is—strangers who by mistake have created a child between them, but strangers still.'

He nodded. He was keeping himself under control, because it was essential to do so. Just as it had been on his journey here—on the flight to Salt Lake City, closer to here than San Francisco, gaining him time on her, and then on the pedal-to-the-metal drive south, guided only by what his security team had uncovered.

She'd never flown to LA. She'd flown via San Francisco instead, then taken another flight to Vegas. Picked up a hire car there. Asked the clerk about winter closures, revealing her destination. Giving him the chance to get here in time.

To say what he had to say.

On which so much hung.

More than I ever knew. Could ever know. Until she walked away from me.

'Yes,' he said now, his tone still measured, his hands plunged deep into his pockets, where she could not see them clench with the exertion of the emotion that it was so essential to keep from her.

For now—or else for ever.

'Yes, strangers. The aristocratic Donna Francesca and the *nouveau riche* Nicolo Falcone.' He took a breath, felt the cold air rushing into his lungs. 'But there are two people who *aren't* strangers.'

He paused again. He had to get this right. He had only one chance, and on it everything depended. *Everything.*

'Two people,' he went on, his eyes never leaving her, 'who met as strangers but parted as lovers. Nic Rossi and Doc Fran.'

Doc Fran. The sound of his affectionate name for her rang in her ears, clutched at something inside her. She wanted to cry out, but was silent. Silent as she stood there, unable to move, unable to do anything but hear his words, as still he spoke to her.

His eyes were fixed on hers, willing her to listen. To believe. Believe what he was telling her, what he *must* tell her. His voice took on an intensity that caught at her, made her take a breath in.

'Fran, why—*why*—when we first met, do you

think we never told each other who we were? Why did we want to be the person each of us presented ourselves as being? Because,' he spelt it out now, finally, urgent to make her understand, 'we didn't want to be weighed down by the rest of who we are! We wanted to be free of that.' She must understand him, surely she must—

Her eyes were widening, wondering, taking in his words. Letting them make sense inside her.

Then she heard herself answer him.

'Here in the USA I've never had to be *Donna Francesca*,' she said. 'I could just be…myself.' She looked at him. 'The person I would have been but for an accident of birth. With no expectations on me to marry a man like Cesare, to be his Contessa, fulfilling my mother's dreams instead of my own.'

He nodded slowly, his eyes never leaving hers, filling with new self-knowledge. 'I liked it that you thought me just one of the security team. It meant I didn't have to be Nicolo Falcone, endlessly proving the world wrong about me. Proving I could outsoar Viscari.'

Her expression changed. She was reminiscing. 'I remember how you said it was defeatist to accept the universe as it is.'

His blue-eyed gaze drifted across her face. 'I remember the fire in your eyes as you talked to me about the stars. The passion in your voice.' His expression changed again—changed to one that started to melt the bones in her body. 'And not just a passion for the stars.'

She gave a smothered cry, backing away. 'But that's gone. You made it clear enough that night I came to your hotel.'

His eyes flashed. 'I was telling Donna Francesca.' He took a shuddering breath, making himself say what he knew now was the truth. The truth he had tried to twist into knots inside him. 'I used it—used your being Donna Francesca—to send you away.' He shook his head slowly, as if clearing something from it. 'But that wasn't the reason. I was lying to myself—to you.'

His mouth set and his gaze turned inward.

'All my life,' he said slowly, finding the familiar thoughts that had controlled him all his life hard to put into bare, bald words, 'I have feared being as my father was—a man who left my mother pregnant with me. It was why I was so insistent that we marry. All my life I have vowed I would not be like him. And the simplest, surest way to not be like that was never to let any woman close to me. So I would always part from women, thankful to do so, thankful they had not come to rely on me, to hope for what I dared not offer them. And that,' he said, 'is what I did with you—as I have with all the other women who have passed through my life.'

His face worked.

'Except you were never like any of those women. Right from the start you were different.' He paused. 'Special. Like no other woman I've known.'

He took another breath.

'So when I saw you again, that night in London—

saw you again when I had thought never to do so—all I knew was an overwhelming rush of something I had never felt before, never allowed myself to feel. You made every other woman in the world disappear for me. And that showed me…' His voice changed, dropped. 'Showed me the danger I was in—'

He broke off.

'I had to find something—anything—to keep you at bay. So I used the revelation of who you were as a way of doing that.'

Fran's eyes shadowed. She had her own truth to face. One that she had hidden from herself.

'I told myself that night when I came to your hotel that I simply wanted to make my peace with you—that I couldn't bear your cold rejection just because I hadn't told you the truth about myself, because I'd seemed so friendly with Vito Viscari. But I was lying to myself. I know that now. I came to you for one reason only.'

Her voice changed, became charged with intensity.

'I came to you because the first emotion that leapt in me when I saw you again was *joy*, Nic. Overwhelming joy. And I wanted to find you again—the Nic I'd known here, in our time together. That's why I came to you that night…the true reason that I blinded myself to.'

Emotion filled her, full, and choking, so that she could hardly breathe. Could not look at him.

She walked away from him, moving to the low wall that separated the terrace from the rough ground beyond, where it started its precipitous plunge a mile deep into the earth. She gazed out across the gaping distance to the rim so far away. Where once they had stood together, hand in hand.

But now…?

The question hung in the air—hung in the great gap of space that yawned over the plunging canyon.

Nic spoke behind her quietly, his voice low. 'We never made it here, to the North Rim, did we?' he said. He paused, and in the silence stretched all that he had come here for. 'But we're here now.'

She did not answer—could not. He came to stand beside her and she felt the powerful sense of his presence at her side.

'We're here now,' he said again.

And still she could not answer.

He spoke again, in that quiet, deep voice.

'What are names? Nic Rossi or Nicolo Falcone. Doc Fran or Donna Francesca. What are names compared with who *we* are? And why…?' He drew a breath. 'Why should they imprison us? Why should *we* imprison ourselves? Why should I let my poor mother's fears be fulfilled in me? Why would I be as faithless as my father, abandon my own child as he did? If I think it's defeatist to stick with the universe as is, then it's even more defeatist for me to think I would be like my father.'

He took another breath, drawing cold air into his lungs.

'Because of that I let you go, telling myself it

was the right thing to do. And I did not seek you out again.'

Fran spoke, finding the words to say. 'I thought to make contact again, but I couldn't find you—and you had made no contact with me. I had to accept it was over. That I had to move on. I told myself you had been the confirmation of my decision not to marry Cesare. Told myself that because letting go of Cesare had been easy it would be just as easy to let go of you, too—'

She broke off.

'It wasn't easy. *Isn't* easy.' She looked at him, her face strained. 'It wasn't easy to tell you I wouldn't marry you.'

She sensed his body, so close to her but not touching, tense.

'So why not ask yourself *why* it isn't easy?'

The question came from him. Not accusing. Only setting it between them. Needing an answer.

She could not give one. For tears were spilling, silently, and she could not stop them, could do nothing but stand there, full of so much she could not speak of.

Silence netted them. Silence and the chill wind blowing down from the north.

Nic spoke. His eyes fixed on the far horizon to the south.

'Your answer is the same answer I will give,' Nic said, in that quiet, deep voice. 'The answer that brought me here to join you, to where you, too, have come. For the same reason I have come here, giving the same answer to the same question. Come here to the destination we never made it to on our road trip together.'

There was a sudden unbearable tightening in his throat, and as if of its own volition, his hand reached for hers, meshing their fingers tightly.

'The destination we've reached now. Here…' He paused. 'Together.'

A sob choked from her, impossible to stifle, to deny, as impossible to stop as it was to stop her fingers clutching at his, crushing them with hers, desperate and clinging. Instantly his own grip tightened on her hand and he swept her bodily into him. Folding her to him as she wept against him, sobs racking from her, breaking free at last of all that had held them back, bringing to her a release that flooded through her.

He let her weep, cradling her against him, his strength supporting her in her storm of tears.

His arms tightened about her as words broke from him. 'Don't leave me. I can't bear it if you leave me.'

The cry came from deep inside, from a place he'd never acknowledged could ever exist. But it blazed within him now.

She couldn't speak—not in words. But her hands clutched at his body, convulsing over the thick material of his jacket.

'Fran, *this* is us. This is who we are. We knew that, felt it when we were together, but we did nothing about it. We let life take us in different directions. But we should never have let that happen.'

He was guiding her forward, sitting her down on the bench she'd leapt from at his approach, lowering himself down beside her, his arm still around her shoulder. She buried her face in his chest, tears still streaming uncontrollably.

His mouth smoothed the golden tresses of her hair. 'Shall I say it first? Say what the truth is between us that we have been too blind to face?'

He lifted her face from his shoulder, let his blue, blue gaze pour into hers.

'You said we were good when we were together, but we were more than good. We were *right* for each other. Right as only two people who should spend the rest of their lives together are right for each other. *That's* what we had—that's what we recognised in each other but never said out loud. Well, now I *do*. I say it out loud—to you, here and now.'

He took a ragged breath, never letting go her gaze as she lifted it to his, yearning for his. He was filled with an emotion so strong it overpowered him, yet through it he spoke again. And each word bound him to her with bonds that would never break, *could* never break. Not now. Not ever.

'I know, Fran, with every fibre of my being, that you recognised that too and still do.' He paused, and she could hear the catch in his voice, felt her heart turn over at it. 'And you always will. For we have it again, and more, that rightness between us. The rightness of our love.'

He cupped her face with his hands, cradling it

between his strong, tender fingers. His eyes pouring into hers.

'The love of Nic Rossi for Doc Fran—*and*, yes, the love between the people we also are, if we can accept it in each other. Nicolo Falcone and Donna Francesca. They too can love each other now.'

His voice changed, became edged with the bitterness engendered in him long, long ago.

'I know I will hardly be welcomed by your family—a self-made, fatherless slum kid—'

Her fingers flew to his mouth to silence him. Emotion was streaming through her as strong as the dazzling radiance of the universe, joy and wonder and a rapture she had never known till now. But she had to speak. To counter what he'd just said. Set it to rest for ever.

'How can you *say* that? You're a billionaire hotelier! You could probably buy and sell my father ten times over.'

Her voice changed, became strained, and her eyes searched his painfully as she lifted his hands away, folding them within her own, impressing upon them the fearful emotion she felt suddenly.

'I don't want you despising me for an accident of birth. I can't help being who I was born, any more than you can.'

'I know that,' he acknowledged heavily. His expression became shadowed. 'But I've had to fight for everything I ever had, and I've always despised those who have it handed to them on a plate, despised everything they stand for. All that the likes of Vito

Viscari stand for. I have done right from the moment he appeared, fresh out of university and wet behind the ears, and his uncle gave him the managerial position I had worked my guts out to deserve in years of hard, unrelenting slog. Right to the moment his wife's mother gave him back the shares I'd seized from him in my takeover bid.'

She rested her forehead against the strong wall of his chest, his hands still folded within hers, feeling his heart pounding within. Then, abruptly, she lifted her head away.

'Nic.' Her voice was urgent. 'You *have* to let go of such feelings.' She guided his right hand, deliberately sliding it beneath the thick quilting of her jacket, across the soft warmth of her body beneath. She felt him start, but ignored it. She pressed her own hand over his, keeping it there.

'Our baby, Nic,' she said. 'Our baby will be born to *both* our heritages. Its grandfather will be a *marchese*, its great-grandfather a duke, and it will be heir to *your* billions. Are you going to despise *it* for the circumstances of its birth?'

She nodded slowly as she went on, his silence giving her the answer she knew he must give.

'You see?' she said softly.

She slid her fingers into his, rounded on her still slender frame within which their baby nestled, safe and protected. Growing to become the child they had created between them.

Our baby is real. Growing and living.

Wonder filled her, and a feeling of thankfulness that was an embrace to the baby deep within her.

A baby...a mother...a father. A family.

Emotion caught at her throat and she leaned into the strong body of the man with whom she had created such a miracle. A sense of peace possessed her now, after the tumult of her tears. A peace so profound and a sense of wonder so radiant in her mind, her heart, that she could scarcely bear it.

She had come here, to the destination they had never reached on that road trip that had ended before it should, to say goodbye to him. But now—ah, now—

Joy flamed in her—the same sudden blaze that had filled her when she'd seen him after all those months in London, but more...oh, so much more!

Could they really, truly be here together? United like this?

His hand was on her belly, and her hand was on his, and beneath them both the baby they had made was growing silently and secretly. For the first time she gave a little gasp of wonder. For the first time it was real to her. And as she cradled the tiny being, and he did too, for the first time she felt the wondrous reality of conception like a flower opening within her.

We've made it real. Made it real because now we are real together too! Nic and Fran... Nicolo and Francesca. And we are all the family we shall make together, when our baby is born to us.

Love poured through her—love for her baby, love

for the man she had created it with. Love that she had never known nor had thought to feel. But now it was alight in her—a flame that could never be quenched.

She lifted her face to his, all that she felt blazing in her gaze, clinging to him, their arms around each other.

'Am I dreaming this?' There was a smile in her eyes, a yearning.

His sapphire eyes burned down to hers. And in them she could see, with glory in her heart, that same emotion she felt for him. Pouring from him.

'Whatever name you call me by I am here for you. My own, my beloved, my most beautiful and exquisite Donna Francesca and my incandescent Doc Fran, who sets the heavens ablaze with her passion for them and sets me ablaze too.'

She caught his face with her hands, cupping his strong jaw, her thumbs on the mouth that could smile like a desert wolf but could also kiss with the velvet touch that had melted her from the first time he had ever taken her into his strong arms.

Her eyes poured into his. 'I told you I didn't like you, Nicolo Falcone, but that isn't true. For you are still Nic, and you always will be. Nic Rossi—the man I fell for, the man I went *Wow!* over the first time he came across to chat me up. And if I admired and respected you then…' there was a little choke in her voice '…knowing you'd made good out of the rubbish childhood you had—well, how much more do I admire and respect you for the dizzying heights you've climbed as Nicolo Falcone? You've fought such battles and won them all.'

An acerbic glint showed in his blue, blue eyes. 'I lost my takeover of Viscari,' he corrected her.

She waved it away with her hand. 'And I'm glad you did. You don't have to prove anything to him any more. Or to anyone. Let Vito have his hotels and you have yours.'

She paused for a moment, wanting to say what it was important for him to hear.

'Nic, I know from my own field that all each of us needs is the zeal to excel. I don't have to prove I'm better than any other researcher. I just have to find out that bit more about the universe than anyone knows at the time when I publish my latest paper. I don't have to resent any other researcher for doing the same with their new bit of knowledge.'

Her voice changed.

'You have nothing more to prove to Vito! Nothing more to resent in him. You've got your fabulous empire, made all by yourself, through your own efforts and talents—now just *enjoy* it.' She smiled at him. A warm, true smile. 'Let's just enjoy it *all*, Nic—everything that life has blessed us with. I've won my own battles too. I've got my research career, and it's all I ever wanted to achieve. But now—'

She broke off. Took his hand, placed it once more where their child was growing silently, invisibly.

'Now I have even more. *We* have so much more! We have each other and we have our baby.' She gave a little choke, realising another truth. 'The baby brought us back together, Nic, and that is worth more than any number of research papers, any number of luxury hotels!'

His eyes held hers, so blue, so long-lashed, so absolutely precious to her.

'My wise, wise beloved,' he said.

His hand splayed across her slow-ripening body, splayed upwards to touch the soft swell of her breasts. She felt her heart begin to quicken as his expression changed, the glint in his eyes now blissfully familiar. As blissfully familiar as it was in her own.

He said her name—a low growl now—and she lifted her face to his, her heart full, lips parting in a sigh of expectation, of fulfilment to come.

His kiss was like slow velvet, playing on her lips, opening her mouth to him, soft and sweet and sensual. She felt her pulse quicken more, and warmth spread in her body as her hand slid under his jacket to feel the muscled strength of him, so blissful to remember, to have again for ever now.

She murmured his name, felt her eyelids fluttering helplessly. She wanted only him, wanted everything he wanted, for all time.

And suddenly he was sweeping her up, leaping to his feet, whirling her around as if she were a feather, then striding off with her.

Breathless, she cried out, 'Nic! Where are you going?'

His eyes were alight with desire. With hunger for her. Urgent and possessing. 'To book us in to the lodge—right now!'

She gave another cry, half-laughing, half-rueful. 'Nic, it's closed for winter. It's day visitors only at this time of year.'

He lowered her abruptly, disbelievingly. She pressed herself against him, hugging him close. She was as light as the very air.

'We'll have to find somewhere outside the park,' she told him.

She stepped away, fishing her car keys from her purse. 'First person to reach a motel warms the bed!' she cried, and raced for the car park and her car.

He caught her before she'd even opened the door, sweeping her back to him.

'We'll take mine,' he said, brooking no argument. 'I'll send someone to collect yours. Because from now on…' his blue, blue eyes poured into hers, and what she saw in them melted her all the way down to her fast-beating heart '…wherever we go, my adored, Fran, we go *together*.'

He scooped her up, lowering her into his own hire car, then climbing in himself.

'Ready to start our next road trip?' he asked. His sapphire eyes were ablaze for her and her alone as he reached across to kiss her, to seal with her the union that they were making that would bind them one to each other, all their days. 'The one that will last a lifetime and beyond,' he said.

She gave a sigh of happiness and joy and a contentment that would never leave her. 'Let's go,' she said, 'wherever the road leads us.'

She smiled, with love in her eyes, her heart, her

very being. Nic, *her* Nic, was hers for ever. The man she knew she loved and always would.

'Together…' she breathed. 'Always together.'

He gunned the engine, turning his flashing desert wolf smile at her, the one that turned her heart over and over.

'Sounds good to me,' he said, in the laconic, laid-back way she loved so much. He headed out towards the road. 'But we stop at the first motel we find, OK?'

His glinting glance at her, so rich with bone-melting promise, brooked no disagreement.

Fran laughed. As carefree as the wind.

'Definitely!' she agreed. 'The very first.'

EPILOGUE

THE VAST GREAT HALL at Beaucourt Castle, its bare stone walls bedecked with a fearsome array of medieval weaponry, was freezing—despite the half a tree trunk burning in the cavernous fireplace to one side.

Fran and Nic, newly arrived, walked up to the elderly man standing four-square by the hearth. As Fran kissed him on the cheek, then greeted her aunt, uncle and cousins, his gimlet eyes skewered the man standing beside her.

'So,' announced His Grace the Duke of Revinscourt, 'you think you're going to marry my granddaughter, do you?'

'Yes,' said Nic.

'Hmmph! Well, you've plenty of money, so I hear, but nothing of anything else!'

'No,' agreed Nic.

'Hotels, they tell me?' His Grace expanded.

'Yes,' said Nic again.

He was holding his ground. Fran had told him to, but he'd have done it anyway. No way was he being put down. Not now. Not ever.

'And you intend to hold the wedding in one of them—is that it?'

'I didn't want to upstage Adrietta's wedding at home,' Fran put in. 'So Nic's given me the pick of all his properties.'

'She's opted for one that's on a private island in the Caribbean,' elaborated Nic.

'Caribbean? What's wrong with whatever you've got in town here? Mayfair, so I'm told—perfectly respectable!' the Duke expostulated irately.

'The Caribbean is warmer at this time of year,' Nic explained.

'Well, don't expect me to fly out there!' His Grace barked testily. 'Not at my time of life!'

'We understand that, Gramps,' Fran put in placatingly, not mentioning that that was exactly the reason her father had suggested it, knowing the occasion would be a lot more comfortable without the crotchety old Duke there. 'But we're holding an engagement party at the Falcone Mayfair, and of course we want you *there*.'

'Hmmph,' said His Grace—again. His eagle eyes skewered his prospective grandson-in-law. 'Falcone, eh?'

His eyes lifted to the lofty armorial hatchment over the cavernous stone fireplace. Above the ducal coronet carved into the stone a fierce falcon hovered. Firelight glimmered on the same image on the Duke's signet ring. Then the grey eyes snapped back to Nic. Something in them had changed.

'Well, I don't hold with signs and portents, and

I could do without you being another damned foreigner, like your father-in-law, but there it is. She'll do what she wants, this granddaughter of mine, just like her mother did. Marry who she wants and do what she wants. A doctor of astrophysics... What use is that, eh? Just like there's quite enough hotels in this world for my liking. But if the two of you want each other, that's enough. If you've come from nothing, then you've clearly got grit, and that counts for a lot.'

He shot a look towards his grandson, Harry, whose expression was a study as he tried to catch Fran's eyes and see her roll them along with his own at their grandfather's inquisition.

'And besides, this young idiot—who, one day, God help us all, is going to be running this place—tells me he's going to rope you in for rugby.' The gimlet grey eyes turned approving and he nodded. 'Definitely a forward. Just what we need.'

Harry grinned, explaining, 'Castle versus village—the annual derby. Village always thrashes us. You, however, are going to be our secret weapon!'

'Happy to be of use,' replied Nic dryly.

His hand tightened on Fran's and she squeezed it back, throwing him a covert smile. He'd come through with flying colours, just as he had with her parents. Much to his astonished surprise.

Instead of the disdain and open disapproval he'd expected, the Marchese had shaken Nic vigorously by the hand, immediately asking his advice on how to transform an unused *palazzo* he happened to own into a luxury hotel.

As for Fran's young brother, Tonio—he'd declared it 'seriously cool' to have a brother-in-law with a police mugshot on file, and he couldn't wait to tell his cousin Harry. Fran's sister, Adrietta, had promptly informed him, with her prettiest smile, that she was determined to have her forthcoming honeymoon at the Falcone Seychelles, because she'd looked it up on the Internet and it was 'positively divine'.

As for her mother, Lady Emma, La Marchesa had simply exclaimed, 'Thank heavens Francesca's agreed to marry *someone* at last!' and warned Nic not to let her daughter jilt him, as was her habit with men she was engaged to.

'No, dearest Mama,' Fran had said sweetly, dropping a kiss on her mother's cheek. 'I won't be doing that. Because, you see, I love Nic and he loves me.'

Then, taking a breath, she'd explained the reason for her rush to the altar ahead of Adrietta.

Her surprise at her mother's reaction had equalled Nic's at her father's reaction to his becoming his son-in-law. A shriek of excitement had sounded from the Marchesa, accompanied by renewed vigorous pumping of Nic's hand by her father at the news that he and the Marchesa were to become grandparents.

With shock, Nic had realised that his presence in the di Ristori family was actually going to be *welcomed.*

It was a welcome that was being extended now by her maternal relatives too.

Fran's aunt, the Marchioness, had stepped forward. 'Come along, everyone! I am *not*,' she said decidedly, 'going to freeze here any longer if you are starting on about rugby! The drawing room is *much* warmer, and it's time to toast the happy couple!'

With quiet but practised management of her irascible father-in-law, she shepherded them through to where vintage champagne was awaiting them, installing the Duke in a vast winged chair by the fireside.

As Nic and Fran started to thaw they turned to each other.

'Told you Gramps would like you!' she whispered. 'Despite his manner, he likes people who aren't cowed by him. And I do so hope,' she said, 'that you will like them all too—all my family.'

He could see the emotion in her eyes and she made a little face.

'They really can't help being aristocrats, you know.' There was a mix of humour and wariness in her voice.

'I will do my best to ignore their unfortunate origins,' Nic promised her solemnly, for he would promise her the world now—and fetch it for her too.

For a moment Fran's expression wavered, then she landed a soft fist on his chest and laughed.

Emboldened, she added, 'Now all you have to do,' she gave a wry laugh '—apart from trying *not* to refer to Cesare as "the illustrious Conte" in that sardonic tone you always use about him—is make peace with Vito Viscari.'

This time his face darkened, his eyes hardening automatically.

But Fran held her ground. 'Nic, you can't go on feuding for ever. Vito isn't responsible for his having inherited the Viscari hotels, nor for his mother-in-law buying your half back, and nor was he responsible when his uncle handed him the management job you were after, way back when. Speaking of which...' she took a breath '...I've been putting my head together with Carla and Eloise—yes, I have, so don't make that face at me.'

Nic's expression was wary. 'And what have the three of you cooked up?' he enquired.

He had a feeling he was being outmanoeuvred, but for some strange reason—probably to do with the fact that he'd have laid down his life for the woman speaking to him, so much did he love her—he let her continue. Which she did.

'Well,' she said, encouraged, 'it's this...'

Her eyes gleamed with the same enthusiasm he was so familiar with when she talked about her beloved cosmology.

'We think the two of you—you and Vito—should start an international programme of apprenticeships for disadvantaged young people, just as *you* once were, Nic, and train them in all aspects of the hotel trade. Not just things like cheffing and housekeeping, but management and finance as well. Almost like a global university for the hospitality industry.'

Nic's eyes narrowed in consideration. 'The Falcone Foundation...' he mused. He liked the sound of it. Liked the concept.

'Well, I suppose it really ought to be the Viscari-Falcone Foundation,' Fran put in.

'You mean the Falcone-Viscari Foundation,' Nic corrected her.

Fran waved a hand. 'Whatever! You two can argue it out—or each have foundations of your own, if you insist. It doesn't matter. What matters is that you *co-operate*, Nic. You and Vito. For a common goal.' Her voice changed, softened. 'It's what brought you to what you are today—a man made good. Made very, *very* good.'

There was a little choke in her voice and Nic caught her hand, pressed his mouth against it, then against his heart. '*You've* made me good, *mio amore*.'

His eyes poured into hers and hers gazed up into his. She felt her heart flowering with the love she had for him. The rest of the world disappeared.

Then a voice beside them sounded. 'Save your canoodling for later, you two love birds, and have some champagne.'

Her aunt's voice was genial, and she was handing them two brimming flutes. Then, looking at her niece, she hesitated a moment.

'Should you?' she queried. 'I had a *very* excited phone call this morning from my sister-in-law. Telling me she's going to be a grandmother.'

'What's this?' Harry sauntered up, catching the last of the sentence. 'Fran—you're *never* preggers, are you? Wow, fast work, Falcone. Still, all the more champers for me!' he said cheerfully, helping himself to Fran's glass.

Then he looked across at Nic.

'Don't overdo it on the fizz tonight, old chap. There's a training session first thing tomorrow morning—we need to see what position is best for you. Put you through your paces. Dad and I are thinking forwards, definitely, but just where is the question. I'm thinking back row, so—'

Fran silenced him with a hand over his mouth. 'Shut up, Harry,' she said amiably.

'OK,' he said good-naturedly, removing her hand. 'So, tell me more about this private island for the wedding? Sounds cool. I can't wait to party there.'

Fran laughed. 'Well, you won't be partying with us, Harry. We'll be in the honeymoon *cabana* at the far end of the island! *Totally* private,' she warned with a smile.

Her uncle was approaching, bearing a glass of orange juice which Fran took gratefully. Then the Marquess called for silence. 'I believe my father has a few words to say,' he announced.

Immediately everyone dutifully turned towards the Duke, seated as if he were enthroned.

'Raise your glasses, if you please,' he instructed, in his must-be-obeyed fashion. Everyone duly did, apart from Fran and Nic. 'And now,' he continued, in his stentorian voice, belying his years and his frailty, 'I am formally welcoming the newest member to our family. He's shown the amazingly good sense to choose my granddaughter for his wife, and for that alone I approve of him.'

A ripple of laughter went around the room.

'As for my granddaughter—well…' His voice changed, and with a sense of shock Fran realised he was suppressing emotion. 'Any man who can start with nothing and end up with a great deal more than anyone in *this* family has must have something to him. And whatever that is my granddaughter has had the good sense to see it, want it, and wish to marry him for it.'

He took a breath, held all their eyes. Then gave his toast.

'To Francesca and her husband-to-be. And…' there was a discernible note of satisfaction in his voice now '…to my next descendant—my great-grandchild!'

There was a general echoing of his toast, with much joviality, especially on his grandson's part, and then Fran was turning towards Nic. Her eyes were lambent with the emotion that she would always feel for him. Joy. Pure, overwhelming, incandescent joy.

'To us, Nic. To you and me and our precious, precious baby. Together for *ever*.'

Nic's sapphire eyes were for her and her alone. 'To us both,' he breathed. 'To us *all*.'

And then his glass was tilting against hers, and hers to his, and their toast was simple.

'To love,' they said in unison.

As it always would be, now and for all eternity.

The sun was setting over the Caribbean. Nic and Fran stood hand in hand as the priest said to them the words that would unite them in holy matrimony.

In the little open-air chapel, just behind her, Fran

could hear her mother sobbing quietly. She knew, too, that her father would not have a dry eye either. Apart from her elderly grandfather, the Duke, all her family were here, on her father's side and her mother's, and though she knew they were all here for them both, she had spoken quietly to Nic before the ceremony.

'I want this to be for your mother too, Nic—the mother who raised you to be the man you are now. Strong and courageous and determined. I want—' her voice had choked a little '—I want this to be, as well, for the father you never knew. We don't know, Nic, just what made him turn his back on you, and maybe there were reasons neither you nor your poor mother knew about, but one thing I do know…' her voice had been fervent '…is that *you* are going to be the father to *your* child—*our* child—that he should have been. *Your* child and its siblings yet to come will have a father to be so proud of. So beloved. We'll make that happen, Nic. You and I. Together. And whether our children grow up to be star-gazers like me, or hoteliers like you, or something completely different, we shall love them for all their lives. And we shall love each other too.'

Her words echoed now in his head as, with a smile, the priest said the words that every bride and groom longed to hear.

'You may kiss the bride.'

Which was just what Nic did—long and sweet and tender and passionate. And Fran, his bride, his beloved, beautiful bride, who took his breath away with every glance at her, kissed him right back as the golden glow of the setting sun bathed them both in its glorious light.

* * * * *

The Greek's Secret Son

MILLS & BOON

DEDICATION

To all care-workers everywhere. And how grateful we are to them. Thank you to you all.

CHAPTER ONE

A FINE DRIZZLE was threatening. Low cloud loured over the country churchyard and the wintry air was damp and chill as Christine stood beside the freshly dug grave. Grief tore at her for the kindly man who had come to her rescue when the one man on earth she'd most craved had been lost to her. But now Vasilis Kyrgiakis was gone, his heart having finally failed as it had long threatened to do. Turning her from wife to widow.

The word tolled in her mind as she stood, head bowed, a lonely figure. Everyone had been very kind to her for Vasilis had been well regarded, even though she was aware that it had been cause for comment that she had been so much younger than her middle-aged husband. But since the most prominent family in the neighbourhood, the Barcourts, had accepted their Greek-born neighbour and his young wife, so had everyone else.

For her part, Christine had been fiercely loyal—grateful—to her husband, even at this final office for him, and felt her eyes misting with tears as the vicar spoke the words of the committal and the coffin was lowered slowly into the grave.

'We therefore commit his body to the ground, earth to earth, ashes to ashes, dust to dust, in sure and certain hope of the Resurrection...'

The vicar gave his final blessing and then he was guiding her away, with the soft thud of earth falling on wood behind her.

Eyes blurred, she felt herself stumble suddenly, lifting her head to steady herself. Her gaze darted outwards, to the lychgate across the churchyard, where so lately her husband's body had rested before its slow procession from the hearse beyond into the church.

And she froze, with a sense of arctic chill.

A car had drawn up beside the hearse—black, too, with dark-tinted windows. And standing beside it, his suit as black as the hearse, his figure tall, unmoving, was a man she knew well. A man she had not seen for five long years.

The last man in the world she wanted to see again.

Anatole stood motionless, watching the scene play out in the churchyard. Emotions churned within him, but his gaze was fixed only on the slight, slender figure, all in black, standing beside the priest in his long white robe at the open grave of his uncle. The uncle he had not seen—had refused to see—since the unbelievable folly of his marriage.

Anger stabbed at him.

At himself.

At the woman who had trapped his vulnerable uncle into marrying her.

He still did not know how, and it had been *his* fault that she had done so.

I did not see what ambition I was engendering.

It was an ambition that had spawned her own attempt to trap him—when thwarted, she had catastrophically turned on his hapless uncle. The uncle who—a life-long bachelor, a mild-mannered scholar, with none of the wary suspicions that Anatole himself had cultivated throughout his life—had proved an easy target for her.

His gaze rested on her now, as she became aware of his presence. Her expression showed naked shock. Then, with an abrupt movement, he wheeled about, threw himself inside his car and, with a spray of gravel, pulled away, accelerating down the quiet country lane.

Emotion churned again, plunging him back into the past.

Five long years ago…

Anatole drummed his fingers frustratedly on the dashboard. The London rush-hour traffic was gridlocked and had come to a halt, even in this side street. But it was not just the traffic jam that was putting him in a bad mood. It was the prospect of the evening ahead.

With Romola.

His obsidian-dark eyes glinted with unsuppressed annoyance and his sculpted mouth tightened. She was eyeing him up as marriage material. *That* was precisely what he did not welcome.

Marriage was the last thing he wanted! Not for him—no, thank you!

His eyes clouded as he thought of the jangled, tangled mess that was his own parents' lives. Both his parents had married multiple times, and he had been born only seven months after their wedding—evidence they'd both been unfaithful to their previous spouses. Nor had they been faithful to each other, and his mother had walked out when he was eleven.

Both were now remarried—yet again. He'd stopped counting or caring. He'd known all along that providing their only child with a stable family was unimportant to them. Now, in his twenties, his sole purpose, or so it seemed, was to keep the Kyrgiakis coffers filled to the brim in order to fund their lavish lifestyles and expensive divorces.

With his first class degree in economics from a top university, his MBA from a world-famous business school and his keen commercial brain, this was a task that Anatole could perform more than adequately, and he knew he benefitted from it as well. Work hard, play hard—that was the motto he lived by—and he kept the toxic ties of marriage far, far away from him.

His frown deepened and his thoughts of Romola darkened. He'd hoped that her high-flying City career would stop her from having ambitions to marry him, yet here she was, like all the tedious others, thinking to make herself Mrs Anatole Kyrgiakis.

Exasperation filled him.

Why do they always want to marry me?

It was such a damn nuisance…

A dozen vehicles ahead of him he saw the traffic light turn to green. A moment later the chain of traffic was lurching forward and his foot depressed the accelerator.

And at exactly that moment a woman stepped right in front of his car…

Tia's eyes were hazed with unshed tears, her thoughts full of poor Mr Rodgers. She'd been with her ill, elderly client to the end—which had come that morning. His death had brought back all the memories of her own mother's passing, less than two years ago, when her failing hold on life had finally been severed.

Now, though, as she trudged along, lugging her ancient unwieldy suitcase, she knew she had to get to her agency before it closed for the day. She needed to be despatched to her next assignment, for as a live-in carer she had no home of her own.

She would need to cross the street to reach the agency, which was down another side street across the main road, and with the traffic so jammed from the roadworks further ahead she realised she might as well cross here. Other people were darting through the stationary traffic, which was only moving in fits and starts.

Hefting her heavy suitcase with a sudden impulse, she stepped off the pavement…

With a reaction speed he had not known he possessed, Anatole slammed down on the brake, urgently sounding his horn.

But for all his prompt action he heard the sickening thud of his car bumper impacting on something solid. Saw the woman crumple in front of his eyes.

With an oath, he hit the hazard lights then leapt from the car, stomach churning. There on the road was the woman, sunk to her knees, one hand gripping a suitcase that was all but under his bumper. The suitcase had split open, its locks crushed, and Anatole could see clothes spilling out.

The woman lifted her head, stared blankly at Anatole, apparently unaware of the danger she'd been in.

Furious words burst from him. 'What the hell did

you think you were doing? Are you a complete idiot, stepping out like that?'

Relief that the only casualty seemed to be the suitcase had flooded through Anatole, making him yell. But the woman who clearly had some kind of death wish was perfectly all right—except that as he finished yelling the blank look vanished into a storm of weeping.

Instantly his anger deflated, and he hunkered down beside the sobbing woman.

'Are you OK?' he asked.

His voice wasn't angry now, but his only answer was a renewed burst of sobbing.

Obviously not, he answered his own question.

With a heavy sigh he took the disgorged clothes, stuffed them randomly back into the suitcase, and made a futile attempt to close the lid. Then he took her arm.

'Let's get you back on the pavement safely,' he said.

He started to draw her upright. Her face lifted. Tears were pouring in an avalanche down her cheeks, and broken, breathless sobs came from her throat. But Anatole was not paying attention to her emotional outburst. As he stood her up on her feet, his brain, as if after a slow motion delay, registered two things.

The woman was younger than he'd first thought. And even weeping she was breathtakingly, jaw-droppingly lovely.

Blonde, heart-shaped face, blue-eyes, rosebud mouth...

He felt something plummet inside him, then ascend, taking shape, rearranging everything. His expression changed.

'You're all right,' he heard himself say. His voice was much gentler, with no more anger in it. 'It was a narrow escape, but you made it.'

'I'm so sorry!' The words stuttered from her as she heaved in breath chokily.

Anatole shook his head, negating her apology. 'It's all right. No harm done. Except to your suitcase.'

As she took in its broken state her face crumpled in distress. With sudden decision Anatole hefted the suitcase into the boot of his car, opened the passenger door.

'I'll drive you to wherever you're going. In you get,' he instructed, all too conscious of the traffic building up behind him, horns tooting noisily.

He propelled her into the car, despite her stammering protest. Throwing himself into his driver's seat, he turned off the hazard lights and gunned the engine.

Absently, he found himself wondering if he would have gone to so much personal inconvenience as he was now had the person who'd stepped right out in front of his car not been the breathtakingly lovely blonde that she was…

'It's no problem,' he said. 'Now, where to?'

She stared blankly. 'Um…' She cast her eyes frantically through the windscreen. 'That side street down there.'

Anatole moved off. The traffic was still crawling, and he threw his glance at his unexpected passenger. She was sniffing, wiping at her cheeks with her fingers. As the traffic halted at a red light Anatole reached for the neatly folded clean handkerchief in his jacket pocket and turned to mop at her face himself. Then he drew back, job done.

Her eyes were like saucers, widening to plates as she looked back at him. And the expression in them suddenly stilled him completely.

Slowly, very slowly, he smiled…

Tia was staring. Gawping. Her heart was thudding like a hammer, and her throat was tight from the storm of weeping triggered by the man whose car she had so blindly, stupidly, stepped in front of when he had laid into her for her carelessness. But it had been building since the grim, sad ordeal of watching an elderly, mortally ill man take his leave of life, reminding her so much of the tearing grief she'd felt at her mother's death.

Now something else was overpowering her. Her eyes were distended, and she was unable to stop staring. Staring at the man who had just mopped her face and was now sitting back in his seat, watching her staring at him with wide eyes filled with wonder…

She gulped silently, still staring disbelievingly, and words tumbled silently, chaotically in her head.

Black hair, like sable, and a face as if...as if it was carved... Eyes like dark chocolate and smoky long, long lashes. Cheekbones a mile high... And his mouth...quirking at the corner like that. I can feel my stomach hollowing out, and I don't know where to look, but I just want to go on gazing at him, because he looks exactly as if he's stepped right out of one of my daydreams... The most incredible man I've ever seen in my life...

Because how could it be otherwise? How could she possibly, in her restricted, constricted life, during which she had done nothing and seen nothing, ever have encountered a man like this?

Of course she hadn't! She'd spent her teenage years looking after her mother, and her days now were spent in caring for the sick and the elderly. There had never been opportunity or time for romantic adventures, for boyfriends, fashion, excitement. Her only romances had been in her head—woven out of time spent staring out of windows, sitting by bedsides, attending to all the chores and tasks that live-in carers had to undertake.

Except that here—right now, right here—was a man who could have sprung right out of her romantic fantasies…everything she had ever daydreamed about.

Tall, dark and impossibly handsome.

And he was here—right *here*—beside her. A daydream made real.

She gulped again. His smile deepened, indenting around his sculpted mouth, making a wash of weakness go through her again, deeper still.

'Better?' he murmured.

Silently, she nodded, still unable to tear her gaze away. Just wanting to go on gazing and gazing at him.

Then, abruptly, she became hideously aware that although *he* looked exactly as if he'd stepped out of one of her torrid daydreams—a fantasy made wondrously, amazingly real—*she* was looking no such thing. In fact the complete, mortifying opposite.

Burningly, she was brutally aware of how she must look to him—the very last image a man like him should see in any daydream, made real or not. Red eyes, snuffling nose, tear runnels down her cheeks, hair all mussed and not a scrap of make-up. Oh, yes—and she was wearing ancient jeans and a bobbled, battered jumper that hung on her body like a rag. What a disaster…

As the traffic light changed to green Anatole turned into the side street she'd indicated. 'Where now?' he asked.

It came to him that he was hoping it was some way yet. Then he crushed the thought. Picking up stray females off the street—literally, in this case!—was not a smart idea. Even though…

His glance went to her again. *She really is something to look at! Even with those red eyes and rubbish clothes.*

A thought flashed across his mind. One he didn't want but that was there all the same.

How good could she look?

Immediately he cut the thought.

No—don't ask that. Don't think that. Drive her to her destination, then drive on—back to your own life.

Yes, that was what he *should* do—he knew that perfectly well. But in the meantime he could hardly drive in silence. Besides, he didn't want her bursting into those terrifyingly heavy sobs again.

'I'm sorry you were so upset,' he heard himself saying. 'But I hope it's taught you never, *ever* to step out into traffic.'

'I'm so, *so* sorry,' she said again. Her voice was husky now. 'And I'm so, *so* sorry for…for crying like that. It wasn't you! Well, I mean…not really. Only when you yelled at me—'

'It was shock,' Anatole said. 'I was terrified I'd killed you.' He threw a rueful look at her. 'I didn't mean to make you cry.'

She shook her head. 'It wasn't because of that—not really,' she said again. 'It was because—'

She stopped. All thoughts of daydream heroes vanished as the memory of how she'd spent the night at the bedside of a dying man assailed her again.

'Because…?' Anatole prompted, throwing her another brief glance. He found he liked throwing her glances. But that he would have preferred them not to be brief…

Perhaps they need not be—

She was answering him, cutting across the thought he should not have. Most *definitely* should not have.

'It was because of poor Mr Rodgers!' she said in a rush. 'He died this morning. I was there. I was his care worker. It was so sad. He was very old, but all the same—' She broke off, a catch in her voice. 'It reminded me of when my mother died—'

She broke off again, and Anatole could hear the half-sob in her voice. 'I'm sorry,' he said, because it seemed the only thing to say. 'Was your mother's death recent?'

She shook her head. 'No, it was nearly two years ago, but it brought it all back. She had MS—all the time I was growing up, really—and after my father was killed I looked after her. That's why I became a care worker. I had the experience, and anyway there wasn't much else I could do, and a live-in post was essential because I don't have a place of my own yet—'

She broke off, suddenly horribly aware that she was saying all these personal things to a complete stranger.

She swallowed. 'I'm just going to my agency's offices now—to get a new assignment, somewhere to go tonight.' Her voice changed. 'That's it—just there!'

She pointed to an unprepossessing office block and Anatole drew up alongside it. She got out, tried the front door. It did not open. He stepped out beside her, seeing the notice that said 'Closed'.

'What now?' he heard himself saying in a tight voice.

Tia turned to stare at him, trying to mask the dismay in her face. 'Oh, I'll find a cheap hotel for tonight. There's probably one close by I can walk to.'

Anatole doubted that—especially with her broken suitcase.

His eyes rested on her. She looked lost and helpless. And very, very lovely.

As before, sudden decision took him. There was a voice in his head telling him he was mad, behaving like an idiot, but he ignored it. Instead, he smiled suddenly.

'I've got a much better idea,' he said. 'Look, you can't move that broken suitcase a metre, let alone trail around looking for a mythical cheap hotel in London! So here's what I propose. Why not stay the night at my flat? I won't be there,' he added immediately, because instantly panic had filled her blue eyes, 'so you'll have the run of it. Then you can buy yourself a new suitcase in the morning and head to your agency.' He smiled. 'How would that be?'

She was staring at him as though she dared not believe what he was saying. 'Are you sure?' That disbelief was in her voice, but her panic was ebbing away.

'I wouldn't offer otherwise,' Anatole replied.

'It's incredibly kind of you,' she answered, her voice sounding husky, her eyes dropping away from his. 'I'm being a total pain to you—'

'Not at all,' he said. 'So, do you accept?'

He smiled again—the deliberate smile that he

used when he wanted people to do what he wanted. It worked this time too. Tremulously she nodded.

Refusing to pay any attention to the voice in his head telling him he was an insane idiot to make such an offer to a complete stranger, however lovely, Anatole helped her back into the car and set off again, heading into Mayfair, where his flat was.

He glanced at her. She was sitting very still, hands in her lap, looking out through the windscreen, not at him. She still looked as if she could not believe this was really happening.

He took the next step in making it real for her. For him as well.

'Maybe we should introduce ourselves properly? I'm Anatole Kyrgiakis.'

It was odd to say his own name, because he usually didn't have to, and certainly when he did he expected his surname, at least, to be recognised instantly. Possibly followed by a quick glance to ascertain that he meant *the* Kyrgiakis family. This time, however, his name drew no reaction other than her turning her head to look at him as he spoke.

'Tia Saunders,' she responded shyly.

'Hello, Tia,' Anatole said in a low voice, with a flickering smile.

He saw a flush of colour in her cheeks, then had to pay attention to the traffic again. He let her be as he drove on, needing to concentrate now and wanting her to feel a little more relaxed about what was happening. But she was still clearly tense as he pulled up outside his elegant Georgian town house and guided her indoors, carrying her broken suitcase.

The greeting from the concierge at the desk in the

wide hallway seemed to make her shrink against him, and as they entered his top-floor apartment she gave a gasp.

'I can't stay here!' she exclaimed, dismay in her voice. 'I might mess something up!'

Her eyes raced around, taking in a long white sofa, covered in silk cushions, a thick dove-grey carpet that matched the lavish drapes at the wide windows. It was like something out of a movie—absolutely immaculate and obviously incredibly expensive.

Anatole gave a laugh. 'Just don't spill coffee on anything,' he said.

She shook her head violently. 'Please, don't even *say* that!' she cried, aghast at the very thought.

His expression changed. She seemed genuinely worried. He walked up to her. Found himself taking her hand with his free one even without realising it. Patting it reassuringly.

'Speaking of coffee… I could murder a cup! What about you?'

She nodded, swallowing. 'Th…thank you,' she stammered.

'Good. I'll get the machine going. But let me show you to your room first—and, look, why not take a shower, freshen up? You must have had a gruelling night, from what you've said.'

He relinquished her hand, hefted up the broken suitcase again, mentally deciding he'd get a new one delivered by the concierge within the hour, and carried it through to one of the guest bedrooms.

She followed after him, still glancing about her with an air of combined nervousness and wide-eyed amazement at her surroundings, as if she'd never seen anything like it in her life. Which, he realised, she probably never had.

An unusual sense of satisfaction darted within him. It was a good feeling to give this impoverished, waiflike girl, who'd clearly had a pretty sad time of it—both parents dead and a poorly paid job involving distressing end-of-life care—a brief taste of luxury. He found himself wanting her to enjoy it.

Setting down the suitcase, which immediately sprang open again, he pointed out the en suite bathroom, then with another smile left her to it, heading for the kitchen.

Five minutes later the coffee was brewing and he was sprawled on the sofa, checking his emails—trying very, very hard not to let his mind wander to his unexpected guest taking her shower…

He wondered just how far her charms extended beyond her lovely face. He suspected a lot further. She was slender—he'd seen that instantly—but it hadn't made her flat-chested. No, indeed, Even though she was wearing cheap, unflattering clothes, he'd seen the soft swell of her breasts beneath. And she was petite—much more so than the women he usually selected for himself.

Maybe that was because of his own height—over six foot—or maybe it was because the kind of women he went out with tended to be self-assured, self-confident high-achieving females who were his counterparts in many ways, striding through the world knowing their own worth, very sure of themselves and their attractions.

Women like Romola.

His expression changed. Before Tia had plunged in

front of his car he'd made the decision to cut Romola out of his life—so why not do that right now? He'd text her to say he couldn't see her tonight after all, that something had come up, and that it was unlikely he'd be back in London any time soon, Say that perhaps they should both accept their time together had run its course…

With a ruthlessness that he could easily exercise whenever he felt himself targeted by a woman wanting more of him than he cared to give, he sent the text, softening the blow with the despatch of a diamond bracelet as a farewell gift as a sop to Romola's considerable ego. Then, with a sense of relief, he turned his thoughts back to tonight.

A smile started around his mouth, his eyes softening slightly. He'd already played out King Cophetua and the Beggar Maid in offering Tia the run of his flat, so why not go the whole hog and give her an evening she would always remember? Champagne, fine dining—the works!

It was something he'd take a bet that she'd never experienced in her deprived life before.

Of course it went without saying that that would be *all* he'd be offering her. He himself would not be staying here—he'd make his way over to the Mayfair hotel where his father kept a permanent suite. Of course he would.

Anything else was completely out of the question—however lovely she was.

Completely out, he told himself sternly.

CHAPTER TWO

TIA STOOD IN a state of physical bliss as the hot water poured over her body, foaming into rich suds the shampoo and body wash she'd found in the basket of expensive-looking toiletries on the marble-topped vanity unit. Never in her whole life had she had such a lavish, luxurious shower.

By the time she stepped out, her hair wrapped up in a fleecy towel, another huge bath sheet wrapped around her, she felt reborn. She still hadn't really got her head around what was happening because it all just seemed like a fairytale—swept off by a prince who took her breath away.

He's just so gorgeous! So incredibly gorgeous! And he's being so kind! He could just as easily have left me on the pavement with my broken suitcase. Driven away and not cared!

But he hadn't driven away—he'd brought her here, and how could she possibly have said no? In all her confined, unexciting life, dedicated to caring for her poor mother and for others, when had anything like this *ever* happened except in her daydreams?

She lifted her chin, staring at her reflection, resolve

in her eyes. Whatever was happening, she was going to seize this moment!

She whirled about, yanking off the turban towel, letting her damp hair tumble down, then rapidly sorting through her clothes, desperate to find something—anything—that was more worthy of the occasion than her ancient jeans and baggy top. Of course she had nothing at all that was remotely suitable, but at least she had something that was an improvement. She might never hope to be able to look like a fairytale princess, but she'd do her damnedest!

As she walked back into that pristine, palatial lounge her eyes went straight to the darkly sprawling figure relaxed on the white sofa. Dear Lord, but he was unutterably gorgeous!

He'd shed his formal business jacket and loosened his tie, undone his top button and turned up his cuffs. And through her veins came that same devastating rush she'd felt before, weakening her limbs, making her dizzy with its impact.

He rose to his feet. 'There you are.' He smiled. 'Come and sit down and have your coffee.'

He nodded to where he'd set out a plate of pastries, extracted from the freezer and microwaved by his own fair hand into tempting, fragrant warmth. Two had already been consumed, but there were plenty left.

'Are you on a diet?' he asked convivially. 'Or can I tempt you?'

Anatole watched with a sense of familiarity as the colour rushed into her face and then out again. Maybe he shouldn't have used the word 'tempt'. He had the damnedest feeling that it wasn't the thought of the pastries that were making her colour up like that.

Snap!

Because if *she* was experiencing temptation, then he knew for sure that he was as well. And with good reason…

She'd changed her clothes and, although they were still clearly cheap and high street, they were a definite improvement. She'd put on a skirt—a floaty cotton one, in Indian print—and topped it with a turquoise tee shirt that gave her a whole lot more figure than the baggy jumper she'd had on previously. On top of that, her freshly washed hair was loose now, still damp, but curling in a tousled mane around her shoulders. The redness had finally gone from her eyes, and her skin was clear and unblemished. Her lips rosy, tender…

Still the ingénue, definitely…but no longer a sad waif.

With an expression of intense self-consciousness on her face, she gingerly sat herself down on the sofa, slanting her slender legs. He saw her hands were shaking slightly as she took the coffee he'd poured with a low murmur of thanks.

She drank it thirstily, hoping it would steady her wildly jangling nerves, and her eyes jumped again to Anatole to drink in the gorgeous reality of his presence. Her eyes met his and she realised he was watching her, a smile playing around his mouth. It was a smile that sent little quivers shimmering through her and made her breath shallow.

'Have a pastry,' he said, pushing the plate towards her.

Their warm, yeasty cinnamon scent caught at her, reminding her that she'd not had a chance to eat all day. She took one, grabbing a thick, richly patterned paper napkin as she did so, terrified of dropping buttery flakes on the pristine upholstery or the carpet.

Anatole watched her polish off the pastry, letting his eyes drift over the sweet perfection of her heart-shaped face, the cerulean eyes, the delicate arch of her brows, the soft curls of her fair hair.

She is breathtakingly lovely—and she is taking my breath away just looking at her...

He glanced at his watch. It was coming up to seven, though the evenings were still light. They could drink champagne on his roof terrace. But first…best to order dinner.

He reached for his laptop, brought up the website for the service he used when dining in, then tilted the screen towards her. 'Take a look,' he invited, 'and see what you'd like for dinner. I'm going to order in.'

Immediately—predictably—she shook her head. 'Oh, no, please—not for me. I'm absolutely fine just eating these pastries.'

'Yes, well, I'm not,' he rejoined affably. 'Come on—take a look. What sort of food do you like best? And do *not*,' he added sternly, 'say pizza! Or Indian. Or Chinese. I'm talking gourmet food here—take your pick.'

Wide-eyed, Tia stared at the long page of menu options on the screen. She couldn't understand most of them. She swallowed.

'Will you let me choose for you?' Anatole asked, realising her dilemma.

She nodded gratefully.

'Anything you're allergic to?' he asked.

She shook her head, but all the same he chose relatively safe options—no shellfish, no nuts. A midnight dash to A&E was *not* the way he wanted this evening to end.

And you're not going to let it end the way you're thinking right now either! his conscience admonished him sternly.

Not even when he was leaning towards her, and she towards him, so they could both read the screen, and he could catch the fresh scent of her body. All he would have to do to touch her would be to lift his hand, let it slide through those softly drying curls, splay his fingers around the nape of her neck and draw that sweet, tender mouth to his…

He straightened abruptly, busying himself with putting the order through, then closing his laptop. Time to fetch the champagne.

He returned a few moments later, with a bottle at the perfect temperature from his thermostatically controlled wine store and two flutes dangling from his hand. He crossed to the picture window, sliding it open.

'Come and see the view,' he said invitingly.

Tia got to her feet, following him out on to a roofline terrace with a stone balustrade along it. She was still in a daze. Was he really intending to have dinner with her? Drink champagne with her? Her heart was beating faster, she knew, just at the very thought of it.

As she stepped out the warm evening air enveloped her. Sunshine was still catching the tops of the trees visible in the park beyond. Nor was that the only greenery visible—copious large stone pots adorned the terrace, lush with plants, creating a little oasis.

'Oh, it's so lovely!' she exclaimed spontaneously, her face lighting up.

Anatole smiled, feeling a kick go through him at her visible pleasure, at how it made her eyes shine, and set down the champagne and flutes on a little ironwork table flanked by two chairs.

'A private green haven,' he said. 'Cities aren't my favourite places, so when I'm forced to be in them—which is all too often, alas—I like to be as green as I can. It's one of the reasons,' he went on, 'that I like penthouse apartments—they come with roof terraces.'

He paused to open the champagne with a soft pop of the cork, then handed her one of the empty flutes.

'Keep it slightly tilted,' he instructed as he poured it half full, letting the liquid foam, but not too much. Then he filled his own glass and lifted it to her, looking down at her. She really was petite, he found himself thinking again. And for some reason it made him feel…protective.

It was an odd thought. Unfamiliar to him when it came to women.

He smiled down at her. She was gazing up at him, and the expression in her eyes sent that kick through him again. He lifted his glass, indicating that she should do the same, which she did, glancing at the foaming liquid as if she could not believe it was in her hand.

'Yammas,' he said.

She looked confused.

'It's *cheers* in Greek,' he elucidated.

'Oh,' she said, '*that's* what you are! I knew you must be foreign, because of your name, but I didn't know what—'

She coloured. Had she sounded rude? She hadn't meant to. London was incredibly multicultural—there had been no reason to say he was 'foreign'. He was probably as British as she was—

'I'm sorry,' she said, looking dismayed. 'I didn't mean to imply—'

'No,' he said, reassuringly. 'I *am* foreign. I'm a Greek national. But I do a lot of work in London because it's a major financial hub. I live in Greece, though.' He smiled again, wanting to set her at her ease. 'Have you ever been to Greece? For a holiday, maybe?'

Tia shook her head. 'We went to Spain when I was little,' she said. 'When my dad was still alive and before mum got MS.' She swallowed, looking away.

'It's good to have memories,' Anatole said quietly. 'Especially of family holidays as a child.'

Yes—it *was* good to have such memories. Except he didn't have any. His school holidays—breaks from boarding at the exclusive international school in Switzerland he'd attended from the age of seven—had been spent either at friends' houses or rattling around the huge Kyrgiakis mansion in Athens, with no one except the servants around.

His parents had been busy with their own more important lives.

When he'd reached his teens he'd taken to spending a few weeks with his uncle—his father's older brother. Vasilis had never been interested in business or finance. He was a scholar, content to bury himself in libraries and museums, using the Kyrgiakis money to fund archaeological research and sponsor the arts. He disapproved of his younger brother's amatory dissoluteness, but never criticised him openly. He was a lifelong bachelor, and Anatole had found him kindly, but remote—though very helpful in coaching him in exam revision and for university entrance.

Anatole had come to value him increasingly for his wise, quiet good sense.

He cleared his thoughts. 'Well, here's to your first trip to Greece—which I'm sure you'll make one day.' He smiled, tilting his glass again at Tia, then taking a mouthful of the softly beading champagne. He watched her do likewise, very tentatively, as if she could not believe she was doing so.

'Is this real champagne?' she asked as she lowered her glass again.

Anatole's mouth twitched. 'Definitely,' he assured her. 'Do you like it?'

And suddenly, out of nowhere, a huge smile split her face, transforming the wary nervousness of her expression. 'It's gorgeous!' she exclaimed.

Just like you are!

Those were the words blazing in her head, as she gazed at the man who was standing there, who had scooped up the crumpled heap she'd made on the road and brought her here, to this beautiful apartment, to drink champagne—the first champagne she'd ever tasted.

Should I pinch myself? Is this real—is this really, really real?

She wanted it to be—oh, how she wanted it to be! But she could scarcely believe it.

Maybe the single mouthful of champagne had made her bold. 'This is so incredibly kind of you!' she said in a rush.

Kind? The word resonated in Anatole's head. *Was*

he being kind? He'd told himself he was, but was the truth different?

Am I just being incredibly, recklessly self-indulgent?

He lifted his glass again. Right now he didn't care. His only focus was on this lovely woman—so young, so fresh, so breathtakingly captivating in her simple natural beauty.

She is practising no arts to attract me, making no eyes at me, and she asks nothing of me—

He smiled, his expression softening, a tinge of humour at his mouth. 'Drink up,' he said, 'we've a whole bottle to get through!'

He took another mouthful of the fine vintage, encouraging her to do likewise.

She was looking around her as she sipped, out over the rooftops of the houses nearby. 'It's nice to think,' she heard herself say, 'that even though up here used to be the attics, where the servants lived, they got this view!'

Anatole laughed. 'Well, the attics have certainly gone up in the world since then!' he answered, thinking of the multi-million-pound price tag this apartment had come with. 'And it's good that those days are gone. Any house staff these days get a lot better than attics to live in, and they are very decently paid.'

Probably, he found himself adding silently, *a lot more than you get as a care worker...*

He frowned. Essential though such work was, surely it would be good if she aspired to something more in her life?

'Tell me,' he said, taking some more of his champagne, then topping up both their glasses, 'what do you want to do with your life? I know care work is important, but surely you won't want to do it for ever?'

Even as he asked the question it dawned on him that never in his life had he come across anyone from her background. All the women he knew were either in high-powered careers or trust fund princesses. Completely a different species from this young woman with her sad, impoverished, hard-working life.

Tia bit her lip, feeling awkward suddenly. 'Well, because I was off school a lot, looking after Mum, I never passed my exams, so I can't really go to college. And, though I'm saving from my wages, I can't afford accommodation of my own yet.'

'Have you no family at all to help you?' Anatole frowned.

She shook her head. 'It was just Dad, Mum, and me.'

She looked at him. Nearly a glass down on the champagne and she was definitely feeling bold. This might be a daydream, but she was going to indulge herself to the hilt with it.

'What about you?' she asked. 'Aren't Greek families huge?'

Anatole gave a thin smile. 'Not mine,' he said tersely. 'I'm an only child too.' He looked into his champagne flute. 'My parents are divorced, and both of them are married to other people now. I don't see much of them.'

That was from choice. His and theirs. The only regular Kyrgiakis family gathering was the annual board meeting when all the shareholders gathered—himself, his parents and his uncle, and a few distant cousins as well. All of them looked to him to find out how much more money he'd poured into the family coffers, thanks to his business acumen.

'Oh,' Tia said, sympathetically, 'that's a shame.'

An unwelcome flicker went through her. She didn't want to think that fantasy males like this one could have dysfunctional families like ordinary people. Surely when they lived in fantastic, deluxe places like this, and drank vintage champagne, they couldn't have problems like other people?

Anatole gave another thin smile. 'Not particularly,' he countered. 'I'm used to it.'

Absently, he wondered why he'd talked about his family at all. He never did that with women. He glanced at his watch. They should go indoors. Dinner would be arriving shortly and he didn't want to think about his family—or his lack of any that he bothered about. Even Vasilis, kindly though he was, lived in a world of his own, content with his books and his philanthropic activities in the arts world.

He guided his guest indoors. Dusk was gathering outside and he switched on the terrace lighting, casting low pools of soft light around the greenery, giving it an elvish glow.

Once again, Tia was enchanted. 'Oh, that's so pretty!' she exclaimed, as the effect sprang to life. 'It looks like a fairyland!'

She immediately felt childish saying such a thing, even if it were true, but Anatole laughed, clearly amused.

The house phone rang, alerting him that dinner was on its way up, and five minutes later he and Tia were seated, tucking in to their first course—a delicate white fish terrine.

'This is delicious!' she exclaimed, her face lighting up as she ate.

She said the same thing about the chicken bathed in a creamy sauce, with tiny new potatoes and fresh green beans—simple, but beautifully cooked.

Anatole smiled indulgently. 'Eat up,' he urged.

It was good to see a woman eating with appetite, not picking at her food. Good, too, to see the open pleasure in her face at dining with him, her appreciation of everything. Including the champagne as he topped up her glass yet again.

Careful. He heard the warning voice in his head. *Don't give her more than she can handle.*

Or, indeed, more than he could handle either—not when he still had to get to the hotel for the night. But that wasn't yet, and for now he could continue to enjoy every moment of their evening.

A sense of well-being settled over him. Deliberately, he kept the conversation between them light, doing most of the talking himself, but drawing her out as well, intent on making her feel relaxed and comfortable.

'If you do ever manage to get to Greece for a holiday, what kind of thing would you most like doing? Are you a beach bunny or do you like sightseeing? There's plenty of both across the mainland and the islands. And if you like ancient history there's no better place in the world than Greece, to my mind!' he said lightly.

'I don't really know anything about ancient history,' she answered, colouring slightly.

She felt uncomfortable, being reminded of her lack of education. Such realities got in the way of this wonderful, blissful daydream she was having. This real-life fairytale.

'You've heard of the Parthenon?' Anatole prompted.

A look of confusion passed over Tia's face. 'Um… is it a temple?'

'Yes, the most famous in the world—on the Acropolis in Athens. A lot of tall stone pillars around a rectangular ruin.'

'Oh, yes, I've seen pictures!' she acknowledged, relieved that she'd been right.

'Well, there you are, then.' He smiled, and went on to tell her the kind of information most tourists gathered from a visit to the site, then moved on to the other attractions that his homeland offered.

Whether or not she took it all in, he didn't know. Mostly she just gazed at him, her beautiful blue eyes wide—something he found himself enjoying. Especially when he held her gaze and saw the flush of colour mount in her cheeks, her hand reaching hurriedly for the glass of iced water beside her champagne flute.

As they moved on to the final course—a light-as-air pavlova—he opened a bottle of sweet dessert wine, calculating that she would find it more palatable than port.

Which, indeed, she did, sipping the honeyed liquid with appreciation.

When all the pavlova was gone, Anatole got to his feet. He'd set coffee to brew when he'd fetched the dessert wine, and now he collected it, setting it down on the coffee table by the sofa.

He held his hand out to Tia. 'Come and sit down,' he invited.

She got up from the table, suddenly aware that her

head was feeling as if there was a very slight swirl inside it. Just how much of that gorgeous champagne had she drunk? she wondered. It seemed to be fizzing in her veins, making her feel breathless, weightless. As if she were floating in a blissful haze. But she didn't care. How could she? An evening like this—something out of fairyland—would never come again!

With a little contented sigh she sank down on the sofa, the dessert wine glass in her hand, her light cotton skirt billowing around her.

Anatole came and sat down beside her. 'Time to relax,' he said genially, flicking on the TV with a remote.

He hefted his feet up onto the coffee table, disposing of his tie over the back of the sofa. He wanted to be totally comfortable. The mix of champagne and sweet wine was creaming pleasantly in his veins. He hoped it was doing so in Tia, as well, allowing her to enjoy the rest of the evening with him before he took himself off to his hotel.

Idly, he wondered whether he should phone and tell them to expect him, but then he decided not to bother. Instead he amused himself by channel-surfing until he chanced upon a channel that made his unexpected guest exclaim, 'Oh, I *love* this movie!'

It was a rom-com, perfectly watchable, and he was happy to do so. Happy to see Tia curl her bare feet under her skirt on the sofa and lean back into the cushions, her eyes on the screen.

At what point, Anatole wondered as he topped up her glass again, had he moved closer to her? At what point, as he'd stretched and flexed his legs, had he also stretched and flexed his arms, so that one of them was now resting along the back of the sofa, his fingertips grazing the top of her shoulder?

At what point had his fingers started idly playing with the now dry silky-soft pale curls around her neck?

At what point had he accepted that he had no desire—none whatsoever—to go anywhere else tonight?

And all the caution and the warnings sounding in his head, in what remained of his conscience, were falling on ears that were totally, profoundly deaf…

The film came to its sentimental end, with the hero sweeping the heroine up into his arms, lavishing an extravagant kiss upon her upturned face, and the music soared into the credits. A huge sigh of satisfaction was breathed from Tia, and she set down her now empty glass, turning back towards Anatole.

Emotion was coursing through her, mingling with the champagne and with that deliciously sweet wine she'd been drinking, with the gorgeous food she'd eaten—the best she'd ever tasted—all set off by candles and soft music and with her very own prince to keep her company.

It was foaming in her bloodstream, shining from her eyes. The rom-com they'd watched was one of her favourites, sighed over many times, but this—this now, *here*, right now—with her very own gorgeous, incredibly handsome man sitting beside her, oh, so tantalisingly close, was *real*! No fairytale, no fantasy—*real.* She'd never been this physically close to a man before—let alone a man like this! A man who could make fairytales come true…

And she knew how fairytales culminated! With the hero kissing the heroine…

Excitement, wonder—*hope*—filled her, and her eyes were shining like stars as she gazed up into the face of this glorious, gorgeous man who represented to her everything she had ever longed for, dreamt of, yearned for.

The man who was looking down at her, his dark eyes lustrous, his lashes long and lush, his sculpted mouth so beautiful, so sensual—

She felt a little thrill just thinking of it, her breath catching, her eyes widening as she looked up to his.

Anatole looked down at her, seeing the loveliness of her face, of the loose, long pale hair waving like silk over her slender shoulders, seeing how the sweet mounds of her breasts were pressed against the contours of her cotton tee shirt, how her soft tender lips were parted, how her celestial blue eyes were wide, gazing at him with an expression that told him exactly what she wanted.

For one long, endless moment he stayed motionless, while a million conflicting thoughts battled in his head over what he should do next. What he *should* do versus what he wanted to do.

Yet still he held back, knowing that what he wanted so badly to do he should not. He should instead pull back, make some gesture of withdrawal from her, get up, get to his feet, increase the distance between them. Because if he didn't right now, then—

Her hand lifted, almost quivering, and with trembling fingers she let the delicate tips touch his jaw, feather-light, scarcely making contact, as if she hardly dared believe that this was what she was doing. She said his name. Breathed it. Her eyes were pools of longing. Her lips were parted, eyes half closed now. Waiting—yearning… For him.

And Anatole lost it. Lost all remaining shreds of conscience or consciousness.

He leaned towards her. The hand behind her head grazed her nape, his other hand slid along her cheek, his fingers gentle in her hair, cupping her face. Her eyes were wide, like saucers, and in them starlight shone like beacons, drawing him into her, into doing what she so blazingly wanted him to do.

His eyes washed over her, his pulse quickening. She was so lovely. And she so wanted him to kiss her… He could see it in her eyes, in her parted lips, in the quivering pulse in her delicate white throat.

His lashes swept down over his eyes as his mouth touched hers, soft as velvet, tasting the sweet wine on her lips, the warmth of her mouth as he opened it to his questing silken touch. He heard her give a little moan, deep in her throat, and he felt his own pulse surge, arousal spearing within him.

She was so soft to kiss, and he deepened his kiss automatically, instinctively, his hand sliding down over the curve of her shoulder, turning her towards him as he leant into her, drawing her to him, drawing her across him, so that her hand now braced itself against the hard wall of his chest, so that one slender thigh was against his.

He heard her moan again and it quickened his arousal. He said her name, told her how sweet she was, how very lovely. If he spoke in Greek he didn't realise it—didn't realise anything except that the wine was coursing in his bloodstream, recklessness was heady in his smitten synapses, and in his arms was a woman he desired.

Who desired him.

Because that was what her tender, lissom body was telling him—that was what the sudden engorgement of her breasts was showing him in the cresting of her nipples that were somehow beneath the palm of his hand.

Without realisation, she was winding her hand around his waist. He laid her back across his lap, half supported on his arm as he kissed her still, one hand palming her swelling breast until she moaned, eyes closed, her face filled with an expression of bliss he would have had to be blind not to see. He lifted his mouth from hers, let his eyes feast on her a moment, before his mouth descended yet again to graze on the line of her cheekbones, to nip at the tender lobes of her ears.

He let his hand slip reluctantly from her breast and then slide languorously along her flank to rest on her thigh, to smooth away the light cotton of her skirt until his hand found the bare skin beneath. To stroke and to caress and to hear her moan again, to feel her thigh strain against him—feel, too, his own body surge to full arousal.

Desire flamed in him…strong, impossible to resist…

And yet he *must*. This was too fast, too intense. He was letting his overpowering desire for her carry him away and he must draw back.

Heart pounding, he set her aside.

'Tia—' His voice was broken, his hand raised as if to ward her off. To hold himself back from her.

He saw her face fill with anguish. It caught at him like a blow.

'Don't…don't you want me?' There was dismay in her voice, which was a muted whisper.

He gave a groan. 'Tia—I mustn't. This isn't right. I can't take advantage of you like this!'

Immediately she cried out, 'But you aren't! Oh, please, *please* don't tell me you don't want me! I couldn't bear it!'

Her hand flew to her mouth and her look of anguish intensified. Her breathing was fast and breathless and she felt bereft—lost and abandoned.

He caught her face between his hands. 'Tia—I want you very, very much, but—'

But there's more than one bedroom in this apartment and we have to be in separate bedrooms tonight—we just have to be! Because anything else would be...would be...

Her face had lit like a beacon again. 'Please… *please*!' she begged. Her face worked. 'This whole evening with you has been incredible! Fantastic! Wonderful! And now…with you…it's like nothing I've ever experienced in all my life! You are like no one I've ever met! I'll never meet anyone else like you again, and this…all this…'

She gestured at the room, softly lit with table lamps, at the candles still on the dining table, the empty bottle of champagne, the glow of the lights on the terrace beyond.

'All this will never happen to me again!' She bit her lip, mouth quivering. 'I want this *so* much,' she said huskily, her eyes pleading with him, her hand fastening on his strong arm as if she might draw him back to her again. *'Please,'* she begged again. 'Please don't turn me away—*please*!'

And yet again Anatole lost it.

Unable to resist what he did not want to resist, what he could not bear to resist, he swept her back up to him, his mouth descending to taste again the honeyed sweetness of her mouth which opened to his instantly, eagerly…hungrily.

She wants this—she wants this as much as I do. And, however briefly we have known each other, my desire for her is overpowering. And so is hers for me. And because of that…

Because of that, with a rasp deep in his throat, he hefted to his feet, holding her in his arms, his hand sweeping under her knees to cradle her against him as he carried her away.

Away not to the guest room but to his own master suite, where he ripped back the bedcovers to lay her gently upon cool sheets. She was gazing up at him, blindness in her eyes, her pupils flared, lips bee-stung, breasts straining against the moulding of the cotton tee.

He wanted it gone. Wanted all her clothes gone, and all his—wanted no barriers between himself and this lovely woman he wanted now…*right* now…

CHAPTER THREE

TIA GAZED UP at him—at this incredible, unbearably devastating man—her mind in whiteout. Her body seemed to be on fire, with a soft, velvet flame, glowing with a sensual awareness that was possessing her utterly. She reached her arms up to him, yearning for him, beseeching him to take her back in his arms, to kiss and caress her, to sweep her off into the gorgeous bliss of his touch, his desire for her.

He was stripping off his clothes and she could feel her eyes widen as his shirt revealed the smooth, taut contours of his chest. And then his fingers were at his belt, snaking it free…

She gave a little cry, turning her head into the pillow, suddenly desperately shy. She had never dreamt that a man like this would ever be real in her life, and he was suddenly only too real.

Then she felt the mattress dip, felt his weight coming down beside her, heard him murmur soft words, urgent words, seductive, irresistible…and then his hand was curving her face back towards his, and he was so close to her, so very close, and in his eyes was a light she had never seen in a man's eyes before. She'd never seen a man's eyes so filled with blazing, burning fire…

I can't stop this—I can't stop it—and I don't want to! Oh, I don't want to!

She wanted it to happen, wanted what would happen now—what must happen now—wanted it with all her being, yearned and longed for it. It had come out of nowhere—just as the whole encounter with this amazing, fabulous man had come out of nowhere.

And I can't say no to it. I can't and I don't want to. I want to say yes—only yes....

Her eyes fluttered closed and she felt his mouth feather-light on hers, like swansdown. She felt his hands move to her waist, lift the material of her tee shirt from her, easing it over her head with hardly a pause in his sweet kissing. She felt his hands—warm, strong, skilled—slide around her back, unfasten her bra and slip it from her, discarding it somewhere. She knew not where and she did not care—did not care at all except that now he was doing the same with her skirt, skimming it from her, and then… Oh, then he was easing her panties from her quickening thighs.

He lifted himself from her, one hand splaying into her hair as it spread in tumbling golden curls across the pillow. His eyes burned into hers. 'You are so, so beautiful,' he said. 'So beautiful…'

She could say nothing, could only gaze upwards, hearing her mind echoing his words… *He* was beautiful! He with his sable hair and his sculpted cheekbones, with eyes you could drown in. His hard, lean body that her hands were now lifting themselves to of their own accord.

Her fingertips traced every line, every contour of the smooth, honed muscles. He seemed to shudder and she felt his muscles clench, as if what she was doing was unbearable, and then his mouth descended again.

Hungry…oh, so hungry.

And there was a hunger in her too. A ravening hunger that was as instinctive, as overpowering, as her need to be held and kissed and caressed by this most blissfully seductive of men. It was making her body arch to his, the blood rush like a torrent in her veins, drowning her senses, turning her into living flame. Never had she imagined that passion could feel like this! Never had her daydreams known what it was to be like this, in the arms of a man filled with urgent desire.

And she desired him.

She clung to him, not knowing what she was doing, only that it was what she burned to do. Her body arched to his, her thighs parting. She heard him say something but was lost to all coherence.

He seemed to pause, pull away from her, and it was unbearable not to have his warm, strong body over hers. And then, with a rush of relief, she felt him there again, kissing her again, his hands urgent, every muscle in his body tautening. She felt his body ease between hers, felt his hips move against hers, felt—

Pain! A sudden, piercing stab of pain!

She cried out, freezing, and he froze too. He gazed down at her, his eyes blind, then clearing into vision. Words escaped him. He was shocked.

He lifted from her and the pain vanished. Her hands reached for him, her head lifting blindly to catch his mouth again. But he was still withdrawn from her.

'I didn't know—I didn't realise—' The words fell from him. Shocked. Abrupt.

She could only gaze up at him. Devastation was flooding through her.

'Don't you want me?' It was all that was in her head now—the devastation of his rejection before.

'Tia…' He said her name again. 'I didn't realise that I would be the first man for you—'

Her hands pressed into his bare shoulders. 'I *want* you to be! Only you! Please—oh, *please*!'

Conflict seared in him. He burned for her, and yet—

But she was pressing her body against his, crushing her breasts against the wall of his chest. Lifting her hips to his in an age-old invitation of woman to man, to possess and be possessed.

'Please…' she said, her voice a low husk, a plea. 'Please—I want this so much—I want *you* so much.'

Her hand slid around the base of his skull, pressing against it, drawing his head down. She reached up with her mouth, feeling as her lips touched his a relief go through her that sated all her ardent yearning, all her desperate desire.

She opened his mouth under hers and Anatole, with a low, helpless groan, abandoned all his inner conflict, let himself yield to what he so wanted to do… to make her his.

It was morning. The undrawn curtains were letting in the light of dawn. Drowsily, wonderingly, Tia lay in Anatole's arms. There had been no more pain, and he had been as gentle with her as if she were made of porcelain—though the soft tenderness of her body now proclaimed that she was flesh and blood. But there was only a fading ache now, and in the cocoon of his strong arms it mattered not at all.

His arm was beneath her shoulder, her head lax upon it, and she smiled up at him, bemused, enchanted. His dark eyes were moving over her face, his other hand smoothing the tendrils of her silken hair from her cheeks. He was smiling back at her—a smile of intimacy, endearment. It made her feel weak with longing.

Bliss enveloped her, and a wonder so great that she could scarcely dare to believe that it was true, what had happened.

'Do you *have* to return to work?' Anatole was asking her.

She frowned a little, not understanding. 'The agency will open again at nine,' she said.

Anatole shook her head. 'I mean, do you have to take up another position? Are you booked to be a carer for someone else?'

Her frown deepened. She was understanding even less.

He smoothed her silken hair again, his eyes searching her face. 'I don't want you to go,' he said to her. 'I want you to stay with me.'

He watched her expression change. Watched it transform before his very eyes. Saw her cerulean blue eyes widen as she took in the meaning of what he'd said.

His smile deepened. Became assured. 'I have to go to Athens this week. Come with me—'

Come with me.

The words echoed in his head. He was sure of them—absolutely, totally sure. He felt a wash of desire go through him—not for consummation but for continuation.

I don't want to let her go—I want to keep her with me.

The realisation was absolute. The clarity of his desire incontrovertible.

'Do you mean it?'

Her words were so faint he could hardly hear them. But he could hear the emotion in her voice, see how her expression had changed, how her eyes were flaring wide, and in them hope blazed, dimmed only by confusion.

He brushed her parted lips. 'I would not ask you otherwise,' he said, knowing that to be true.

His arm around her tightened. She was so soft in his arms, so tiny, it seemed to him, nestling up against him.

He smiled at her. 'Well?' he asked. 'Will you come with me?'

The shadow of confusion, of fear that she had misunderstood, that he did not really mean what he'd said, vanished. Like the sun coming out, her smile lit up her face.

'Oh, yes! Yes, yes, *yes*!'

He laughed. He had had no fear that she would say no—why should she? The night they had spent together had been wondrous for her—he knew that—and he knew that he had coaxed her unschooled body to an ecstasy that had shocked her with its intensity. Knew that her ardent, bemused gaze in the sweet, exhausted aftermath of his lovemaking betokened just what effect he'd had on her.

And if he wanted proof of that today—well, here

it was. She was gazing at him now with a look on her face that spread warmth through his whole being.

He brushed her lips with his again. Felt arousal—drowsy, dormant, but still present—start to stir. He deepened his kiss, using slow, sensuous, feather-light touches to stir within her an answering response. He would need to be gentle—very careful indeed—and take account of the dramatic changes to her body after their first union.

He felt her fingertips steal over his body, exploring...daring...fuelling his arousal with every tentative touch and glide...

With a deep, abiding satisfaction he started to make love to her again.

It was several days before they went to Athens. Days in which Tia knew she had, without the slightest doubt, been transported to a fantasy land.

How could she be anywhere else? She had been transported there by the most gorgeous, the most wonderful, the most shiveringly fabulous man she could ever have imagined! A man who had cast a glittering net of enchantment over her life.

That first morning, after he had made love to her again—and how was it possible for her body to feel what it did? She'd never known, never guessed that it was so—they'd breakfasted out on the little terrace, with the morning sun illuming them.

Then he'd whisked her off to one of the most famous luxury department stores in the world, from which she'd emerged, several hours later, with countless carrier bags of designer clothes and a new hairstyle—barely shorter, but so cunningly cut it had felt feather-light on her head, floating over her shoulders. Her make-up had been applied by an expert, and Anatole had smiled in triumphant satisfaction when he saw her.

I knew she could look fantastic with the right clothes and styling!

His eyes had worked over her openly, and he'd seen the flush of pleasure in her face. The glow in her eyes. Felt the warmth of it.

I've done the right thing—absolutely the right thing.

The certainty of that had streamed through him. This breathtakingly lovely creature that he'd scooped off the road and taken into his life was exactly right for him.

And so it had proved.

Taking Tia to Athens would only be the first of it.

He'd sorted out a passport for her—or rather, his office had—and they were now flying out…first class obviously.

For the entire flight she sat beside him in a state of stupefied bliss, sipping at her glass of champagne and gazing out through the porthole with a look of enchanted disbelief that this could really be happening to her.

In Athens, his chauffeured car was waiting to take him to his apartment—he did not use the Kyrgiakis mansion, far preferring his own palatial flat, with its stunning views of the Acropolis.

'Didn't I tell you that you should see the Parthenon one day?' he quizzed her smilingly, indicating the famous ruins visible from all around. 'It's not in the best of shape because the Ottomans used it as a gunpowder store, which exploded…' He grimaced. 'But it's being preserved as well as possible.'

'Ottomans?' Tia queried.

'They came out of what is now Turkey and conquered Greece in the fifteenth century—it took us four hundred years to be free.' Anatole explained.

Tia looked at him uncertainly. 'Was that Alexander the Great?' she asked tentatively, knowing that the famous character must come into Greek history somewhere.

Anatole's mouth twitched. 'Out by over two thousand years, I'm afraid. Alexander was before the Romans. Greece only became independent in modern times—during the nineteenth century.' He patted her hand. 'Don't worry about it. There's a huge amount of history in Greece. You'll get the hang of it eventually. I'll take you to the Parthenon while we're here.'

But in the end he didn't, because instead, business matters having been attended to, he decided to charter a yacht and take her off on an Aegean cruise.

His father had commandeered the Kyrgiakis yacht, but the one upon which he and Tia sailed off into the sunset was every bit as luxurious, and it reduced Tia to open-mouthed, saucer-eyed amazement.

'It's got a *helicopter!*' she breathed. 'And a swimming pool!'

'And another one indoors, in case it ever rains,' Anatole grinned. 'We'll go skinny-dipping in both!'

Colour flushed in her cheeks, and he found it endearing. He found everything about her endearing. Despite the fact that after a fortnight together she was *way* past being the virginal ingénue she'd been that first amazing night together, she was still delightfully shy.

But not so shy that she refused to go for a starlit swim with him—the crew having been ordered to keep well below decks—nor declined to let him make love to her in the water, until she cried out with a smothered cry, her head falling back as he lifted her up onto his waiting body.

For ten days they meandered around the Aegean, calling in at little islands where he and Tia strolled along the waterfront, lunching in harbourside restaurants, or drove inland to picnic beneath olive groves, with the endless hum of the cicadas all about them.

Simple pleasures…and Anatole wondered when he had last done anything so peaceful with any female. Certainly not with any female who was as boundlessly appreciative as Tia was.

She adored everything they did together. Was thrilled by everything—whether it was taking the yacht's sailing dinghy to skim over the azure water to a tiny cove on a half-deserted island, where they lunched on fresh bread and olives and ripest peaches and then made love on the sand, washing off in the waves thereafter, or whether, like today, it was drinking a glass of Kir Royale and watching the sun set over a harbour bar, before returning to the yacht, moored out in the bay, for a five-course gourmet meal served on the upper deck by the soft-footed, incredibly attentive staff aboard, while music played from unseen speakers all around, the yacht moved on the slow swell of the sea and the moon rose out of the iridescent waters.

Tia gazed at Anatole across the damask tablecloth, over the candlelight between them.

'This is the most wonderful holiday I could ever have imagined!' she breathed.

Adoration was obvious in her eyes—for how could it not be? How could she not reveal all that she felt for this wonderful, incredible man who had brought her here? Emotion swelled within her like a billowing wave, almost overpowering her.

Anatole's dark eyes lingered on her lovely face. A warm, honeyed tan had turned her skin to gold, and her hair was even paler now from the sun's rays. He felt desire cream within him. How good she was for him, and how good he felt about her…about having her in his life.

'Tell me,' he said, 'have you ever been to Paris?'

Tia shook her head.

Anatole's smile deepened. 'Well, I have to go there on business. You'll love it!'

It felt good to know that he would be the first man to show her the City of Light. Just as it had felt good to take her on this cruise, to see her enjoy the luxury of his lifestyle. Good to see her eyes widen, her intake of breath—good to bestow his largesse upon her, for she was so appreciative of it.

King Cophetua, indeed.

But he liked the feeling. Liked it a lot. For her sake, obviously, he was finding pleasure in bestowing upon her the luxury and treats that had never come her way in her deprived life. But not just for her sake—he was honest enough to admit that. For himself too. It was very good to feel her ardent, adoring gaze upon him. It made him feel—warm.

Loved.

His mind sheered away from the word, as if hitting a rock in a stream. His expression changed as he negated what he'd just heard in his mind.

I don't want her to love me.

Of course he didn't! Love would be a completely unnecessary complication. They were having an affair, just as he'd had with all the women who had been in his life…in his bed. It would run its course and at some point they would part.

Until then—well, Tia, so unlike any other woman he'd known, was just what he wanted.

His only source of disquiet was that she remained so clearly uncomfortable whenever they were in company, wherever they travelled. He didn't want her feeling out of her depth in the inevitably cosmopolitan, sophisticated and wealthy circles he moved in, and he did his best to make things easier for her, but she was always very quiet.

Thoughts flickered uneasily in his head. Had anyone ever thought to ask the Beggar Maid how she'd felt after King Cophetua had plucked her up into his royal and gilded life?

And yet when they were alone she visibly relaxed, coming out of her shell, talkative and at ease. Happy just to be with him and endlessly appreciative. Endlessly desirous of him.

He was in no hurry, he realised, to part with her.

Will I ever be? he thought. Then he put the question out of his head. Whenever that time came, it was not now, and until it did he would enjoy this affair—enjoy Tia—to the full.

Tia sat at the vanity unit in the palatial en suite bathroom, gazing at her reflection. She was wearing one of the oh-so-many beautiful dresses Anatole had bought for her over the past months of their relationship. His generosity troubled her, but she had accepted it because she knew she couldn't move in his gilded world in her own inexpensive clothes.

And besides, none of these outfits are really mine! I wouldn't dream of taking them with me when—

Her mind cut out. She didn't want to think about that time. She didn't want it spoiling this wonderful, blissful time with Anatole.

Anatole! His very name brought a flush to her cheeks, a glow to her eyes. How wonderful he was—how kind, how *good* to her! Her heart beat faster every time she thought of him. With every glance she threw at him or he at her, she felt emotion burn in her, coursing through her veins.

She felt her expression change, and even as it did so her gaze became more troubled still, her eyes shadowing.

Be careful! Oh, be careful! There is only one way this affair can end when it does end—like fairy gold turning to dust at dawn! And the end will be bad for you—so, so bad.

But it would be worse—and the shadow in her eyes deepened, a chill icing down her veins—much, much worse, if she let her heart fill with the one emotion that it would be madness to feel for Anatole.

I long for the one thing that would keep me in Anatole's life for ever...

Anatole's mood was tense. They were back in Athens, and the annual Kyrgiakis Corp board meeting was looming. It never put him in a good mood. His parents would pester him for more money—sniping at each other across the table—and only the calming presence of his Uncle Vasilis would be any balm.

Putting in long hours at the Kyrgiakis Corp headquarters, closeted with his finance director going through all the figures and reports before the meeting, meant he'd had little time to devote to Tia lately, but when he did spend time with her he could sense that something was troubling her.

He'd had no time to probe, however—he'd told himself he would get this damn board meeting out of the way and then take her on holiday somewhere. The prospect had cheered him. But not enough to lift the perpetually grim expression on his face as he'd prepared for the coming ordeal.

Now, today, over breakfast, he was running through his head all that had to be in readiness for the meeting that morning,

As well as the official business his family would expect a lavish celebratory lunch, to be held at one of the best hotels in Athens where his father liked to stay. His mother, predictably, never stayed there, but at a rival hotel. They ran up huge bills at both, for they both put their stays on the business account—much to Anatole's irritation.

But his parents had always been a law unto themselves, and since he wanted as little to do with them as possible he tolerated their extravagance, and that of their current respective spouses, with gritted teeth. The only person he actually wanted to see was Vasilis, who'd been preoccupied in Turkey for some time now, helping one of the museums there in salvaging ancient artefacts from the ravages of war in the Middle East.

He'd invited Vasilis to lunch the day after the board

meeting, knowing that even though his scholarly uncle would be far too academic for Tia his kindly personality would not be intimidating to her.

He reached for his orange juice and paused. Tia was looking at him, her fingers twisting nervously in the handle of her coffee cup, with an expression on her face he'd never seen before in the many weeks they'd spent together.

'What is it?' he asked.

She didn't answer. Only swallowed. Paled. Her fingers twisted again.

'Tia?' he prompted.

Was there an edge in his voice? He didn't mean there to be, but he had to get on—time was at an absolute premium today, and he needed to eat breakfast and be gone. But maybe his tone *had* been a bit off, impatient, though he hadn't intended it to be, because she went even whiter. Bit her lip.

'Tell me,' he instructed, his eyes levelling on her.

Whatever was troubling her, he would deal with it later. For now he'd just offer some reassuring words—it was all he had time for. He set down his orange juice and waited expectantly. An anguished look filled her eyes and he saw her swallow again, clearly reluctant to speak.

When she did, he knew why. Knew with a cold, icy pool in his stomach.

Her voice was faint, almost a stammer.

'I… I think I may be pregnant…'

CHAPTER FOUR

CHRISTINE CLIMBED OUT of the car. Her legs were shaking. How she'd get indoors she did not know. Mrs Hughes, the housekeeper, was there already, having left the church before the committal, and she welcomed her in with a low, sad voice.

'A beautiful service, Mrs K,' she said kindly.

Christine swallowed. 'Yes, it was. The vicar was very good about allowing him a C of E interment considering he was Greek Orthodox.' She tried to make her voice sound normal and failed.

Mrs Hughes nodded sympathetically. 'Well, I'm sure the Good Lord will be welcoming Mr K, whichever door he's come into heaven through—such a lovely gentleman as he was, your poor husband.'

'Thank you.'

Christine felt her throat tighten, tears threaten. She went into her sitting room, throat aching.

The pale yellow and green trellis-pattern wallpaper was in a style she now knew was *chinoiserie*, just as she now knew the dates of all the antique furniture in the house, who the artists were of the Old Masters that hung on the walls, and the age and subject of the artefacts that Vasilis had so carefully had transferred from Athens to adorn the place he had come to call home, with his new young wife.

This gracious Queen Anne house in the heart of the Sussex countryside. Far away from his old life and far away from the shocked and outraged members of his family. A serene, beautiful house in which to live, quietly and remotely. In which, finally, to die.

Her tears spilled over yet again, and she crossed to the French window, looking out over the lawn. The gardens were not extensive, but they were very private, edged with greenery. Memory shot through her head of how she'd been so enchanted by the green oasis of Anatole's London roof terrace when he'd switched the lights on, turning it into a fairyland.

She sheared her mind away. What use to think… to remember? Fairyland had turned to fairy dust, and had been blown away in the chill, icy wind of reality. The reality that Anatole had spelt out to her.

'I have no intention of marrying you, Tia. Did you do this to try and get me to marry you?'

A shuddering breath shook her and she forced her shoulders back, forced herself to return to the present. She had not invited anyone back after the funeral—she couldn't face it. All she wanted was solitude.

Yet into her head was forced the image of the grim-faced, dark-suited man standing there, watching her at her husband's grave. Fear bit at her.

Surely he won't come here? Why would he? He's come to see his uncle buried, that's all. He won't sully his shoes by crossing this threshold—not while I'm still here.

But even as she turned from the window there came a knock on the door, and it opened to the housekeeper.

'I'm so sorry to disturb you, Mrs K, but you have a visitor. He says he's Mr K's nephew. I've shown him into the drawing room.'

Ice snaked down Christine's back. For a moment she could not move. Then, with an effort, she nodded.

'Thank you, Mrs Hughes,' she said.

Summoning all her strength, and all her courage, she went to confront the man who had destroyed all her naive and foolish hopes and dreams.

Anatole stood in front of the fireplace, looking around him with a closed, tight expression on his face, taking in the *objets d'art* and his uncle's beloved classical statuary, the Old Masters hanging on the panelled walls.

His mouth twisted. *She's done very well for herself, this woman I picked up from the street—*

Anger stabbed in him. Anger and so much more.

But anger was quite enough. She would be inheriting all Vasilis's share of the Kyrgiakis fortune—a handsome sum indeed. Not bad for a woman who'd once had to take any job she could, however menial and poorly paid, provided it came with accommodation.

Well, this job had certainly come with accommodation!

The twist of his mouth grew harsher. He had found a naïve waif and created a gold-digger…

I gave her a taste for all this. I turned her into this.

Sourness filled his mouth.

There were footsteps beyond the double doors and then they opened. His eyes snapped towards them as she stood there. He felt the blade of a knife stab into him as he looked at her. She was still in the black, tailored couture suit. Her hair was pulled back off her face into a tight chignon—no sign of the soft waves that had once played around her shoulders.

Her face was white. Stark. Still marked by tears shed at the graveside.

Memory flashed into his head of how she'd stood trembling beside the bonnet of his car as she broke down into incoherent sobs when he yelled at her for her stupidity in walking right in front of his car. How appalled he'd been at her reaction…how he'd wanted to stop those tears.

The blade twisted in him…

'What are you doing here?'

Her question was terse, tight-lipped, and she did not advance into the room, only closed the double doors behind her. There was something different about her voice, and it took Anatole a moment to realise that it was not just her blank, hostile tone, but her accent. Her voice was as crisp, as crystalline, as if she had been born to all this.

Her appearance echoed that impression. The severity of the suit, her hairstyle, and the poise with which she held herself, all contributed.

'My uncle is dead. Why else do you think I'm here?' His voice was as terse as hers. It was necessary to be so—it was vital.

Something seemed to pass across her eyes. 'Do you want to see his will? Is that it?'

There was defiance in her voice now—he could hear it.

A cynical cast lit his dark eyes. 'What for? He'll

have left you everything, after all.' He paused—a deadly pause. 'Isn't that why you married him?'

It was a rhetorical question, one he already knew the answer to.

She whitened, but did not flinch. 'He left some specific items for you. I'm going to have them couriered to you as soon as I've been granted probate.'

She paused, he could see it, as if gathering strength. Then she spoke again, her chin lifting, defiance in her voice—in her very stance.

'Anatole, why have you come here? What for? I'm sorry if you wanted the funeral to be in Athens. Vasilis specifically did not want that. He wanted to be buried here. He was friends with the vicar—they shared a common love of Aeschylus. The vicar read Greats at Oxford, and he and Vasilis would cap quotations with each other. They liked Pindar too—'

She broke off. Was she *mad*, rabbiting on about Ancient Greek playwrights and poets? What did Anatole care?

He was looking at her strangely, as if what she had said surprised him. She wasn't sure why. Surely he would not be surprised to find that his erudite uncle had enjoyed discussing classical Greek literature with a fellow scholar, even one so far away from Greece?

'The vicar is quite a Philhellene…' she said, her voice trailing off.

She took another breath. Got back to the subject in hand. Tension was hauling at her muscles, as if wires were suspending her.

'Please don't think of…of… I don't know…disinterring his coffin to take it back to Greece. He would not wish for that.'

Anatole gave a quick shake of his head, as if the thought had not occurred to him as he'd stood there, watching the farce playing out in the churchyard—Tia grieving beside the grave of the man she'd inveigled into committing the most outrageous act of folly—marrying her, a woman thirty years his junior.

'So what *are* you doing here?'

Her question came again, and he brought his mind back to it. What was he doing here? To put it into words was impossible. It had been an instinct—overpowering—an automatic decision not even consciously made. To… To what?

'I'm here to pay my respects,' he heard his own voice answer.

He saw her expression change, as if he'd just said something quite unbelievable.

'Well, not to *me*!' There was derision in her voice—but it was not targeted at him, he realised. He frowned, focussing on her face.

He felt his muscles clench. *Thee mou*, how beautiful she was! The natural loveliness that had so enchanted him, captivated him, that had inspired him so impulsively to take her into his life, had matured into true beauty. Beauty that had a haunting quality. A sorrow—

Does she feel sorrow at my uncle's death? Can she really feel that?

No, surely there could be only relief that she was now free of a man thirty years her senior—free to enjoy all the money he had left her. Yet again that spike drove into him. He hated what she had become. What he himself had made her.

'Anatole, I know perfectly well what you think of

me, so don't prate hypocrisies to me! Tell me why you're here.' And now he saw her shoulders stiffen, her chin rise defiantly. 'If it's merely to heap abuse on my head for having dared to do what I did, then I will simply send you packing. I'm not answerable to you and nor—' the tenor of her voice changed now, and there was a viciousness in it that was like the edge of a blade '—are you answerable to me, either. As you have already had occasion to point out!'

She took another sharp intake of breath.

'Our lives are separate—you made sure of that. And I… I accepted it. You gave me no choice. I had no claim on you—and you most certainly have no claim on me now, nor *any* say in my decisions. Or those your uncle made either. He married me of his own free will—and if you don't like that…well, get over it!'

If she'd sprouted snakes for hair, like Medusa, Anatole could not have been more shocked by her. Was *this* the Tia he remembered? This aggressive harpy? Lashing out at him, her eyes hard and angry?

Tia saw the shock in his face and could have laughed savagely—but laughing was far beyond her on this most gruelling of days. She could feel her heart-rate going insane and knew that she was in shock, as well as still feeling the emotional battering of losing Vasilis—however long it had been expected—and burying him that very day.

To have in front of her now the one man in the entire world she had dreaded seeing again was unbearable. It was unbearable to look at the man who had once been so dear to her.

She lifted a hand, as if to ward him off. 'Anatole, I don't know why you've come here, and I don't care—

we've nothing left to say to each other. Nothing!' She shut her eyes, then opened them again with a heavy breath. 'I'm sure you grieve for your uncle… I know you were fond of him and he of you. He did not seek this breach with you—'

She felt her throat closing again and could not continue. Wanted him only to go.

'What will you do with this place?'

Anatole's voice cut across her aching thoughts.

'I suppose you'll sell up and take yourself off to revel in your ill-gotten inheritance?'

She swallowed. How could it hurt that Anatole spoke to her in such a way? She knew what he thought of her marriage to Vasilis.

'I've no intention of selling up,' she replied coldly, taking protection behind her tone. 'This is my home, with many good memories.'

Something changed in his eyes. 'You'll need to live *respectably* here…' there was warning in his voice '…in this country house idyll in an English village.'

'I shall endeavour to do so.' Christine did not bother to keep the sarcasm out of her voice. Why should she? Anatole was making assumptions about her…as he had done before.

A stab went through her, painful and hurtful, but she ignored it.

Again something flashed in his eyes. 'You're a young woman still, Tia—and now that you have all my uncle's wealth to flaunt you can take your pick of men.' His voice twisted. 'And this time around they won't need to be thirty years older than you. You can choose someone young and handsome, even if they're penniless!'

His tone grew harsher still.

'I'd prefer it if you took yourself off to some flash resort where you can party all night and keep your married name out of the tabloid rags!'

Christine felt her expression harden. Was there any limit to how he was going to insult her? 'I'm in mourning, Anatole. I'm not likely to go off and party with hand-picked gigolos.'

She took another heaving breath, turning around to open the double doors.

'Please leave now, Anatole. We've nothing to say to each other. *Nothing.*'

Pointedly, she waited for him to walk into the wide, parquet-floored hall. There was no sign of Mrs Hughes, and Christine was glad. How much the housekeeper—or anyone else—knew about the Kyrgiakis clan, she didn't know and didn't want to think about. Providing everything was kept civil on the surface, that was all that mattered.

Anatole was simply her late husband's nephew, calling to pay his respects on his uncle's death. No reason for Mrs Hughes to think anything else.

With his long stride Anatole walked past her, and Christine caught the faint scent of his aftershave. Familiar—so very familiar.

Memory rushed through her and she felt her body sway with emotion. For a second it was so overwhelmingly powerful she wanted to catch his hand, throw herself into his arms, and sob. To feel his arms go about her, feel him hold her, cradle her, feel his strong chest support her, feel his closeness, his protection. Sob out her grief for his uncle—her grief for so much more.

But Anatole was gone from her. Separated from her as by a thousand miles, by ten thousand. Separated from her by what she had done—what he had *thought* she had done. There was nothing left to bring them together again—not now. Not ever.

This is the last time I shall set eyes on him. It has to be—because I could not bear to see him again.

There was a tearing pain inside her as these words framed in her head—a pain for all that had been, that had not been, that could never be…

He didn't look at her as he strode past her, as he headed for the large front door. His face was set, closed. She had seen it like that before, that last terrible day in Athens, and she had never wanted to see him look like that again. Like stone, crushing her pathetic hopes.

A silent cry came from her heart.

And then, from the top of the staircase that swept up from the back of the wide hallway to the upper storey of the house, came another cry. Audible this time.

'Mumma!'

Anatole froze. Not believing what he had heard. Froze with his hand on the handle of the door that would take him from the house, his heart infused with blackness.

Slowly he turned. Saw, as if in slow motion, a middle-aged woman in a nanny's uniform descending the stairs, holding by the hand a young child to stop him rushing down too fast. Saw them reach the foot of the staircase and the tiny figure tear across the hall to Tia. Saw her scoop him up, hug him, and set him down again gently.

'Hello, munchkin. Have you been good for Nanny?'

Tia's voice was warm, affectionate, and something about it caused a sliver of pain in Anatole's breast, penetrating his frozen shock.

'Yes!' the little boy cried. 'We've done painting. Come and see.'

'I will, darling, in a little while,' he heard her answer, with that same softness in her voice—a softness he remembered from long, long ago, that sent another sliver of pain through him.

The child's eyes went past her, becoming aware of someone standing by the front door.

'Hello,' he said in his piping voice.

His bright gaze looked right at Anatole. Clearly interested. Waiting for a response.

But Anatole could make none. Could only go on standing there, frozen, as knowledge forced itself into his head like a power hose being turned on.

Theos—she has a son.

He dragged his eyes from the child—the sable-haired, dark-eyed child—to the woman who was the boy's mother. Shock was in his eyes still. Shock, and more than shock. An emotion that seemed to well up out of a place so deep within him he did not know it was there. He could give it no name.

'I didn't know—' His voice broke off.

Did her hand tighten on the child's? He could see her face take on an expression of reserve, completely at odds with the warmth of a moment again when she'd been hugging her child.

'Why should you?' she returned coolly. Her chin lifted slightly. 'This is Nicky.' Her eyes dropped to her son. 'Nicky, this is your—'

She stopped. For a second it seemed to Anatole that a kind of paralysis had come over her face.

It was he who filled the gap. Working out just what his relationship was to the little boy. 'Your cousin,' he said.

Nicky cast him an even more interested look. 'Have you come to play with me?' he asked.

Immediately both his nanny and his mother intervened.

'Now, Nicky, not *everyone* who comes here comes to play with you,' his nanny said, her reproof very mild and given as if it were a routine reminder.

'Munchkin, no—your...your cousin is here because of poor Pappou—'

The moment she spoke Christine wished desperately that she hadn't. But she was in no state to think straight. It was taking every ounce of what little remaining strength she had just to remain where she was, to cope with this nightmare scenario playing out, helpless to stop it. Helpless to do anything but hang on in there until finally—dear God, *finally*—the front door closed behind Anatole and she could collapse.

'Pappou?'

The single word from Anatole was like a bullet. A bullet right through her. She stared, aghast at what she'd said.

Grandfather.

She could only stare blindly at Anatole. She had to explain, to make sense of what she'd said—what she'd called Vasilis.

But she was spared the ordeal. At her words Nicky's little face had crumpled, and she realised with a knife in her heart that she had made an even worse mistake than saying what she had in front of Anatole.

'Where is he? I want him—I *want* him! I want Pappou!'

She dropped to her knees beside him, hugging him as he sobbed, giving him what comfort she could, reminding him of how Pappou had been so ill, and was now in heaven, where he was well again, where they would see him again one day.

Then, suddenly there was someone else hunkering down beside her and Nicky. Someone resting his hand on Nicky's heaving shoulder.

Anatole spoke, his voice a mix of gentleness and kindness, completely different from any tone she'd heard from him so far in this nightmare encounter. 'Did you say that you've been doing some painting with Nanny?'

Christine felt Nicky turn in her arms, look at the man kneeling down so close. She saw her son nod, his face still crumpled with tears.

'Well,' said Anatole, in the same tone of voice but now with a note of encouragement in it, 'why don't you paint a picture especially for...for Pappou?'

He said the word hesitantly, but said it all the same. His tone of voice changed again, and now there was something new in it.

'When I was little, I can remember I painted a picture for...for Pappou. I painted a train. It was a bright red train. With blue wheels. You could paint one too, if you like, and then he would have one from both of us. How would that be?'

Christine saw her son gaze at Anatole. Her throat

felt very tight. As tight as if wire had been wrapped around it—barbed wire that drew blood.

'Can my train be blue?' Nicky asked.

Anatole nodded. 'Of course it can. It can be blue with red wheels.'

Nicky's face lit up, his tears gone now. He looked across to his nanny, standing there, ready to intervene if that were needed. Now it was.

'What a good idea!' she said enthusiastically. 'Shall we go and do it now?'

She held out her hand and Nicky disengaged himself from his mother, trotting up to his nanny and taking her hand. He turned back to Christine. 'Nanny and me are going to paint a picture for Pappou,' he informed her.

Christine gave a watery smile. 'That's a lovely idea, darling,' she said.

'Will you show it to me when you've done it?' It was Anatole who'd spoken, rising to his feet, looking across at the little boy.

Nicky nodded, then tugged on his nanny's hand, and the two of them made their journey back up the stairs, with Nicky talking away animatedly.

Christine watched them go. Her heart was hammering in her chest, so loudly she was sure it must be audible. A feeling of faintness swept over her as she stood up.

Did she sway? She didn't know—knew only that a hand had seized her upper arm, was steadying her. A hand that was like a vice.

Had Anatole done that only to stop her fainting? Or for another reason?

She jerked herself free, stepped back sharply. To have him so close—so close to Nicky…

He spoke, his voice low, so as not to be within earshot of the nanny, but his tone was vehement.

'I had no idea—*none*!'

Christine trembled, but her voice was cool. 'Like I said, why should you? If Vasilis chose not to tell you, *I* was hardly likely to!'

Anatole's dark eyes burned into hers. She felt faintness drumming at her again. Such dark eyes…

So like Nicky.

No—she must not think that. Vasilis's eyes had been dark as well, typically Greek. And brown was genetically dominant over her own blue eyes. Of course Nicky would have the dark eyes of his father's family.

'Why does the boy call my uncle *pappou*?' The demand was terse—requiring an answer.

She took a careful breath. 'Vasilis thought it… wiser,' she said. Her mouth snapped closed. She did not want to talk about it, discuss it, have it questioned or challenged.

But Anatole was not to be silenced. 'Why?' he said bluntly.

His eyes seemed to be burning into hers. She rubbed a hand over her forehead. A great weariness was descending on her after the strain of the last grim months—Vasilis's final illness, the awfulness of the last fortnight since he'd died, and now, the day of her husband's burial, the nightmare eruption into her life of the man who had caused her marriage to Vasilis.

'Vasilis knew his heart was weak. That it would give out while Nicky was still young. So he said…' Her voice wavered and she took another difficult breath, not wanting to look at Anatole but knowing she *must* say what she had to. 'He said it would be…kinder for Nicky to grow up calling him his grandfather.'

She had to fight to keep her lips from trembling, her eyes from filling with tears. Her hands clenched each other, nails digging into her palms.

'He said Nicky would miss him less when the time came, feel less deprived than if he'd thought of him as his father.'

Anatole was silent but his thoughts were hectic, heaving. And as troubled as a stormy night. Emotion writhed within him. Memory slashed across his synapses. He could hear Tia's voice—his own.

'I have no intention of being a father—so do not even think of forcing my hand!'

Christine looked at him, her expression veiled. Seeing his—guessing what he was remembering.

'Given what has happened,' she said quietly, 'Vasilis made the right decision. Nicky will have only dim memories of him as he grows, but they will be very fond ones and I will always honour Vasilis's memory to him.'

She swallowed, then said what she must.

'Thank you for suggesting he paint Vasilis a picture. It was a very good idea—it diverted him perfectly.'

'I can remember—just—painting the picture for my uncle that I told Nicky about. He'd come to visit and I was excited. He always brought me a present and paid attention to me. Spent time with me. Later I realised he'd come to talk to my father, to tell him that, for my sake, my father should…mend his ways.' His mouth twisted. 'He had a wasted journey. My father was incapable of mending his ways.'

He frowned, as if he had said too much. He took a ragged breath, shook his head as if to clear it of memories that had no purpose any more.

Then he let his eyes rest on Tia.

'We need to talk,' he said.

CHAPTER FIVE

CHRISTINE SAT ON the chintz-covered sofa, tension racking her still as Mrs Hughes set out a tray of coffee on the ormolu table at her side. Her throat was parched and she was desperate for a shot of caffeine—anything to restore her drained energy levels.

In her head, memory cut like a knife.

'I could murder a cup of coffee.'

Anatole had said that the very first afternoon he'd picked her up off the street where she'd fallen in front of his car and brought her back to his flat. Was he remembering it too? She didn't know. His expression was closed.

As her eyes flickered over him she felt emotion churn in her stomach. His physical impact on her was overpowering. As immediate and overwhelming as it had been the very first time she'd set eyes on him. The five years since she had last set eyes on him vanished.

Panic beat in her again.

I've got to make him go away. I've got to—

'You realise that this changes everything—the fact that Vasilis has a son?'

She started, staring at Anatole. 'Why?' she said blankly.

He lifted an impatient hand, a coffee cup in it, before drinking. 'Don't be obtuse,' he said. 'That is, don't be stupid—'

'I know what obtuse means!' she heard herself snap at him.

He paused, rested his eyes on her. He said nothing, but she could see that her sharp tone had taken him by surprise. He wasn't used to her talking to him like that. Wasn't used to hostility from her.

'It changes nothing that he has a son.' Her voice trembled on the final word. Had Anatole noticed the tremor? She hoped not.

'Of course it does!' he replied.

He finished his coffee, roughly set the cup back on the tray. He was on the sofa opposite her, but he was still too close. His eyes flickered over her for a moment, but his expression was still veiled.

'I will not have Nicky punished for what you did.' He spoke quietly, but there was an intensity in his voice that was like a chill down her spine, 'I will not have him exiled from his family just because of you. He needs his family.'

Her coffee cup rattled on its saucer as her hand trembled. 'He *has* a family—*I* am his family!'

Anatole's hand slashed down. 'So am I! And he cannot be raised estranged from his kin.' He took a heavy breath. 'Whatever you have done, Tia, the boy must not pay for it. I want—'

Something snapped inside her. 'What *you* want, Anatole, is irrelevant! *I* am Nicky's mother. I have sole charge of him, sole guardianship. *I*—not you, and not anyone else in the entire world—get to say any single thing about how he grows up, and in whose company, or any other detail of his life. *Do you understand me?*'

She saw his face whiten around his mouth. Again, it was as if she had sprouted snakes for hair.

Stiffly, he answered her. 'I understand that you have been under considerable strain. That whatever your…your feelings you have had to cope with Vasilis's final illness and his death. His funeral today. You are clearly under stress.'

He got to his feet.

How tall he seemed, towering over her as she sat, her legs too weak, suddenly, to support her in standing up to face him.

He looked at her gravely, his face still shuttered.

'It has been a difficult day,' he said, his voice tight. 'I will take my leave now…let you recover. But…'

He paused, then resumed, never taking from her his dark, heavy gaze that pressed like weights on raw flesh.

'But this cannot be the end of the matter. You *must* understand that, Tia. You must accept it.'

She pushed herself to her feet. 'And *you*, Anatole, must accept that you have nothing to do with my child. *My* child.'

The emphasis was clear. Bitter. Darkness flashed in her eyes, and she lifted her chin defiantly, said the words burning in her like brands.

'I don't want you coming here again. You've made your opinion of me very, very clear. I don't want you coming near my son—*my* son! He has quite enough to bear, in losing Vasilis, without having your hatred of me to cope with. I won't have you poisoning his ears with what you think of me.'

She took a sharp breath, her eyes like gimlets, spearing him.

'Stay away, Anatole. Just *stay away*!'

She marched to the drawing room doors, yanking them open. Her heart was thumping in her breast, her chest heaving. She had to get him out of her house—right now.

Wordlessly, Anatole strode past her. This time—*dear God*—this time she would get him out of the house.

Only at the front door did he turn. Pause, then speak. 'Tia—'

'That is no longer my name.' Christine's voice was stark, biting across him, her face expressionless. 'I stopped being Tia a long time ago. Vasilis always called me Christine, my given name, not any diminutive. I am Christine. That's who I am—who I always will be.'

There was a choke in her voice as grief threatened her. But grief was not her greatest threat. Her greatest threat was the man it always had been.

Her nails pressed into her palms and she welcomed the pain. She turned away, leaving him to let himself out, rapid footsteps impelling her towards the door of her sitting room. She gained it, shut the door behind her, leaning against it, feeling faintness threatening. Her eyes were stark and staring. That barbed wire garrotting her throat.

I will never be Tia again. I can never be Tia again.

The barbed wire pressed tighter yet. Now it was drawing blood.

Anatole drove up the motorway, back towards London. He was pushing the speed limit and did not care. He needed to put as much distance as he could between himself and Tia.

Christine.

That was what she called herself now, she'd said. What his uncle had called her. His eyes shifted. He did not want to think about his uncle calling Tia… Christine…anything at all. Having anything to do with her.

Having a child with her.

His mind sheared away. No, he could not think about that—about the creation of a child between Tia and his uncle—his erudite bachelor uncle who'd never had a romance in his life.

And still never had, either—whatever lures Tia had cast over him.

His expression changed. No, that was the wrong way to look at it—they could not have been lures. Vasilis would have been immune to anything so crude.

She would just have come across as helpless and vulnerable. Cast aside by me—

His mind shifted away again. He still did not want to think about it. Didn't want to remember that day five long years ago.

Yet memory came, all the same…

'I… I think I may be pregnant.'

The words fell into the space between them.

Anatole could feel himself freezing, hear himself responding.

'So are you or aren't you?'

That was what he said. A simple question.

He saw, as if from a long way away, her face blanch.

'I'm not sure,' she whispered, expression strained. 'My period is late—'

'How late?' Again, a simple question.

'I… I think it's about a week late. I… I'm not sure. It may be longer.'

Anatole found himself trying to calculate in his head when she'd last been…indisposed. Could not quite place it. But that wasn't relevant. Only one thing mattered now.

His voice seemed to come from a long way away. A long way from where she was sitting, gazing at him, her expression like nothing he had ever seen before. Like nothing he wanted to see.

'You'd better do a test.' The words came out clipped, completely unemotional. 'With luck it's a false alarm.'

Without luck—

His mind sheared away. He would not think about the alternative. But even as he steeled himself he narrowed his eyes, resting them on her face. There was a stricken look on it, but something more, too.

She's hiding something.

Every instinct told him that. She was concealing something, pushing it back inside her, so that he could not tell what it was. But he knew—oh, he knew.

I haven't given her the right answer—the answer she wanted to hear. I've caught her out by not giving her that answer, and she doesn't know how to react now.

He knew what she'd wanted his reaction to be. It was obvious. He was supposed to have reacted very differently from the way he had.

I was supposed to look amazed—thrilled. I was supposed to sweep her up into my arms. Tell her she was the most treasured thing in the universe to me, carrying my oh-so-precious child! I was supposed to tell her that I was thrilled beyond everything—that she'd given me the best gift I could ever have dreamt of!

And then, of course, he was supposed to have gone down on one knee, taken her hand in his, and asked her to marry him.

Because that was what they *all* wanted, didn't they? All the women who passed through his life. They wanted him to marry them.

And he was so tired of it—so bored, so exasperated.

All of them wanted to be Mrs Kyrgiakis. As if there weren't three of them already—his father's current wife and his two exes. Even his mother had coupled her new husband's name to Kyrgiakis, to ensure so she got kudos from the family connection as well as her hand in the Kyrgiakis coffers.

So, no, with quite enough Mrs Kyrgiakises in the world, he did not want another one.

Not another one who had only become one because she was pregnant—the way his mother had become Mrs Kyrgiakis the Second. Giving her the perfect opportunity to dump her unwanted first husband and snap up a second. Not that she'd wanted his father for long, or he her. They'd both got bored and taken lovers, and then another spouse each. Creating yet another Mrs Kyrgiakis.

And so the circus had gone on.

I will not perpetuate it.

Not willingly. *Never* willingly—

His eyes rested on Tia, his expression veiled. She was looking pale and nervous. He reached out a hand as if to touch her cheek, reassure her. Then he pulled back. What reassurance could he give her? He didn't want to marry her. That would hardly reassure her, would it?

'Did you do it deliberately? Take a chance that you might get pregnant?'

The words were out of his mouth before he could stop them. He heard her gasp, saw her face blanch again. As if he had slapped her.

But he could not unsay them—un-ask the question he'd pushed at her.

'Well?' he persisted.

His eyes were still resting on her, no expression in them, because he did not want to let his feelings show. He needed to keep them banked down, suppressed.

He saw her swallow, shake her head.

'Well, that's something,' he breathed. 'So, how did it happen? How is it even a possibility?'

She'd been on the Pill for months now. Ever since he'd made the decision to keep her in his life. So what had gone wrong?

He saw her drop her eyes, her face convulse. 'It was when we went to San Francisco. The changing time zones muddled me.'

He gave a heavy sigh. He should have checked—made sure she hadn't got 'muddled'.

'Well, hopefully it hasn't screwed things up completely.'

Her expression changed. Anxiety visible. But there was another emotion too. One he could not name. Did not want to.

'Would it?' Her voice was thin, as if stretched too far. Her eyes were searching his. '*Would* it screw things up completely?'

He turned away. Reached for his briefcase. It was

going to be a long, draining day—getting through the annual board meeting, seeing his parents again, watching them pointedly ignore each other, pointedly show demonstrations of affection to their current new spouses, glaring testimony to the shallow fickleness of their emotions, constantly imagining themselves in love, rushing into yet another reckless, ill-considered marriage.

No wonder he didn't want to marry—didn't want to be cornered into marrying by any woman prepared to do anything to get his ring on her finger. Including getting herself pregnant.

I didn't think Tia was like that. I thought what we had suited her, just like it suited me. I thought that she was fond of me, as I am of her—but there's nothing about love. Nothing about marriage. And, dear God, nothing about babies!

But it looked as if he'd been wrong—

He didn't answer her. Couldn't answer her. Instead he simply glanced at his watch—he was running late already.

He looked back at her as he headed for the door, not meeting her eyes. 'I'll have a pregnancy testing kit delivered,' he said—and was gone.

There was a tight wire around his throat. He felt its pressure for the rest of the day. All through the gruelling board meeting—his parents behaving just as he'd known they would, constantly pressing for yet more profits to be distributed to them. And after the meeting was the even more gruelling ordeal of an endlessly long lunch that went on all afternoon.

'You seem distracted, Anatole. Is everything all right?'

This was his Uncle Vasilis, taking the opportunity to draw him aside after the formal meal had finally finished and everyone was milling about, lighting up cigars, drinking vintage port and brandy.

'Call me old-fashioned,' Vasilis said, 'but when a young man is distracted it is usually by a woman.'

He paused again, his eyes studying Anatole even though Anatole had immediately, instinctively, blanked his expression. But it did not silence his uncle.

'You know,' Vasilis continued, 'I would so like you to fall in love and marry—make a *happy* marriage! Yes, I know you are sceptical, and I can understand why—but do not judge the world by your parents. They constantly imagine themselves in love with yet another object of their desire. Making a mess of their lives, being careless of everyone else's. Including,' he added, his eyes not shifting from Anatole's face, 'yours.'

Anatole's mouth tightened. *Making a mess of their lives...* Was that what *he* was going to do too? Had he already done it? Was he simply waiting to find out whether it was so?

Does she have the results already? Does she know if she's messed up my life—and I hers?

But a darker question was already lurking beneath those questions. Would being pregnant by him mess up Tia's life or achieve a dream for her? Attain her goal—her ambition.

Have I given her a taste for the life I lead, so that now she wants to keep it for herself, for ever?

Having a Kyrgiakis child would achieve that for her. A Kyrgiakis child would achieve a Kyrgiakis husband. Access to the Kyrgiakis coffers. To the lavish Kyrgiakis lifestyle.

'Anatole?'

His uncle's voice penetrated his circling thoughts, his turbid emotions. But he could not cope with an inquisition now, so he only gave a brief smile and asked his uncle about his latest philanthropic endeavour.

Vasilis responded easily enough, but Anatole was aware of concern in his uncle's eyes, a sense that he was being studied, worried over. He blanked it, just as he was blanking the question that had been knifing in his head all day. Did Tia have her results, and—dear God—what were they?

He wanted to phone her, but dreaded it too. So much hung in the balance—his whole future depended on Tia's answer.

As everyone finally dispersed from the hotel—Vasilis departing with a smile and saying he was looking forward to accepting his nephew's lunch invitation the next day, an invitation Anatole now wished he'd never made—he found that he actually welcomed his father catching him by the arm and telling him, in a petulant undertone, that thanks to the booming profits Anatole had just announced his latest wife had suddenly decided to divorce him.

'You've made me too rich!' he accused his son ill-temperedly. 'So now I need you to find a way to make sure she gets as little as possible.'

He dragged Anatole off to a bar, pouring into his son's ears a self-pitying moan about greedy ex-wives, and how hard done by he was by them all, while he proceeded to work his way through a bottle of whisky.

Eventually Anatole returned him to his hotel room

and left him. Finally heading back to his apartment, he felt his heart start to hammer. He could postpone finding out Tia's results no longer.

Yet when he reached his apartment, close to midnight, Tia was asleep. He did not disturb her. Could not. Of the pregnancy test kit there was no sign, and he had no wish to search for it in the bathroom, to see the result—to know what his future would be. Not now, not yet…

With that wire tightening around his throat, he stood gazing down at her. She looked so small in the huge king-sized bed. Emotions flitted across the surface of her mind. Emotions he had never had cause to feel before. Thoughts he had never had to think before.

Is she carrying my child? Does it grow within her body?

Those emotions flickered again, like currents of electricity, static that could not flow, meeting resistance somewhere in the nerve fibres of his brain.

Yet he could feel the impulse to let it flow, connect, let it overcome him—so that almost, almost he stripped off his clothes to lie own with her, take her into his arms, not to make love to her, but to hold her slender, petite body, to slide his hand across her abdomen where, right now, secret and safe, their baby might be taking hold of life. To hold them both, close and cherishing…

He stepped away. He must not let himself succumb. Must do what he was doing now—walking away, taking himself off to another bedroom, sleeping there the night, his dreams troubled and troubling.

He woke the next morning to see Tia standing in

the doorway, her body silhouetted in her nightgown by the morning sun.

'I'm not pregnant,' she said to him. 'I've just got my period.' There was no emotion in her voice. Nor in her face.

Then she turned and left.

Anatole lay motionless, his open eyes staring at the ceiling, where sunlight played around the light socket. It was very strange. Her announcement should have brought relief. Should have made everything well between them.

Yet it had ended everything.

CHAPTER SIX

CHRISTINE SAT AT the desk in Vasilis's study. She could feel the echo of him here still—here where he had spent so much of his time—and found comfort in it.

The weeks since his death had turned into months. Slow, painful, difficult months of getting used to a house empty of his quiet presence. It had been difficult for her, difficult for Nicky. Tears and tantrums had been frequent as the little boy had slowly, unwillingly come to terms with the loss of his beloved *pappou*.

Pappou—the word stabbed into Christine's head, and again she heard Anatole's shock. Her mind closed, automatically warding off the memory of that nightmare encounter with the man she had fled. Who had not wanted her as she had wanted him. Who thought of her as nothing more than a cheap adventuress…a gold-digger who had married his uncle for the wealth he could bestow upon her.

Pain hacked at her at the thought of how badly Anatole regarded her. How much he seemed to hate her now.

She had been right to send him packing. Anything else would have been unbearable! Unthinkable. Yet even as she felt that resolve she felt another emotion too. Powerful—painful. Nicky had done the painting of a train for his *pappou* and he wanted to know when his 'big cousin' was going to come and see it.

She had given evasive answers—he lived in Greece, Pappou's homeland, and he was very busy, working very hard.

After a while Nicky had stopped asking, but every now and then he would still say 'I *want* to see him again! Why can't I see him again? I painted the picture! I want to show it to him!' And then he'd become tearful and difficult.

Guilt stabbed at Christine. Her son was going through so much now. And he always would. He would be growing up without Vasilis in his life, without the man he thought of as his grandfather.

Growing up without a father—

Her mind sheared away. What use was it to think of that? *None.* Instead, she took a breath, focussing her attention on what she needed to do right now.

Probate had finally been completed—a lengthy task, given that Vasilis's estate was large, his will complex, and it had involved the setting up of both a family trust and a philanthropic foundation to carry on his work.

It was the latter that preoccupied her now. At the end of the week she was going to have to perform her first duty as Vasilis's widow—to represent him at the opening of an exhibition of Greek art and antiquities at a prestigious London museum. Though she had always accompanied him to the events he'd sponsored, this was the first time she would be alone. It was a daunting prospect, but she was resolved to perform to the best of her ability. She owed it to Vasilis to do so.

Now, in preparation, she bowed her head to read through the correspondence and the detailed notes from the curator, to make sure she knew what she must know in time for the event.

This is for Vasilis. For him who gave me so much!

It was a fraction of what she owed him—the man who had rescued her when her life had been at its lowest, most desolate ebb.

Anatole was in a business meeting, but his mind was not on the involved mesh of investments, profits and tax exposure that was its subject. Instead he was focussed mentally on the request he had received that morning from his uncle's lawyers in London. They wanted him to contact them. Probate, apparently, had now been completed.

His mouth thinned. So now he would find out just how rich Vasilis's young widow would be. Just how much she had profited from marrying his middle-aged uncle. Oh, she had done very well indeed out of convincing him to marry her. To rescue her from Anatole, the man who had lifted her—literally—off the street!

I thought she was so devoted to me. But all along it was just the lifestyle I gave her. She couldn't wait to ensure it for herself by getting Vasilis's wedding ring on her finger after I'd made it clear to her that any hope she might have had of letting herself get pregnant to get me to marry her was out of the question.

That old familiar stab came again. It was anger—of *course* it was anger! What else could it be? It was anger that he felt when he thought about Tia abandoning him to snap up his uncle. Only anger.

Restlessly, Anatole shifted in his seat, impatient for

the meeting to be done. Yet when he finally was free to get back to his office, to phone London, he knew he was reluctant to do so.

Did he really want to stir up in himself again those mixed emotions that his uncle's death had caused? That his rash visit to England on the day of the funeral had plunged him into? Shouldn't he just leave things be? He could not alter his uncle's will—if his widow had all Vasilis's money to splurge, so what? Why should he care?

Except that—

Except that it is not just about Tia, is it? Or about you. There's someone else to think about.

Vasilis's son. Nicky. The little boy he'd known nothing about—never guessed existed.

That scene burned in his head again—himself hunkering down to offer solace to the heartbroken child. Emotion thrust inside him, but a new one now—one that seemed to pierce more deeply than the thought that the woman he had once romanced, made love to, taken into his life, had abandoned him. It was a piercing that came from the sobs of a bereft child, that made him want to comfort him, console him.

He stared sightlessly across his office. Where did that emotion come from? *Never* had he thought about children—except negatively. Oh, not because he disliked them, but because they had nothing to do with him. Could never have anything to do with him. What he'd said to Tia, that grim day when she'd thought she was pregnant, was as true now as it had been then.

And yet—

What instinct had made him seek to comfort the

little boy? To divert him, bring a smile to his face, light up his eyes?

It's because he's Vasilis's son. Because he has no one else to look out for him now. Only a mother who married his father just to endow herself with a wealthy lifestyle she could never have aspired to otherwise.

His expression changed. Turned steely. He had told Tia that Nicky's existence changed everything but she had rejected what he'd said. Sent him from her house. Banned him from making any contact with Nicky. His eyes darkened. Well, that was not going to happen. *Someone* had to look out for Vasilis's child, and now that his widow had a free rein with her late husband's wealth she could do anything she wanted with it! What security would there be for Vasilis's son when his mother was an ambitious, luxury-loving gold-digger?

The phone on his desk sounded, indicating the call to London was ready for him. Grim-faced, he picked it up. Whatever he had to do, he would ensure that his vulnerable young cousin was not left to the mercy of his despised mother.

I'll fight her for justice for her son—for Vasilis's son.

Yet when he slowly hung up the phone, some ten minutes later, his expression was different. Very different. He called through to his secretary.

'Book me on the next flight to London.'

Christine sat back in the car that was taking her up to London for the evening. Her nerves were jittery, and not just because she would be representing Vasilis at the exhibition's opening. It was also because this would be the first time she'd been to London since he'd died—and London held memories that were of more than her husband.

She felt her mind shear away. No, she must not think—must not remember how she had met Anatole, how he had swept her into his life, how she had fallen head over heels for a man who had been to her eyes like a prince out of a fairytale!

But he hadn't been a prince after all. He'd been an ordinary person, however rich and gilded his existence, and he'd had no desire for her to be a permanent part of his life. No desire at all for a baby…a child.

It was Vasilis who'd wanted that. Had wanted the child who'd given him a joy that, as Christine sadly knew, he'd never thought to have.

The knowledge comforted her.

However much he gave me—immense though that was, and eternally grateful though I am—I know that I gave him Nicky to love…

Now she was all Nicky had.

Her nerves jangled again. She must not think of Anatole, must only be grateful that he'd accepted her dismissal. Had made no further attempt to get in touch. Make contact with Nicky.

Her mouth set. Eyes stark.

His knowing of Nicky's existence doesn't change anything. And I won't—I won't!—have anyone near Nicky who thinks so ill of me, poisoning my son's mind against me…

For the remainder of the journey she forced herself to focus only on the evening's event.

Later, when the moment came, she felt a sudden tightening of her throat as she was introduced as Mrs

Vasilis Kyrgiakis, then she took a measured breath and began her short, carefully written speech. She said how pleased her husband had been to support this important exhibition of Hellenistic art and artefacts, so expertly curated by the museum—giving a smiling nod to the director, Dr Lanchester—and then diverted a little on descriptions of some of the key exhibits, before concluding with a reassurance that despite Vasilis Kyrgiakis's untimely death his work was being entrusted to a foundation specifically set up for that purpose.

After handing over to Dr Lanchester she stepped away, and as the formal opening was completed started to mingle socially with the invited guests.

Everyone was in evening dress, and although, of course, her dress was black, her state of mourning did not prevent her from accepting a proffered glass of champagne. She sipped it delicately, listening to something the director's wife was saying, and smiling appropriately. She knew both the director and his wife, having dined with them together with Vasilis, before his final illness had taken its fatal grip on him.

She was about to make some remark or other when a voice behind her turned her to stone.

'Won't you introduce me?'

She whipped round, not believing her eyes. But it was impossible to deny who she was seeing.

Anatole.

Anatole in a black tuxedo, like all the other male guests, towering over her.

Shock made faintness drum in her head.

How on earth? What on earth?

He gave a swift, empty smile. 'I felt it my duty to represent the Kyrgiakis family tonight,' he informed her.

If it was meant as a barb, implying that *she* could not possibly do so, she did not let her reaction show. She gave a grave nod.

'I'm sure Vasilis would have appreciated your presence here,' she acknowledged quietly. 'He worked hard to ensure this exhibition would be possible. Many of the artefacts have been rescued from the turmoil in the Middle East, to find safety here, for the time being, until eventually they can be securely returned.'

She indicated with a graceful gesture towards some of the exhibits to which she was referring, but Anatole was not looking. His eyes were only on her. Taking her in. The woman standing there, in a black silk evening gown, with long sleeves and a high-cut neckline, was every inch in mourning, but she was not a woman Anatole recognised.

He'd arrived to see her take centre stage, and had not believed it could be Tia—*Christine*—Vasilis's widow. Poised, elegant, mature—and perfectly capable of addressing a room full of learned dignitaries and opening an exhibition of Hellenistic archaeology.

No, she was definitely not the socially nervous, timid Tia he remembered.

Nor was it the Tia he remembered who was turning now towards the museum's director.

'Dr Lanchester—may I introduce Vasilis's nephew, Anatole Kyrgiakis?'

If there was any tremor in her voice Anatole did not hear it. Her composure was perfect. Only the sudden masking in her eyes as she'd first seen him there had revealed otherwise. And that masking came again as the museum director smiled at Anatole.

'Will you be taking on your uncle's role?' he asked.

'Alas, I will be unable to become as directly involved as he was, but I hope to be one of the trustees of the foundation,' Anatole replied easily. 'Along with, I'm sure, my…' He hesitated slightly, turning to Christine. 'I'm not sure quite what our relationship is,' he said.

Was that another barb? She ignored it, as she had the first. 'I doubt it has a formal designation,' she remarked, with dogged composure. 'And, yes, I shall be one of the foundation's trustees.'

Her mouth tightened. *And no way on earth will I let you be one too!*

The very thought of having to attend trustees' meetings with Anatole there—she felt a cold chill through her. Then he was speaking again. He was smiling a courtesy smile, but she could see the dark glint in his eyes.

'I do hope, then, that you no longer believe Alexander the Great to be contemporary with the Greek War of Independence!' he said lightly.

Did he mean to wound her? If he did, then it only showed how bitter he was towards her.

Before, when she had been Tia—ignorant, uneducated Tia, who'd spent her schooldays nursing her mother—he'd never been anything other than sympathetic towards her in her lack of knowledge of all that he took for granted with his expensive private education.

But he'd meant to wound her now, and she would not let him do so.

So she only smiled in return, not looking at him but at the others. 'Before I married Vasilis,' she explained, 'I was completely ignorant of a great deal of history. But I *do* now know that in the fourth century BC Alexander was pre-dating the Battle of Navarino in 1827 by quite some time!'

Her expression was humorous. It had to be. How else could she deal with this?

'I think—at least, I *hope*!—that now, thanks to Vasilis's tuition, I can recognise the Hellenistic style, at least in obvious examples. Speaking of which…' she turned to the curator of the exhibition and bestowed an optimistic smile upon him '… I wonder if I might impose on you to guide me around the exhibits?'

'I'd be delighted!' he assured her, and to her profound relief she was able to move away.

Nevertheless, as she was conducted around she was burningly conscious of Anatole's presence in all the rooms.

She prayed that she would not have to talk to him again. Why had he turned up? Had he meant it, saying he wanted to be one of the foundation's trustees? What power would she have to prevent him? After all, he was a Kyrgiakis—how could she object?

But perhaps he only said it to get at me. Just like he made that reference to how ignorant I once was…

She felt a little sting inside her. Did he truly hate her so much? Her throat tightened. Of course he did! Hadn't he said it to her face, the day of Vasilis's funeral, calling her such vile names?

But you didn't want me, Anatole—and Vasilis did! So why berate me for accepting what he offered with such kindness, such generosity?

The answer was obvious, of course. Five long years of anger were driving him, and Anatole believed that she had manoeuvred Vasilis into marrying her so that she could enjoy the lavish Kyrgiakis lifestyle he provided. For no other reason.

A great sense of weariness washed over her. The strain of having to represent Vasilis tonight, the poignancy of the occasion and then the shock of Anatole intruding, the barbs he had directed at her—were all overpowering her.

Forcing herself to make some kind of appropriate response to the curator as he introduced each exhibit, she counted the minutes until she could decently call a halt. She had to get away—escape.

Finally, murmuring her excuses—readily accepted, given her mourning status—she was treading through the empty corridors towards the museum's entrance.

'Leaving so soon?'

The voice behind her on the wide stone staircase echoed in the otherwise deserted building, well away from the exhibition gallery.

This time she was more collected in her reaction. 'Yes,' she said.

'I'll drive you back,'

Anatole's footsteps quickened and he drew level with her. Moved to take her arm. She avoided it, stepping aside.

'Thank you, but my car is waiting.'

Hurriedly, she went out, stepped onto the wide pavement, thankful to see her chauffeured car at the kerbside.

She turned back to Anatole. He seemed taller than

ever, more overpowering. She lifted her chin. 'Don't let me keep you, Anatole,' she said.

It was nothing more than an expression, and yet she heard it echo savagely in her head. No, she had not been able to *keep* Anatole, had she?

Because I committed the cardinal sin in his book. The one unforgivable crime.

Her mind sheared away. Why remember the past? It was gone, and gone for ever.

She headed determinedly towards her car, but Anatole was there before her, opening her door. Then, to her consternation, as she got inside as quickly as her long gown permitted Anatole followed.

'I've dismissed my own car. I'll see you to your destination. Where are you staying?'

He realised he had no idea. Had Vasilis acquired a London base? He did not use his father's hotel suite—that he knew.

The suite I never went to that fatal night I took Tia into my arms—into my life.

No, don't remember that night. It was over, gone—nothing was left of that life now.

He heard her give with audible reluctance the name of a hotel. It was a top hotel, but a quiet one—not fashionable. Ideal for his uncle, Anatole acknowledged.

He said as much, and Christine nodded.

'Yes, Vasilis always liked it. Old-fashioned, but peaceful. And it has a lovely roof garden—you'd hardly know you were in London—'

She stopped. Memory sprang, unwanted, of Anatole's verdant roof terrace at his London apartment, of him saying that he did not care for cities.

There was a moment of silence. Was Anatole remembering too?

Well, what if he is? So what?

Defiance filled her, quelling the agitation that had leapt automatically as he'd got into the car. She was sitting as far away as possible, and even knowing the presence of Mr Hughes behind his glass screen was preventing complete privacy with Anatole, her heart was beating hectically. She tried to slow it—she must retain control, composure. She *must*!

I am Vasilis's widow. He can protect me still simply by virtue of that. That is my identity now.

She pulled her mind back—Anatole was speaking.

'I wanted to tell you,' he was saying, his voice stiff, as if the words did not come easily, 'how impressed I was with you tonight. You handled the occasion very well.' He paused. 'You did Vasilis proud.'

Christine's turned her head, her eyes widening. Had Anatole really just said that? Anatole who thought her the lowest of the low?

'I did it for him,' she said quietly, and looked away, out of her window, away from Anatole.

She could feel his presence in the car as something tangible, threatening to overpower her. How many times had she and he driven like this, through the city night? So many nights—so many cities…

It was so long ago—five years ago. A lifetime ago. And I am not the same person—not by any measure. Even my name is different now. I have been a wife, and now I am a widow—I am a mother. And Anatole can mean nothing to me any more. Nothing!

Just as she, in the end, had meant nothing to him.

Memory stabbed at her of how Anatole had sat her

down, talked to her, his face tense, the morning she had told him she wasn't pregnant after all.

'Tia—this is something you have to understand. I do not want to marry and I do not want to have children. Not with you—not with anyone. Now, if either or both of those things is something you do want,' he'd continued in the same taut voice, 'then you must accept that it is not going to happen with me. Not *voluntarily*.'

His voice had twisted on that word. He'd been sitting opposite her, leaning forward slightly, his hands hanging loosely between his thighs, an earnest expression on his face as if he were explaining something to someone incapable of understanding.

And that was me—I couldn't understand. So I learned the hard way....

He'd taken a breath, looked her straight in the eyes. 'I like you Tia. You're very sweet, and very lovely, and we've had a really great time together, but...' He'd taken another breath. 'What I will not tolerate is any attempt by you to...to get pregnant and force me to the altar. I won't have that, Tia—I won't have it.'

He'd held her eyes, making her hear what he was telling her.

'So from now on make sure there is no chance of another scare like this one, OK? No more getting "muddled up" over time zones.' And then an edge had come into his voice, and his eyes had had a look of steel in them. 'If that is what really happened.'

He'd got to his feet, his six-foot height dwarfing her seated figure, and she'd looked up at him, her throat tight and painful, her hands twisted in her lap.

'If you want a baby, Tia, accept that it cannot be

with me.' His expression had hardened. 'And if it's me you want one with—well, then you had better leave, right away, because it's over between us—*over*.'

He'd left the apartment then, heading to his office, and she'd watched him go. Her vision had grown hazy, and she'd felt feel sobs rising. The moment he'd gone she had rushed into the bathroom, releasing the pent-up tears, hating it that Anatole was being like that—hating it that she'd given him cause.

What she longed for so unbearably was what he did *not* want, and her heart felt as if it was cracking in pieces.

Her red-rimmed eyes had fallen on the little rectangular packet by the basin. It had been delivered the day before but she had dreaded using it. Dreaded finding out. Finding out whether what she had once thought would be a dream come true was instead turning into a nightmare. Was she forcing a child on Anatole—forcing him into a loveless, bitter marriage he did not want to make.

Then her period had arrived after all, making the test unnecessary.

She'd stared at the packet. Fear in her throat.

I've got to be sure—absolutely, totally sure—that I'm not pregnant. Because that's the only way he'll still want me.

She'd shut her eyes. She needed Anatole to want her on any terms at all. *Any* terms.

So she had done the test. Even though she hadn't needed to. Because she hadn't been able to bear not to.

She had done the test…and stared at the little white stick…

* * *

Christine's car was pulling up at the hotel. Anatole leant across, opening her door for her. The brush of his sleeve on her arm made her feel faint, and she had to fight to keep her air of composure, dangerously fragile as it was.

She turned to bid him goodnight. But he was getting out too. Addressing her.

'I need to speak to you.' He glanced at the hotel entrance. 'In private.'

He took her elbow, moved to guide her inside. Unless she wrested herself away from him, made a scene in front of Mr Hughes and the doorman tipping his hat to them, she must comply.

The moment she was indoors, she stepped away.

'Well?' she said, lifting her eyebrows, her expression still unyielding.

His eyes had gone to where a small bar opened up off the lobby, and she walked stiffly to one of the tables, sat herself down. The place was almost empty, and she was glad. She ordered coffee for herself and Anatole did likewise, adding a brandy.

Only when the drinks arrived did he speak. 'I've heard from Vasilis's London solicitors,' he opened.

Christine's eyes went to him. She was burningly conscious of him there—of his tall, effortlessly elegant body, of the achingly familiar scent of his aftershave, of the slight darkening of his jawline at this advanced hour of the evening.

How she had loved to rub her fingers along the roughening edges, feeling passion start to quicken…

Yet again, she hauled her mind away. Anatole's

voice was clipped, restrained as he continued. She realised he was tense, and wondered why.

'Now that probate has been granted they have told me the contents of Vasilis's will.' The words came reluctantly from him, his mouth tight. His eyes rested on her face, looking at her blankly. Then his expression changed. 'Why did you let me think you would inherit all my uncle's personal fortune for yourself?'

Christine's eyes widened. 'I didn't,' she said tightly. '*That*, Anatole,' she added, her voice sharp, 'was something you assumed entirely on your own!'

He half lifted his hand—as if her objection were irrelevant. As if there were more he had to say.

'My uncle's wealth has been left entirely in trust for his son—you get only a trivial income for yourself. Everything else belongs to Nicky!'

Her eyes flickered and her chin lifted. 'I wouldn't call my income *trivial*. It's over thirty thousand pounds a year,' she replied.

'Chickenfeed!' he said dismissively.

Her expression tightened. 'To you, yes. To me it's enough to live on if I have to—more than enough. I was penniless when I married Vasilis—as you reminded me. Of *course* everything must go to Nicky. And besides—' she allowed a flash of cynicism to show in her eyes '—as I'm sure you will point out to me, I will continue to reap the benefits of Nicky's inheritance while he's a minor. I get to live in a Queen Anne country house, and I'll have all of Nicky's money to enjoy while he grows up.'

A hand lifted and slashed sideways. 'But you will have no spending money other than your own income.'

Her composure snapped. 'Oh, for heaven's sake,

Anatole. What am I going to spend money on? I have enough clothes to last me a lifetime. And I've told you I have no ambition to racket around the world causing scandals, as you so charmingly accused me of wanting to do. I simply want to go on living where I do now—for my sake as much as Nicky's. It's where he's grown up so far, where I have friends and know people who knew Vasilis and liked him, valued him. If I want to take Nicky on holiday, of course funds will be made available to me. I shall want for nothing—though I'm sure you'll be the first to accuse me of the opposite!'

She saw him reach for his brandy, take a hefty mouthful before setting it down on the table with a decisive click.

'I can accuse you of nothing.' He took a breath—a deep, shuddering breath—and focussed his eyes on her. Emotion worked in his face. 'Instead—' He stopped, abruptly. His expression changed. So did his voice. 'Instead,' he repeated, 'I have to apologise. I said things to you that I...that were unfair—'

He broke off again. Reached for his coffee and downed it. Then he was looking at her again. As if she were not the person he had thought her to be.

But she isn't. She's not the avaricious, ambitious gold-digger I thought. It was she who insisted on Vasilis leaving his personal fortune to Nicky, his lawyers told me, with nothing for her apart from that paltry income.

It was not what he'd expected to hear. But because of it...

It changes everything.

It was the same phrase that had burst from him when he'd discovered the existence of Vasilis's son, and now it burned in his head again, bringing to the fore the second thing he had to tell her. The imperative that had been building up in him, fuelled by that strange, compelling emotion that had filled him when he'd crouched down beside the little boy to console and comfort him.

'I would like to see Nicky again—soon.'

Immediately Christine's face was masked.

'He is my blood,' he said tightly. 'He should know me. Even if—' He stopped.

She filled the gap, her face still closed. Her tone was acid. 'Even if *I* am his mother?'

Anatole's brows drew together in a frown. 'I did not mean—' Again he broke off.

He'd just told her he couldn't accuse her of wanting her husband's fortune—but she'd still persuaded a man thirty years older than her to marry her in order to acquire the lavish lifestyle she could never have achieved otherwise. That alone must condemn her. What other interpretation could there be for what she had done when she had left him to marry his uncle?

Conflict and confusion writhed in him again.

'Yes, you did,' Christine retorted, her tone still acid. 'Anatole, look—try to understand something. *You* may not have wanted to marry me, to have a child with me—but your uncle did. It was his *choice* to marry me. You insult him if you think otherwise and your approval was not necessary.'

She saw his hand clench, emotion flash across his face, but she didn't want to hear any more. She got to her feet, weariness sweeping over her. She longed for Vasilis's protective company, but he was gone. She was alone in the world now. Except for Nicky—her beloved son.

The most precious being in the universe to her.

The very reason she had married.

Anatole watched her walk out—an elegant, graceful woman. A woman he had once held in his arms, known intimately—and yet now she was like a stranger. Even the name she insisted on calling herself emphasised that.

Emotion roiled within him in the confusing mesh that swirled so confusingly in his head, that he could make no sense of.

But there was one thing he *could* make sense of.

Whatever his conflicting thoughts about Tia—or Christine, as she now preferred to be known—and whatever she had done…abandoning him, marrying his uncle, remaking her life as Vasilis's oh-so-young wife…she'd gone up in the world in a way that she could never have imagined possible the day she had trudged down that London street with a heavy suitcase holding all her possessions.

Now she was transformed into a woman who was poised and chicly dressed, who was able—of all things!—to introduce an exhibition of ancient artefacts as if she were perfectly well acquainted with such esoteric knowledge. Yes, whatever she had done in these years when he had never seen her, there was one thing he could make sense of.

Nicky. The little boy who had lost the man he'd thought of as his grandfather—who would now be raised only by his mother, knowing nothing of his paternal background or his heritage.

Anatole's face steeled. Well, he would ensure that did not happen. He owed it to Vasilis—to the little boy himself—to play *some* part in his life at least.

A stab of remorse—even guilt—pierced him. In the five long years since Tia had left him he'd received, from time to time, communications from his uncle. Careful overtures of reconciliation.

He'd ignored them all—blanked them.

But he could not—*would* not—ignore the existence of Vasilis's young son.

I want to see him again!

Resolve filled him. Something about the child called to him.

Again that memory filled his head of how he'd distracted the little boy, talking about painting a picture of a train, just as he himself had once done for his uncle in that long-ago time when it had been he himself who'd been the child without any kind of father figure in his life to take an interest in him. When there had only been occasional visits from Vasilis—never his own father, to whom he had been of no interest at all.

Well, for Nicky it would not be like that.

He'll have me. I'll make sure of it!

And if that meant seeing Tia—Christine—again, well, that was something he would have to endure.

Unease flickered in him. *Can I cope with that? Seeing her in the years to come with Nicky growing up?*

It was a question that, right now, he did not want to think about.

CHAPTER SEVEN

'MUMMA, *LOOK*!'

Nicky's excited voice called to her and Christine finished her chat to Nanny Ruth and paid attention to her son.

They were out in the garden now that spring was here, and Nicky was perched on a bench beside a rangy young man who was showing him photos on his mobile phone.

As Nanny Ruth went off to take her well-earned break Christine went and sat herself down too, lifting Nicky onto her lap. 'What have you got there, Giles?' she asked with a smile.

The young man grinned. 'Juno's litter,' he said. 'They arrived last night. I couldn't wait to show Nicky.'

'One of them is going to be mine!' Nicky piped up excitedly. 'You said, Mumma, you *said*!'

'Yes, I did say,' Christine agreed.

She'd talked it through with Giles Barcourt and his parents. They were the village's major landowners from whom Vasilis had bought the former Dower House on the estate. They had always been on very friendly terms, and now, they were recommending to Christine that acquiring a puppy would help Nicky recover from losing his beloved *pappou*. She was in full agreement, seeing just how excited he was at the prospect.

'So,' Giles continued, 'which one shall it be, do you think? It will be a good few weeks before they're ready to leave home, but you can come and visit them to make your final choice.'

He grinned cheerfully at Nicky and Christine, and she smiled warmly back. He was a likeable young man—about her own age, she assumed, with a boyish air about him that she suspected would last all his life. He'd studied agriculture at Cirencester, like so many of his peers, and now ran the family estate along with his father. A born countryman.

'By the way,' he went on, throwing her a cheerful look again, 'Mama—' he always used the old-fashioned moniker in a shamelessly humorous fashion '—would love you to come to dinner next Friday. My sister will be there, with her sproglets and the au pair, so Nicky can join the nursery party. The sproglets are promised one of the pups too, so there'll be a bunfight over choosing. What do you say?'

Christine smiled, knowing the invitation was kindly meant. It would be poignant to be there without Vasilis. But at some point she must start socialising again, and the Barcourts had always been so kind to her. And Nicky would love it.

'That would be lovely—thank you!' she exclaimed, and Giles grinned back even more warmly.

She was aware that he was probably sweet on her—as he might have called it, had any such introspection occurred to him—but he never pushed it.

'Great!' he said. 'I'll let her know.'

He was about to say something else, but at that moment there was the sound of footsteps on the gravel path around the side of the house. She looked up, startled.

A mix of shock and dismay filled her. 'Anatole…' she said faintly.

This time there had not even been any warning from her housekeeper. Anatole must have parked his car, heard voices, and come across the gardens. Now he was striding up to them. Unlike last time he was not in a black business suit, nor in a tuxedo as he had been in London. This time he was wearing jeans, a cashmere sweater and casually styled leather jacket.

He looked…

Devastating.

A thousand memories drummed through her head, swooping like butterflies. Like the butterflies now fluttering inside her stomach as he stood, surveying the group. Her grip was lax suddenly, and she felt Nicky wriggle off her lap.

Excitement blazed from Nicky's face and he rushed up to Anatole. 'You came—you *came*!' he exclaimed. 'I did that painting! I painted it for Pappou, like you said.'

Anatole hunkered down. 'Did you?' He smiled. 'That's great. Will you show it to me later?'

There was something about the ecstatic greeting he was receiving that was sending emotion coursing through him. His grin widened. How could he possibly have stayed away so long when a welcome like this was coming his way?

'Yes!' cried Nicky. 'It's in my playroom.' Then something even more exciting occurred to him. 'Come and see my puppy!'

He caught at Anatole's hand, drew him over to the bench where Giles had got to his feet.

'Puppy?' queried Anatole.

He was focussing on Nicky, but at the same time he was burningly conscious of Tia's presence. Her face was pale, her expression clearly masked. She didn't want him there—it was blaring from her like a beacon—but he didn't care. He wasn't here for *her*, but for Vasilis's son. That was his only concern.

Not the way that her long hair was caught back in a simple clip…nor how effortlessly lovely she looked in a lightweight sweater and jeans.

Was her blonde loveliness the reason her current visitor was there? Anatole's eyes snapped across to the young man who'd stood up, and was now addressing him.

'Giles Barcourt,' he said in an easy manner, oblivious to what Christine instantly saw was a skewering look from Anatole. 'I'm a neighbour. Come to show young Nicky Juno's pups.' He grinned, and absently ruffled Nicky's hair.

Christine saw Anatole slowly take Giles's outstretched hand and shake it briefly.

'Giles—this is…' she swallowed '…this is Vasilis's nephew, Anatole Kyrgiakis.'

Immediately Giles's expression changed. 'I'm sorry about your uncle,' he said. 'We all liked him immensely.'

There was a sincerity in his voice that Christine hoped Anatole would respect. She saw him give a tight nod.

'Thank you,' he said.

His glance moved between her and Giles assessingly. She felt her spine stiffen. Then he was speaking again.

'A puppy sounds like a very good idea,' he said.

Was he addressing her or Giles? Whichever it was, it was Giles who answered.

'Absolutely,' he said. 'Take the little guy's mind off...well, you know.' His glance went back to Christine. 'I'll take myself off, then,' he said cheerfully. 'We'll see you on Friday week. Come a bit earlier, so the tinies can have some playtime together and inspect the puppies.'

His glance encompassed Anatole.

'Dinner with my parents,' he explained, adding without prompting, 'You'd be most welcome to join us.' He smiled with his usual unaffected good humour.

Christine waited for Anatole to make some polite but evasive reply. To her shock, he did the exact opposite. 'Thank you—that's very good of you.'

'Great! Well, see you, then. Cheers, you guys!' He loped off, waving at Nicky, and disappeared.

Anatole watched him go. He'd wondered who the muddy-wheeled four by four in the parking area behind the house belonged to, and now he knew.

He turned back to Christine. 'An admirer?' he said silkily. But beneath the silk was another emotion, one he did not care to name.

Anger flashed in her eyes. Raw, vehement. But she did not deign to honour his jibe with a reply. Instead, she said, 'What are you doing here Anatole?'

Nearly a fortnight had passed since that second encounter with him in London, and she had hoped that he'd taken himself off again, abandoned his declared intention to have anything more to do with her. With Nicky.

But his next words only confirmed that intention. He looked at her. 'I told you I wanted to see Nicky again.'

All too conscious of her son's presence, of the fact that he was tugging at Anatole to get his attention, Christine knew she could not do anything other than reply with, 'Did you not think to ring first?'

'To ask *permission* to see Vasilis's son?' His voice was back to being silky. Then he turned his attention back to Nicky. 'OK, so how about showing me your painting, then?' he asked.

'Yes—yes!' Nicky exclaimed.

Christine took a breath. 'I'll take you up. Nanny Ruth is having her break now.'

She led the way indoors. She was trying hard to stay composed, though her heart was hammering. Behind her she could hear Anatole's deep voice, and Nicky's piping one. She felt her heart clench.

Inside, she headed up the wide staircase and then along the landing to where another flight of stairs led to the nursery floor beneath the dormer windows.

Nicky's playroom was lavish—Anatole's glance took in a rocking horse, a train set, a garage and toy cars, plus a large collection of teddy bears and the like. The walls were covered in colourful educational posters, and the plentiful bookshelves were full of books.

A large table was set by the dormer window, and on a nearby wall there was a wide noticeboard which held a painting of a blue train with red wheels. There were some other paintings pinned up too, and in alphabet letters was spelled out the phrase, *Paintings for my pappou*. A lot of kisses followed.

Anatole felt his throat close, a choke rising. This was clearly the nursery of a much-loved child.

'There it is!' Nicky cried out, and ran to the noticeboard, climbing up on a chair and pointing to the painting.

Then he pointed to the others—a red car, a house with chimneys and a green door, and a trio of stick people with huge faces. Smiling faces. Underneath each of the stick people was a name, painstakingly written out in thick pen around dotted guidelines: *Pappou*, *Mumma* and *Nicky*. The stick people were surrounded by kisses.

'That's my *pappou*,' Nicky said. 'He lives in heaven. He got sick. We'll see him later.' He cast a quivering look at Christine. 'Won't we, Mumma?'

It was Anatole who answered. 'Yes, we will,' he said decisively. 'We all will. We'll have a big, big party when we see him.'

The quivering look vanished from his little cousin's eyes. Then they widened excitedly. 'A party? With balloons? And cakes?'

'Definitely,' said Anatole. He sat himself down at the table on the other chair. 'Now,' he said to Nicky, 'how about if we do some more painting. Do you know…' he looked at Nicky '…there isn't a picture of me here yet, is there?'

'I'll do one now,' Nicky said immediately, and grabbed at the box of paints and some of the drawing paper piled on the table. He looked at Anatole. 'You do one of *me*,' he instructed, and gave some paper and a brush to his big cousin, who took them smilingly.

'You'll need some water,' Christine said.

She went into the bathroom leading off the playroom, which linked through to Nicky's bedroom next to Nanny Ruth's quarters. As she filled the jar she swallowed, blinking. But she soon went back, set the filled jar down on the table.

'Thank you, Mumma,' said Nicky dutifully.

Nanny Ruth was very keen on manners.

'You have fun, munchkin,' she said.

She left the room. She had to get out of there—had to stop seeing her son and Anatole, poring over their labours, their heads bent together—both so dark-haired, dark-eyed. So alike…

She clattered down the stairs to the main landing. How long would Anatole be here? Did he expect to stay the night?

He can't stay here—he can't!

Panic rose in her throat, then subsided. No, of course he would not want to stay here. It would not be *comme il faut* for her to have such a guest, even if he *was* her late husband's nephew. Even *without* anyone knowing their past relationship.

But if he wasn't heading back to town tonight he'd have to stay at the White Hart in the nearby market town. It was upmarket enough, in this well-heeled part of England, not to repel him, and they should have vacancies this time of year. She realised her mind was rambling, busying itself with practical thoughts so that she didn't have to let in the thought she most desperately wanted to keep at bay.

Anatole and Nicky…heads together…so alike…so very, very alike.

No! Don't go there! Just don't go there! That was

a past that never happened. Anatole did not want a child...did not want a child by me...did not want me for a wife...

Emotion rose up inside her in a billowing wave of pain. Pain for the idiot she'd been, her head stuffed full of silly fairytales!

With a cutting breath, she headed downstairs into her sitting room to phone the White Hart, and then let Mrs Hughes know they might have an unexpected guest for dinner. Her thoughts ran on—hectic, agitated.

She rubbed at her head. If only Anatole would go away. He'd kept away while Vasilis was alive. As if she were poison…contaminated. But if he was set on seeing Nicky—who seemed so thrilled that he'd come, so animated and delighted…

How can I stop Anatole from visiting, from getting to know Nicky? How can I possibly stop him?

She couldn't think about it—not now, not here.

With a smothered cry she made her phone call, put her housekeeper on warning, then got out the file on Vasilis's foundation and busied herself in the paperwork.

It was close on an hour later when the house phone went. It was Nanny Ruth, back on duty for the evening, wanting a decision about Nicky's teatime.

'Well, why not let him stay up this evening?' Christine said. That way, if Anatole was assuming he would dine here, she would have the shield of her son present. Surely that would help, wouldn't it?

Some twenty minutes later her housekeeper put her head round the door.

'Nicky and Mr Kyrgiakis are coming downstairs,' she said, 'and dinner's waiting to be served.'

Christine thanked her and got up. She would not bother to change. Her clothes were fine. Anatole would still be in his jeans and sweater, and Nicky would be in his dressing gown.

She went into the dining room, saw them already there. Anatole was talking to Nicky about one of the pictures on the wall. It was of skaters on a frozen canal.

'Brrr! It looks freezing!' Anatole was shivering exaggeratedly.

'It's Christmas,' explained Nicky. 'That's why it's snowy.'

'Do you have snowy Christmases here?' Anatole asked.

Nicky shook his head, looking cross. 'No,' he said disgustedly.

Anatole looked across at Christine, paused in the doorway. 'Your mother and I had a snowy Christmas together once—long before you were born, Nicky. Do you remember?'

If he'd thrown a brick at her she could not have been more horrified. She was stunned into silence, immobility.

With not a flicker of acknowledgement of her appalled reaction, he went on, addressing her directly. 'Switzerland? That chalet at the ski resort I took you to? We went tobogganing—you couldn't ski—and I did a black run. We took the cable car up, I skied down and you came down by cable car. You told me you were terrified for me.'

She paled, opening her mouth, then closing it again.

He was doing it deliberately—he *had* to be. He was referring to that unforgettable Christmas she'd spent with him and the unforgettable months she'd spent with him—

'What's tobogganinning?' Nicky asked, to her abject relief.

Anatole answered him. He was glad to do so. Had he gone *mad*, reminding Tia—reminding himself—of that Christmas they'd spent in Switzerland?

I'm not here to stir up the past—evoke memories. It's the future that is important now—the future of Vasilis's son. Only that.

He answered the little boy cheerfully. 'Like a sledge—you sit on it, and it slides down the hill on the snow. I'll take you one day. And you can learn to ski, too. And skate—like in the picture.'

'I like that picture,' Nicky said.

'It's worth liking,' Anatole said dryly, his eyes flickering to Christine. 'It's a minor Dutch Master.'

'Claes van der Geld,' Christine said, for something to say—something to claw her mind out of the crevasse it had fallen into with the memory of that Christmas with Anatole.

They'd made love on Christmas Eve, on a huge sheepskin rug, by the blazing log fire…

Anatole's eyes were on her, with that same look of surprise in them, she realised, as when she'd mentioned Vasilis discussing Aeschylus and Pindar with the vicar.

She gave a thin smile, and then turned her attention to Nicky, getting him settled on his chair, then taking her own place at the foot of the table. Anatole's place had been set opposite Nicky. The head of the table was empty.

As she sat down she felt a knifing pang in her heart at Vasilis's absence, and her eyes lingered on the chair her husband had used to sit in.

'Do you miss him?'

The words came from Anatole, and she twisted her head towards him. There was a different expression on his face now. Not sceptical. Not ironic. Not taunting. Almost…quizzical.

Her eyes narrowed. 'What do you think?' she retaliated, snatching at her glass, and then realising it had no water in it.

He reached for the jug of water on the table, filled her glass and then his own. 'I don't know,' he said slowly. His mouth tightened. 'There's a lot I don't know, it seems. For example…' his tone of voice changed again '… I didn't know that you knew about Dutch Old Masters. Or anything about Hellenistic sculpture. Or classical Greece literature. And yet it seems you do.'

She levelled a look at him. There was no emotion in it. 'Your uncle was a good teacher,' she said. 'I had nearly five years of personal tuition from him. He was patient, and kind, infinitely knowledgeable, and—'

She couldn't continue. Her voice was breaking, her throat choking. Her eyes misted and she blinked rapidly.

'Mumma…?'

She heard Nicky's voice, thin and anxious, and shook her unshed tears away, making herself smile and reach for her son, leaning forward to drop a kiss on his little head.

'It's all right, darling, Mumma's fine now.' She made her face brighter. 'Do you think Mrs H has made pasta?' she asked. It was no guess—Mrs Hughes always did pasta for Nicky when he ate downstairs.

'Yes!' he exclaimed. 'I *love* pasta!' he informed his cousin.

Anatole was grinning, all his attention on Nicky too. 'So do I,' he said. 'And so,' he said conspiratorially, 'does your mumma!'

His gaze slid sideways. He was speaking to her again before he could stop himself. Why, he didn't know. He only knew that words were coming from him anyway.

'We always ate it when you cooked. Don't you remember?'

Again, she reeled. Of *course* she remembered!

I remember everything—everything about the time we spent together. It's carved into my memory, each and every day!

She reached for her water, gulping it down. Then the door opened and Mrs Hughes came in, pushing a trolley.

'Pasta!' exclaimed Nicky in glee as Christine got to her feet to help her housekeeper serve up.

Nicky did indeed have pasta, but for herself and Anatole there was more sophisticated fare: a subtly flavoured and exquisitely cooked ragout of lamb, with grilled polenta and French beans.

There was no first course—Nicky wouldn't last through a three-course meal and he was eager to start eating straight away—but, again, Nanny Ruth's training held fast.

Christine put a few French beans on a side plate,

arranging them carefully into a tower to make them more palatable.

'How many beans can you eat?' she asked Nicky, and smiled. 'Can you eat ten? Count them while you eat them,' she said, draping his napkin around his neck—she knew Mrs Hughes's pasta came with tomato sauce.

She turned back to put more dishes on the table, only to see Mrs Hughes lift two bottles of red wine and place them in front of Anatole.

'I've taken the liberty,' she announced, 'of bringing these. But of course there is all of Mr K's cellar if you think these won't do—that's why I haven't opened them to breathe. I hope that's all right with you?'

Christine said nothing, but bitter resentment welled up in her. Mrs Hughes was treating Anatole as if he were the man of the house. Taking her husband's place. But she said nothing, not wanting to upset her.

Nor, it seemed, did Anatole. 'Both are splendid,' he said approvingly, examining the labels, 'but I think this one will be perfect.' He selected one, handed back the other. 'Thank you!'

He cast her his familiar dazzling smile, and Christine could see its effect on her housekeeper.

Mrs Hughes beamed. 'Good,' she said. Then she looked at Christine. 'Will Mr Kyrgiakis be staying tonight? I can make up the Blue Room if so—'

Instantly Christine shook her head. 'Thank you, but no. My husband's nephew has a room reserved at the White Hart in Mallow.'

'Very well,' said Mrs Hughes, and took her leave.

Christine felt Anatole's eyes upon her. 'Have I?' he enquired.

'Yes,' she said tightly. 'I reserved it for you. Unless you're driving back to town tonight, of course.'

'The White Hart will do very well, I'm sure,' replied Anatole.

His voice was dry, but there was something in it that disturbed Christine. Disturbed her a lot.

She turned to Nicky. 'Darling, will you say Grace for us?'

Dutifully, Nicky put his hands together in a cherubic pose. 'Thank you, God, for all this lovely food,' he intoned. Then, in a sing-song voice he added, 'And if we're good, God gives us pud.' He beamed at Anatole. 'That's what Giles says.'

Anatole reached for the foil cutter and corkscrew, which Mrs Hughes had set out for him, and busied himself opening the wine, pouring some for Christine and himself. Nicky, he could see, had diluted orange juice.

'Does he, now?' he responded. Wine poured, he reached for his knife and fork, turning towards Christine, who had started eating, as had Nicky—with gusto. 'This dinner party next Friday…tell me more.'

'There isn't much to tell,' she replied, keeping her voice cool.

She hadn't missed the dry note in Anatole's voice. But she didn't care. Let him think what he would about her friendship with Giles Barcourt. He would, anyway, whatever she said. She was condemned in his eyes and always would be.

'Don't expect a gourmet meal—but do expect hospitality. The Barcourts are very much of their type—landed, doggy and horsy. Very good-natured, easy-going. Vasilis liked them, even though they are completely oblivious to the fact that their very fine Gainsborough portraits of a pair of their ancestors need a thorough cleaning. He offered to undertake it for them, but they said that the sitters were an ugly crew and they didn't want to see them any better. Their Stubbs, however,' she finished, deadpan, 'is in superb condition. And they still have hunters in their stable that are descended from the one in the painting.'

Anatole laughed.

It was a sound Christine had not heard for five long years, and it made a wave of emotion go through her. So, too, did catching sight of the way lines indented around his sculpted mouth, the edges of his dark, gold-flecked eyes crinkled.

She felt her stomach clench and her grip on her knife and fork tighten. She felt colour flare out along her cheeks. Memory, like a sudden kaleidoscope of butterflies, soared through her mind. Then sank as if they'd been shot down with machine gun fire.

'I look forward to meeting them.' His eyes rested on Christine. His tone of voice changed. Hardened. 'Giles Barcourt would not do for you,' he said. 'As a second husband.'

She stared. Another jibe—coming hard at her. Dear God, how was she to get through this evening if this was what he was going to do? Take pot-shots at her over everything? Wasn't that what she'd feared? That his blatant animosity towards her would start to poison her son?

'I am well aware of that,' she said tightly. She took a mouthful of wine, needing it. Then she set it back, stared straight at Anatole. 'I am also well aware,

Anatole…' she kept her voice low, and was grateful that Nicky was still enthusiastically polishing off his plate of pasta, paying no attention to anything but that '…that I am not fit to be the wife of a man whose family have owned a sizeable chunk of the county since the sixteenth century!'

'That's not what I meant!' Anatole's voice was harsh, as if he were angry.

His expression changed, and Christine saw him take a mouthful of wine, then set the glass down with a click on the mahogany table. 'I meant,' he said, 'that your years with Vasilis have…have *changed* you, Tia—Christine,' he amended. He frowned, then his expression cleared. 'You've changed almost beyond recognition,' he said.

'I've grown up,' she answered. Her voice was quiet, intent. 'And I am a mother.' Her gaze went to Nicky. 'He gives my life meaning. I exist for him.'

She could feel Anatole's eyes resting on her. Feel them like a weight, a pressure. She saw him ready himself to speak.

But then, with an exaggerated sigh of pleasure, Nicky set down his miniature knife and fork and announced, 'I'm finished!' He looked hopefully at his mother. 'Can I have my pudding now? Is it ice cream?'

'*May* I,' corrected Christine automatically, her voice mild. 'And, yes, I expect so. But you'll have to wait a bit, your…your cousin and I are still eating.'

Had she hesitated too much on the word cousin? She hoped not.

'It's odd to think of myself as Nicky's cousin,' Anatole commented. 'When I'm old enough to be his—'

He stopped abruptly. Between them the unspoken

word hung like a bullet in mid-air. He reached for his wine, drank deeply, poured himself another glass. Emotion clenched in him, but he would not give it room.

Yet his eyes went back to Vasilis's son.

The son who could have been his if—

No, don't go there. It didn't happen. Accept it. And the fact that it did not was what you wanted.

His mouth tightened, eyes hardening. But by the same token it was what Tia *had* wanted. And because she hadn't been able to get it from him—well, she'd gone and got it from his uncle.

In his head, he heard Christine's words.

You may not have wanted to marry me, to have a child with me—but your uncle did! It was his choice to marry me—

He felt his mind twist. Could it possibly be *true*? Could his lifelong bachelor uncle actually have *wanted* a child? A son?

But even if that *were* true, why take someone like Tia for a wife—of all women! His own nephew's ex-lover—thirty years his junior! If he'd wanted a wife there would have been any number of women in their own social circle, of their own nationality, far closer to him in age, and yet still young enough for child-bearing.

His eyes went to Christine.

She'd trapped him. It was the only explanation. She'd played on his good nature, his kindness—evoked his pity for my spurning of her, of what she wanted from me.

His mind twisted again, coming full circle. What did it matter now how Tia had got his uncle to marry her? All that was important to him now was the little boy sitting there, who was going to have to grow up without a father. Without the father he should have had.

A loving, protective father who would have devoted himself to his son, made him centre stage of his life, the kind of father that every boy deserved…

Thoughts moved in his head, stirred by emotions that welled up from deep within. He lifted his wine glass, slowly swirled the rich, ruby liquid as if he could see something in those depths. Find answers to questions he did not even know he was asking—knew only that he could not answer them. Not yet.

His eyes lifted, went to the woman at the foot of the table. Her attention was not on him, but on her son, and Anatole felt emotion suddenly kick through him. Gone was the strained, stiff expression she always had on her face when he himself was talking to her, as if every moment in his company was an unbearable ordeal. Now, oblivious of him, she was talking to her little boy, and her expression was soft, her eyes alight with tender devotion.

Once, it was me she looked at like that—

His gaze moved over her, registering afresh her beauty, her youthful loveliness now matured. A beauty that would be wasted unless she remarried.

Instantly the thought was anathema to him. Urgently he sought reasons for his overwhelming rejection of Tia remarrying—or even having any future love-life at all. Sought them and found them—the obvious ones.

I won't have Vasilis's fatherless son enduring a stranger for a stepfather. Worse, a succession of 'uncles'—Tia's lovers!—parading in and out of his life. Let alone any who crave to share in the wealthy lifestyle that Nicky will have as he grows up—that a stepfather could have too, courtesy of Tia. And Tia could take up with anyone! Anyone at all!

Even if it was some upper-class sprig like Giles Barcourt—there was no harm in a man like that—he'd never make a good husband for Tia…not for the woman she'd become. And besides—another thought darkened his mind,—any man she married would want children of his own, children who would displace Nicky. Yet it was impossible to think she could live in lonely widowhood for ever. She was not yet thirty!

His eyes went to her again, drawn to rest on her as she talked to her son. *Thee mou*, how beautiful she was! How exquisitely lovely—

Emotion kicked again. Something was forming in his mind, taking shape, taking hold. Yes, she would marry again. It was inevitable. Unavoidable. But no stranger that she married could be the father that Nicky needed. No *man* could be the father that Nicky needed.

Unless…

From deep within, emotion welled. In the flickering synapses of his brain currents flowed, framing the thought that was becoming real, forcing its way into his consciousness. There was only one man who could be the father Nicky needed. One obvious man…

Nicky was all but falling asleep as he polished off his ice cream, and Christine abandoned her slice of *tarte au citron* to go and lift him up, carry him to bed. But

Anatole was been there before her, effortlessly hefting Nicky into his arms.

Christine followed them upstairs, her face set. It was hard—*very* hard—to see Anatole carry Nicky so tenderly, so naturally.

Into her head sounded those bleak words he'd spoken to her that final harrowing morning.

'I don't want to marry and I don't want children.'

Her face twisted. Well, maybe a young cousin was different. Maybe that was OK for Anatole.

Something rose in her throat, choking her. An emotion so strong she could not bear it.

As she settled her son into bed, kissed him goodnight, Anatole stepped forward, murmuring something to him in Greek. Christine recognised it as a night-time blessing, and felt her throat tighten with memory. It was what Vasilis had said to bless his son's sleep.

And his son had recognised it too. 'That's what my *pappou* says,' Nicky said drowsily. His little face buckled suddenly. 'I want my *pappou*,' he cried, his voice plaintive.

Instinctively Christine stepped forward, but Anatole was already sitting himself down beside Nicky, taking his hand.

Anatole thought how strange it was to feel the feather-light weight of this cousin of his, to feel the warmth of his little body, to feel so protective of him.

It isn't his fault that he is now bereft, he thought. *Or that his mother inveigled Vasilis into marrying her. None of that is his fault. And if it was truly Vasilis's choice—however bizarre, however unlikely that seems—to marry Tia, then my responsibility to my uncle's child is paramount!*

But *was* it just a case of responsibility? That sounded cold, distant. What he felt for this little boy was not cold or distant at all—it welled up in him… an emotion he'd never felt before. Never known before. Strong and powerful. Insistent.

'How about if you had me instead, Nicky?' he said, carefully choosing his words, knowing he absolutely must get this right. 'How about,' he went on, 'if your *pappou* had asked *me* to look after you for him? Would that do?'

Dark, wide, long-lashed eyes stared up at Anatole. He felt his heart clench. He didn't know why, but it did. He stroked the little boy's hair, feeling his throat tighten unbearably.

'Yes, please,' Nicky whispered. He gazed up at Anatole. 'Promise?'

'Promise,' Anatole echoed gravely. And it was more than a word. It had come from deep within him.

Yet even as the word echoed he wondered if it could really be true, after his own miserable childhood, that he could make such a promise? All his life he'd resolved never to tread this path—but here he was, dedicating himself to this boy who seemed to be calling to something inside him he had not known he possessed. Had always thought was absent from him.

He watched Nicky's face relax, saw sleep rushing upon him. 'Don't forget…' were his slurring last words.

'No,' Anatole said gravely, stroking the fine silky hair. 'I won't.'

He felt his heart clench once more. What was this

emotion coursing through him that he had never known he could feel?

A sharp movement behind him made him turn his head. Christine was turning down the night light so that it would give a soft glow, but not be so bright as to disturb. But her eyes were fixed on Anatole.

Anatole was sitting on Nicky's bed, stroking his hair. And she saw an expression on his face that put barbed wire around her throat.

I can't bear this—I can't... I can't—

She walked out of the room, went downstairs to the hall, pacing restlessly until Anatole drew level with her. She opened her mouth to tell him that he should go, but he spoke pre-emptively.

'Come back into the dining room—I need to talk to you.' His voice was clipped, yet it had an abstracted tone to it.

'Anatole, I want you to go now—'

He ignored her, striding back into the dining room. Christine could only follow. He sat himself down at his dinner place, indicating that she should sit down too.

As if it's his house, his dining room—

Protest rose in her throat, but she sat down all the same.

'Well?' she demanded. Her heart-rate was up, emotions tearing at her. Anatole was looking at her, his gaze veiled, but there was something in it that made her go completely still.

'You heard Nicky,' Anatole said. His voice was taut, but purposeful. 'You heard his answer to my question about taking over from his *pappou*. You *heard* it, Christine—heard him say, *"Yes, please."* Well…'

He took a breath, and she saw lines of tension around his mouth.

'That is what I am going to do.' His eyes flared suddenly, unveiled. 'I am going to take Vasilis's place in his life. I am going to marry you.'

CHAPTER EIGHT

HAD THE WORLD just tilted on its side? Had an earthquake just happened? Her vision was blurred…her heart seemed to have stopped.

'What?'

The word shot from her like a bullet. A bullet that found its target in the blankness of Anatole's face.

'Are you *insane*?' she shot again.

He lifted a hand. It was a jerky movement, as if designed to stop more bullets. As if to silence her.

'Hear me out,' he said. 'It's the obvious solution to the situation!'

Christine's eyes flashed. It felt as if her heart had still not started beating yet. 'What *situation*?' she demanded. 'There *is* no situation! I am Vasilis's widow. He has left me *perfectly* well provided for and even more so his son—a son who will before long no longer be so sad at the loss of his *pappou* and who will grow up adored by me and protected by Vasilis's wealth. What on earth about that needs a *solution*?'

Anatole's expression shifted. Something moved in his eyes. But his words, when he spoke, were stony. 'Nicky needs a father. All children do. With Vasilis gone, irrespective of whether Nicky thought of him as his grandfather, another man must take the role he played in his son's life.'

His eyes rested on Christine, shifting in their regard.

'You are not yet thirty, Tia—Christine—and it is impossible to envisage you not remarrying at some point.' He lifted his hand again. 'I take back what I said,' he said stiffly, 'about your likely dissolute lifestyle as the wealthy widow of a deceased much older husband.'

He felt the fury of Christine's eyes hurling daggers on him, even for saying that, even with his stiff apology, but he kept on speaking. It was vital he do so. Imperative.

'But it *is* inevitable that you will remarry,' he persisted. Something flashed darkly in his eyes. 'That neighbour of yours, Barcourt, would be only too eager—or any other man! And I do not mean that as an insult. I mean it as a compliment, Christine.'

He gritted his teeth.

'I appreciate that you would never marry anyone who would not be a doting stepfather to Nicky. And Barcourt—I give him this freely—is clearly cut out to be an excellent father. But he would not, as I said, make a good husband for you.'

His eyes rested a moment on her, his face taut, his eyes implacable.

'I would,' he said.

He took an incised breath.

'I would make an excellent husband for you. Think about it…'

He leant forward a little, as if to give emphasis to what he was saying—what he had to say to make her hear. Accept what had forced its way into his head and now could not be banished.

Urgently, he forged on. 'I am the closest relative to Nicky on his father's side. I discount my own father. He would be as little interested in Nicky as he was in me,' he said scathingly.

Christine could hear something in his voice that for the first time since he had tilted the world sideways for her with what he had said, stopping the beating of her heart, shifted her to react. There had been dismissal in his voice, but something else too. Something that she recognised. Recognised because she herself had been possessed by it totally and absolutely five years ago.

Pain—pain at rejection…at not being wanted.

But Anatole was speaking still, making her listen to him.

'Who better to be a father to Nicky than myself—his closest blood kin? And who better to be your husband, Christine…' his voice changed suddenly, grew huskier '…than me?'

His eyes washed over her—she could feel it like a silken brush over her senses.

'Who better than me?' he said again, his voice lower, that brush across her senses coming again.

She felt fatal faintness drumming at her again. She desperately wanted to speak, but she was voiceless. Bereft of everything except the sensation of his gaze washing over her, weakening her, dissolving her.

She tried to fight it—oh, dear God, she tried! Tried to remember all the pain he'd caused her.

But his eyes were washing over her now as they had done so many times, so long ago.

'I *know* you, Tia,' he said now, and the name he'd always called her by came naturally to him…as naturally as the wash of his eyes over her. 'And you know me. And we both know how compatible we are.'

He took another breath.

'And now we're much more so. You have matured into this woman you have become—poised, elegant, able to hold your own in company that would have terrified you five years ago! Five years ago you were young and inexperienced. Oh, I don't just mean sexually…'

He'd said the word casually, but it brought a heat to Christine's cheeks she would have given a million pounds for them not to have, and she beat it back as desperately as she could,

'I mean in all the ways of the world.'

His eyes slipped away, stared out as if into the past, a frown folding his brow.

He spoke again—with difficulty now. 'I didn't want to marry you then, Tia. I didn't want to marry anyone. Not just you—anyone at all. There was no reason for me to marry, and many not to. But now…' His eyes came back to her, sweeping in like a beacon, skewering her helplessly. 'Now there is every reason. To make a stable family for Nicky, a loving family—' He broke off, as if that had been hard for him to say.

For a moment Christine could not answer. Too much was pouring through her head—far, far too much. Then, with a scissoring breath, she said, 'I will not have a husband who despises me.'

It was tersely expressed, vehemently meant.

She saw him shake his head.

'I don't,' he answered. 'I don't despise you—'

Her eyes flashed blue fire. 'Don't lie to me, Anatole! You called me a cheap little adventuress! You thought me a scheming, ruthless gold-digger, who manipulated your hapless uncle into putting a wedding ring on my finger! And you thought I tried exactly the same thing on you—was perfectly prepared to get myself *pregnant*—' her mouth bit out the word as if it was rotten '—to make you marry me!'

His face turned stony. 'Whatever your motives for marrying Vasilis, I accept that you have not profited from his death and that you are devoted to your son.'

His eyes shifted again, and a troubled look drifted across them as a new thought formed—one that he had not had before. Had she wanted a baby so much that she'd been happy to marry a man so much older than her? Could it possibly be that it had not been his wealth that had made her marry his uncle? Had his riches *not* been the driving force behind her desire to marry Vasilis? Otherwise, why would she have insisted on not being the main beneficiary of his will?

He looked at her now—directly, eye to eye.

'Why did you marry my uncle?'

The strained look was instantly back in her face. 'I don't wish to discuss it. Think what you want, Anatole. I don't care.'

There was weariness in her voice, resignation.

With a jerking movement she got to her feet. 'It's time you left,' she said, her voice terse.

He stood also. Seeming to tower over her as Vasilis had never done.

Memory drummed in her, fusing the past with the present, making it impossible to separate them. Ramming home to her just how vulnerable she was to the man who stood there, a man who had always been able to melt her bones with a single glance from his deep, dark eyes. Who quickened her senses, heated the blood in her veins.

He wants to marry me—

The words were in her head—unbelievable, impossible. Yet they were there.

'You haven't given me your answer yet,' Anatole said.

His dark gaze was fixed on her. But this was the present, not the past. The past was over, would never return. *Could* never return.

With a summoning of her strength, she pulled herself together. 'I gave it to you instantly,' she countered. 'What you are proposing is insane, and I will treat it as such. And in the morning, Anatole, if you have any brain cells left in your head, you will agree with me.'

She walked out into the hall, moving to the front door, opening it pointedly.

He followed her out of the dining room. 'Are you really throwing me out of my uncle's house?' he said.

There was an edge in his voice that cut at her.

She pressed her lips together. 'Anatole, my husband was thirty years older than me. Do you think I haven't learnt to be incredibly careful about my reputation?' Her voice twisted. 'I know that my reputation can mean nothing to you, but for Nicky's sake have the decency to leave.'

He walked towards her. There was something in the way he approached her that made all the nerve fibres in her body quiver. Suddenly the space between them was charged with static electricity, flickering with lightning.

He looked at her speculatively. 'Do I tempt you, Tia?'

There was a caress in his voice, intimacy in the way his eyes washed over her. A caress and an intimacy that had once been as familiar to her as breathing. That she had not experienced for five long years. That was now alive between them again.

She could not breathe, could not move.

His hand reached for her and he drew one finger gently, oh-so-gently, down her cheek, brushing it across her parted lips. It felt like silk and velvet, and faintness drummed in her ears.

So long...it's been so long...

She felt her heart cry out his name, but it was from far away. Oh, so long ago. Echoing down the years to now—to this unbearable moment.

'You are more beautiful now than you ever were,' he said softly.

His eyes were holding hers, dissolving hers.

'How could I forget how beautiful you are? How could I not want you again, so incredibly beautiful, so very lovely…?'

She felt her body sway, had no strength to hold herself upright. It was as if all that was keeping her standing was his eyes, holding hers.

'So beautiful…' he murmured, his voice as soft as feathers.

Slowly, infinitely slowly, his mouth descended and his lips touched hers, grazed hers, moved slowly across her sweet, tender mouth. She made no move, not one—could not…would not. Dared not…

He drew back, his eyes searching hers. 'Once, Tia, you would have melted into my arms.'

He smiled—a warm, embracing smile that crinkled

the corners of his eyes, that made her remember all that had once been between them.

With that single, long, casual finger he tilted up her chin. 'So tiny, so petite…' He smiled again. His expression changed. 'You'll melt for me again, sweet Tia.'

He let his finger drop, took a breath, gave another final smile. Of confidence…of certainty.

What he wanted was right—was obvious. It was absolutely what should happen between them. It was an impulse, yes, but it had been impulse that had made him pile her into his car that afternoon all those years ago, drive off with her, take her to his apartment… his bed.

And had he not done so she would not be here now—his uncle's widow, the mother of a fatherless child, a young boy who needed a loving father as every child needed one, as every child needed a loving mother too, who made their child the centre of their universe. That was what he could do for Nicky—his uncle's child. Forge for him a loving family, keep him safe in that love all through his childhood… All his life.

I did not have that. Nicky will.

He smiled again, seeing how everything would resolve itself. Nicky would have himself, Anatole, to raise him, and he would have Tia—recreated now as Christine. Once, marriage had seemed impossible to him—fatherhood out of the question. But now, as emotion swept up in him, he knew that everything had changed for ever.

The future was crystal-clear to him and it was centred on this woman—this woman who was back in his life. It made clear, obvious sense all round. His desire for her was stronger than it had ever been. Her mature beauty drew him now even more than her *ingénue* loveliness had moved him—on that count there could be no doubt.

He spoke again to her, his final words for this evening, his tone a low, sensual husk, his eyes a caress.

'You'll melt, Christine,' he said, with promise in his voice, 'on our wedding night.'

Christine lay in bed, sleepless, her eyes staring up at the ceiling. Thoughts, emotions, confusion—all whirled chaotically around in her head. She could make sense of nothing. Nothing at all. Every now and then she would try and snatch at the whirling maelstrom, to try and capture it, but it always eluded her. Fragments skimmed past her again, just out of range.

He wants to marry me.

He despises me.

He kissed me.

None of it made sense—none of it—yet round and round the fragments whirled.

She tossed and turned, and found no rest at all.

But in the morning, when finally she awoke from the heavy, mentally exhausted slumber into which she'd fallen in the small hours, only one fragment was vivid in her head.

Temptation.

Oh, she could tell herself as much as she liked that it was insane that a man who had thrown the accusations at her that he had, a man who had told her to her face that he never wanted to marry her, should now be offering to do just that. Of his own free will.

It was insane that she should pay even the slightest attention to what he'd said. What he'd done. And yet tendrils of something writhed through her brain, finding soft, vulnerable places to cling to, to penetrate. She could feel it spreading in her mind…something so dangerous it terrified her.

Temptation.

Deadly, fatal temptation.

She had felt it once before—just as strong, just as dangerous. Once before she had been about to do something that with every instinct in her body she had known to be wrong. And the conflict had almost destroyed her. Would have destroyed her had it not been for Vasilis.

She had poured it all out to him that desperate day in Athens, when Anatole had made it so ruthlessly clear how little she meant to him—had set out the only terms under which he was prepared to continue with her, and what the consequences would be if she rejected those terms, broke them.

And Vasilis had listened. Had let her weep and sob and pour out all her misery and desperation. And then kindly, calmly and oh-so-generously, he had put forward another possibility for her.

He saved me. He saved me from the danger I was in of yielding to that overpowering temptation, that nightmare torment, that desperate desolation of realising that Anatole was a million miles away from what I yearned for.

Restlessly now, all these years later, she crossed to the window of her bedroom to look down over the gardens. She loved this house—this quiet, tranquil house that was so redolent of her marriage to Vasilis. He had brought her peace when her life had been in pieces.

Her eyes moved to the door set in the wall that led into a little dressing room, and from there into Vasilis's bedroom. A room that was now empty of him.

I miss him. I miss his kindness, his company, his wisdom.

Yet already, in the long months since she'd stood at his bleak graveside, he was beginning to fade in her head. Or perhaps it was not that he was fading, but that another was forcing himself into her consciousness. Into the space that had once been her husband's.

Just as her husband had once taken the space that had belonged to the man now replacing him.

I worked so hard to free myself of Anatole. Yet now he is back in my head, dominating everything.

And he was offering her now, with supreme, bitter irony, what he had never wanted to offer her before.

'Do I tempt you?'

Anatole had taunted her with those words and she had felt the force of them…the temptation to let herself be tempted. And then she had felt the touch of his mouth on hers…

With a smothered cry of anguish she whirled about, forcing herself to get on with the day—to put aside the insanity that Anatole was proposing, force it out of her head.

But when, mid-morning, she went up to Nicky's nursery to spend some time with him and let Nanny Ruth have a break, the first thing Nicky did was ask where Anatole was. She gave some answer—she knew not what—and was dismayed to see his little face fall.

Even more dismayed to discover that he remembered what he'd said so sleepily the night before. What Anatole had said.

His little face quivered. 'He said my *pappou* sent him to look after me. But where *is* he?'

She did her best to divert him, practising his reading and writing with him, until suddenly his eyes brightened and Christine, too, heard a car arriving—crunching along the front drive.

A bare few minutes later, rapid, masculine footsteps sounded outside, the nursery door opened, and there was Anatole.

With a whoop of glee Nicky rushed to him, to be swung up into Anatole's arms. Christine could only gaze at them, emotion scything inside her powerfully at the sight of her son's blazing delight at Anatole's arrival—and Anatole, his face softening, showed in every line of his body his gladness to see Nicky.

He turned to Christine, with Nicky held effortlessly in the crook of his arm, one little hand snaked around his neck, and the pair of them smiled broadly at her.

So like each other…

There was a humming in her ears, blood rushing, and she could only blink helplessly. Then Anatole was speaking…

'Who wants to go on an adventure today?' he asked.

Nicky's eyes lit up. 'Me! Me!' came the excited reply.

Anatole laughed and swung him down on his feet again, his eyes going to Christine.

'It's a glorious day out there—how about an outing? All three of us?'

She opened her mouth to give any number of objections, but in the face of Nicky's joyous response could not voice them. 'Why not?' she said weakly. 'I'll let Nanny know.'

She made her escape, finding Nanny Ruth in her sitting room, watching a programme about antiques on the TV and finishing off a cup of tea.

'What a good idea!' she said, beaming when Christine told her of Anatole's plans. She looked at her employer. 'It will distract Nicky. And, if I might say…' Christine got the impression that she was picking her works carefully '… I am very glad that young Mr Kyrgiakis is finally in touch.' She nodded meaningfully. 'He's clearly very fond of Nicky already. It will be important for Nicky to have him in his life.'

Her eyes never left Christine's and then she took a breath, as if having said enough, and got to her feet.

'Now, where does young Mr K plan on going today? I'll make sure Nicky has the right clothes.'

She headed into the playroom, leaving Christine feeling outmanoeuvred on all fronts. With deep misgiving she went downstairs, fetching a jacket for herself.

A whole day in Anatole's company—with only Nicky to shelter behind.

Tension netted her, and she felt her heart-rate increasing. She knew what was causing it to do so. Knew it and feared it.

CHAPTER NINE

'THIS,' ANNOUNCED NICKY with a happy sigh, 'is the best day *ever*!' He sat back in his chair, a generous smear of chocolate ice cream around his mouth.

Christine laughed—she couldn't help it. Just as she hadn't been able to help herself laughing when she'd realised just where Anatole was taking them.

'A holiday camp?' she'd exclaimed disbelievingly as they'd arrived in Anatole's car.

He'd somehow procured a child's booster seat, and Nicky had stared wide-eyed with dawning excitement as they parked.

'Day tickets,' Anatole had replied. He'd looked at Nicky. 'Do you think you'll like it?'

The answer had been evident for over six hours now. From the incredible indoor swimming paradise—towels and swimwear for all three of them having been conveniently purchased from the pool shop—with its myriad slides and fountains and any number of other delights for children, to the outdoor fairground, finishing off the day with a show based on popular TV characters.

Now they were tucking into a high tea of fish and chips and, for Nicky, copious ice cream. Christine leant forward to mop his face. Her mood was strange. It had been impossible not to realise that she was enjoying herself today. Enjoying, overwhelmingly, Nicky's excitement at everything. And Anatole's evident pleasure in Nicky's delight.

His focus had been on her little boy, and yet Christine had caught herself, time and time again, exchanging glances with Anatole over Nicky's expressions of joy at the thrills of the day. Brief glances, smiles, shared amusement—as the day had gone on they had become more frequent, less brief.

The tension that had netted her before they'd set off had evaporated in a way she could not have believed possible, and yet so it was. It was as if, she suddenly realised with a start, the old ease in his company, which had once been the way she was with him until the debacle that had ended their relationship, was awakening as if after a long freezing.

It was disturbing to think of it that way. Dangerous!

As dangerous as it had been when, emerging with Nicky from the changing rooms at the poolside, her eyes had gone immediately to Anatole's honed, leanly muscled form, stripped down to swim shorts. Memory had seared in her and she'd had to drag her eyes away. But not before Anatole had seen her eyes go to him—and she knew that his had gone to her.

Although she'd deliberately chosen, from the range available in the on-site shop, a very sporty swimsuit, not designed in the slightest to allure, consciousness of her body being displayed to him had burned in her as she'd felt his gaze wash over her.

Then, thankfully, Nicky, his armbands inflated, had

begun jumping up and down with eagerness to be in the water and the moment had passed.

That consciousness, however, resurfaced now as, tea finished and back in the car for their return journey, she realised that Nicky had fallen asleep, overcome with exhaustion after the day's delights. In the confined intimacy of the car, music playing softly, Anatole's presence so close to her was disturbing her senses.

She felt his eyes glance at her as he drove. Then he spoke. 'What I said last night—has today shown you how good it would be, making a family for Nicky?'

His tone was conversational, as if he'd asked her about the weather and not about the insanity of marrying him.

She was silent for a moment. Though it seemed to her that her heavy heartbeat must be audible to him, as it was to her. She tried to choose her words carefully. One of them had to be sane here—and it had to be her.

'Anatole, think about it rationally. You're running on impulse, I suppose. You've only just discovered about Nicky, and Vasilis is barely in his grave. For you—for *either* of us!—to make any kind of drastic alteration to our lives at such a time would be disastrous.' She looked at him. 'Everything I've read about bereavement urges not to take any major decisions for at least a year.'

Would that sufficiently deter him? She could only hope so. Pray so. Yet in the dimming light of the car she could see a mutinous look on his face. He was closing down—closing out what she'd said.

'It's the right thing to do,' he said.

There was insistence in his voice, and he could

hear it himself. How could she not see the obvious sense of what he was proposing? The rightness of it. Yes, he was being impulsive—but that didn't mean he was being irrational. In fact the very opposite! It was so clearly, unarguably right for him to make a family for this fatherless boy by marrying his mother—the very woman who'd once wanted a child by him… the woman he'd desired from the first moment he'd set eyes on her.

And I desire her still! And she desires me too. There is no doubt of that—no doubt at all!

Yet still she was denying it. As her blunt answer proved.

'No,' she answered. 'It isn't.'

Her head dipped, and she stared at her hands, lying in her lap. What more could she say without ripping apart the fragile edifice of her life—plunging herself back into the desperate torment she had once known with Anatole? The torment that had raked her between temptation and desolation?

She felt him glance at her. Felt the pause before he answered, with a tightness in his voice that she could not be deaf to.

'I'm not used to you disagreeing with me,' she heard him say. There was another pause. 'You've changed, Tia—Christine.'

Her head lifted, and she threw him a look. 'Of *course* I've changed,' she said. 'What did you expect?'

She took a breath that was half a sigh, remembering, for all her defiant words, how she'd used to love watching him drive, seeing how his hands curved so strongly over the wheel. How she'd drink in his profile, the keen concentration of his gaze. How she'd always loved gazing at him, all the time, marvelling over and over again at how wonderful, how blissful it was that he wanted her at all, how he had taken her by the hand and led her into the fantasy land where she'd dwelt with him…

He caught her eye now, and there was a glint in it that was achingly familiar.

'You used to gaze at me like that all the time, Tia. I could feel it, know it—sense it.'

His voice had softened, and though there was a trace of amusement in it there was also a hint of something she had not heard from him at all since the moment he'd stalked into her life again.

Tenderness.

She felt her throat catch and she dragged her eyes away, out over the road, watching the cars coming towards them, headlights on now as dusk gathered in the countryside.

'That was then, Anatole,' she said unsteadily. 'A long time ago—'

'I've missed it,' he answered her.

She heard him take a breath—a ragged-sounding one.

'I missed *you,* Tia, when you left me. When you walked out on me to marry my uncle, to become his pampered young bride.' There was an edge in his voice now, like a blade.

Her eyes flew to him, widening. '*I* didn't leave *you*!' she exclaimed. '*You* finished it with *me*! You told me you refused to have a relationship with someone who wanted to marry you, to get pregnant by you!'

She saw a frown furrow his brow, and then he threw a fulminating look at her, his hands tightening on the wheel. 'That didn't mean you had to *go*,' he retaliated. 'It just meant—' He stopped.

'You just meant that I had to give up any idea of meaning anything to you at all—let alone as your wife or the potential mother of your children. Give up any idea of making a future with you!'

Christine's voice was dry, like sandpaper grating on bare skin. She shut her eyes for a moment, her head swirling, then opened them again, taking another weary breath.

'Oh, Anatole,' she said, and her voice was weary, 'it's all right. I get the picture. You were young, in the prime of your carefree life. I was an amusing diversion—a novelty! One that lasted a bit longer than you probably intended at first, when you scooped me off the road. I came from an entirely different walk of life from you—I was pretty, but totally naïve. I was so blatantly smitten by you that you couldn't resist indulging yourself—and indulging *me*. But I know that didn't give me any right to think you might want me long-term. Even if…'

She swallowed painfully, knowing she had to say it.

'Even if there hadn't been that pregnancy…scare…' she said the word with difficulty '…something else would have ended our affair. Because…' Her throat was tight. 'Because an affair was all it was. All it could ever be.'

She knew that now—knew it with the hindsight of her greater years. She had been twenty-three… Anatole had been the first man in her life—and a man such as she had never dreamt of, not even in her girlish fantasies! He'd taken her to fairyland—and even in her youthful inexperience she had feared that it would all be fairy gold and turn to dust.

And so it had. Painfully. Permanently.

'But now I want more,' he replied, and his words and the intensity of his voice made her eyes fly to him again. 'I want much, much more than an affair with you.'

He took a breath, changing gear, accelerating on an open stretch of road as if that would give escape to the emotion building up inside him. Emotion that was frustration at her obstinacy, at her refusal to concede the rightness of what he was proposing.

'Christine, this *works*—you, me and Nicky! You can see it that works. Nicky likes me, trusts me…and, believe me, I meant exactly what I said to him last night. That he can believe that his *pappou* sent me to look after him in his place. To become his father—'

He could have been my son! Had Tia been pregnant then—five years ago—Nicky would be my son. A handful of months older...no more.

Emotion rolled him over. Over and over and over—like a boulder propelled down a mountainside by an overwhelming, unstoppable force. Emotion about what might have been, about what had never been, that silenced him until they arrived at Vasilis's house—now Christine's home.

The home she kept for her son—his uncle's son—just as the legacy of Vasilis's work, his endless endeavours to preserve the treasures of the past, would pass to her guardianship.

And she will guard it well. How strange that I can trust her to do that, that I know now that I can trust her.

Yet it was not strange at all—not now that he had

seen her in London, at the exhibition opening, and here as chatelaine of this gracious house. She had grown into it—into a woman who could do these things, *be* these things.

Just as I have grown into what I am doing now. Accepting that I want a wife. A child.

He scooped up the sleeping boy, cradling his weight in his arms as he walked indoors with him. Christine opened the front door, leading the way upstairs in the quiet house—both Mrs Hughes and Nanny Ruth were out for the evening.

In his bedroom, they got Nicky into bed, still fast asleep, exhausted by the day's delights. For a moment, Anatole stood beside her as they gazed down at the sleeping child, illumined only by the soft glow of the night light.

His hand found Christine's. She did not take it away. She stood with him as they looked down at Nicky. As if they were indeed a family indeed…

Was there a little sound from her? Something that might have been a choke? He did not know. Knew only that she'd slipped her hand from his and was walking out of the room. He looked after her, a strange expression on his face, then back at Nicky, reaching almost absently to smooth a lock of dark hair from his forehead, to murmur a blessing on the night for him.

Then he turned and went downstairs.

Christine was waiting in the hall by the front door. Her head was lifted, her expression composed.

'Thank you for a lovely day,' she said.

She spoke calmly, quelling all the emotion welling up inside her. What use to feel what was inside her? It was of no use—it never could be now.

She opened the door, stepped back. He came up to her, feeling that strange, strong emotion in him again. This time he made no attempt to kiss her.

'It's been good,' he said.

His voice was quiet. His eyes steady. Then, with a quick smile, the slightest nod of his head, he was gone, crunching out over the gravel beneath the mild night sky.

As he opened his car door he heard the front door of the house close behind him.

Shut it, if you will—but you cannot shut me out. Not out of Nicky's life—or yours.

Certainty filled him as to the truth of that.

In the week that followed Christine did her best to regain the state of mind she'd had since her marriage to Vasilis. But it had gone—been blown away by the return of Anatole into her life. His invasion of it.

It was an invasion that had been angrily hostile, and he had been scathing in his denunciation of her behaviour. And the searing irony of it was that anger and hostility from him was so much easier for her to cope with. What she couldn't cope with—what she was pathetically, abjectly unable to cope with—was the way he was with her now.

Wooing!

The word stayed in her head, haunting her.

Disturbing her. Confusing her.

Changing her.

And she didn't want to change. She'd made a new life for herself—made it in tears and torment, but she was safe inside it. Safe inside the life Vasilis had given her. *That* was what she wanted to cling to.

Anatole is my past. I can't—I won't—have him as my future!

She dared not. Too much—oh, far too much—was at stake for her to allow that. More than she could bear to pay again.

Her resolve was put to the test yet again the following Friday—the day the Barcourts had invited her and Nicky over. Her hope that Anatole had forgotten proved to be in vain. He arrived in time to drive them over. And at the rambling Elizabethan mansion the Barcourts' welcome to Anatole could not have been friendlier.

'I'm glad you could come this evening, Mr Kyrgiakis. We were all so sorry to hear about your uncle—he was well liked, and very well respected.' Mrs Barcourt smiled kindly at Anatole as she greeted him, then led the way into the oak-panelled drawing room.

Nicky was scooped up by the nursery party, who were rushing off to see the puppies with the nanny, and Giles's sister Isabel, as cheerful as her brother, launched into a panegyric about the beneficial effects a puppy had on childhood, adding that Nicky should also learn to ride—as soon as he could. Giles agreed enthusiastically, volunteering their old pony, Bramble, for the job.

'Don't you agree?' Isabel said to Anatole.

'I'm sure my young cousin would love it,' he answered. 'But it is Christine's decision.'

He glanced at her and she smiled awkwardly. What the Barcourts were making of Anatole, she had no idea—knew only that they were asking no questions about him and seeming to take his presence for granted.

But her relief lasted only until after dinner, when their hostess announced they would leave the menfolk to their port and drew Christine and Isabel off to the drawing room. There, a bottle of very good madeira was produced, and Isabel went off to see her children.

Mrs Barcourt, Christine realised with dismay, was about to start her interrogation.

'My dear, *what* a good-looking young man! *Such* a shame we've seen nothing of him until now!' she exclaimed. She bent to absent-mindedly stroke the ancient, long-haired cat lounging on the hearth rug. 'I take it we'll be seeing a lot more of him now?'

Her smile was nothing but friendly. The question was clearly leading…

Christine clutched her glass. 'He *would* like to get to know Nicky,' she managed to get out.

Her hostess nodded sympathetically. 'Very understandable,' she said. 'And very good for Nicky too.' She paused. 'It's early days, I know, but you *will* need to think of the future, Christine—as I'm sure you realise.'

She stroked the cat again, then looked at her guest, her expression open.

'A stepfather would be excellent for Nicky—but you must choose wisely.' She made a face and spoke frankly, as Christine had known she would. 'Not Giles,' she said, with a little shake of her head. 'Fond though he is of Nicky, you wouldn't suit each other, you know.'

Christine's expression changed. 'No, no… I know that.'

Her hostess nodded. 'I know you do, my dear, and I'm glad of it.' She sat back, picking up her glass.

'You and Anatole seem to get on very well...' She trailed off.

Christine had no idea what to say, but Mrs Barcourt did.

'Well, I shall say no more except that I can see no reason not to look forward to getting to know him better. You must both come over again before long. Ah, Isabel—there you are!' she exclaimed as her daughter breezed in. 'How is little Nicky?'

'Begging for a sleepover, and my brood are egging him on! What do you say, Christine?'

Christine, abjectly grateful for the change of subject, could only nod. 'If you're sure it's no trouble?'

'Not in the least,' Isabel answered cheerfully. 'And tomorrow morning he can try out Bramble, if you're all right with that. Loads of kiddie riding kit here!'

Christine nodded weakly. But belatedly she realised that if Nicky slept here tonight she would be without his protective presence herself.

It was something she felt more strongly at the end of the evening, when she sat beside Anatole in his car, heading home.

He glanced at her. She'd looked enchanting all evening, wearing a soft dark blue velvet dress, calf-length in a ballerina style, with a double strand of very good pearls—presumably a gift from his uncle—and pearl ear studs. Her hair was in a low chignon, with pearl clips. Simple, elegant—and breathtakingly lovely.

Young Giles Barcourt had thought so too, Anatole thought, with an atavistic male instinct. Was that why he'd felt the need to make a point of emphasising his family link with Christine? Staking his claim to her?

Re-staking it.

She is mine. She's always been mine!

Certainty streamed through him. Possessiveness. Remorse and regret.

Why did I let her go—why did I not rush to her and claim her from Vasilis before he married her? Instead I gave in to anger and to my determination not to be forced into marriage and fatherhood.

Well, he hadn't been ready then—but he was ready now. More than ready. All he needed was to persuade Christine that he was right. And if words could not do so, then other means might.

He made some anodyne remark to her now—about the evening, about the pair of Gainsboroughs hanging in the dining room that Vasilis had itched to see cleaned—and said that he agreed with their hosts that perhaps they were best left covered in thick varnish. He had the gratification of hearing Christine chuckle, and then she asked if he'd spotted the very handsome Stubbs in pride of place over the fireplace.

'Indeed,' he replied. 'Do you think Bramble is one of the descendants?' It was a humorous remark, and intended to be so.

'I hope not!' Christine returned. 'That Stubbs stallion looks very fearsome!'

'Do you mind Nicky learning to ride?' Anatole asked as he steered the car along the dark country lanes back to the house.

She shook her head. 'I'm very grateful to Giles and Isabel,' she acknowledged. 'I want Nicky to grow up here, so riding will certainly make him feel at home. And he's very attached to Giles—'

The moment she spoke, she wished she hadn't. Even in the dim interior she could see Anatole's face tighten. She recalled Mrs Barcourt's words to her—not about her son, who was perfectly well understood between them, but about Anatole. Dear God, surely she and Anatole weren't coming across as a couple, were they? Please, *please* not! The very last thing she could bear was any speculation in that direction.

It was bad enough coping with the pressure from Anatole, let alone any expectations from the Barcourts. Consternation filled her about how she was going to handle Anatole's comings and goings—even if they were only to see Nicky. Talk would start—it was inevitable in a small neighbourhood. People would have them married off before she knew it.

Turmoil twisted in her, keeping her silent.

Anatole, too, was silent for the remainder of the short journey.

When they arrived back at her house she got out, preparing to bid him goodnight before he drove back to the White Hart. But instead he said, in a perfectly conversational voice, 'I could do with a nightcap. As the designated driver I got very little of that excellent claret over dinner—and none at all of the port that Barcourt Senior tried to press on me! So I could still have one more.' He glanced expectantly at Christine. 'He mentioned that he gave Vasilis a bottle at Christmas…'

Reluctantly, she let Anatole follow her inside. The house was very quiet—the Hugheses were in their apartment in the converted stables, and Nanny Ruth was away for the weekend. In the drawing room she switched on the table lamps, giving the elegant room a soft warm glow, and extracted the requisite bottle and two port glasses from a lacquered cabinet, setting them down with a slight rattle on a low table by the silk-upholstered sofa.

Anatole strolled across and seated himself, but Christine chose the armchair opposite, spreading her velvet skirts carefully against the pale blue fabric. He poured her a generous measure, and himself as well, then raised his glass to her. His gaze was speaking.

'To us, Christine—to what we can make together.'

His eyes held hers—dark, long-lashed, deep and expressive. She felt their power, their force. The long-ago memories they kindled within her. Emotion swirled, dark and turbid, troubling and disturbing.

It was as disturbing as feeling Anatole's lambent gaze upon her, which did not relinquish her as he took a mouthful of the sweet, strong, rich ruby port. She took a mouthful herself, needing its strength to fortify her.

The bottle had not been opened before—Vasilis's health had worsened steadily, remorselessly after Christmas, and he'd openly prepared her for the coming end. She felt her eyes blur with a mist of tears.

'What is it?' Anatole's voice was quiet, but she could hear the concern in it. 'You're not worrying about Nicky, are you?'

She shook her head. 'No—I'm used to leaving him for a night or two. He never fretted when I went to London with Vasilis.'

Her voice trembled over her late husband's name. Anatole heard the emotion in it and it forced a recognition in him. One he had held back for many years.

'You cared for him didn't you? My uncle?' he said.

His voice was low. Troubled. As if he were facing

something he didn't want to face. Something he'd held at bay for five long bitter, angry years.

'Yes—for his kindness,' she said feelingly. 'And his wisdom. His devotion to Nicky—'

She broke off. Thoughts moved within Anatole's mind—thoughts he did not want to think. His uncle—decades older than Tia and yet she'd had a child with him.

His mind blanked. It was impossible, just *impossible*, to envisage Nicky's conception. It was wrong to think of Tia with anyone else in the whole world except himself. Not his uncle, not young Giles Barcourt—no one!

The same surge of possessiveness he'd felt in the car swept over him again as his eyes drank her in, sitting there so close to him, looking so beautiful it made his breath catch.

How did I last this long without her?

It seemed impossible that he had. Oh, he'd not been celibate, but there had been only fleeting liaisons, deliberately selected for their brevity and infrequency. He'd put that down to having had such a narrow escape with Tia, when she'd so nearly trapped him into marriage—into unwanted fatherhood—exacerbating his existing resistance to women continually seeking to marry him. And yet now that he *did* want to marry her—the same woman who'd once dreamt of that very thing—she was refusing him.

Her words to him echoed in his head, giving him a reason for her obduracy that he could not accept. *Would* not.

'But that does not mean you cannot marry again!' he said.

Her gaze shifted away. 'Anatole—please. Please don't.'

Her voice was a thread. It was clearly unbearable to her that he should say such a thing. But he could not stop.

'Did he…care…for *you*?'

He did not like to think of it. It was…*wrong*. As wrong as Tia having feelings for a man who had probably been older than her own father, had he lived.

'He was fond of me,' she said. Her eyes went to him. 'And he adored Nicky.' She took a breath. 'That was what I valued most—that I was able to give him Nicky. He would never otherwise have had a child had he not married me.'

There was defiance in her voice, and Anatole knew the reason for it. Felt the accusation. Knew he had to answer it. That it was time to face what he had said, what he had done.

He took a breath—a difficult one—and looked her in the face, his expression sombre. 'I'm sorry, Christine. Sorry that when we were together I did not want a child. That I welcomed the fact you were not pregnant after all.'

He took a mouthful of port, felt it strong and fiery in his throat.

'I was not ready to be a father.' His eyes met hers. Unflinching. 'But now,' he said, 'I am. I want to be the father to Nicky that Vasilis did not live to be. I feel,' he swallowed 'I feel my uncle would want that. And I want so much for you to want it too.'

There was a choking noise from Christine and immediately Anatole was there, his port glass hastily set down, kneeling on the Aubusson carpet before Christine's chair, taking her hand. The mist of tears in her eyes was spilling into diamond drops on her lashes.

'Don't cry, Tia,' he said softly, lifting a finger to brush away the tears. 'Don't weep.'

His hand lifted the hand he was holding, which was trembling in his grasp, and he lifted it to his lips, smoothing his mouth across her knuckles.

'We can make this work—truly we can. Marry me—make things as right between us as they were wrong before. Make a family for your son with me—for his sake, for my uncle's sake. For my sake. For your sake.'

His eyes were burning into hers and she was gazing down into their depths, tears still shimmering. He took the half-empty glass from her trembling hand, then retained that hand, getting to his feet, drawing her with him. Light from the table lamp illumined her and his breath caught. How lovely she was…how beautiful.

His mouth lowered to hers. He could not stop—could not prevent himself. Desire streamed within him, and the memory of desire, and both fused together—the past into the present. Her lips were honey to his questing mouth, sweet and soft, and he felt arousal spring within him, strong and instant. His kiss deepened and he heard her make a low noise in her throat, as if she could not bear what was happening. As if she could not bear for him to stop.

His hands slipped from hers, sliding around her slender waist, pulling her gently, strongly, against him. He felt the narrow roundness of her hips against his. Felt his own arousal surge yet more. His blood coursed through him and he deepened his kiss as passion and desire drove him on.

She was quickening in his arms—he could feel it—

and he remembered, with a vividness that was like a flash of searing lightning, how she had always responded when he kissed her like this…how her slender body trembled, strained against him…how her eyes grew dazed as they were dazed now, with a film of desire glazing them as her pupils flared with arousal and the sweet peaks of her breasts strained against the wall of his chest.

He felt her nipples cresting, arousing him. She was kissing him back now—ardently, hungrily. As if she had not kissed anyone for a long, long time. As if only he could sate her hunger.

The last of his control broke. He swept her up into his arms. She was as light as a feather, as thistledown, and the soft material of her skirts draped over his thighs as he carried her from the room, up the wide sweep of stairs into the waiting bedroom. He laid her down on the bed, came down beside her.

How his clothes were shed he did not know—he knew only that her hair had been loosened from its pins and was spilling out upon the pillows, that he was parting the long zip of her dress and peeling it from her body so that her pale, engorged and crested breasts, so tender and so tempting, were exposed to him.

Memory knifed through him of all the times he had made love to her—to Tia, his lovely Tia—so soft in his arms, so yielding to his desire. And she was his again! His after so, *so* long. All that was familiar flooded back like a drowning tide, borne aloft by passion and desire, by memory and arousal.

His palm cupped her breast and he heard her moan again, low in her throat. The dazed look in her distended eyes was dim in the shadows of the night. His mouth lowered to her breast, fastening over her crested nipple, and his tongue worked delicately, delectably, around its sensitive contours.

The moan came again, more incoherent, and he felt her hands helpless on his back. Her neck was arched against the pillows, her throat exposed to him, and he drew his fingers down the length of it, stroking softly, holding her for himself as he moved his mouth to her other breast, to lave it with the same ministrations.

But her sweet ripened breasts were not enough. He wanted more. He felt a low, primitive growl, deep in his being.

He drew her dress from her completely, revealing tiny panties, slipping her free of them. Her thighs slackened and the dark vee between was a darker shadow. He propped himself on one elbow, taking her mouth with his again, feasting on it with slow, arousing sensuality, splaying his free hand on her soft pale flank.

He smiled down at her in the darkness. 'Tell me you do not want this. Tell me you do not want *me*,' he said to her. His voice was low. Driven. 'Tell me to go, Tia—tell me now, or do not tell me at all.'

It was impossible for her to give such an order. Her resistance was gone. How could it persist when his mouth, his hands, his tongue, his lips, his body and all his being were taking her where she should not be going, to what she should not be yielding to?

And yet she *was* yielding. Was succumbing hopelessly, helplessly, to what her body was urging her to do. It was taking her over, demolishing, drowning what her head was telling her. Her head was telling her that it was madness, insanity, to do what she was doing. But she could not stop. It was impossible to do so—impossible not to let the muscles of her thighs slacken, not to tighten her fingers over his strong, warm shoulder as delirium possessed her, as her body swept away the long, empty years since Anatole had last made love to her, had last taken her with him to that place only he could take her to. Where he was taking her again…now, oh, *now*!

She moaned again, her head starting to thresh, her spine arching, the muscles in her legs tautening. Her body ripened, strained as he readied her for his possession. The possession she yearned for, craved, was desperate for.

She heard her voice call his name, as if pleading with him. Pleading with him to complete what he had begun, to lift her to that plane of existence where fire and sweetness and unbearable light would fill her, where the rapture that only he could release in her would be.

He answered her, but she knew not what he said—knew only that his body was moving over hers, the strong, heavy weight of it as familiar as it had ever been, and her arms were snaking around him, enclosing him as her hips lifted to him, yearning for him, craving him, wanting only him, only this.

He thrust into her, a word breaking from him that she did not know but remembered well. The past and present fused, melded, became one. As if no years separated them. As if there had been no parting.

His possession filled her and her body enclosed his, embracing his even as her arms wrapped him to her. The strength of his lean, muscled form, the weight of it upon her, was crushing and yet arousing, even as his slow, rhythmic movements were arousing, and her legs wound about his as each thrust of his body pulsed the blood through her heated, straining body.

She wanted him—oh, dear God, how she wanted him—wanted this—wanted everything—everything he could give her.

He cried out—a straining roar—and as if it were a match to tinder she felt her body flood with him, with her, and she was lifted up, up, soaring into that other world that existed only at such times, forced through a barrier that was invisible, intangible in mortal life, but which now, in Anatole's arms, in his passion and embrace and the utter fusion of their bodies, was their sole existence. On and on she soared, crying into the wind as the heat of the sun in that other world burned down upon her.

Then, like the wind subsiding, she was drawn back down, panting, exhausted. *Sated.* Her whole body purged and cleansed in that white-hot air. She was shaking, trembling, and he was smoothing her hair, talking to her, withdrawing from her and yet folding her back against him, so that she was not alone, not bereft. She was crushed against him, his limbs enfolding hers, his arms wrapped tight around her, and his breath was warm on her shoulder, his hand curving around her cheek, his voice murmuring. She could feel the shuddering of his chest, the thudding of his heart that was in tune with hers.

He was saying her name, over and over again. The name he'd always called her. 'Tia, my Tia. *Mine.*'

And she *was* his. She was, and she always had been—she always would be. Always.

Sleep rushed over her, as impossible to resist as

if it had been slipped into her bloodstream like an overpowering drug. Her eyes fluttered closed. Muscles slackening, her body slumped into the protective cradle of his arms.

They tightened close around her.

CHAPTER TEN

MORNING WAS BREAKING over the gardens, reaching pale fingers of sun across the dew-drenched lawn. Christine stood at the window of her bedroom, a silk *peignoir* wrapping her, gazing blindly out. Her face was sombre, her thoughts far away into the past. The past that had become the present. The present she could not deny. Nor could she deny that she had allowed something to happen that should *never* have happened.

I called it insanity when he said we should marry. But what I've just done is insanity.

How could it be anything else? She turned her head, looking back towards the sleeping figure in her bed, the bedclothes carelessly stretched around his lean, golden-skinned body so that she could see the rise and fall of his chest—the chest she had clung to in that madness, that insanity of last night, as she had clung so often in that long-ago time that should have been *gone* for ever!

It has to be gone—it has to be! It's over!

And she could not, *must* not, allow it to be anything else. Whatever the unbearable temptation to do otherwise—a temptation that Anatole had made a million times more devastatingly powerful after what had happened last night.

I can't be what Anatole is telling me to be. Urging me to be. It's impossible—just impossible!

Impossible for so many reasons.

Impossible for just one overwhelming reason.

The same reason it's always been impossible.

Pain constricted her throat as she stared across at him now, where he lay sleeping in her bed.

There can be no future between us now—none. Just as there could be no future for us then.

She felt the breath tight in her lungs and moved to turn away. But as she did so she heard him stir, saw his hand reaching across the bed, his face registering her absence. His eyes sprang open and he saw her standing there. Emotion speared in his face but it was she who spoke first.

'You have to go! Right now! I can't have Mrs Hughes realising you spent the night here.'

His expression changed. 'But I did—and in your arms.'

He was defying her to deny it, his eyes holding hers. He sat up, reaching for her, catching her hand. Resting his hand on her flank, warm through the cool silk. Looking up at her.

'It's far too late for pretence,' he said softly. 'Didn't last night prove that to you?'

He drew her to him.

'Doesn't this prove it to you?'

His mouth lowered to hers. His kiss was like velvet—the kiss of a man who had taken possession of the woman he desired. She felt honey flow through her, felt her limbs tremble with it.

His eyes poured into hers, rich and lambent. 'It's happened, Tia.' His voice was as intimate, as hushed as if they were the only two people in the world. 'It's happened, and there's no going back now.'

She tried to pull away. Tried to free herself.

'There *has* to be!' she cried. 'I can't do what you want, Anatole. I can't—I *can't*!'

I mustn't! I daren't! What you are offering me is a temptation beyond my endurance. But I must endure it—I must.

She had endured it before—she must do so again. Must find refuge somehow. Find the strength to keep refusing him. Even now, after she had burned in his arms, in his embrace.

Now more than ever. Now that I know how weak I am...how helpless to resist you. Now that I know how hopelessly vulnerable I am to you. Now that I know the danger that stands before me.

Raggedly, she pulled free of him. 'I won't marry you, Anatole,' she said doggedly, each word tugged from her. 'I will not. Whatever you say to me—I will *not*.'

Who was she speaking to? Him or herself? She knew the answer. And she knew what that answer told her—knew the danger it proved her to be in.

Frustration flared in his eyes. 'Why? I don't understand? *Why*, Tia? How can you possibly deny what there is between us?'

She would not reply—could not. All she could do, with a desperate expression on her face, was beg him yet again to go. For an instant longer Anatole just stood there, then abruptly he stood up, seized up his discarded clothes, and disappeared into the en suite bathroom.

Rapidly, Christine got dressed too—pulling on a pair of jeans and a lightweight sweater, roughly brushing out the tangled hair that waved so wantonly around her shoulders, echoing her bee-stung lips in its sensuality…

With a smothered cry she whirled around to see Anatole emerge, wearing his clothes from the night before, but only the shirt and trousers. He looked… she gulped…he looked incredibly, devastatingly *sexy*. There was no other word for it—no other word to describe the slightly raffish look about him, compounded by the lock of raven hair falling across his forehead, the cuffs of his shirt pushed back casually, the dark shadow along his jawline.

She could not take her eyes from him—could feel her pulse quicken, the blood surging in her, colour flushing across her face, lips parting…

He saw her reaction and smiled. A slow, sensual smile, full of confidence.

'You see?'

It was all he said. All he needed to say. He walked towards her. *Strolled.*

She backed away, panic suddenly replacing her betraying reaction to his raw sexuality. 'No—Anatole, *no*! I won't let you do this to me—I *won't*!'

She held her hands up as if to ward him off. He halted, his expression changing. When he spoke there was frustration in his voice, and challenge, in equal measure.

'Tia, you cannot ignore what has happened.'

'I am *not* Tia! I am not her any more—and I will *never* be her again!'

The cry of her own voice, its vehemence, shocked

her. It seemed to shock Anatole as well. His eyes narrowed, losing that blatantly sexy half-lidded look with which he'd stared at her before. For a moment he did not speak. Just looked at her pale face, the cheekbones etched so starkly. Saw the tremble in her upheld hands.

'No,' he said quietly. 'You're not Tia. I've accepted that. I've accepted that you are Christine Kyrgiakis—Mrs Vasilis Kyrgiakis.'

The use of the description made her start. Made her hear the rest of what he said.

'The widow of my uncle—the mother of his son—the mother of my cousin.' He paused again, as if assessing her, the way she was reacting. 'I have made my case, *Christine*—' deliberately he used the name of the woman she was now, the woman she would always be going forward '—and I have given you the reasons why we should marry. And I believe I have done it in more than words.'

For a second that look was back in his eye—that heavy, half-lidded look that made her tremble as nothing that he could say could make her tremble, making her limbs turn boneless, her heart catch in mid-beat. Then he held up a hand, as if she had tried to interrupt him.

'But for now I'll leave it be. I understand, truly, that you must have time to get used to it. Time to come to terms with it. To see it as being as inevitable as I see it to be.' He took a breath, his tone changing. 'But for now the subject is closed. I accept that.'

He turned away, fetching his jacket, so carelessly thrown on a chair last night, and shrugging it on, tugging his cuffs clear and fastening them, then looking across at Christine again.

'I'll go now—to preserve the appearances that are, I know, so important to you right now.' There was no bite in his words, only acknowledgement. 'But I'll be back later. We have Nicky to collect—and, no, please don't tell me not to come with you. He'll be disappointed if I don't.'

She nodded in dumb acquiescence. It seemed easier than contesting his assertion. All she wanted—desperately—was for him to be out of here, finally to be able to collapse in a state of mental and emotional exhaustion, her body aching and spent.

She sheared her mind away—*no, don't think, not now. Not ever...*

But it was impossible not to think, not to feel, for the rest of the day, and when Anatole returned late in the afternoon—as he'd told her he would—so they could drive over to collect Nicky from the Barcourts, she felt a leap of unbearable emotion as her eyes went to his. And his to hers.

For a moment, as their eyes met, she felt as if she had been transported back in time and was poised to do what she had once done so automatically and spontaneously—run into his arms that would open to her and fold her to him.

Then his eyes were veiled and the moment passed. As he helped her into the car he made some pleasantry about the weather, to which she replied in kind. They chatted in a desultory way during the short journey, and Christine told herself she was thankful.

And she was even more thankful that as they arrived there was a melee to greet them: Elizabeth

Barcourt's grandchildren, their mother and their grandmother, all chattering to them madly.

As for Nicky—he was only too eager to regale them both with the delights of his day.

'I rode a pony! Can I have a pony—*can* I? Can I?' he pleaded, half to Anatole, half to Christine.

A spike drove into her heart as she saw the way her son addressed them both. As if he accepted her and Anatole as a unit. She tensed, and it was noticed by Elizabeth Barcourt, who drew her a little aside as Anatole crouched down to Nicky's level to get the full account of the joys of his day and the thrill of riding a pony for the first time.

'My dear, I'm glad Anatole is able to spend time with you—the more the better.' She cast a look at Christine, and then at Nicky. 'He's a natural with him! One might almost think—'

She broke off, as if conscious she had said too much, then stepped away, quietening her noisy grandchildren and telling them it was time for Nicky to head home.

As they finally set off Nicky's chatter was all of ponies and puppies and the fun he'd had with the other children.

'I'm going to paint a picture of a pony and a puppy,' he announced as they arrived, and then belied his intention by giving a huge yawn, indicating how little actual sleep his exciting sleepover had involved.

'Bath first,' said Christine, and then hesitated.

What she wanted to do was tell Anatole it was time for him to leave, to go away, to leave her alone with her son. But her hesitation was fatal.

'Definitely bath time,' Anatole said, adding with a grin, 'I'll race you upstairs!'

With a cry of excitement Nicky set off up the wide staircase and Anatole followed—as did Christine, much more slowly, her face set.

OK, so the two of them would bath Nicky, and see him to bed and *then* she'd tell Anatole it was time he left. That was her intention—her absolute resolve. Because no way was he going to spend the night here again.

And not in my bed!

Her face flushed with colour, her features contorting.

He's got to go—he's just got to.

Close to an hour later, with Nicky tucked up in bed and falling asleep instantly, she walked back downstairs with Anatole. She paused at the foot and turned to him.

'Are you staying at the White Hart tonight or heading straight back to London?' Her voice was doggedly bright, refusing to acknowledge there was any other possibility.

He looked at her. His gaze was half lidded, as if he knew why she was saying what she was.

'Once,' he said, 'you were not so rejecting of me.'

The expression in his eyes, the open caress in his voice, brought colour to stain her cheekbones, and her fingers clenched at her sides.

'Once,' she replied, 'I was a different person.'

He gave a swift shake of his head, negating her denial. 'You're still that person—whether you call yourself Tia or Christine, you're still her. And last night showed me that. It showed *you* that! So why deny it?

Why even *try* to deny it? Why try to deny that our marriage would work?'

And now the caress was back in his voice, almost tangible on her skin, which was suddenly flushing with heat.

'Last night showed how alive that flame that was always between us still is. From the moment you saw me, Tia, you wanted me—and I wanted you. I wanted you then and I want you now. And it is the same for you. It blazes from you, your desire for me.'

He reached a hand towards her, long lashes sweeping down over his eyes, a half-smile pulling at his mouth.

'Don't deny it, Tia,' he said softly. 'Don't deny the truth of what we have. We *burn* for each other.' His voice dropped to a sensual husk.

She took a jerky step backwards—an instinctive gesture of self-protection against what he wanted. He didn't like it that she did so, and he stilled. She lifted her chin. Looked straight at him. She must tell him what she needed to say. What he needed to hear.

Her eyes met his unflinchingly, with a bare, stark expression in them. 'I know that, Anatole! Dear God, of *course* I know it! How could I not?'

She shook her head, as if acknowledging a truth she could not deny. Then her eyes reached his, hung on to his, trying to make him hear, understand.

'It was always like that—right from the first. And, yes, it's still there. Last night did prove it, just as you say. But, Anatole, listen—*listen* to me. I can't let myself be blinded by passion! And nor can you! A marriage can't be built on passion alone, and nor can it be based on just wanting to make a family for Nicky. You *have* to see that!'

There was a tremor in her voice, intensity in her face—but in his there was only blank rejection of her rejection of him.

'All my life,' he said slowly, 'women have wanted to marry me. You included, or so I supposed way back then. And yet now, when I *want* to marry, the woman I want to marry is turning me down.' He gave a laugh. There was no humour in it. 'Maybe that's some kind of cosmic karma—I don't know.'

He pressed his lips together, as if to control his words, his emotions. Emotions that were streaming through him in a way he had never known before. A kind of disbelief. Even dismay.

His eyes rested on her. 'So, what *can* a marriage be built on? Tell me what else there needs to be.'

She looked at him, and there was a deep sadness in her voice as she answered. 'Oh, Anatole, the fact that you have to ask tells me how impossible marriage would be between us.'

'Then *tell* me!' he ground out.

She shut her eyes for a moment, shaking her head before she opened them again. She looked at him, her features twisting. 'I can't,' she said. 'But…' She paused, as if profoundly reluctant to speak, yet she did so. 'You would know it—'

She broke off, turned away, walked unevenly towards the front door to open it for him to leave. Marriage between them was as impossible now as it had been when she'd thought she lived in fairyland.

Emotion was pressing upon her—unbearable, agonising—but she would not yield to it. Opening the door, she turned back to him. He hadn't moved. He was just looking at her.

Determinedly, she met his gaze. 'Anatole—please—' She indicated the open doorway.

He walked towards it, pausing beside her. 'We'd make a good couple,' he said. 'We'd have each other and Nicky. Maybe a child of our own one day.'

A smothered cry came from her. '*Go!* Go, Anatole, and leave me alone!'

She closed the door on him, not caring that she'd all but pushed him out. Only when the lock clicked, cutting out the sound of his footsteps on the gravelled drive, muffling the sound of his car door slamming, the engine starting, did she turn, leaning back on the closed front door, shutting him out—out of her house, out of her life.

A child of our own...

That muffled cry came again. That was what she had longed for so long ago—before the glowing fairy dust she'd sprinkled over her life had turned to bitter ashes.

Slowly, bleakly, she headed upstairs to kiss her sleeping son a silent goodnight.

The only person she could love.

Could allow herself to love.

CHAPTER ELEVEN

'MY DEAR, IT'S good to see you again. How are you bearing up?'

It was the vicar's wife, welcoming her into the vicarage where her husband offered her a dry sherry.

'I miss my weekly symposia with Vasilis,' he said, after his wife had asked after Nicky, and how he too was bearing up.

This kind of kind enquiry had continued to come her way, and Christine always answered as best she could. But it was difficult. How could she possibly tell people that Anatole had offered her marriage in order to make a family for Nicky? An offer she could not accept, however overwhelming the temptation.

That temptation still wound itself inside her head even now—despite all she felt, all she told herself, all she had forced herself to feel, not to feel, in the endless month that had passed since Anatole had driven away that last time.

It had been a month filled with anguish and torment over what she had done. A month of missing Anatole.

And that was the worst of it—the most dangerous sign of all—telling her what she so desperately did not want to be told. She longed to be able to put him out of her mind, but it was impossible. And made more so by Nicky's repeated mentions of him, his constant questioning about when Anatole would be back.

'I want him to come!' he would say plaintively, and Christine and Nanny Ruth would be hard pressed to divert him, even though summer was coming and the weather warm enough for them to think of driving to the coast, for a day at the beach.

'But I want Cousin Anatole to come too!' had been Nicky's only response when she'd told him. 'Why can't he come? *Why?*'

Christine had done her best. 'Munchkin, your cousin works very hard—he has lots to do. He has to fly to other countries—'

'He could fly *here*,' Nicky had retaliated. He'd looked across at his mother. 'He could *live* here. He said he was coming to look after me—he *said*. He said my *pappou* told him to!'

His little face had quivered, and Christine's heart had gone out to him. Pangs had pierced her.

If she married Anatole—

No! It was madness to think of yielding. Worse than madness. It would be sentencing herself to a lifetime of anguish.

Instead she had to sentence her beloved son to missing Anatole.

When the first postcard had arrived, she'd been grateful. It had been from Paris, showing the Eiffel Tower and a popular cartoon character. Anatole had written on the back.

Will you do me a painting of the Eiffel Tower, with you and me at the top?

Nicky, thrilled, had rushed off to get his paints.

More postcards had arrived, one every week, from different parts of the globe. And now a month had turned into six weeks. Six endless weeks.

The imminent arrival of his puppy was a source of cheer, and learning to ride, being taught as promised by Giles, helped keep Nicky busy—as did the open day at the pre-prep school he would start at in the autumn.

After meeting some of the other boys there who would be his classmates Christine had arranged some play dates. She'd even thought about taking Nicky away on holiday for a week somewhere. Perhaps a theme park. Perhaps the seaside in Brittany or Spain.

She didn't know. Couldn't decide. Couldn't think. Couldn't do anything except let one day slip by into another and feel a kind of quiet, drear despair seep over her.

Was this to be her life from now on? It seemed so lonely without Anatole.

I miss him!

The cry came from deep within, piercing in its intensity. She tried to think of Vasilis, to use his calm, comforting memory to insulate herself—but Vasilis was fading. His presence in the house, her life, was only a fragile echo.

She felt him most when she attended to the business of his foundation, but that was intermittent, with the meat of the work being carried out by his handpicked trustees, who followed the programme her husband had set out for them. She did her bit, played her part, had gone twice to London for meetings, but on her return there was only one man she thought about.

Only one.

The one she could not have.

The one she had sent away.

And the one whom she missed more and more with every passing day.

Anatole was back in Athens again. He'd spent weeks flying from one city to another, relentlessly restless, driven onwards by frustration and a punishing need to keep occupied and keep moving, putting out of his mind all that he had left behind.

The only times he let it intrude was when he paused in airports to buy a postcard for Nicky of wherever he happened to be, scrawling something on it for the boy.

But it did not do to think too much of Nicky. Still less of Christine. Instead, he made himself focus on what had landed on him here in Athens.

His face set in a grim expression. Both parents had demanded that he visit, and both visits had been hideous. His father intended to get yet another divorce, and wanted a way of getting out of the pre-nup he'd so rashly signed, and his mother wanted him to get back a villa on the Italian lakes she regretted allowing her most recent ex to have.

He was interested in neither demand, nor in the flurry of social invitations that had descended upon him to functions at which women would make a beeline for him, as they always did, his unmarried status a honeypot to them. It had always been like that and he was fed up with it—more fed up than he'd ever been in his life.

I don't want any of this. I don't want to be here. I don't want these people in my life.

Neither the women fawning over him, trying to get his interest, nor his parasitic parents, who only contacted him when they wanted something from him and otherwise ignored his existence, were anything other than repellent to him. And as he headed back to his apartment—alone—he knew with a kind of fierceness that ran like fire in his veins that in all the six punishing weeks he'd spent travelling the world there had been only one place he wanted to get back to. Only one place he wanted to be.

He walked out on to his balcony and the heat of the city's night seemed suffocating. Clogging his lungs. Memory sliced through him, pushing a different balcony high up in the London rooftops into his mental vision. A greenish glow lit the greenery…a soft voice exclaimed at the sight.

A soft voice that had cried out to him again after so many years as they had reached ecstasy together once more. Before that same voice, soft no longer, had banished him.

A vice seemed to close around him, crushing him. He had lost her once before, through his own blindness. Now he had lost her again and he could not endure it.

I have to see her again. I have to try again—I can't give up on her. I want a family—a family with her, with Nicky.

And why should she not want that too? What impediment could there be?

Across his mind, her words drifted like a ghost intent on haunting him.

'You would know it—'

What had she meant? What did she want that he

was not offering her? What was necessary to a good marriage other than what he had set out in plain words, in every caress that he had lavished upon her?

It made no sense.

He shook the thoughts from him, impatient to be gone, to close the yawning space between where he was and where she and Nicky were.

Within hours, those parting miles had vanished, and as he sped out of Heathrow, heading south, gaining open countryside, for the first time since he had left he felt his spirits lighten, his breathing ease.

Elation filled him. And hope renewed. This time—surely this time—he would persuade Christine to finally make her future with him.

This time she won't refuse me.

Hope, strong and powerful, streamed within him.

Christine turned in between the wrought-iron gates, the wheels of her car crunching over the gravel. She'd just collected Nicky from another riding lesson at the Barcourts', and now he was imparting Giles's equine wisdom to his mother.

'You mustn't let ponies eat too much grass,' he informed her. 'It blows them up like a balloon. They might pop!'

'Oh, dear,' said Christine dutifully.

'And you have to groom them after *every* ride. I groom Bramble—but not his tail. Giles does that. Ponies can kick if they get cross.'

'Oh, dear,' Christine said again, thankful that Giles had performed that tricky office.

'I did his mane. I stood on a box to reach,' continued Nicky. 'Bramble is a strawberry roan. He's thirteen hands. That means how high he is. When I'm grown up I'll be too big for him. Now I'm almost just right.'

Murmuring appropriately, Christine rounded the bend in the drive, emerging from the shade into the sunshine that was bathing the gracious frontage of the house, with its pleasing symmetry and the dormer windows in the roofline. The sunshine that was gleaming off the silver-grey saloon car just drawing up ahead of her.

She felt her stomach clench. Her pulse leap. Her breath catch. Anatole was emerging from the car, looking round as he heard her approach, lifting a hand in greeting.

Nicky stopped in mid-word and cried out, ecstatic delight and excitement in his voice, 'He came—he *came*! I wanted him to and he has!'

The next few minutes passed in a blur as, trying urgently to quell the tumult inside her, Christine drew her car up beside Anatole's. Nicky, overjoyed, scrambled out to hurl himself at Anatole, who scooped him in a single sweep up into his arms, clutching him tightly.

Exhilaration streamed through Anatole at the feel of the little lad embracing him. It was good, *so* good to see him again—more than good. Wonderful!

'Oof!' he exclaimed laughingly. 'You're getting heavier and heavier, young man!'

He ruffled the dark hair—as dark as his own, thought Christine, and felt the familiar ache shooting inside her—then lowered Nicky to the ground. He looked across at Christine.

'Hi,' he said casually. Determinedly casually. Determinedly suppressing the urge, the overpowering desire to do to her as he'd done to Nicky—sweep her up into his arms and hug her tightly! But he must not do that. He must be calm, casual. Friendly, nothing but friendly.

For now.

His expression changed slightly. 'Sorry to drop in unannounced. I hope it's OK.' He paused, then said deliberately, 'I'm booked in at the White Hart.'

He wanted to give her no excuse for sending him away again. To do nothing to scare her off.

Wordlessly, she nodded, feeling relief for that, at least. She was trying to get her composure back, but it was impossible. Impossible to do anything but feel the rapid surge of her blood, the hectic flare of colour in her cheeks as her eyes hung on him.

He was in casual clothes—designer jeans and a sweater with a designer logo on it, and designer sneakers. He looked totally relaxed and like a million dollars. She felt her heart start to thump.

'I'd better let Mrs Hughes know you'll be here for dinner,' she said, finally managing to speak.

He tilted an eyebrow at her. 'Not if you have other plans.'

She had no plans—nothing except helping Nanny Ruth with Nicky's tea, bath time and bed. Then her own TV supper in her sitting room.

She made herself smile. 'I'm sure Nicky will want to eat with you.'

'Yes! *Yes!*' Her son tugged at Anatole's jeans. 'Come and play with me. I've been for a ride. And I groomed Bramble. Giles says I'm going to be jumping him soon!'

'Are you, now?' Anatole grinned, letting himself focus on the lad.

He didn't look again at Christine. It would not have been wise.

She was looking…*beautiful*—that was what she was looking. Beautiful, with her hair pushed off her face by a band, wearing a summery skirt in a blue-printed material, gathered at the waist, and a pale yellow blouse with a short cardigan in a deeper yellow. Her legs were bare, showing golden calves, and her narrow feet were in espadrilles.

He felt desire leap instantly within him. And an emotion that he could not name kicked through him, powerful and unfamiliar. He wanted to go on looking at her. More than look. Wanted to close the distance between them, take her face in his hands and kiss her sweet, tender mouth—as a husband would a wife.

Determination swept through him. *I have to make her mine. I have to persuade her, convince her how right it is for us to marry! Overcome her objections…*

Into his head came her words again—the words he could not understand but needed to understand, about just what it was that she was holding out for.

'You would know it—'

Frustration ground at him again. *What* would he know? What was it she wanted of him that he was not offering her?

I have to find out.

And that was why he had come, wasn't it? To try again—and again.

I'll never give up—never!

The knowledge seared in him, infusing every brain cell with its power. But then Nicky was tugging at him again, chattering away, reclaiming his attention—which he gave with a leap of his emotion to see the boy so eager to be with him. He grinned down fondly at him, and let Nicky drag him off.

Christine watched them go indoors, feeling as if a sledgehammer had just swiped her sideways. Jerkily, she put her car away in the garage, went indoors via the kitchen to seek out Mrs Hughes about revising dinner plans, then she hurried to the sanctuary of her bedroom, her heart hammering, her emotions in tumultuous free fall.

She knew she couldn't keep Anatole out of Nicky's life indefinitely, but how could she possibly bear to keep on seeing him turn up like this…turning her upside down and inside out all over again?

Of their own volition her eyes went to her bed—the bed where she had made love with Anatole in that insane yielding to her own impossible desire for him.

Biting her lip, as if to bite off a memory she must not allow, she headed for her bathroom.

Her cheeks were far too hot. And there was only one cause of that…

As Mrs Hughes wheeled in dinner, it was like *déjà vu* for Christine, as she remembered that first time—so long ago now, it seemed—when Anatole had invited himself.

Nicky, in fine fettle and fresh from bath time, in pyjamas and dressing gown, was exclaiming to Anatole that it would be pasta for dinner. Anatole was saying it would liver and spinach.

'No! No!' cried Nicky, unconvinced. 'That's for *you*!' He gave a peal of laughter.

'Yummy!' retorted Anatole, rubbing his midriff. 'My favourite!'

'Yucky-yuck-yuck!' Nicky rejoined, repeating it for good measure, with another peal of laughter.

Christine calmed him down—getting him over-excited was not sensible. But then, dining here with her son and Anatole was not sensible either, was it? It was the very opposite of sensible. It was little short of criminally stupid.

But how could she deprive her son of what he was clearly enjoying so much? Emotion slid under skin. If she succumbed to Anatole's proposal, this might be their way of life…

For a moment she saw the glitter of fairy dust over the scene. She and Anatole, Nicky with them, day after day, night after night. A family. A fairytale come true.

Into her head she heard the words that Elizabeth Barcourt had spoken. *'He's a natural with him!'* And the half-sentence that had followed. *'Almost as if—'*

No! The guillotine sliced down again and she busied herself helping Mrs Hughes.

In yet another replay of that first time Anatole had dined here, the housekeeper proffered wine for Anatole's inspection—and this time it did not grate with her, Anatole taking his uncle's role.

Vasilis seemed so very far away now—and she found it hurt her to realise just how long ago their marriage seemed. As if she were leaving him behind.

'You're thinking of my uncle, aren't you?'

Anatole's voice was quiet and his eyes were on her, Christine realised, as Mrs Hughes left the room.

She nodded, blinking. Then she felt a gentle pressure on her arm. Anatole had leant across to press his hand softly on her sleeve. The gesture was simple, and yet it made Christine stare at him, confusion in her gaze. There was something in his eyes she'd never seen before. Something that made her throat tighten.

For a moment their eyes held.

'Mumma, *please* may I start?' Nicky's voice broke the moment.

'Yes—but say Grace first,' said Christine with a smile at her son. A smile that somehow flickered to Anatole as well, and was met with an answering flicker.

In his sing-song voice Nicky recited Grace, with an angelic expression on his face and his hands pressed together in dutiful reverence, rounding off with Giles Barcourt's reminder that puddings came to those who were good.

Anatole laughed and they all tucked in—Nicky to his beloved pasta, Christine and Anatole to a delicious chicken fricassee. As she sipped her wine she felt the difference in atmosphere at this meal from the meal when Anatole had first descended on them.

How much easier it was now.

How much more natural it seemed.

As if it's right for him to be here.

She felt the pull of it like a powerful tide, drawing ever closer. A dangerous tide of overwhelming temptation. But if she indulged—

She tore her mind away, focussing on the moment, on Nicky's chatter, on Anatole's easy replies and her own deliberately neutral contributions when necessary.

As the meal ended, with pudding consumed, Nicky started to yawn copiously. Between them, she and

Anatole carried him up to bed, saw him off to sleep, then slowly headed downstairs.

The Greek words of the night-time blessing Anatole had once again murmured over the sleeping child, resonated in Christine's head. And, as if it did in his too, Anatole spoke.

'What arrangements are being made to ensure that Nicky grows up bilingual? I'm sure Vasilis would have wanted that. Obviously I'll do my best, but if I only visit occasionally he may well lose what he has already.'

There was no criticism in his voice, only enquiry.

Christine nodded, acknowledging his reasonable concern. 'Yes, something must be arranged.' She gave a slight smile. 'Our vicar promised Vasilis that he'd teach Nicky classical Greek in a few years, but that won't be enough, I know. I can manage a little modern Greek—enough to teach him the alphabet, but nothing more. Maybe…' she glanced cautiously at Anatole '…maybe you could chat to him regularly over the Internet? And ensure he has contemporary Greek language children's literature to read?'

She started to walk downstairs again. It was not unreasonable to encourage Nicky to keep up his Greek with Anatole—surely it wasn't?

I have to learn to live in harmony with Anatole. Whatever happens, I can't refuse him that.

Her mind skittered away, not wanting to think about the rest of her life with Anatole interacting with Nicky over the years. It was too difficult.

Instead, she went on, 'I could have a word with his headmaster—see if he can recommend a tutor in modern Greek when he starts school in September?'

'School?' Anatole frowned.

'Yes—Vasilis enrolled him at the nearby pre-prep school. It's the same one Giles Barcourt went to. Very traditional, but very well regarded. We both liked it when we visited—and so did Nicky. He's looking forward to starting.'

'Is it a boarding school?' There was a harsh note in Anatole's sharp question.

Christine stared at him. 'Of course it isn't! I wouldn't *dream* of sending him to boarding school! If he actually *wants* to board, when he's a teenager, then fine—but obviously not till then…if at all.'

She saw Anatole's face relax. 'My apologies. It's just that—' He broke off, then resumed as his heavy tread headed downstairs ahead of her. 'I was packed off to boarding school when I was seven. I was a nuisance to my parents, and they wanted shot of me.'

There was harshness in his voice. More than harshness. *Pain.*

She caught up with him as he reached the hall, grabbed his arm. 'Oh, Anatole, that's awful! How could they *bear* to?' There was open shock and sympathy in her voice.

A hollow laugh was her answer. 'I wasn't a priority for them—'

He broke off again, and into Christine's head came a memory from five years ago, when she'd told him how much she missed her father, and he'd told her she was lucky to have any good memories of him at all.

'In a way,' he said, and there was a twist in his voice that was very audible to her, 'Vasilis cared more for me in his abstract manner than either of my parents did. Maybe,' he went on, not looking at her, but looking inwardly, 'that's why I so want Nicky to have me in his life. So I can be to Vasilis's son what he was to me. But…more so.'

His eyes went to her, and there was a veiled expression in them.

'I want you both, Christine. You *and* Nicky. That will not change.'

His eyes held hers, and what she saw in them told her why he had come here.

She made herself hold his gaze. Made herself speak to him. 'And nor will my answer, Anatole.' Her voice was steady, though she felt her emotions bucking wildly inside her. But she must hold steady. She *must*.

Frustration flashed across his features. '*Why?* It makes such *sense* for us to marry!'

Her throat was tight, and her hands were clasping each other as she faced him. 'It made sense for me to marry Vasilis. At least…' she took a painful breath '…it seemed to at the time.' Her eyes were strained, her cheekbones etched. 'I won't—' She swallowed, feeling the tightness in her throat. 'I won't marry again for the same reason.'

And not you, Anatole! Not you over whom I once sprinkled fairy dust only to have it turn to ashes.

She lifted up her hands in that warding off gesture she had made last time. It made him want to step towards her, deny her negation of him. Frustration bit in him, and more than frustration. A stronger emotion he could not name.

But she was speaking again, not letting him counter her, try to argue her down, make her accept what he could see so clearly.

'Anatole, *please*!' There was strain in her voice now, and her face was working. 'Please. I cannot—*will* not—marry you to make a family for Nicky!' She gave a weary sigh. 'Oh, Anatole, we're going round in circles. I don't want what *you* want.'

'Then what *do* you want?' he cried out, with a frustration that shook him in its intensity.

Yet even as he spoke he heard her words, spoken to him the last time they'd stood here, going round in the circles they were caught in, round and round, repeating the impasse of their opposition.

'You would know it—'

The words mocked him, taunted him. He wanted to knock them to the floor, get them out of the way, because they came between him and what he wanted so much—to crush her to him and smother her with kisses, to sweep her up the stairs and into her room, her bed. To make her his own for ever!

But he did not. For yet again they were caught in that endless loop they were trapped in, and she was doing what he had seen her do before.

He saw her walk to the door, open it, to usher him out—out of her life again. As she always did. Always had from the very moment she had left him to marry his uncle.

On heavy tread he did as she bid him, feeling as though gravity were crushing him.

'May I visit tomorrow?' The words sounded abrupt, though he did not mean them to be.

She nodded. Nicky would expect it. Long for it. How could she deprive her son of what gave him such delight?

How can I deprive him of what Anatole is offering?

Like a serpent in her veins, temptation coiled in its dangerous allure. Tightening its fatal grip on her.

'Thank you,' Anatole said quietly.

He paused, looked at her in the doorway. Behind her in the hall he could hear the grandfather clock ticking steadily, measuring out their lives. Their *separate* lives. The thought was anguish to him.

Then he made himself give her a flickering smile, bid her goodnight. He walked out into the summer's night, heard an owl calling from the woodlands, smelled the scent of honeysuckle wafting at him.

From the doorway she watched him go…watched the car drive off, its headlights sweeping through the dark, cutting a path of light. And then he was gone. Gone yet again.

Was this what her life was to be now? Anatole arriving and departing? Spending time with her only to see Nicky, watching him grow up as year followed year? How could she bear it?

In the quiet hallway she heard the clock ticking past the seconds, the months, the years ahead.

A sudden smothered cry broke from her and she turned away, heading back indoors, shutting the door.

Alone once more.

So alone.

CHAPTER TWELVE

ANATOLE STOOD BY the open window in his bedroom, looking out over the walled garden of the White Hart. Dawn was stealing in, heralding the new day. But not new hope.

His expression was sombre and drawn. His journey here had been in vain. It was pointless to have made it. She had refused him again. Had told him she would always refuse him.

She does not want me.

That was what it came down to. Her rejection of him. She had rejected him when she'd left him to marry Vasilis. She was rejecting him still.

A bitter twist contorted his lips as he stood staring bleakly. He should be used to rejection. Should have got used to it from a young age. He had been rejected by his own parents—who had never wanted him, never loved him.

His mind sheared away from ancient pain. Why was he thinking about that now? He'd always known he wasn't important to them. Had learnt to insulate himself from it. Learnt to ignore it. Discard it. Do without it. He had always lived his life without love. Without wanting love.

He frowned. Why waste his thoughts on his parents? They were not important to him. It was Tia who was important. Tia and her son Nicky.

His expression softened, the twist of his lips relaxing, curving into a fond, reminiscent smile that lit up his eyes as he recalled how wonderful it had been to be greeted by his young cousin so eagerly, to spend the evening with him, absorbed in his world. As Nicky had hurtled towards him, and as he'd caught him up into his arms, an emotion so fierce had swept him, rushing through him like a freight train. Overwhelming him.

What was it, that emotion that had possessed him? A joy so intense, a lifting of his heart that he felt again now, even in recalling it? What *was* that emotion? He'd felt nothing like it before—never in his life.

And it had stayed with him, intensified, curving right through him as his eyes had gone to Christine—so beautiful, so lovely, and so very dear to him.

How can I live without her? Without them both?

He couldn't. It was impossible.

I can't live without them. I need them to breathe, to keep my heart beating!

His expression changed as he rested his gaze on the deep-shadowed garden.

Why? *Why* did he need them to breathe, to keep his heart beating? *Why* did that fierce, protective emotion possess him when he hefted Nicky into his arms? When he gazed at Christine? What *was* it that he felt with such burning intensity?

On the far side of the garden, towards the east, the sky was lightening, tipping the outlines of the ornamental trees and the edges of their silhouetted branches with light. He stood staring at them, feeling inside that same emotion building again, filling him, confusing him, bewildering him.

He heard his own voice calling silently inside his head.

Tia, tell me! Tell me what it is I feel about you. About Nicky.

And in his head he heard her, answering him with the words she'd said that had so confused him, bewildered him.

'You would know it—'

He heard the words that completed what she'd said. What she had not said.

If you felt it.

Slowly, oh-so-slowly, as if the whole world had turned about, the two phrases came together—fused.

You would know it if you felt it.

And suddenly, out of nowhere—out of an absence in his being that had been there all his life—he was filled: filled with a rush, a flood of realisation. Of understanding, of knowledge.

That was why he needed her to keep his heart beating! That was why he needed her to breathe!

That was the emotion that he felt—the emotion he knew because he felt it.

It was an emotion he had never known in his life, for no one had ever felt it about *him*—no one had ever taught him how to recognise it.

Accept it.

Feel it.

That was the emotion he felt when he thought about Christine, about Nicky. *That* was what had brought him here to be with them, to beg her to let him stay with her and Nicky all his life. To make a family together.

That was the emotion that filled him now—filled him in every cell in his body—the emotion that was turning his heart over and over and over as realisation poured through him.

He stood there breathless with it, stunned with it. Stood stock-still as he gazed out into the garden which was filling now with gold…with the risen sun.

As he stood there, with the world turning to gold around him, turning to gold within him, he knew there was only one thing to be done right now. To find Christine and tell her.

'You would know it—' she had told him.

Triumph and gratitude, wonder and thankfulness seared him. Well, now he knew—and it was time to tell her. Oh, time to tell her indeed!

Pulling away from the window, he hurried to dress.

•

Christine was having breakfast on the little stone-paved terrace beyond her sitting room, with Nicky seated opposite her. Nanny Ruth was upstairs, packing for her weekend away to visit her sister. The morning was warm already, the garden filled with sunshine and birdsong, rich with the scent and colour of flowers.

Nicky was chattering away, talking to her about what they would do when Anatole arrived. 'Can we go to the holiday park again? Can we? Can we?' he asked eagerly.

'I don't know, munchkin—let's wait and see,' she temporised.

Her mood was torn. Hammered down under a barrier as impenetrable as she could make it, battering to be let out, was an emotion she must not feel. The raw, overpowering eagerness to see Anatole again, to let her eyes light upon him, drink him in. But she must not let that emotion break through. If it did—

I might crack, and yield. Give in to what I so long to do, which would bring me nothing but misery and anguish.

No, all she could do was what she was trying so hard to do now—crush down that desperately dangerous longing, suppress it tightly, keep it leashed so that it never broke through.

I've got to be careful! Oh, so careful!

She had to learn how to school herself, how to manage what would from now on be the routine of her life. She had to learn to face seeing Anatole on and off, whenever he visited Nicky through all the years ahead—years that stretched like a torment before her. Wanting so much…yearning for what she could not have. What she had always yearned for but had never had.

She reached for her coffee as Nicky munched his toast, still happily chattering. Lifted her cup to her mouth to take a sip. And stilled in mid-lift.

Anatole was striding across the gardens towards her.

He'd come from the direction of the boundary wall, and the woodland beyond, and a dim part of her mind wondered why. But the rest of her consciousness was leaping into ultra-focus, her gaze fastening on him, that emotion leaping within her that she must not feel but could not suppress as he drew closer. Her clinging gaze took in his ruffled hair, the soft leather jacket he was wearing over a dark blue sweater, his long, lithe jeans-clad legs covering the dew damp lawn in seconds.

He came up to them. Nicky, sitting with his back to him, hadn't noticed him.

Anatole's eyes went to her in a sudden, flickering gaze that was only brief, but she felt a tingle of shock go through her. In it had been something she had never seen before—but an instant later it had gone…gone before she could even wonder at it. She only know that as his gaze flicked away she felt a sense of empty desolation in her so strong she almost sobbed.

Then a grin was slicing his face, and his hands were sliding around Nicky's eyes. 'Guess who?' he said.

Nicky squealed in delight, grabbing Anatole's hands and clambering down to rush around the chair to hug his legs and greet him deliriously.

Then he pulled away sharply. 'You're all wet!' he said indignantly.

Anatole hunkered down beside him to hug him. His heart was pounding, and not just from the long walk he'd had. 'I came on foot,' he said, 'and there's a lot of long damp grass in those fields!'

Christine stared weakly. 'But it's five miles!' she exclaimed.

He only shrugged, for a second making that flickering eye contact with her again that left her reeling and then desolate when he broke it, and laughed.

'It's a glorious morning—it was a joy to walk!' He pulled out one of the ironwork chairs at the table and sat himself down. 'I could murder a coffee,' he said.

Like an echo, piercing and sibilant, memory stabbed into Christine. He'd used those same words five long years ago, when he'd taken her to his London apartment.

Numbly, she got to her feet. 'I'll… I'll go and make some fresh,' she said, her emotions in turmoil at his unexpectedly early arrival.

In the kitchen, she tried to calm herself. What use was it for her heart to leap the way it did when she set eyes on him? What use at all? What use to feel that dreadful, desolate ache inside her?

Forcibly, she took deep breaths, and when she went back out with a fresh cafetière of coffee, plus toast and some warmed croissants, she felt a little less agitated.

But it only took the sight of Anatole sitting with Nicky at the table, laughing and smiling, to make her feel weak again, to know how useless her attempts to cope with this would be.

'We're going to the beach! We're going to the beach!'

Her son's excited piping made her turn her attention to him.

'Beach?' she echoed vaguely, her mind still churning.

'We can make a day of it.' Anatole grinned. Then his expression changed. 'If that's acceptable to you?'

She nodded. Now that the magic word 'beach' had been uttered it would be impossible to withdraw it without tears from Nicky.

'I'll need to get our beach things packed up,' she said.

Getting away from him again would give her respite, allow her to steady her nerves, arm herself against his presence.

But his arm reached out. 'Don't rush off,' he said.

He took a breath. Met her eyes. That same strange, unreadable flicker was in them that had caught at her so powerfully. She felt herself tense. Something had changed about him, but she didn't know what.

Then he was turning to Nicky. 'Why don't you run upstairs and tell Nanny Ruth we're going to go to the beach?' he said, making his voice encouraging.

Excited, Nicky hared off.

Anatole turned back to Christine. For a second—less than a second—there was complete silence. It seemed to fill the space, the world between them. Then he spoke.

'I need to talk to you,' he said.

There was an intensity in his voice, in his expression, that stilled her completely.

'What is it?' she asked, alarm in her words.

There was something in his eyes that was making her heart suddenly beat faster—something she'd seen in that brief second when he'd arrived.

'Can we walk across the garden?' he asked.

Numbly, she nodded, and Anatole fell into place beside her.

An intense nervous energy filled him. So much depended on the next few minutes.

Everything depends on it—my whole life—

'Anatole, what's wrong?'

Christine's voice penetrated his hectic thoughts. There was a thread of anxiety audible in her tone.

He didn't answer until they'd crossed the lawn into a little dell of beech trees dappled with sunlight, where there was a rustic wooden bench. She sat down, and so did he, wanting to take her hand, but not daring to. His heart was slugging in his chest.

Christine's eyes were on him, wide with alarm. 'Anatole…' she said again, faintly.

Something was wrong—the same dread that had assailed her that nightmare morning when she'd had to tell him she thought she was pregnant was rising up to bite in her lungs.

'Christine…' He took a breath, a ragged one, wanting to look at her, but not wanting to, instead fixing his gaze on the beech mast littering the ground. 'Last night…' He paused, then forced himself on. 'Last night you said you would never marry me just because it made sense to do so, just to make a family for Nicky. And the time before—that morning after,' he said, daring, finally, to steal a glance at her, seeing in a brief instant how still her face was, how taut with tension—how beautiful.

Emotion sliced through him, but he had to blank it. Had to get the words out he needed to say.

'You said you would never marry me just because… because of how good we are together.'

He did not spell it out further—the flush in her cheeks showed him he did not need to.

'You told me…' He drew another breath, 'You told me that there was only one reason you would marry again. And that I would know it…'

He paused again, hearing birdsong in the trees, rustling in the undergrowth. The sounds of life were going on all around him and the world was stretching from here to eternity, all in absolute focus—while he was putting to the test the single thing that would mean everything to him for the rest of his life.

'I know it,' he said quietly.

At his side he felt her still—still completely, as if her very breathing had ceased.

'I know it,' he said again.

And now his eyes went to her, his head turning. Her face was a mask, the pallor in it draining all the blood from her skin. Her eyes were huge. Distended in her face. And in them was something he had never seen revealed before. He felt it like a sudden stabbing of his heart.

But it was there, and he knew it for the very first time in his life—because for the very first time in his life it was in his own eyes, in his face, in his very being as well.

'It's love, isn't it, Tia?' He said her old name without conscious thought, only with emotion. An emotion he had never felt before, never recognised, never believed in.

Until now.

'Love,' he said again. 'That's what you said we needed. The only reason to marry.'

He lifted a single finger to her cheek, felt the soft silk of its texture.

'Love,' he said again.

It was strange…the tip of his finger was wet, and he lifted it away. There was the faintest runnel of moisture on her cheek, below her eye. Another came from the other side. He saw her blink, saw another diamond catch the light and spill softly, quietly.

'Tia!' His voice was filled with alarm. 'Oh, Tia—I don't mean to make you weep!'

But it was too late. Far too late. A cry broke from her—a cry that had been five long years in its engendering. A cry that broke the deadly, anguished turmoil of her heart.

His arms swept around her, hugging her to him,

holding her close until she wept no more. Then he sat back, catching up her hands and pressing them with his as if he would never let them go.

He would never let *her* go—never again.

'I ask you to forgive me,' he said, his eyes searching hers, fusing with hers. 'For not understanding. For not knowing. For being so hopeless at realising what you meant.'

His hands pressed hers more tightly yet. Entreaty was in his eyes, his face.

'Forgive me, I beg you, but I didn't recognise love because I've never known it till this moment! Never in all my life experienced it.'

His eyes flickered for a moment, old shadows deep within them.

'They say,' he said slowly, 'that we have to be taught to love. And that it is in being loved that we learn to love.'

His gaze broke from her, looking past the trees around them, looking a long way past.

'I never learnt that essential lesson,' he said.

His eyes came back to her and she saw in them a pain that made her heart twist for him.

She pressed his fingers. 'Vasilis told me a little of your parents,' she said carefully, feeling her way. 'It made me understand you better, Anatole. And you yourself sometimes dropped signs about how unloving your parents were. Still are.' She gave a sad smile. 'Vasilis let me see how I'd wanted more from you than you could give me. He helped me to accept that you could not feel for me what I felt for you.'

'Felt?' The word dropped from his lips, fear audible.

She crushed his hands more tightly yet. Emotion

was streaming through her, pouring like a storm, a tidal wave, overwhelming her with its power. But she must find her way through it—find the words to tell him.

'Oh, Anatole, I *made* myself fall out of love with you! I had to! I had no choice. You didn't love me. You *could* not love me! And I had to save myself. Save—'

She broke off. Then, with a breath, she spoke again, her eyes clinging to his as she told him what had been in her heart for so long.

'I fell in love with you, Anatole, when I was new to you—when I was Tia. I knew it was unwise—but how could I have stopped myself when you were so wonderful to me, like a prince out of a fairytale?'

She looked away for a moment, her eyes shadowing, her voice changing as she looked back at him knowing she must say this too. However difficult.

'Anatole, I give you my word that I never deliberately sought to get pregnant. But…' She took a sharp breath, made herself say it. 'But when I thought I was, I knew that I hoped so much that it was true! That I was going to have your baby. Because…' She took another breath. 'Because then surely you would realise you were in love with me too and would want to marry me, make a family with me.'

She felt her hands clenching suddenly, spasming.

'But when you spoke to me—told me to my face that if that was what I was hoping it would never happen, *could* never happen, that the only marriage you could ever make would be an unwilling one, then… Oh, then something died within me.'

A groan of remorse broke from him. 'That gruesome lecture I gave you!'

Anatole's voice was harsh, but only with himself. He held her gaze, his eyes troubled, spoke again.

'Tia—Christine—I make no excuses for myself, but…' He paused, then continued, finding words with difficulty. 'I can only tell you how much I dreaded being made to be a father when the only one I knew—my own—was so totally and absolutely unfit to be one! Fatherhood was something I never wanted because I feared it so much. I feared that I would be as lousy a father as mine had been. But I've changed, Tia! I've changed totally!'

His voice softened.

'Meeting Nicky—feeling that rush whenever I see him, that incredible kick I get when I'm with him—oh, that's shown me just how much I've changed! Shown me how much I want a family of my own.'

She nodded slowly, her face working. 'I know—I *do* know that. Truly I do. But, Anatole, do you understand now why I had to refuse you when that was all you were offering me? I wanted to accept—dear God, how I longed to accept you!—but I did not dare.'

Her hands slipped from his now and she shifted her position, turning her shoulders away, her body language speaking to him of what speared him to the quick.

'I loved you once, Anatole, and lost you. I married Vasilis—not out of love, but… Well, it suited us.'

Did he hear evasion in her voice? She hurried on.

'All I knew was that to marry you simply to make a family for Nicky would have become hell on earth for me. Hell to know that I had fallen in love with you all over again and that all I was to you was a mother for Nicky, and a partner in your bed…' Her voice twisted. 'To be so close to heaven and yet outside the door still…'

He turned her to him, his hands warm on her shoulders. His voice was firm and strong, filled with a strength that came from the heart.

'I will make heaven for you, Tia. My adored Tia. My Christine—my beautiful, beloved Christine. My love for you will make heaven for you—for us both.'

Tears broke from her in a heart-rending sob and she was swept against him again. She clutched him and kissed him, his cheeks, his mouth, long and sweet and filled with all that she'd had to hold back from him. All that she need never hold back again.

He held her tight, returned her embraces, then sat back a little.

'Heaven for us *all*,' he said. 'You and me and Nicky.' His breath choked him suddenly. 'Nicky whom I will love as if he were my own.'

She stilled as if every cell in her body were turning to stone. Keeping her as silent as she had been for five long years. Then, beneath his gaze, she spoke. Said what she had to say.

Slowly, infinitely slowly, she picked each word with care. 'I have to tell you why I married Vasilis.'

She saw his features twist. Heard him make his own admission. So long denied.

'It hurt,' he said. 'I did not realise it, thought myself only angry with you. But that was because you'd left me for him—rejected me when I still wanted you. On my own terms, yes, but I wanted never to let you go.' He swallowed 'You wanted to leave me. And what he could offer you, I now understand, was more than I could offer.'

He took a ragged breath, met her troubled gaze.

'You wanted a child and so did Vasilis. It was that simple.'

She shook her head. A violent, urgent shaking. 'No—no, it was *not* that simple! Oh, God, Anatole, it was not that simple at all!'

Her voice was vehement, stormy with emotion.

'Anatole… That nightmare morning, when I told you I was not pregnant and you lectured me on how I must never let that happen, well…' Her throat closed, but she forced the words through. 'I was so terrified that I… I used the pregnancy test I'd been too scared to use before! I knew I didn't need to—that I had got my period—but I was so distraught that I wanted every proof I could grasp at! So I did the test—'

She stopped. Silenced by the truth she must tell him now. Her heart was like lead within her.

'It showed positive.'

There was silence. Silence all around. Even the birds were silent. Then…

'I don't understand.'

'Neither did I.' Her voice came as if from far away. 'Apparently it's not that unusual, though I had no idea at the time. There can still be a show of blood. Even when you're pregnant.'

His eyes were on her—staring, just staring. She went on—had to—had no choice but to do so.

'I was beside myself with terror. I knew I would have to tell you when you returned. How horrified you would be. And that was how your uncle found me,' she said, and swallowed, 'when he arrived for lunch with us.' Her face worked. 'He was so kind…so incredibly, wonderfully kind! He sat me down, calmed me down, got the whole dreadful tale out of me. How I'd fallen in love with you, but you hadn't with me, how you'd have felt you *had* to marry me, and how that would have condemned me to a lifetime's misery—condemned *you* too, ruining your life! How I loved you and knew I'd be forcing you to have a child you did not want, forcing you to marry me when you did not want to. And then…' she half closed her eyes '…then he made his suggestion.'

Another deep breath racked through her.

'He said that in the circumstances I needed time—time to think, to accept what had happened. Time to come to terms. To make my decision. Whether to tell you or to raise the child myself. So, as you know, he took me back to London, where I had more doctor's appointments to confirm that, yes, I was, indeed pregnant. And then…' She looked at Anatole. 'And then, knowing what I'd told him, and knowing you as he did, he offered me one other possibility.'

From far away she heard Anatole speak.

'To marry him so he could raise my son—the son I did not want. Marry the woman I did not want to marry.'

The accusation in his voice—against himself—was unbearable for her to hear. The pain was like a spear in her heart.

Her eyes flew to him. 'He did it for *you*, Anatole! To give your son a home, a loving and stable family, to provide for him and for me as his mother, in a way that was the very best way to do it!'

Her expression changed, infused with sadness now.

'He knew he would not live to see Nicky grow up, that he could only be a temporary figure in his life. That's why, as I told you, to Nicky he was his *pappou*. And for that very reason…' she swallowed again, making herself look at Anatole, hard though it was '…he knew that one day he would not be here. That one day—' she took a painful, harsh breath '—I would have to tell you. When the time was right.'

She was silent for a moment.

'And now that time has come, hasn't it, Anatole? Please, *please* tell me it has?' Her voice dropped to a whisper. 'Can you forgive me, Anatole, for what I did?'

His eyes were bleak. 'I am to blame,' he said. 'I brought it on myself.'

'You could not help the way you felt—the way you *didn't* feel!' Her negation of his lacerating self-accusation was instant.

He caught her hands. 'You are generous, Tia, but the fault is mine. That you did not even dare to tell me—' He broke off, anguish in his face.

She crushed his fingers in hers. 'Anatole, please! I understand. And maybe I *should* have told you. Maybe I should have had the courage, the resolution to do so. I've deprived you of your son—'

He cut across her. 'I didn't deserve him.'

His eyes clung to hers and she saw them change from self-accusation to something new.

Hope.

She said the words he needed to hear. 'But you deserve him *now*, Anatole,' she said quietly, from her heart. 'You have come to love him, and that is all a child needs. All that *you* were never given. And now,' she said, and her voice was choked with the emotion running through it, 'now Nicky is *yours*. Your son to love as he should be loved. As he *is* loved!'

She got to her feet, drawing him with her though she was so petite against his height. She gazed up at him, never letting go of his hands.

'And you will have a wife to love you too,' she said.

She lifted her mouth to his and his eyes softened, with a tenderness in them that lit her like a lamp.

'And you will have a husband to love you back,' he said gently.

His lips were a brush upon hers. His hands holding hers fast.

'Nicky is my son.' It was a statement—a truth that seemed to him to be opening the sky in a glory of brightest sunlight, blazing down on him. 'Nicky is *my* son!'

He gave a sudden great exclamation of joy, sliding his arms around her waist, lifting her up and twirling her round and round, laughing, exclaiming until he put her down again, breathless with joy.

'Dear God,' he said, 'can such happiness exist? To have discovered my love for you, for Nicky—and now to discover that you love me back, that the boy I've come to love is mine!'

His expression changed. Grew grave.

'But he is my uncle's child too. I will never forget that, Christine. I owe him that. And I will always be thankful to him for what he did for Nicky and for you.'

She felt her eyes fill with tears. 'He was a good man, my dear Vasilis. A *good* man.' And now her gaze was full upon him, 'Though he was never my husband in anything but name—he would not have wanted anything else, nor I.'

He was looking down at her, taking in the implications of what she'd said.

She gave a sad little smile. 'Did you never wonder why your uncle remained a bachelor? He was in love once, you know, when he was a student. But the woman he wanted to marry did not come from your world, and his parents objected. He resolved to get his teaching qualifications and marry her, be independent of the Kyrgiakis wealth. But...' Her voice became sadder. 'But, unbeknownst to him, while he was studying in England she found she was pregnant and developed eclampsia. They both died—she and the baby with her.'

She took a pained breath.

'I think, you know, that is partly why he offered to make me his wife—because he remembered how alone the woman he loved had been.'

Anatole folded her to him. 'Let us hope and pray,' he said quietly, 'that they are all finally together now. He and the woman he loved, and his own child.' He held her back, his eyes pouring into hers. 'As *we* are together, Tia—my beloved, my dearest adored Christine—as we are together now. You and me and our most precious son—together for ever. Nothing can part us now.' His voice seared with emotion. *'Nothing!'*

He kissed her again, sweetly and passionately, warmly and lovingly, and the world around them turned to gold.

It was Christine who drew back first. 'This is all very wonderful...' she said.

And there was a smile in her voice even as tears were in her eyes—tears of the radiant, unbreakable happiness and joy that swelled her heart until it was bursting within her at the miracle that had happened, at the gift she had been given that she had never hoped to have: the love of the man she loved…

'All very wonderful,' she repeated, her eyes starting to dance, 'but I really think we have to get back to the house. We have a trip to the beach to undertake! Or our son, Anatole—' did her voice choke over the word 'our'? She thought it did, and rejoiced in it '—our son will never forgive us!'

He gave a laugh as warm as the fire of happiness blazing within him and laced an arm around her. They walked back to the house—shoulder to shoulder now, and in all the days to come—ready to start their family life together.

EPILOGUE

THE LITTLE CHURCH was filled with flowers. But the guests were few and very select.

The Barcourts—with Giles's mother and sister looking particularly satisfied with events—occupied the front pew, and on the other side the vicar's wife sat with Mr and Mrs Hughes and Nanny Ruth.

As Christine progressed slowly up the nave, her pale lavender gown emphasising her slender beauty, she was followed by Nicky, holding her short train. He was followed by Isabel Barcourt's daughter as flower girl.

At the altar rail stood Anatole, waiting for his bride. As she reached him Christine smiled, turning to beckon Nicky to stand beside her. The vicar, his expression benign, began the service.

In Anatole's head Christine's words echoed. *'You would know it...'*

And now he did. He knew the power of love—the power that had brought him here, to this moment, where the woman he loved and the child he loved would be his for all eternity—as he was theirs.

Gravely he spoke the words that would unite them, heard Christine's clear voice echoing, until his ring was on her finger and hers on his.

'You may kiss the bride.' The vicar smiled.

She lifted her face to Anatole—to her husband, the man she loved. She let their mouths touch, exchanging their love. And then, with a graceful dip of her knees, she lifted Nicky. Anatole took him from her, hefting him effortlessly into the crook of his arm, and they both turned round.

The organ music surged, the bells pealed out, and the congregation burst into applause as the flower girl threw rose petals over them. Laughing and smiling, the three of them—husband and wife, mother and father and precious son—headed down the aisle and out into the golden sunshine of their lives beyond.

* * * * *

Keep reading for an excerpt of a new title
from the Modern series,
FORBIDDEN ROYAL VOWS by Caitlin Crews

CHAPTER ONE

QUEEN EMILIA OF LAS SOSEGADAS was perfect.

She made sure of it.

Las Sosegadas was a tiny country between France and Spain, all mountains and sparkling alpine lakes. Her family had ruled it for centuries, mostly in peace. And her people were consistently at the top of all the polls that measured the happiest citizens in the European Union.

And unlike some other kingdoms, support of *her* monarchy was always robust.

Because, she knew, she was perfect.

Perfection wasn't simply her job. It was her calling. Her duty.

She spent hours every day discussing exactly how the Queen could appear to her best advantage in all things, not because she had an ego, because she didn't. What she had was a crown and what she owed her subjects was to keep it untarnished.

In private, she could be a person. Even a woman.

In private, she still thought of herself as Mila, the nickname only her sister still called her. Even her mother called her *Your Majesty* now, likely to remind herself as much as anyone else that it was her daughter on the throne now instead of her late husband.

There were a lot of things Mila liked about being *just Mila*, but that was always a temporary state, mostly when she was asleep.

The moment she left her rooms and let anyone lay eyes on her, she was the paragon of a modern queen she always was. In public, Mila was only and ever *the Queen*.

She had promised herself to her country and that was that.

A life of service suited her perfectly, she always said, and she meant it.

Tonight her service to her country had involved the sort of dress fitting that had taken most of the afternoon. It was always necessary to make sure that she looked the part, of course. She had an entire wardrobe team dedicated to the task and they were good at what they did.

What Mila had to do in turn was always and ever appear *relatable*. But not *too* relatable. Subjects wanted to love their Queen, but they certainly didn't want to know her *too* well. A simple flip through the headlines of any European kingdom on any given day told her as much.

Mila had to strike a balance between seeming *almost* approachable while never actually letting anyone near enough to get any fingerprints on the symbol she'd become in her short reign.

Figurative fingerprints, that was. Or the Royal Guards would get involved.

Tonight's event was a banquet to honor service to the crown, an annual gala that also raised money for various charities. It was the usual collection of aristocrats, Mila saw at a glance as she arrived, her foot hitting the exact stone that she had promised it would hit at the exact time it had been announced she would.

Because it was always important to be a *dependable* icon, no matter what else she was.

Sometimes Mila thought it was all she was.

If so, she thought now, *there are far worse things I could be.*

And she did not list off what those things were, as she sometimes did. She already knew that did not lead to perfection. It went the other way, rather precipitously.

She swept through her usual protocols for these things. The selected greetings after her entrance. The few, carefully chosen comments to make it clear that she knew the people she was speaking to. Even a smile now and again.

Mila had always been good at these things. She'd always known how to make these little connections, over so quickly, feel bigger than the sum of their parts. Because she had not been thrown into the royal life in a turbulent fashion. She'd had the gift and curse of knowing that her father was not only going to have to die *someday* for her to succeed him, but that the doctors had given him a date by which they expected that to occur.

There were very few good things about that, but one of them—maybe the only one—was that he had taken the time to prepare her appropriately for what was to come. And not in the abstract, as she'd been taught as a child.

She had no regrets, she told herself.

What was there to regret? She was the Queen.

"You are looking splendid, Your Majesty," said her mother from her side as they left the receiving line and processed through the party, headed for the Queen's usual spot on a dais up near the throne. Mila inclined her head, lest anyone think she was engaging in something as base as small talk or gossip while the trumpets were playing.

Was it ostentatious to have balls take place in front of the throne of the kingdom? Certainly. On the other hand, she had been told many times that most people appreciated the touch of glamour.

Besides, it was expected.

No point going all the way to a palace and not experiencing anything palatial, now, is there? her sister, Carliz, would have said if she was there.

Mila let her lips curve with great serenity as she passed the line of bowing subjects. But inside, she felt that surprising pang again.

She didn't know why it had not occurred to her that she would miss her sister.

When Carliz had gone off to university, the first one in the family to leave the kingdom to do so, she had been younger and consumed with learning her duties as Crown Princess. It wasn't that she hadn't missed her then, because she had.

But it was different this time.

She had gotten used to having Carliz here, was the thing. She had gotten used to her sister slipping into her room at night, when Her Majesty was left at the door and Mila could simply be Mila again. They had spent most of a summer that way and Mila had gotten used to it. She had come to rely on it, even. That was all.

It wasn't that she would change a thing. She was too happy for Carliz, who had gone from being one of the world's greatest sparkling It girls to about the happiest wife and mother Mila had ever seen.

But she could be happy for Carliz and sad for herself, it turned out.

I contain multitudes, she thought as she moved, practicing the dignified inclination of her head which she could often use in place of actual speech, or even a smile.

This was one of the great many ways she got people to forget how very young she was.

Only twenty-seven, though that was rarely mentioned in the way it had been at first, when her father had died and the whole of Europe had acted as if they didn't know what an *heir apparent* was.

Now when they said *"only twenty-seven"* it was in tones of awe, as if no one could quite credit that she was still something less than the formidable dowager of indeterminate years she would be one day. The one she had gotten so good at pretending she already was.

If everything went according to plan, she would simply grow grayer but otherwise remain exactly the same.

The Queen, nothing more and nothing less.

As ageless as the currency she graced.

Her mother was murmuring to her as they walked, the usual comments about this noblewoman's dress or that aristocrat's wandering eye, because nobody minded if the Queen Mother offered commentary. And the dancing had begun, so there was no shortage of things to look at.

"And, of course, we are treated to the next regrettable stop along Lady Paula's road to ruin," her mother was tutting at her side. "I often look at her and think, there but for the grace of God above did your poor sister go."

Mila was entirely too well-trained to react broadly enough that anyone could see it. All she did was slide a look her mother's way. Nothing more. She did not even have to raise an eyebrow.

Still, the Queen Mother blew out a breath, aware that she had stumbled into one of the places she should know better than to go.

As Mila had made her feelings on this clear. As the Queen.

"My sister," Mila said softly, smiling magnificently at a set of honorees as she passed them, dipped down low into their curtseys, "would never dream of embarrassing me. And she never did. Lady Paula, who I think you know I quite like, has a different goal entirely in mind."

She did not go so far as to say, *I support her.*

But she was defending her, so that should have been obvious.

"You may judge me if you like," her mother replied in that particularly aggrieved tone she was so good at pulling out at moments like this, as if Mila had thrown her in the dungeons. If the palace had actually *had* dungeons, which it did not, she might have considered it—for the express purpose of watching expression on her mother's face. But that was childish. And the Queen could never be childish. Even when she'd been a child, it had been discouraged. "But I cannot for the life of me understand what it is Lady Paula is so upset about. Many women of her station are called upon to make life choices that honor their family legacy, not their own wild impulses."

It was well known that Lady Paula's father wished to marry her off to a man of his choosing. Lady Paula had made certain that no one in the whole of the kingdom could think for one moment that this was something she approved. Or would ever approve. She had gone to great lengths to make sure that her disapproval was recorded in the starkest possible terms in every tabloid that could be found.

With as many inappropriate men she could find, to her father's fury.

"Maybe it's time that we allowed women of whatever station to choose their own destinies," Mila said.

Reasonably enough, to her mind.

The look her mother shot her was sharp. Too sharp for a public setting, Mila would have thought. "I hope you do not intend to follow Lady Paula's example. Your Majesty."

That was a shot and they both knew it.

Mila smiled as they came to a stop before the throne, because it was considered gaudy and inappropriate for her to guffaw. Or so she had been told, never having given in to the urge in public before.

"I know my duty, Mother," she said softly. "I daresay I know it better than most."

"Of course you do, my dear," her mother

replied, though they both knew that if it were up to her, the Queen Mother would be planning the sovereign's wedding here and now.

And when she turned away to talk brightly to the people who came up on the other side, as if she hadn't been squabbling with the Queen herself, Mila took a moment to gaze out at the whirling mass of dancers before her, looking for that telltale flash that was always Lady Paula's orange-red hair.

When they'd been girls, Paula had won her friendship forever by wrinkling up her nose and laughing too loudly at a party where they were all attempting to out-ladylike each other, and then announcing quite boldly that as her hair was already problematic, she saw no particular reason not to make sure her behavior matched it.

Mila heard Paula's laugh before she saw her. She was already smiling as she realized her friend had drawn near the way she usually did, moving along the sides of the ball that was in full swing across the floor of the great room. She turned her head, expecting to see what she normally did when Paula attended one of these parties.

Her friend always dressed *almost* inappropriately, but not quite, because it drove her staid and quiet family mad. And she took pride in always presenting herself in the company of some or other wildly inappropriate date, and then presenting said date to her friend—the Queen.

Usually Mila made it worse, according to her mother, by indulging Paula in this. Meaning she only smiled at her friend's behavior when, as queen, she could also have indicated her displeasure.

That would not have stopped Paula, but it would have meant she had one less friend, and Mila had never seen the point.

She had so few as it was.

"Don't start," she warned her mother beneath her breath as Paula drew close.

Her mother sniffed in reply.

But then the crowd parted way and the man Paula was leading toward the throne stepped into full view.

And Mila froze.

She wondered for a moment if she'd simply died where she stood—or possibly it was only that she wished she had.

Because tonight it wasn't just any old inappropriate man on Paula's arm. This or that baronet from some country Mila hardly knew.

Tonight, it was the most inappropriate man Mila had ever met.

And he was looking right at her.

With that trademark near-smirk in the corner of his appallingly sensual mouth.

Because he was the only person in the entire world who knew the truth that Mila preferred to believe only she knew. That Queen Emilia of Las Sosegadas was not the least bit perfect.

He was, in fact, the only one who knew that she was capable of an epic, life-altering, unforgivable error of judgment.

Not just *capable* of it.

He was one of the last great European playboys in the old style, a recent article in a non-tabloid magazine had claimed quite seriously. And had backed it up.

He was famous for his long string of astonishingly beautiful, powerful, and famous lovers, his mesmerizing charm that Hollywood actors tried and failed to replicate on-screen, his deeply mutable moral code that some found charming, and the great fortunes he'd inherited from all branches of his enormously complicated family tree.

A tree, the article had claimed, that has its roots in every grand old family in Europe.

Worse than all that, he was impossibly, disastrously attractive.

A description of him would involve dark hair, dark eyes, and those cheekbones, but it would fail entirely to capture the way he moved through a room like the world was nothing but a crock of creamery butter waiting for the edge of his knife.

And she knew that he always, always, had that knife.

He was always perfectly dressed for every occasion, yet managed to provoke all the same. It was that swagger. It was that hint of a smirk. It was that lazy wit in his gaze, and his inability to show even the faintest bit of humility to stations higher than his own.

It was the fact that he could be so incisive. That he was so intelligent when there should have been nothing but air and smugness between his temples.

It was the formidable way he could gaze at a person and make them forget who they were without even seeming to try—

Mila had to remind herself to maintain her composure. She had to *order herself* not to lose her cool, right here in the middle of a gala.

Something she had not had to do since she

was a child of eight who had accidentally indulged in too much sugar one Christmas.

But he was a whole lot worse than too many sweets at a holiday party.

He was a *catastrophe.*

He was Caius Candriano.

Mila's one and only mistake.

And he was also, though no one knew this but the two of them nor ever would as long as she drew breath, still—legally—her husband.